"My magic...it's gone," she told him with a shrug

Disappointment flashed across his eyes before it quickly faded. Or he masked it. *Come on, Breena, you're supposed to be good at reading people.*

He placed the barest of kisses against her mouth. "Then *tell* me stop, and I'll stop."

How could she, when she ached to finally *live* every emotion and sensation the Osborn of her dreams had promised?

She shook her head. "I can't."

His fingers began to caress the skin below her ears, never thinking how sensitive she was there. Something dark and slightly possessive flashed across his features, turning his features stony. But this wasn't scary. Oh, it was dangerous, and should be a warning, but it was so, so tantalizing....

Breena wanted more.

Don't miss the bonus story, Primal Instincts, *included in this book!*

JILL MONROE

makes her home in Oklahoma with her family. When not writing, she spends way too much time on the internet, completing "research" or updating her blog. Even when writing, she's thinking of ways to avoid cooking.

JILL MONROE

LORD OF RAGE

&

PRIMAL INSTINCTS

ROYAL HOUSE of SHADOWS

Harlequin®

TORONTO NEW YORK LONDON
AMSTERDAM PARIS SYDNEY HAMBURG
STOCKHOLM ATHENS TOKYO MILAN MADRID
PRAGUE WARSAW BUDAPEST AUCKLAND

HARLEQUIN BOOKS

ISBN-13: 978-0-373-83773-1

Recycling programs for this product may not exist in your area.

CONTENTS

LORD OF RAGE

Dear Reader,

Writing *Lord of Rage* was an amazing experience. Not only because I've always been a fan of dark, sizzling paranormal romance, but I also got to work with three amazing and talented authors—Gena Showalter *(Lord of the Vampires)*, Jessica Andersen *(Lord of the Wolfyn)* and Nalini Singh *(Lord of the Abyss)*.

We started out with a single idea—rewrite fairy tales with a mystical twist—and from that, the Royal House of Shadows was born.

And, baby, did we have a blast! Our world is filled with dangerous magic, vampires and werewolves, and I couldn't resist adding one more creature to the mix—an elusive berserker possessed with a strength and rage so intense, his enemies shudder with fear, even though he's the last of his kind. Add in a lost princess desperate to save her brothers and find her kingdom, and watch as the sparks start flying. But can she conquer the Lord of Rage and right the wrongs an evil sorcerer has dealt her?

I'm so excited about this electrifying series, and hope you have as much fun reading as we did writing!

All my best,

Jill

PROLOGUE

ONCE UPON A TIME, in a land unseen by human eye, there was a beautiful princess...destined to wed to further her father's political gains.

Not the kind of fairy tales Princess Breena of Elden grew up reading in the warmth of her mother's solar room. In those stories, the princesses rode glowing unicorns, slept on piles of mattresses, their rest only interrupted by a tiny pea, or lived in towering enchanted castles filled with magical creatures.

Although, none of those princesses could talk to themselves in their dreams.

As far as magical abilities, Breena's gift was pretty worthless. When she was a child, she could talk herself out of a nightmare, which was a bonus to her seven-year-old self, but now, as an adult, it didn't add anything special. Her mother could look into the dreams of men, was able to send fearful emotions into the hearts of her father's enemies or even peer into possible futures.

And once upon a time, Queen Alvina had married Breena's father for her own father's political ambition. Joining her magic to the blood drinker's power. Her oldest brother, Nicolai, could absorb the powers of others, while her other brothers Dayn and Micah could mindspeak with the blood drinkers of their kingdom.

While Breena's dream talking was not powerful... she could always connect to one particular warrior.

That's how she referred to him while awake. War-rior. As she slept, she thought of him as lover. His dark eyes matched his unruly hair that she so liked to slide her fingers through. His broad shoulders begged for her touch. Her lips. Sometimes in her dreams he'd take her in his arms, his body big and powerful, and carry her to the nearest bed. Or down to the hard floor. Sometimes it was even against the wall. Her lover would tear her clothes, ripping them from her body, then cover her skin with the softness of his lips or roughness of his callused palms.

Breena would wake up, her heart pounding and her nipples hard and throbbing. She'd ache all over. She would draw her knees to her chest, trying to suck in air, clearing her mind of the need and the wanting.

Once she caught her breath, and her heartbeat slowed, she was left feeling only frustrated. She spent the time just after waking trying to remember. To get back into the dream. She'd been with her warrior a hundred times in her sleep, but what came after the clothes ripping and touching? Her dreams never told. Nor could she ever fully see his face. While she knew how he smelled, tasted and what he felt like beneath her fingertips, *he* remained elusive. Mysterious. A dream.

But one thing was for sure. If the man barged out of her dreams, through her door and stalked across her chamber, she'd be frightened. He was little more than savage. Fierce and primal. He wielded a sword as eas-ily as she brandished a hairbrush.

Hairbrushing. Now that was important in the life of a princess. Especially one whose sole job was to marry. Breena sighed, and began to pace the confines of her room. Her feet as restless as her spirit.

And she knew those kind of thoughts would lead to danger.

In all the fairy tales her mother had read to her while growing up, a princess always got into the most trouble when she yearned for something more. She'd be tempting—no, challenging—fate, if she strode with a purpose to her window to gaze below, out past the castle gates, to the trees of the forest, and wonder…what if? What's out there? Is there anything more than this?

She might as well swing the doors open wide and invite in disaster and offer it a cup of sweet tea.

Besides, how was she prepared for adventure? Out past the gates, armed with only a few paltry magical abilities, she'd be as lost as that little boy and girl whose trail of bread crumbs was eaten by the birds. If she could defeat a fearsome ogre with a fabulous meal plan, then what lay beyond those gates might not be so worrisome. But giants and ogres wouldn't be impressed that she was competent in more than twenty kinds of dances from all over the realm. Or that she could arrange every detail from the musicians to the amount of candles needed in the great hall for a ball.

She eyed her discarded needlework. That's what a princess should be concerned about. Perfect stitches.

Tomorrow her father would begin the search for her husband. Breena knew King Aelfric had put off the task; he didn't want his daughter living away from him. His life with Alvina had started as a marriage of convenience where love had grown, and they'd forged a close-knit family. But that family was growing up and changing. Her oldest brother, Nicolai, quickly escaped the dinner table after the meal was over, most likely to the bed of a woman. As a gently bred princess of Elden, Breena wasn't supposed to know those kinds of details—but she did. Already approaching the middle of her second decade, Breena was several years older than when her mother had arrived in Elden, ready to fulfill the marriage contract.

That's why she was so restless. Their family could no longer hold back time and the changes a ticking clock brought with it. Soon she'd be leaving her childhood home, to marry, and go to another kingdom. She'd be in the arms of a man whose face she could see clearly, whose features were not fuzzy results of a dream-haze. A man who'd show her what happened after the clothes came off. The time of her dream lover was over. It would be wrong to force him into her dreams once she belonged to another.

But she wasn't married yet. Her fingers found the timepiece her mother had given her on her fifth birthday. She wore it on a necklace around her neck, a sword and shield decorating the front.

"Why a sword?" she'd asked. Though she was more prone to running through the castle than walking gracefully, even her five-year-old self knew weapons of war did not suit a princess.

Her mother had shrugged, secrets darkening her green eyes. "I don't know. My magic forges the time-pieces." The queen bent and kissed Breena's cheek. "But I do know it will aid you on your journey. Your destiny. Make it a good one."

A craving to see her warrior jolted her. Breena should probably be worried that those cravings hit her more and more frequently.

But if her destiny were not to be with her warrior, then she'd take her mother's advice and make her journey a good one. Breena kicked off her delicate slippers and lay down on her soft mattress, not bothering to slip out of her dress or tug the covers up over her chin. She closed her eyes and pictured a door. When her mother tried to teach her how to take over the dreamworld, she'd told her that all she had to do was turn the knob, and walk through. The door would take her anywhere she wished to be.

The door only took her to the mind of her fierce lover, and right now that was the only place she wanted to go.

She found him sharpening the steel of his blade. Breena often found him taking care of his weapons. In her dreams, she was never made nervous by his axes or swords or knives. She relished his ferocity, his ability to protect. Attack. She leaned against a tree and simply watched the play of his muscles across his shirtless back as he slid the cloth around the hilt.

Breena never found much time to simply observe him. The warrior in him was always on alert, and because she was in a dream, his features were never clearly defined. Did lines from his eyes indicate he liked to laugh? Were there lines across his forehead, marking him as a man of intensity and concentration? All she could see were broad brushstrokes. Not the kinds of things that would tell her who he was inside.

A smile curved her lips when his shoulders tensed. Her lover had sensed her presence. The sword and cleaning cloth dropped to the grass at his feet as he turned. Her nipples hardened as his gaze traveled up and down her body, his breath little more than a hiss. Breena squinted, once more trying to peer through the dreamhaze that never seemed to let her see the true angles of his face. Only his eyes. Those intense brown eyes.

His footsteps were silent as he walked over the leaves

and twigs carpeting the ground. She pushed away from the tree, moving toward him, wanting to meet her lover as quickly as she could now that he knew she'd arrived.

This would be their last time together.

Or at least it should be. She should be focusing on her kingdom, and aiding her father in selecting her husband.

Breena twined her hands around her lover's neck to bring his lips down to hers. The man in her dream never kissed her gently, as she suspected a courtier bred to rule over a castle would. No, this man's lips were demanding. His kiss was passionate and filled with primal desire.

"I want you naked," he told her, his voice tight.

She blinked at him, startled for a moment. He had never talked before in her dreams. Breena liked his voice, elemental and filled with hunger for her. He reached for the material at her shoulders, ready to tear, but she stilled his hand. She didn't want him to be the seducer this day, not that his lovemaking would be considered a smooth seduction. No, she wanted to be equal partners this last time. Breena wanted to undress for him.

With a twist of her wrists, she tugged at the ribbon between her shoulder blades and felt the fabric of her bodice give. Propelled by a slow roll of her shoulders, her dress began to fall. His eyes narrowed when her breasts were revealed, her nipples growing even tighter before his eyes. He reached for her. Breena knew what he would do the moment he had her in his grasp, and she laughed.

"Not yet," she teased. Then she picked up her skirts and ran to the tree. She'd never played this game before…never thought to. She knew on some level her warrior lover would savor the chase. He would win, but she had every intention of letting him find her.

Although her lover was silent, Breena sensed he was close. She laughed again when his hand curved around her waist. He tugged her back against the solidity of his chest. The hard ridge of him pressed against her, and something needy and achy made her stomach feel hollow. The urge to tease and run vanished in an instant. Breena wanted—no, she *needed*—his hands on her body and his lips on her breasts.

Something hard clamped across her mouth. Confusion filled his dark eyes and the solid lines of him began to blur. Fade. His hands tightened around her arms, but it was too late.

"Stay with me," he demanded. "What's happening to you?"

She struggled, willing herself farther through the doorway, closer to him. But it was too late.

Breena fought against the force holding her head in place.

"Quiet," a voice ordered.

She shook her head, and reached for her lover's hand. But she grasped only air. Some thing, some force, was taking her away from him. "Help me," she tried to call, but the hand covering her mouth wouldn't let her speak.

And he was gone.

Breena was back in her bedchamber. Rolfe, a member of her parents' personal security, stood over her. "Quiet, princess. The castle's under attack. They've already taken the king and queen."

She sat up, the last vestiges of her dream fading completely. As the meaning behind the guard's words sank in, her fingers began to chill and her heart began to race. "We must help them," she whispered.

Rolfe shook his head. "It's too late for them. They'd want me to get you and your brothers and take you through the secret passageway out of the castle."

"But…" she began to protest. Tears filmed her eyes and her throat began to tighten. The passageway had been built by some long-ago ancestor as a last-resort escape route if the inhabitants of the castle feared there was no other option but flight.

"Come, princess, and hurry. Put on some shoes. We must fetch Micah and Dayn."

"What about Nicolai?"

The guard shook his head.

Fear slammed into her. The enormity of their danger finally penetrated her dreamhaze. This wasn't an attack on the castle, like those easily repelled in the past; this was an all-out onslaught. "He's been taken, too?"

"I cannot find him. Come, we must save who we can."

Breena began to shudder, but took a deep breath. She had to be strong and face whatever danger lay ahead. Her brothers depended on her.

After sliding her feet into the slippers at the foot of her bed, she followed Rolfe down the hallway that led her to Dayn's and Micah's chambers. Below she heard the clash and clang of sword against shield. The war cry. And the sound of death.

She quickened her pace, quietly stealing into Micah's room first as Rolfe went to Dayn's. Earlier they'd celebrated Micah's fifth birthday. It was now up to her to make sure he celebrated another. If she had her mother's abilities, she'd already be placing awakening thoughts in her brother's dreams. Instead, she would have to gently shake him on the shoulder.

"Where's my brother?" she asked the maid after walking into the chamber where her brother slept.

"His nanny took him. To one of the high rooms in the castle."

Breena sagged in relief.

"But what should we do about the little cousin?"

Her hand flew to cover her gasp. Their cousin, Gavin, who wasn't much older than four, had come for the party. She doubted any of the guards would think to check on him. She raced down the hallway to where he slept.

"Gavin, darling," she whispered. "Get dressed. You've got to come with me and Rolfe."

Her little cousin rubbed at his eyes. "Why?" he asked, more asleep than awake.

"We're playing hide-and-seek," she told him with a smile.

He sat up in bed, confused by the timing, but still ready for the game. Gavin was young enough for her to carry. She simply lifted him from the covers and draped him over her shoulder. She sang a soft lullaby in his ear so he wouldn't grow fretful and loud.

Rolfe joined her in the hallway. "Dayn's not in his room."

Fear for her dear older brother made her shake all over again. "Perhaps he's already escaped."

Doubt flickered in Rolfe's eyes for a moment, before the guard quickly masked it. Dayn was in charge of protecting the outer walls of the castle. Of course he'd be involved in any kind of defense. But their defenses had already been breached. That would mean her brother—

No, she would not allow her thoughts to go there. Right now she must take care of Gavin. Rolfe was already rushing toward the corridor that would lead to the escape route no one in Elden had needed in several generations. Who would be attacking them? Why? Their kingdom had been at peace with most every other in the realm.

Rolfe pushed aside a heavy tapestry revealing the door leading to their means of escape. The sounds of fighting still echoed from below, but were growing closer. The hidden door groaned when Rolfe pushed at the ancient wood. When it finally gave way, the hinges objected loudly after their lack of use for years.

"Stop!"

Breena turned to see a hideous creature, one created from evil. Its eight legs, gleaming with razors and dripping with the blood of her people, sped toward her. It would get them all if she didn't do something to distract it.

"You must walk now, Gavin."

"But I want you to carry me," he protested.

"Princess," the monster called to her, baring its fangs. She realized the revolting beast was focused solely on her. Would do anything to get her, including killing her cousin.

"Go!" she screamed, pushing Gavin into Rolfe's side, and slammed the door shut.

"Breena," she heard her little cousin cry. But then she heard a comforting click as Rolfe slid the dead bolt from the inside. Relief made her legs shake. Taking a deep breath, she turned. The monster was almost at her side. Like her mother, this creature wielded magic, except it harnessed the dark powers that came only from corrupting life-sustaining blood.

It shoved her against the wall, one of its razor-adorned legs trapping her in place. It tugged at the handle, but the door didn't budge. "No matter. They can't hide in there forever." Then it looked over at her. Its eyes were cold. She'd never seen eyes so full of... nothingness. It chilled her.

A smile, if one could even call it that, pulled at its upper lip. "Come. The master will want to see you."

It grabbed her arm, and she sucked in a breath as one of the razors pierced her skin. Her captor dragged her to the staircase where the fighting still waged. Only the crash of sword against sword was already fading as it pulled her down to the great hall. The agonized moans of the injured and dying mingled with the terrified weeping of the captured. Then she spotted her parents on the dais where they held court, chained to their thrones. A mocking humiliation.

Anger began to grow in her chest, chasing away the fear. Her father lay slumped where he once ruled proudly. Blood ran down his cheek and pooled at his feet. So much blood. Too much blood. A sob tore from her throat, and she yanked her arm from her captor's grasp. She couldn't let him die like that. Not her father, who ruled with justice, who loved his people.

The blow came from behind. It knocked her to the floor, the cold stone of the hearth cutting her forehead. Blackness began to move across her vision, and she blinked to try to clear it and the pain. She met her father's gaze. He didn't have much longer to live. Breena forced herself to look at her mother. Her beautiful mother with the striking silver hair, now stained red from the blood she'd shed.

Her parents reached for each other, and the gesture comforted her. They'd die together. Dark brown eyes flashed across her mind. Her dream warrior would fight these creatures who practiced blood magic. He'd die trying to save, to avenge. She wished he were here now.

"No!" called a man, his tone cold. He had a voice that sounded like death.

Breena knew without having to be told that the man, or something that had once been a man, who raced toward her parents was the Blood Sorcerer. A legend. A rumor. Tall and skeletal, this was the creature mothers warned of; he took those foolish to leave the safety of Elden and turned them evil.

Something potent swirled between her parents' outstretched hands. They weren't reaching for each other as she'd first thought, they were rallying their powers. Breena reached for the timepiece, her fingers worrying into the sword and shield decorating the front. How ironic, when what she really needed *was* a sword and shield.

And a man who could wield that sword.

Her timepiece began to warm and glow against her skin. A wave of magic shuddered through her entire body, and Breena no longer felt the sting from the cut of her temple or the coldness of the hard stone beneath her body.

Breena's last thought was of her warrior.

CHAPTER ONE

A furore libera nos, Domine!
Deliver us from the fury, O Lord!

Ten Years Ago

OSBORN'S FINGERS TIGHTENED around the smooth handle of his spear. He'd spent countless hours peeling away the bark and sanding the rough wood until it felt easy in his hand. His legs shook in anticipation as he sat at the campfire, watching the logs turn orange and the smoke rise to the stars.

His last night as a child.

Tomorrow he'd follow the path his father—and his father's father and the generations of his forebearers—had once all walked since the beginning of the beginning. Tomorrow he'd meet the final challenge. Tomorrow he'd become a man or he'd die.

"You must sleep," his father told him.

Osborn glanced up. Even in the dimness of the firelight he could recognize the tension bracketing his father's eyes. Tomorrow he'd either join his father as a warrior or his father would be burying another son.

"I'm not tired," he admitted.

With a nod, his father joined him on the ground, the fire warming the chill night air. "Neither could I that night."

Osborn's eyes narrowed. Even though he'd asked a dozen times about his father's Bärenjagd, he'd said little. A father's task was to prepare his son for the fight, but what to expect, how to feel…that battle was left for each boy to face alone. On his own terms. It defined the warrior he'd become.

If he lived.

AN ABRUPT SHAKE TO HIS shoulder awoke Osborn in the morning. Somehow he'd fallen into a deep sleep. "It's time."

The fire had died, and he resisted the urge to pull his pelt around him tighter. Then he remembered.

It was *now*.

A smile tugged at his father's lower lip when he saw the suddenness of Osborn's actions. In a flash of movement he was dressed, bedroll secured and spear in hand.

"It's time," he announced to his father, repeating the words he'd been given.

They were eye to eye now, and still Osborn would grow taller. Later tonight he'd be returning a man, welcomed to take his place among the warriors.

His father nodded. "I will tell you what my father told me, and I suspect his father and the fathers before him. What you must do now, you do alone. Leave your aleskin here, and take no food. Nothing but your weapon. Be brave, but above all, be honorable."

"How will you know when it is done?" he asked.

"I will know. Now go."

Osborne turned on his heel, and trekked silently though the brush as his father had first taught him so many years ago. One of his many lessons. Last night they'd slept on the outskirts of the sacred bear lands. Now was the time he must cross over.

With a deep breath he stepped onto the sacred land, reveling in the unexpected thrust of power that pounded into his body. The surge swelled in his chest, then grew, infusing his limbs, his fingers. With new energy, he gripped his spear and began to run. Running faster than he'd ever run before, he followed that tug of power, trusting his instincts.

Time lost meaning as he ran. He never grew tired, even as the sun continued to rise in the sky. His vision narrowed, and the heavy tang of musk scented the air. Bear musk.

The time was *now*.

Every muscle, every sense, tightened. Instinct again told him to turn his head, and then he saw it.

The bear was a giant. Towering more than two feet above Osborn, its fierce claws curved, its dark brown fur pulled tight over taut muscles. Osborn met the fearsome creature's eyes. Again something powerful slammed into him, and his muscles locked. His body froze.

The bear growled at him, a thunderous sound that made the earth beneath his feet rumble. Osborn felt his eyes widen, but he still could not move.

The time was *now*.

Osborn forced his fingers to shift, his arm to relax. Then, with a flowing arc he'd practiced alongside his father hundreds of times, he sent his spear soaring. The sound of its sharpened tip whizzed through the air. The animal roared when Osborn's weapon sank into his chest. Blood darkened its coat.

With a guttural cry, Osborn sprinted to where the bear had stumbled to the ground, pawing at the wood lodged inside its body. The animal went wild as Osborn neared, striking toward him with those killer claws. A wave of fear shuddered down his spine. The rusty, salty scent of blood hit his nostrils. The breathy, angered groaning of the bear made Osborn shake his head, trying to clear the sound. The bear rolled to its feet, once more towering above him, and close. So close.

He steeled his resolve. He was to be a warrior. A brave one. Osborn reached for the spear. One weapon was all a boy was allowed to take. The bear swiped at him, his claws ripping through the cloth of his shirt, tearing the skin of his biceps. With a mighty blow, the animal sent Osborn to the ground, the air knocked out of his lungs by the force.

Forget the pain. Forget the blood. Forget the fear.

Once again, Osborn's focus narrowed. He reached for the spear again, this time dragging it from the bear's body. But not without a price. The mighty animal clawed at him again, leaving a trail of torn flesh crossing from his shoulder down to his hip. The pain was agony, and his vision blurred, but he steadied his hand and aimed at the animal's throat.

The animal fell to the ground again, but Osborn knew it would not be getting back to its feet. He met those dark brown eyes of the bear. A wave of anguished compassion settled into Osborn. *This* was why the warriors never told of their experiences.

The bear took a labored breath, blood trickling from its nose. Osborn squeezed his eyes tight, fighting the nausea that threatened. His glance drifted to the pain-glazed eyes of the bear. He was dishonoring this great animal's spirit by letting it suffer. The bear's soul clamored for its release. Its next journey.

The time was *now*.

Osborn grabbed the spear once more, then plunged it directly in the bear's heart, ending its life. A rush of energy slammed into him, almost knocking him backward. He fought it, but it was ripping and tearing through his soul. The *ber* energy fused with his own nature, turning him into the warrior the rest of the realm referred to as *berserkers*.

He felt his muscles begin to quiver, feeling weak from his loss of blood. But the wounds would heal. He'd be stronger than ever before. Osborn gulped in air and stumbled his way back to the place where he'd parted from his father.

Intense relief passed across his father's face, and his brown eyes warmed when he saw Osborn approach. Osborn immediately straightened despite the pain. He was a warrior; he'd greet his father that way. But his father hugged him, grabbed him and held him tight to his chest. For a few moments he basked in his father's pride and love before his father broke away and began packing away their camp supplies.

"It was harder than I thought. I didn't think I'd feel this way," Osborn blurted out for no reason he could guess. He regretted his rash words instantly. That was a boy's sentiments. Not a man's. Not a warrior's.

But his father only nodded. "It's not supposed to be easy. Taking of a life, any life, should never be something done without need and compassion." He stood, slinging his pack over his shoulder. "Guide me to the bear. We must prepare it."

They trekked silently together, crossing into the sacred land to where the bear had taken its final breaths. His father taught him to honor the bear in the ancient ways, then they set to work.

"Now you possess the heart of the bear. As a warrior of Ursa, you will carry the bear's spirit with you. Your *ber* spirit will always be there, waiting silent within you, ready for your call. The strength of the bear comes to you when you wear your Bärenhaut," his father told him, lifting up the bear pelt. "Do not don your pelt without thought and careful consideration. You will be able to kill, Osborn, and kill easily. But only with honor."

"I will, Father," he vowed with a humble sense of pride. "What do we do now?"

"We take the meat back so our people can eat. The claws we use for our weapons. We don't waste what the bear has given us. We revere its sacrifice." His father ran a finger down the bear's fur. "But the pelt, that belongs to you. You wear it only when you go into battle and must call upon the spirit of the bear."

As he'd observed with his father, and the dozen of Ursa warriors who guarded their homeland. Now he was joining their elite ranks.

THEY CAME AT NIGHT. But then vampires were strongest at night. Attacking when all would be asleep. While the warriors and their sons were on Bärenjagd. A coward's choice.

The cries of women filled the night air. The blaze of burned homes and barns and grain silos lit up the sky. Father and son took in the scene below. Osborn's mother was down there. His sister.

His father shucked his clothing, grabbing for his Bärenhaut and sword, which were never far out of reach. Osborn's own bear pelt wasn't ready, not yet dried by the sun, but still he reached for the fur, drawing it about his bare shoulders. Blood and sinew still clung to the pelt, and seeped into Osborn through the wounds on his arm and down his body. A powerful rage took him over. He felt nothing else. No sadness over the bear, no worry or concern for his brothers or sister and mother, no anguish over the loss of the food stores that would keep his people alive through the harsh winter. Osborn felt nothing but the killing rage.

With a war cry, he charged down the hill, to his village, his people. To do battle. Not heeding the warning of his father. A vampire turned at his call, blood dripping from his chin, a chilling smile on his cruel lips.

The anger, the force of his rage, overpowered him. He charged the vamp, grabbing for his throat, tearing at his flesh, ripping at the creature's body with his bare hands. He didn't need a stake, only his fist, slamming through skin, bone, to the heart below. The vamp collapsed at his feet.

Osborn turned, ready to kill another. And he did. Again and again. But the Ursa warriors were outnumbered. Armed with clubs, the vampires waited to ambush the father-and-son pairs slowly returning, easy and unaware targets. The creatures knew what they were doing, fighting his people with neither blade nor fire.

The bodies of his neighbors lay among the blood drinkers he'd killed. In the distance, he still saw his father in the fight, easily taking on two vamps, his *berserkergang* a trusted ally. But then he saw his father fall. Vamps were ready to suck the last of his life force. His spirit.

"No," he cried, his rage growing, building. He grabbed a sword from one of the fallen vamps as he ran. The blade might not do damage to his flesh, but it would soon find a home in a vampire's bitter, dark heart.

The blood drinker at his father's throat lost his head without knowing the threat approaching. The second vampire was able to put up a fight, fueling Osborn's anger. He laughed into the dawn as the vampire fell at his feet. He turned ready for more, to kill more. His rage only soothed by the death of his enemy. But he was surrounded.

Vampires moved at incredible speeds to join those slowly encircling him. Even with his *berserkergang* upon him, the spirit of the bear filling him, he knew he could not defeat this many vampires. The vampires had made sure there was no one to help him.

He'd just make sure he took as many as he could with them when he died. He raised his sword, preparing to do battle.

Just as quickly as the vampires had moved to surround him, they stopped. Light began to filter through the leaves of the trees. One by one the vampires left, faster than his eyes could track.

"Come back and fight," he called to them.

The sound of the wind rustling over the grass was his only answer.

"Fight, cowards."

But his rage was fading, only anguish left in its place. His pelt began to slip off his shoulders.

Those vampires still left dying on the ground began to sizzle. Smoke rose to the sky from their bodies, and soon they were nothing but ash. The smell was horrific, and he turned away, sinking to the ground by his father's prone body.

He lifted his father's hand. It was cold, lifeless. Tears pricked at his eyes, but he blinked them back, in honor of the spirit of the man who'd died to save his people.

The vamp Osborn had relieved of his head left nothing behind but his tunic. Under the cover of the night, he hadn't realized the attackers had been similarly dressed. His own people did not dress alike when they engaged in battle. But one kingdom of the realm did. The magical vampires of Elden. He recognized the navy and purple colors of Elden's royal military guard.

It made no sense. Nothing made sense. There'd been peace between his people and Elden for generations. The king only had to ask, and the Ursan warriors would fight at his side.

Only one thing made sense in Osborn's mind—every last resident of Elden would die by his hand.

THE DAY WAS FILLED WITH hard, gruesome work. He carefully gathered the bodies of his people, trying to remember them as they were—his neighbors, his school buddies, not these lifeless bodies covered in blood and desecrated by bloodthirsty vampires. He found his mother cradling the small, lifeless body of his sister, protecting her even in death. His sister's favorite bear doll in its frilly pink dress lay nearby. Trampled.

By the time the sun was overhead, his grisly task was nearly complete. Tradition dictated the funeral pyre should be set at dusk, burning into the night. But he suspected his family would forgive him for not making himself an easy target for vampires waiting to rip out his throat. Except there were two members of his family unaccounted for. His two younger brothers, Bernt and Torben.

For the first time since his *berserkergang* left him, and he was free to see the carnage left in Elden's wake, did Osborn feel a small twinge of hope. His younger brothers played marathon games of hide-and-seek, but this time their skill at not being found might have saved their lives. And their older brother knew their favorite place. Picking up his steel and pelt, Osborn took off at a sprint.

The earthen smells of the cave was a welcome re-

lief from the smoky ash and blood and death where
he'd been working. He whistled into the cave. He heard
no returning sound, but he sensed they were in there.
Wanted them to be. Needed it. Osborn had never understood his younger siblings' fascination for this place. He
hated the enclosed, dark hole that was the cave, but after
chores, his brothers would spend hours in the shelter of
the rock. He hoped it held true this time. Osborn took
a step inside. "Bernt, are you here? Torben? Come out,
brothers," he urged quietly.

He heard the quick intake of breath, and a relief like
no other made his throat tighten.

"It's Osborn. Take my hand," he suggested as he
forced his fingers deeper into the cave with dread and
hope.

He was rewarded by small fingers encircling his
hand. Two sets of hands. Thank the gods.

He gently drew them outside the cave, their dirty
faces blinking in the harsh sunlight so welcome.

"Mom told us to hide," Bernt said, guilt already hardening his young face.

"We wanted to fight," Torben defended. "But she
made us promise."

He gave a quick squeeze to each of their shoulders.
The way his father would. "You did the right thing. Now
you will live to fight another day." As he had lived. As
he would fight.

After gathering what stores they could find and
carry, his brothers helped Osborn light the pyre, saying a prayer for the spirits of their people.

THE THREE OF THEM TRAVELED far away from Ursa, crossing through the various kingdoms of their world. Osborn spent his days hustling for food, trying to keep his

brothers safe and work on their training. But he soon learned the only marketable skills a warrior of Ursa possessed was for that of killing. Hired out as a mercenary. An assassin.

The boy who'd once mourned the death of a fearless animal now enjoyed the killing. The smell of death. The pleas of his prey.

Osborn thrived under the threat of his imminent death. Not even the pleasure found between a woman's legs could quell the blood fury. Only when he faced the steel of another's blade did his senses awake. Only when the sting of pain lashed through him did he feel… anything.

Only when he witnessed his life's blood pumping from his body with each beat of his heart did he hear the echoing pulse of his ancestors'. Now gone. All dead. Except him. He always survived.

But the royals of the various kingdoms of their realm grew worried and fearful of this man they'd once hired. A man who took jobs without question was not a man to be trusted.

Now he was the hunted.

And once again, eight years since fleeing his homeland, Osborn gathered his younger brothers and fled, this time deep into the woody plains of the sacred bear, a place where no one but an Ursa warrior would dare to tread. And those warriors were all gone.

CHAPTER TWO

BREENA STUMBLED THROUGH the tall grass and bramble. Large thorns tore at the delicate skin of her bare legs, but she no longer cried out in pain. If she were at home in Elden, she could blunt the pain with her magic, force it through some door in her mind and slam it shut. But that power eluded her in this unfamiliar place. Here, wherever she was, she had to endure it. Push through the throbbing of her tired muscles and the sting from the cuts and abrasions running up and down her arms and legs.

The voluminous folds of her once-ornate skirt, her protection from the harsh wilderness, was now gone, ripped and torn away as she'd traveled. Blood ran down her legs from the scratches, joining the dried layer already caked to her calves. Her knees were skinned, and still she drove herself to put one foot in front of another. She pushed forward as she'd been doing since she'd been ripped from her own realm and thrown... somewhere.

She stepped on a rock, its sharp edge digging into the tender arch of her foot; the dainty slippers she'd been wearing when she'd woken up were long gone. She stumbled again, this time falling to the ground, and, as she landed, she lost the last of her strength. Breena would cry if she had even a tiny sliver of energy. She hadn't eaten in days, the only water she'd had was when she'd sipped off plant leaves. No one looking at her now would ever think she'd once been a princess. One who could do magic.

She pulled her hands together, closed her eyes and concentrated, willing her magic to appear. Produce a trickle of water or a berry to eat. But it did not. Just like it hadn't appeared since she'd arrived with only two thoughts she couldn't chase from her mind. Two seemingly opposing goals.

To survive. To kill.

Breena rubbed at her brows, trying to soothe the sharp ache knotting behind her eyes. Those goals seemed to come from someplace outside of her. Survival from someone warm, caring... Her mother? She hugged her arms around herself—yes, her mother would want her to live.

To avenge. To kill. That thought was masculine. Powerful. Authoritative. Her father.

And yet, she'd not do either. She'd neither live nor live to kill. Unless killing herself by pushing forward counted.

She doubted it was what her father had in mind. Her fingers went to the timepiece that had somehow survived whatever kind of hellish force brought her to this wild place. An unknown vengeance burned deep inside her, and she understood, perhaps since waking up dazed and alone in this strange land, that her parents had done something to her. Why here? Were they de— Pain ripped behind her eyes, making her gasp. Her parents... The throbbing always came when her thoughts lingered too long on them. She didn't even know if they were alive or dead. But each time her attention drifted their way, Breena could see a little more. Until the pain took over.

Breena would die either way, so she might as well keep going.

Bracing for the pain, she pulled herself up off the ground and stood. She took an unsteady step, followed by another.

A bird flew overhead. She'd heard a story once about a lost boy following a bird and it leading him to a beautiful meadow filled with fruit and a pond of cool, delicious water. Of course, the boy got lost there, and never returned home. Breena was sure there was some lesson buried in the story, warning curious children about wandering off, but right now, she could only focus on the drinking and eating part.

Shading her eyes, she decided following the bird was the best plan she had so far. She spotted another skull attached to a tree. This was the third she'd seen just like that.

A bear skull.

She had to be in Ursa. The clan with the affinity to the great bear. Fought like them, she'd heard her father comment, clearly impressed. The Ursan kingdom had been allied to her own since her great-grandfather's time. He'd negotiated the conditions himself. If she could just find them, find their village, perhaps they could help her get back to Elden. No, the Ursans were all gone. If only those warriors could help her with both goals, live and kill. The thoughts she'd woken up with two days ago.

Was it two? Felt like more. Like her home in Elden was a lifetime ago. Time was so hazy. It didn't make sense. Like so many things since she'd woken up. Breena remembered something happening to her home, fear for her brothers. When she closed her eyes tight, images of her mother and father appeared. Performing last magic.

But why did they send her here?

Pain ripped across her chest, and Breena shook her head. She didn't want those images in her mind. But something had happened to her. Traces of magic surrounded her. Someone else's magic. Certainly not hers.

Instead, she tried to replace the images of her parents with that of her warrior. As she slept beneath the protective cover of trees, Breena attempted to walk into his dream. His mind. But just like her missing magic, her warrior was lost to her now, too. She found no door.

So she followed the bird, a hawk, as it made a lazy loop in the sky above her head.

"Please be thirsty," she whispered. *And hungry.*

The bird made a squealing sound and dove. Breena forced energy into her feet. Her legs. Not her misplaced magic, but old-fashioned willpower. She sprinted as she chased the bird. Jumping over a fallen log, avoiding a thorny bush.

She came into a small clearing, only to spy the bird claiming a perch rather than hunting for sustenance. Disappointment cut into her side like a stitch, and she rested her hands on her thighs, dragging in large gulps of air. No meadow, no pond...just a perch. She glanced up to glare at the hawk, and then realized it was perched upon the gable of a cottage. A well-kept cottage.

The clearing around the wood cabin was neat and free of weeds and stones. A small plowed area—a garden, perhaps—lay to one side. That meant there had to be water and food inside.

With a squeal she raced to the door, fearing it would be locked. But she'd break through the window if she had to. She knocked on the door, but no one came to

invite her inside. Polite niceties of etiquette over, she
turned the handle, and thankfully the knob twisted easily and she pushed the door open.

Wholesome grain and cinnamon scented the air.
There, on the stove, stood a large pot of oatmeal. Everything in her body seized. Food. Food. Reaching
for the ladle she began to eat from the large utensil.
Irritated with the awkwardness of it all, she tossed the
spoon on the counter and dug in with her hands, feeding
herself like an animal. Her mother would be appalled.

But then it was her mother who'd wanted her to survive. To live.

Her very empty stomach protested as the food hit,
and she forced herself to slow down. Breena didn't want
to make herself sick. A pitcher stood on the table. She
didn't care what was inside; even if it were blackberry
juice, she was going to drink it. She put the spout to her
lips, and allowed the sweet taste of lemonade to fill her
mouth and slide down her throat.

Despite her efforts to slow down, nausea struck her
and she began to shudder. She took a blind step to the
left, falling down hard on a chair at an awkward angle.
With a sharp crack, the legs gave way and the chair
broke, taking her to the floor.

Breena began to laugh. Tears formed at the corners
of her eyes and fell down her cheeks. She'd found herself a cottage, and she was still stumbling to the ground.
No one would believe her to be a princess with oatmeal
drying on her hands and lemonade dripping down her
chin.

The wave of nausea passed only to be replaced by
a bone-deep weariness. Breena had already eaten this
family's meal and broken their furniture, but she didn't
think she could attempt another thing except lay her

head down and close her eyes. She spotted an open door leading to another room of the cottage. Her spirits lifted; perhaps a bed awaited. With one last surge of strength, she crawled across the wooden floor, delighted to see not one but three beds. None were as grand or ornate as the sleigh bed she had in her tower room in Elden. No heavy draperies hung from hooks above the headboard, nor was the bed covered by mounds and mounds of fluffy pillows in bright colors, but they were flat, clean and looked comfortable. Of course, anything would be comfortable after sleeping on the hard, cold ground for days…weeks? Her perception was off; she couldn't grasp what was real.

What she needed was a good night's sleep. She should leave some kind of a note for the inhabitants, but her eyes were already drooping. The combination of fear, hunger, weakness and displacement finally zapped what was left of her waning strength. She fell across the largest of the beds, too tired to even slip beneath the covers.

Too weary to even attempt dreamtime with the warrior.

IT WAS A GOOD THING they weren't hunting for food because his brothers' loud voices would have scared away any game. Osborn glanced over at Bernt. In a year, he'd be looking him in the eye. Torben wasn't that far behind.

If they still lived in their homeland and he was any kind of good big brother, Bernt would have already tested his strengths as a warrior at his Bärenjagd by now. Guilt slammed into Osborn. He should have prepared his brother better, led him to the rites that would make him a man before his people. Before all of the Ursa realm.

But there was no Ursa realm anymore.

What good was the Bärenjagd, the *berserkergang,* if he couldn't save his people? If it left him hunted like an animal? Nothing better than another man's mercenary?

Yet a restlessness hovered over his brother. A need not fulfilled. Bernt had become prone to taking off into the woods, with dark moods and fits of anger that didn't resemble the avenging rage of a *berserker.*

Unfulfilled destiny.

Osborn would have to do something. And soon. An urgency now laced the air. Doubt after doubt crashed into him. Had he worked with Bernt enough on handling his spear? Keeping his balance in combat? Steadying his nerves?

Osborn scrubbed his hand down his face. More than likely, his thoughts mirrored the worries and reservations of his own father. Thoughts his father must have hidden as he'd stared into the fire while his young son Osborn slept nearby.

Only Osborn wasn't Bernt's father. Didn't possess his wisdom. What could he teach about honor? He'd lost his years ago.

His brothers zipped past him, racing for the door. Bernt was in a good mood today. A rarity. Chopping wood for hours under the blazing sun had bled the aggression from him. For the day. The two crashed through the front door, knocking off each other's hats, and generally being loud. But then when were they not loud? At least he'd given them a childhood of carefree days. At least he'd given them that much.

The pot of oatmeal he'd thought he'd left on the stove now lay on the kitchen table. The ladle lay discarded on the scarred wooden countertop, slops of grain sliding down the sides and waiting to be cleaned.

"Who did that?" he bellowed.

The lemonade pitcher was filthy. Dried glops of oatmeal stuck to the handle and it appeared someone had taken a drink directly from the spout.

"No one's going to want to drink from this now. How hard is it to get a cup?"

And when had he become an old woman?

"I didn't do it," Torben said.

"Me, neither," Bernt replied. Already his shoulders were stiffening, his brighter mood growing stormy.

"I don't care who did it." How many times had he said that since taking over the care and responsibility of his younger brothers? "Both of you can help clean it up." And that?

Osborn moved, and the sound of splintering wood broke the tense silence. "Look at the chair." He pointed to the remnants of Bernt's attempt at furniture.

"There's another one that's busted," Bernt grumbled.

"You'll get the hang of woodworking," Osborn told him, forcing as much reassurance into his voice as he could muster.

Bernt's look grew defiant. "I'm supposed to be a warrior."

Yes, and there lay the problem.

"Well, now you're a would-be warrior who works with wood," he said simply, as if it fixed and explained everything. But how long could the three of them pretend?

Torben crouched and reached for one of the busted chair legs. He tossed it from hand to hand as Osborn had once done with a spear. Osborn had been ignoring the fact that his other brother also exhibited every sign of being a warrior.

"This chair didn't fall apart by itself. It broke with force." His brother met his gaze. "Someone's been here."

"Told you I didn't make the mess," Bernt said, his voice still a mix of defiance and triumph. "Someone's been eating our food."

"And someone's been sitting in our chair," echoed his brother.

But Osborn barely heard. All his senses were focusing. Narrowing. The cold began to creep down his limbs, hardening his muscles. For the first time he noticed the tiny bits of grass leading to their bedchamber.

His fingers slid down his boot for the blade. His brother was already handing him the pack sheltering his *berserker* pelt. The pack was always within reaching distance of one of them.

He crept silently across the wooden floor. Telling his brothers to stay back would be useless. Someone had invaded their home. Any warning Osborn issued to them could not compete with Ursan warrior instincts.

A soft sound, like a moan, drifted from the bedchamber. The chill began to subside. His *berserkergang* sensed whatever made that noise was no threat, and began to stand down. But that moan...it shafted through his body, alerting all his senses in a different manner. As a man.

The three of them peered inside the room.

"Someone's sleeping in your bed. And she's still there."

Osborn stalked into the room. The woman lay on her stomach on his bed, her long blond hair fanning across his pillow. Something primal kicked him in the gut.

"Is she dead?" Torben whispered.

His gaze lowered to the even rise and fall of her

back. He shook his head, relief chasing the last of his *berserker's* nature away. "She's asleep."

Why were they whispering? This woman had invaded their home, messed his kitchen and destroyed his property. But he couldn't work up any sense of outrage.

The woman looked as if she'd fallen onto his bed, and gone to sleep. Like a dream come true for most men.

She sighed, a soft delicate sound, and hiked up her leg. No covers hid her from his view. Her legs were bare, and his gaze followed all the way up.

Holy hell. What was left of her skirt has been ripped away, and he could see the rounded curve of her ass. Desire, hot and heavy, hit him. Hardened him. Sweat broke out along his brow.

He forced his eyes downward once more, this time noticing the deep cuts and abrasions all up and down her legs, marring her delicate skin.

How did—? Who would—?

Something deeply buried rose within him. A force as strong as his bear spirit. Not warring, but mingling. Joining and growing more powerful. *His.*

"Leave," he ordered his brothers.

Neither needed a second command from Osborn. They recognized the chill in his voice. The forces charging through him. They fairly tripped over each other fleeing the room.

A line crossed her brow as the clumsy shuffling footsteps of his brothers escaping the bedroom penetrated her sleep. She rolled over and his gaze traveled down once more. He'd never seen a face so delicate, her bones fine and skin that looked almost too soft to touch. Her chin was another thing—not softly rounded like the rest of her, but stubborn. The flaw only made her more appealing. Pink tipped her cheeks and nose, like someone who'd been in the sun too long. The material of her bodice was dirty and torn, many parts missing, but Osborn could tell it had once been fine. Expensive.

Who was she?

The woman took a deep breath, her breasts rising and drawing his attention. Osborn could not look away. Flashes of her bare skin peeked through the rips of her clothing. His eyes narrowed and he could see the rosier skin of her nipples.

His.

The primal conviction drove a harsh thrust of heat and desire through him. Osborn stepped toward her. Peered down at her sleeping figure in his bed. He could see every line of her face. The dark fan of her eyelashes. The soft curve of her bottom lip. He forced his hands down to his sides. Fisted his hands so he wouldn't be tempted to touch her. Trace his fingers along the skin of her arm. Her cheek. Find out for himself if she was as soft as she looked.

What the hell was he thinking? She wasn't his. One person didn't possess another. He willed his body to back down.

Just then her eyes opened, green and sleepy. His gaze darted to her lips, which were turning into a smile. A smile for him.

"Warrior," she said, and hugged his pillow to her chest, still more asleep than awake.

Everything in him controlled and restrained disappeared. Osborn needed to feel her in his arms, kiss that mouth. He reached for her shoulders, dragging her unresisting body toward him. Her eyes widened as he dipped his head.

He tasted the sweet tartness of the lemonade on her lips. But nothing in this world he'd ever sampled was as good as her. Osborn wound his fingers in the messy strands of her blond hair, drawing her still closer. Smashing the softness of her breasts against his chest.

His heartbeat pounded, and he took advantage of her unresisting lips and plunged his tongue in her mouth, savoring her, twining his tongue with hers. No, nothing he'd ever had tasted this good. Felt this good. Made him feel this good. Except...

Except one thing. The woman who invaded his dreams. Tormented his nights. Left him alone feeling tortured, battling a fierce wanting and hungry for more.

He pulled his mouth from hers. Thrust her away.

The sound of their harsh breathing filled the small bedroom. The woman blinked up at him, confusion pulling her brows together. A flush rose along the delicate cords of her neck and across her collarbone. She'd been as affected by that kiss as much as he had. Satisfaction curled in his gut.

She ran her fingers along her lower lip, and he longed to trace that path with his tongue. Suck those fingers into his mouth. All the torment and hunger and wanting torturing his body when he awoke from his dreams with her was magnified tenfold, a hundredfold, for having the real thing in his arms. This wasn't a dream... was it?

"You're real?" he asked, his voice raw and harsh.

Her nod was slow in coming.

Then he knew. The woman in front of him wasn't some dream girl his imagination had conjured to taunt him in the night. The haze that seemed to surround her in his dreams was gone. She lay before him in sharp focus. Osborn remembered the utter helplessness he'd felt, raged against, when he tried to draw her back to him that last time. How he'd failed.

Somehow she'd put herself there. She was responsible for all the anguished desire he'd felt. All his want. Need. His yearning for something he could never have.

Thought he could never have.

His.

Yes, she was his.

His *berserkergang* was wrong to back down, assessing the woman in his bed posed no risk. Everything about her was a threat to him. And still the chill signaling the approach of his *berserkergang* did not hit him.

Something must have been in his eyes, or the set of his lips must have alerted some self-preservation instinct inside her. He reached for her again.

And that's when she screamed.

CHAPTER THREE

BREENA HAD NEVER BEEN so terrified in her life. She'd always thought that if she actually met up with her warrior in the flesh she'd be frightened…and she was right. The man who'd woken her up—his face tight with desire, outrage and stunned disbelief—was huge. Broad-shouldered with the kind of muscular arms that easily proved he wielded a sword. Fearsome. A fighter.

Although he wasn't fighting, whatever was inside him drove him right at her. He quickly approached her, leaning toward her with determination and intent burning in his eyes.

What he intended to do, she didn't fully know, as her dreams never really went much further than the kissing, but whatever it was…it had to be dangerous.

There was a reason princesses were locked up in towers and hidden away in far-off places, guarded by magical creatures. It was to keep those princesses safe from the kind of danger this man radiated. Because despite her fright, some small part of her wanted to know what all that danger was about. She screamed louder.

His hand covered her mouth to stifle her.

That was the second time someone had muzzled her, and it would be the last. Maybe it was the food, or that she'd finally snatched a bit of rest, or just plain fear, but Breena, princess of Elden, had had enough.

With every last bit of strength she possessed, she

pushed at his shoulders, her scream changing to a grunt, then finally silence.

He didn't budge, but his hand fell away. The sound of her labored breathing filled the tiny space of the bedroom. His dark eyes searched her face, lingered at her breasts and followed down her legs. Then his gaze slammed into hers and he reached for her again.

"That's far enough," she said, scrambling to the floor, putting the bed between their bodies.

He lifted a brow at the protection she'd chosen. A bed—not the safest of barriers.

"Who are you?" she asked.

"I'll ask the questions," he told her, his voice gruff and rumbly.

Breena pursed her lips and nodded. The warrior did have a point, she *had* invaded his home.

"I've dreamed about you," he said, angry wonder lacing his words.

She'd been expecting questions, demands; instead, his statement sealed the connections she had with this man. Her dream lover. *Her* warrior.

She wet her bottom lip with her tongue. "You've been in my dreams, too," she admitted. *Because I put you there.* She'd just leave that little detail out of her explanations. Every instinct told her to be cautious, to not offer him too much information about herself.

"But there's never been fear in your eyes."

No, she could imagine what her gaze had conveyed in his dreams. A woman who wanted. Wanted *him*.

Faster than she thought such a large man could move, he was around the bed that separated them, and at her side. Crowding her. Breena took a step backward. And another. The wood-beamed wall of the cabin cut into her shoulder blades.

He'd backed her into the wall, and there was no escape.

"I've wondered a thousand times what your skin would feel like." The back of his hand smoothed down her cheek. His nearness was devastating to her senses. The scent of him, like the woods and fresh air, made her long to breathe him in deep. Heat radiated from his body, chasing away the chill to her skin from wearing tattered clothing.

Blood pounded through her body, rushed in her ears. Her eyelids fluttered at the first touch of his skin against hers. She'd been so alone for the past few days, so afraid, and his touch made her feel safe for the first time.

He'd wondered what she'd feel like outside of a dream. "So have I," she told him, and her fingers lifted to his face. Touched the line of his jaw.

His large hand captured her exploring fingers, drawing them to his lips. "Tell me your name." It was a gentle command. "I've wondered."

"Breena."

"Beautiful name," he said, his gaze lowering to her lips for a moment, then back to meet her eyes. "You look exactly as you appeared in my dreams." He dropped her hand to pull a twig from her hair, rub away some of the dirt from her cheek. "Who's done this to you?"

The caution she'd felt earlier returned. "The details are fuzzy."

Okay, not truly a falsehood. The fine points of how she'd arrived in this strange kingdom, how long she'd wandered around in the wilderness or even eaten, *were* fuzzy. She tried to concentrate, to come up with some piece of information that would allay his curiosity... but the only picture she could conjure in her mind was the sinister, bony frame. The frightening creature with the eight legs that made a shudder slide down her back. The blood of her parents spilled on the floor of the great hall where they'd once danced and once ruled over a kingdom. That was clear.

She swallowed down a quiet sob, her body quaking, remembering her terror that night.

"In my dreams there was no fear in your eyes. Don't be afraid of me." He reached for her hand again, drew her fingertips to his mouth. The warmth of his tongue sparked a carnal response from deep inside her. Breena found it hard to breathe, hard to concentrate on anything but this man. His warmth. His dark eyes, and what he was doing to her body with his lips.

Breena suspected he meant his actions to be soothing, or to draw her attention away from her fear. Instead, she was more afraid of him than ever.

The warrior drew her hand from his mouth and placed it on his shoulder. She sunk her fingers into the dark strands at the nape of his neck. She gasped when his lips grazed along her collarbone, his tongue teasing the sensitive place beneath her ear.

"Tell me why you're here," he urged.

To survive. To kill.

She shrugged her shoulders, wanting the voices out of her head. Breena leaned her back against the wall, giving him better access to her body. Her skin. Her. "I don't know. I thought it was an accident that I found your cottage, but now…now I wonder if maybe I was drawn here."

He seemed to like her response because he tugged the lobe of her ear into his mouth.

Her throat tightened with relief. The man whose dreams she'd visited was perfect. She'd always dismissed her magic as being weak and inadequate, but her powers must have led her to the door that was the gateway into this man's dreams. A warrior who could help her return to Elden, defeat the invaders...just like those heroic princes from her stories.

"Now you can help me," she said, her body beginning to shiver as he traced the curve of her ear with his tongue. Even the feel of his breath, warm and heavy against her skin as he exhaled, did strange things to her body.

"Don't worry, I'll help you all you want." His voice was a promise.

"You can amass an army?" she asked, daring to run her hands along the broadness of his shoulders, delighting in the dozens of muscles roping his arms.

His lips stopped their exploration of her neck. "An army?" He leaned away from her, his eyes heavy-lidded and filled with desire and confusion. "Just what kind of help are you needing?"

"I only—"

But her warrior was already cutting her words off with a slicing arc of his hand. "My sword is not for sale." His gaze crept down to her breasts. "For any price."

"My family is in danger."

"It's not my concern," he told her, his voice indifferent, his stance nonchalant.

"But... You're supposed to..." she sputtered. He was her warrior. He was supposed to help her. Wasn't this some kind of requirement of the fairy-tale code?

His gaze dropped to her nipples poking at her shredded bodice. "I'll have Bernt try to find you some better clothes. But *you* are leaving."

For the first time since waking up in her bedchamber with Rolfe ushering her to safety, Breena felt completely worn out. Defeated.

Survive.

The command echoed through her head. That's what she was trying to do.

"I need your help."

He cupped Breena between her legs, and her breath lodged in her throat with a hiss. "If the help you need is here, I'm happy to please." His fingers caressed her sensitized skin, her tattered clothing hardly an obstacle. "And I *would* please you, Breena."

Her nipples hardened at the carnal guarantee in his words. Her skin heated, and she felt wetness between her thighs.

Then he dropped his hand. His expression grew hard. "That's all the help I'll be offering."

She watched as the man of her dreams left her to walk away, slamming the door behind her.

FOR MONTHS OSBORN HAD woken up in an agony of frustration and wanting. Hunger and need for one woman. After holding the real thing in his arms, caressing her soft skin, tasting her sweet lips, he knew nothing could ever satisfy him.

Nothing but turning around, tossing Breena on her back and burying himself in her sweet flesh.

He couldn't remember when the dreams had first begun, and now he saw those dreams, those fantasies, for what they really were—nightmares.

His brothers were grouped by the kitchen table. The wood from the broken chair already swept away, the table clean of the leftover dried oatmeal. All traces of Breena's visit gone…except he felt her in his home now. Felt her presence in him.

His skin began to chill. His *berserkergang* grew wilder inside him. The walls of the cabin he'd built alongside his brothers, his sanctuary, now boxed him in and imprisoned him. "I have to get out of here," he told Bernt and Torben, grabbing his pelt bag and ignoring the curious glances of his brothers.

"What about her?" Bernt dared to ask.

Osborn turned on his brother, a roar of anger on his lips. "Get rid of her before I get back."

"But she's…" His younger brother Torben swallowed.

"What?" he bellowed his question.

"She's a girl."

And his cock knew it.

Bernt cleared his throat. "We thought maybe she could stay. Make our meals."

"And clean, and do the laundry. Girls like to do that stuff."

Obviously he'd kept his brothers away from civilization for too long. He could just add it to the list of his faults and deficits where his brothers' raising was concerned. "We're not a houseful of dwarves, and she's sure as hell not staying."

"But—"

Osborn shot his brother a look, and Bernt was smart enough to know when to shut his damn mouth.

"Get her some clothes and get her out of here." Osborn slammed the door behind him, making every beam of wood and pane of glass rattle.

"WHAT DO WE DO?" Torben asked.

Bernt shrugged. "Get her a pair of pants, one you've outgrown. I'll see if I can find an old shirt and shoes small enough to fit her feet."

"I don't see why she can't stay," Torben said, happily defiant when his oldest brother wasn't around.

Bernt only shook his head. Nothing about today made much sense.

The door to the bedchamber opened, and the woman poked her head around the corner.

BREENA HAD HEARD THE VOICES from the other room. But then how could she not? She was pretty sure her warrior had left, and she was also plenty sure the hinges of the front door had taken a beating with his retreat.

Why was he so angry? It just didn't add up. Her magic had drawn her to him; it must have. Why would she be able to put herself into the dreams of a man so powerful, so fierce, one who could surely help her, help her family, if she weren't supposed to use that gift?

Two boys stared at her from the other side of the door. They had to be his brothers. They all shared the same dark hair and dark eyes. Tall and lean, like gangly youths, but soon they'd fill out and be as muscular as their older brother. The youngest might even grow to be taller than her warr—

Okay, she was tired of calling him *warrior*. "What's his name?" she asked.

The youngest looked over at his brother, as if spilling that beast's name could be construed as some kind of betrayal.

"Osborn," the older one said. "And I'm Bernt and this is Torben. We're going to find you something to wear before you leave."

Osborn. She allowed his name to roll around in her mind. In all the nights she'd visited this man as he'd slept, she'd never really thought of him as something other than her lover. The warrior in her dreams. Never imagined him in real life, as a man with a family, and responsibilities and a name.

There was another personality trait many of the princesses shared in the stories she'd read, selfishness, and she'd only ever thought of Osborn as someone to help her.

But was hoping to protect her family selfish? Her kingdom and all her people were dying. In truth, they might even now be dead or enslaved.

Breena squared her shoulders. Osborn might want her far away from him, but she had no plans to go. Her magic had brought them together, and her warrior might be reluctant but he *was* going to help. She eyed the front door. Apparently he wanted his brothers to get rid of her before he returned.

Not going to happen.

Kings and princes might rule through sheer force of will and strength, but as her mother always told her, a queen knew how to get what she desired with nothing but a smile and her brain. And she'd taught those skills to her daughter.

Breena flashed that smile at the boys right now. "Thank you for your hospitality. I'm so sorry I broke your chair, and it was such a fine work of craftsmanship, too."

Bernt's cheeks began to flush. Flattery always worked on men.

Torben laughed. "You thought that chair was goo—"

The younger brother's words were cut off by a smack to his shoulder.

"I've been walking for so many days, and seen so many interesting things, but this cabin is…"

The brotherly irritation lining Bernt's forehead faded. "We haven't been outside our lands since—" he stopped, his brown eyes clouding "—well, for a long time. What's out there?"

Now this was very curious. She didn't know how long she'd roamed, but at least a couple of days, and she'd never once spotted another person. Osborn had apparently hidden himself and his brothers away from civilization for quite some time. Why?

Bernt looked more boy now than youth. She had him. A boy's sense of adventure was universal.

"It's a magical world out there."

Torben's eyes focused. "You've seen magic?"

She lowered her voice and leaned forward as if she was about to impart a great secret. "I can do magic," she told him.

"Show me," he demanded.

Now she had him, too. She only had to draw out his curiosity until her missing magic reappeared.

She stretched her arms above her head. "Oh, I'd love to," she told them. Was she going overboard with the reluctance lacing her voice? "But it seems I have to be on my way." She aimed her steps in the direction of the door.

"Oh, but—"

"Maybe you can stay a little longer."

She flashed them a smile. "You did say something about clothes."

"And we have something that will take away the pain of your cuts and sunburn." The boys left her side in a sprint, Bernt rummaging through an old wooden chest by the window, while Torben vanished into the bedchamber. They both returned with well-worn but clean pants and shirts. About three sizes too big. But if for some reason she was back out wandering the woods again, the rugged material of her new outfit would protect her from the sun and the tree limbs.

"Tell us about what you've seen," Torben urged.

What would intrigue him besides her magic? Food always worked for her. "My favorite day is market day. All the tradespeople and farmers bring their wares and set up booths. Of course everyone gives you a little sample of their food so you'll buy. One walk down the aisle and you're completely full." Or so she'd been told by one of the maids who'd helped her dress. Her parents would never have allowed her to go to market day, so she had something in common with these two brothers who longed to experience something new and different.

"What kind of food?" Torben asked, licking his lips. "All we get here is porridge and meat. Burned meat."

"To a crisp," Bernt added. "Osborn is not a very good cook."

"And if we complain, he'd make us do it. Can you cook?"

She didn't exactly cook, but she knew how to direct a kitchen staff. "My favorite is stew." That wasn't a lie. She didn't specifically say she'd cooked it. "Thick with lots of vegetables and fresh baked bread."

Both boys closed their eyes and moaned.

"But there's more than just the booths. There's singing, traveling acrobats and minstrels and dancing bears."

Bernt's face grew angry. "Bears shouldn't dance."

She'd forgotten she was in Ursan lands. "It was only one time. I'd love to tell you more, but I better change clothes and start walking before it gets dark."

Torben slumped in disappointment. "I'd like to try that bread."

Breena began to finger the frayed edge of the pants

they'd given her. "I'd hate to put on these fresh clothes when I'm so dirty. Is there somewhere I can take a bath?"

She'd only suggested a bath to stall time, but now that she'd said the request out loud, Breena actually longed to be clean. To wash the grass from her hair, the dried blood from her knees.

"We usually just hop in the lake."

"There's no bathing tub?"

The boys just looked at her blankly.

"I'm guessing you wouldn't have shampoo?"

Torben only nodded.

"Okay then, point me in the right direction."

Bernt's brow knotted. "I don't think this is a good idea."

"Technically I'll be out of the house, so he can't get mad," she assured him.

"Oh, he can get mad."

She just bet he could.

OSBORN STALKED THROUGH the woods, crashed though the tall grass and avoided the areas where the bears slept. Sweat slid down his back as he pushed himself to keep going. Away from his home and away from her.

He swiped at a branch closing in on his eye. Clearly he was going crazy. The isolation of his lonely life was making him want things he had no business wanting. What a fool he'd been. He'd clung to the woman who visited him as he slept. He hadn't realized how much until what he'd been fighting so hard to hold on to had been ripped away from him. At first he'd try to force his thoughts to something else during the day. Keeping the area around their cabin clear. Ensuring there was enough food and clean water. Taking care of his brothers.

But finally he succumbed, and he'd work to remember those dream moments with her throughout his day. Although, truthfully, it wasn't very hard. Those moments drew him to his bed at night so he could dream.

But it wasn't special like he'd thought. He'd never imagined her to be real; otherwise, he would have dredged hell to find her. The elemental pleasure that tore through him the moment he'd realized his dream woman slept in his bed, lay in his arms, was alive for him, rivaled only by the primal satisfaction of joining the ranks of Ursan warriors.

Only, the woman in his dreams just wanted him to kill for her. Like all the others who thought coin would keep them clean from the dirty work. Special? What in the hell had he turned into?

The heat and exhaustion finally took him over. Osborn stripped off his shirt to cool down, and his steps slowed. But the sun overhead beat down on him. He changed his course to the lake. How many times had he sought refuge from his thoughts, his responsibilities and the weight of the lives he'd taken in those chilly waters?

The splashing was what put him on guard. He sunk to his knees, reaching for the knife he always kept tucked in his boot. He quietly followed the trail of the intruder. They hadn't worked hard to cover their tracks. Or to be quiet. It sounded like...

He shook his head, but no... It actually sounded to him as if...

Osborn heard the beautiful sounds of a woman singing. His muscles tensed and his cock hardened. He cleared the brush blocking his view, the weapon in his hand forgotten. There, swimming in the blue water of his lake, was Breena. Naked.

Her ripped and worn clothes lay discarded in a heap by the bank. He spotted the pants and shirt loaned to her by his brothers neatly folded and waiting for her on a rock. The long blond strands of her hair floated around her shoulders, billowing in the water like something otherworldly and beautiful. He took a step, ready to touch it, touch her, before he stopped himself.

She'd had him under her spell for too long.

Breena let her feet land on the bottom, standing waist-deep. With a smile, she reached toward the light filtering between the leaves of the trees that protected the lake he'd once thought idyllic. Now she'd invaded it, stamped her impression in this place that was once all his own. Sunlight glinted off the water drops rolling down her skin, and her wet hair plastered against her back, almost long enough to reach the most beautiful ass he'd ever seen.

This was how she was when he was alone with her in his dreams. She turned in the sunlight, beautiful and utterly delectable. Her nipples stood out between the wet strands of her hair, tempting him, drawing him closer. His for the taking.

Why was he the one walking away?

She was *his*.

He reached for the button of his pants, and they joined the clothes she'd tossed aside.

The water chilled his overheated skin as he chased her in the water. Breena turned toward him with a little gasp of surprise. Her cheeks were rosy from her exertion in the lake, her green eyes sparkling from the pleasure of her swim. He knew that pleasure. Now he would know another. In her arms.

She hadn't left his lands. Surely it would be easy enough to find another mercenary to kill whomever she wanted dead. There were plenty after his neck. But she'd stayed. She wanted him. Now he needed to know why. Needed to know almost as much as he needed to find the pleasure her sweet body offered. He grasped her chin, forcing her to look up at him.

"You put yourself in my dreams. Tell me the truth. You did it. You made me think of only you. Want only you."

Her nod was slow in coming.

He squeezed his eyes shut tight at her answer. Even now, some small sliver of hope, desire that she wanted him for more than a sword, still ached in his soul. Idiot. He sucked in a large breath of air. Then his gaze met hers. She pulled her chin from his grasp and shrank lower into the lake, the water sloshing over her lips. She looked more afraid of him than ever.

Good.

He always hunted best when his prey panicked.

CHAPTER FOUR

BREENA BIT BACK THE urge to scream. What good would it do, anyway? From the looks of him, he'd only laugh. Osborn seemed to be pleased by her growing unease. As if he grew stronger from her fear.

Then she just wouldn't be afraid of him.

Ha! Impossible.

Her first, and really her only, instinct had been to shrink away from him, and shield herself with the water. And she wasn't exactly getting the reaction she wanted from him—to back away from her. Still, she wouldn't *show* her fear of him. She was a princess, and one of her singular skills was acting. "Why are you so angry with me?" she asked, deliberately keeping her voice low and laced with the confusion she felt.

"You ask that?"

The man basically roared at her. A pair of birds took to the trees, and the leaves rattled. No one had ever dared to raise their voice to her. Not once in her entire life. Breena found she didn't much care for it.

"Your bellowing is scaring the wildlife."

His lips thinned, as if he were forcing himself to calm. "I don't bellow."

She almost destroyed their uneasy truce by lifting an eyebrow and replying with something verging on sarcasm. Her mother would be appalled at that kind of tone, but she'd learned it from her brother Nicolai.

Her parents would be shocked at some of the stuff her brothers shared with a girl who was supposed to be a gently raised bridal prospect. Another wave of home-sickness racked through her. Breena's throat tightened, but she quickly swallowed away the stiffness along with the sadness.

She needed this man's help. Desperately. Every-thing else she'd attempted to do to gain his attention had failed. Well, not everything. Her body had his full notice. Breena felt herself warm despite the coldness of the water. But he'd already proved she couldn't change his mind with kisses. Neither did the logical approach of simply asking for his help.

But this was her warrior. There was no denying it. Why dream of him? Why did he dream of her, if he were not chosen for her?

Breena smiled sweetly. She'd get him to help her. Somehow and some way. "Of course you didn't bellow. My apologies." Even if she had to lie to make it happen.

His eyes narrowed. His gaze searched hers, obviously looking for signs of deception. Breena held her breath, willing every muscle of her face to remain slack. *I'm completely truthful.* His broad, tense shoulders began to relax.

Either he wasn't very good at spotting deception, or he scared everyone around him so much, no one dared to lie.

Or maybe he knew she was lying, and enjoyed the idea of making her think he believed her every word. She could go around and around with conjecture but what she needed was action.

"I never meant to upset you," she tried again.

The warrior made a scoffing sound. "You didn't upset me."

Yeah, he'd have to actually care in order to be upset. This hard man in front of her didn't appear as if he cared about much.

"Hurt?" she offered, enjoying going further down the path of "upset" when he clearly expected her to go the opposite direction.

He crossed his arms.

"Sad?"

His expression told her she was pushing it.

"Angry?"

"Closer."

"Enraged?"

"Closer still."

But his dark brown eyes no longer held a trace of ire. The tension never returned to those big shoulders of his, and his hands hadn't fisted at his sides. What do you know, the warrior in front of her had a sense of humor.

"Irritated?" she finally questioned.

"Irritated," he said with a nod.

Yes, she just bet he was. If she'd ever been allowed to bet.

"I apologize if I irritated you," she said formally.

Surprise flitted in his gaze until he promptly masked it.

Her mother wouldn't have been able to find fault with her apology. Except the part where she was naked. Wet. And standing in front of what she assumed was an equally naked man with only her hair as any kind of covering.

A princess at the Elden Court was seen but rarely heard.

"Your power comes with marriage," her mother would often instruct Breena, "and the best marriages are arranged with a man who knows nothing about you. Can't know anything about you because you've been silent your whole life. Conduct yourself right, and there will be absolutely nothing any potential bridegroom can object to. Nothing his ambassadors can negotiate over on the marriage contract."

Even at the young age of eight, her mother's tutoring sounded bleak and lonely. Breena hadn't been very good at neutralizing her features then. The pout was already forming, the need to argue quick on her lips.

The memory played on. Queen Alvina squeezed her hand gently. "Once you command your own palace, your own kingdom, then you'll be the woman you were meant to be. Until then, observe. Watch the servers and the cooks and the seamstresses. Listen to their conversations, what concerns them. Learn to read the faces of the hunters and soldiers before they ever report to the king. Knowledge and understanding...that is how you rule." A girl could almost be forgotten when she lived among the shadows. Instincts alone told her when someone's words didn't match their expressions, as often happened with the visitors and foreign dignitaries who spoke with the queen and king in chambers.

Over time, she'd also grown to know the feelings and emotions of her people with only a look, or from a few hushed whispers. Such as when a kitchen maid was sad or one of the young huntsmen was in love. Her family might be vampires or wield powerful magic, but she could uncover what most people wanted to keep hidden. Like the proud man in front of her. Breena suspected this man held a lot of secrets. And she wanted to know all of them.

And wasn't she just bemoaning the dullness of her life not so long ago? Since then she'd been awakened, raced through her home in search of her brothers, been captured and brought before—

Something searing and painful lanced across her mind. Breena blinked back tears, either from the pain or from the memory, she couldn't be sure.

Avenge.

Survive.

The two conflicting commands battled inside her head, until she doubled over, gasping for breath.

"Are you all right?" He grasped her arm with his big hand a little too painfully. Perhaps her warrior was unused to touching females. A tiny thrill shot through her. The warmth of his fingers soothed and actually stopped the commands echoing in her mind.

She looked up at him. A sense of urgency filled her, and she suddenly grew desperate to make him understand. To *want* to help her. His touch could block the pain of her memories, could block the words echoing in her mind.

"What we talked about before…it's all true. My magic led me to you."

He made a scornful noise. His hand fell to his side, and the corner of his lip curled up in disgust. He didn't trust her. She sensed the man didn't trust many. What had made him, his life, so very hard?

But she'd seen him with his guard down.

In her dreams.

There he'd smiled. And laughed. And desired. And shared himself with her. The hard man in front of her now would hack off his own arm before baring his private thoughts, his soul, to anyone. Least of all to her. He probably viewed her as the woman forcing her way into his sleep, when he was most vulnerable. No wonder he didn't trust her and was so very angry with her. But she had to make him believe her.

It seemed her very sanity depended on it.

Breena reached for his hand again, needing the warmth of his touch, even if it wasn't freely given. "Please, you have to believe me. I didn't even realize you were real until I woke up…"

"Nearly naked in my bed." There was his growl again, but it didn't hold the kind of anger as before, but something was definitely pent up inside him. This was more to the man she'd opened her eyes to see earlier today. Much more to this warrior of her dreams. For some reason, that was even scarier.

She took a step backward.

"Good move."

She held her breath.

"But too late." He jerked her closer, and their bodies rubbed together.

Osborn lowered his head. The harsh line of his lips just an inch away from her mouth. Her gaze clashed with his. Fierce anger and hot desire burned in those brown eyes. An anger and desire she suspected simmered just below the surface of him.

"Use your magic on me now, Breena. Make me stop."

"I…I can't." She didn't want him to stop.

His mouth came down hard on hers, and her lips parted. His tongue pushed past her lips and found hers. Osborne's thick arms wrapped around her, and he drew her into the heat of his hard body. Her nipples pebbled against the hairy roughness of his muscled chest, and Breena's heartbeat kicked up to a runner's pace.

He smelled of chestnuts and the earthy scent of the deep woods. Her dreams never detailed how wonderfully he smelled. Or how he tasted of the sweetness of apples, and something unrecognizable to her she could only label it as man. *Him.*

Just when she was about to sink into heaven, Osborn took it away. His lips left, and he rested his forehead against hers. Panting. "Why can't you make me stop?" he asked, pulling away to see her face. His fingers grazed the back of her neck, and sweet sensation tingled along her damp skin.

"My magic…it's gone," she told him with a shrug.

Disappointment flashed across his eyes before it quickly faded. Or he masked it. *Come on, Breena, you're supposed to be good at reading people.*

He placed the barest of kisses against her mouth, and her bottom lip trembled. "Then *tell* me to stop, and I'll stop."

How could she when she ached to be in his arms? To draw his mouth down to hers? To finally *live* every emotion and sensation the Osborn of her dreams promised right now in real life?

She shook her head. "I can't."

His fingers began to caress the skin below her ears, never thinking how sensitive she was there. She watched as the muscles lining his throat worked. Something dark and slightly possessive flashed across his face, turning his features stony. But this wasn't scary. Oh, it was dangerous, and should be a warning, but it was so, so tantalizing.

He lowered his head, and this time she met his kiss, unafraid, and as an equal as when she lay on her bed and joined him in her dreams. The fear and the hunger and the pain of the past few days faded from her mind. Osborne took over. The delicious scent of him filled her. The harsh sounds of his ragged breathing pervaded her ears. The taste of him on her lips…

Breena wanted more.

Standing on tiptoe, she twined her arms around Osborne's neck, drawing him down as close as she could. She sunk her fingers into his long, damp strands of hair and she pressed her mouth to his with equal force.

Osborne groaned, the sound rumbling through his chest. His desire for her made Breena's stomach feel hollow, the way it did in her dreams. His hands began running up and down her back, and when she teased his tongue with hers, his hands finally stopped their quest and grabbed her backside, lifting and fitting her against the hard swell of his arousal.

Breena shivered as a wave of powerful desire sped through her. This incredible sensation was what the chambermaids giggled about at night when they didn't realize they could be overheard by their princess. What the young men of Elden fought battles over in the practice fields outside the castle walls. *This* is what drove her back to her dreams with him whenever she could. For the first time, Breena felt like she was living. Living what *she* wanted to live. Every sense, every pore, every part of her body, ached for more and more.

A harsh gust of wind blew through the trees, rustling the leaves and startling the birds. A shadow fell across the lake as dark clouds barred the sunlight. An eerie chill poured over her exposed skin, despite being wrapped in Osborn's arms.

He lifted his head, and she glanced toward the sky.

Something black and snakelike streaked over the treetops. Breena had never seen its like before, but her stomach tightened and grew queasy at the sight. "What is that…?" she began, but couldn't continue. Another formed in the sky, aiming toward them. She began to shudder, every part of her rejecting the horrifying entity charging for them. The vile thing oozed evil. It swallowed the sanctity of this soothing place, returning only fear and pain and a promise of misery.

Osborn swore, and glanced behind her back toward the pack he'd discarded on the bank. "My weapon," he whispered. "On my count, run toward it. But stay behind me."

They wouldn't make it. The bleak thought appeared in her mind out of nowhere. She shook her head, rejecting the hopelessness invading her soul. She knew the grim conviction in her mind had to be planted by the monsters in the sky.

"Now," he urged, still keeping his voice low so as not to alert the creatures coming for them. He jolted in front of her, spinning her around, and aimed for the bank. This water had once welcomed her, took away for a few moments all the pain she'd felt since she'd awoken in the strange land. Now that lake seemed to turn hostile. Heavy water swirled around her waist, tugging at her feet and dragging her down deeper into the depths.

"Resist," Osborn ordered over the harsh crashing of rushing water. "It senses your fear, but that thing has no power over you."

Breena propelled herself, pushing for each step she took. She had to be slowing Osborn down, preventing him from reaching his pack. "Keep going," she told him.

He shook his head, instead gripping her arm tighter, pulling her behind him. But it was too late. The tip of the entity began to wrap and wind itself around Osborn's free arm. His breath came out in a pained hiss, and she felt his body stiffen.

He dropped her arm and shoved her away from him. "Go, Breena. Get out of here and warn my brothers."

He turned and faced the creature, landing a blow with the kind of force that would have felled a large man. With one last burst of energy, she managed to drag herself onto the bank. The sound of the battle behind her was horrific. The creature shrieked as Osborn rained blow after blow along its snakelike skin, but still the beast never fully released him. His face grew red as he fought with nothing but his brute strength. Vines grew from the snake creature's sides. Osborn hacked at them with his bare hands.

With a hideous shriek, the creature struck Osborn across the side of his face. Blood seeped from a gash across his cheek, and began to bubble from the poison.

How could he fight? How could he win against something so vile? Burns marked where the creature had grazed his skin. Osborn sank to his knees. Struggled to stand.

Dark images flashed across her memory. A creature with razors for fingers. The sounds of the dying in her ears. The smell of death. Her head filled with pain. *No.*

All her muscles tensed and she began to shake. An angry energy began to build inside her. *No.* The word seemed to fill her ears, Blocking out any other noises.

Breena lifted her arms and pointed at the snakelike beast attacking Osborn. "No!" she shouted at the evil thing, and a hot bolt tore from her fingertips. The creature shrieked as if burned. Osborn fell to the ground as the beast turned and aimed straight for her. Fear knifed through her. She almost turned and ran.

But she was done with running away.

Breena locked her knees, faced the evil coming toward her and lifted her hands again.

That thing has no power over you.

If she could prevent the monster from hurting Osborn, she could do more. The thing sped toward her. Another bolt flew into the creature's side and it twisted with a shrill howl. She sent another and another, until sweat filmed her forehead and it grew hard to breathe. Then she sent one more.

With a final shriek, the creature broke apart in a burst of blood. Red gore fell to the churning water, as if the purity of the lake wanted to repel the carnage rather than absorb it. She expected the other creature in the sky to attack next. It circled twice above their heads, then slithered away into the horizon. Finally the water in the lake settled. The wind died down and the sky lightened.

Breena sunk to the ground. Her muscles shook as she struggled to breathe. Whatever energy she'd used to kill the creature sapped her of any strength. She looked around for Osborn. She spotted him still lying where the creature had dropped him. Beaten. Poisoned. Burned. And still he fought to help her get away.

Now he didn't move.

She choked back a sob. Her stomach tightened, and a fluttery panic filled her chest. "Osborn!" she shouted as she crashed through the shallow pools of water and sand, where he lay facedown. "Please be alive. Please." Breena didn't think she could take another death. Certainly not that of her warrior.

With a strength she managed to scrounge up from somewhere, she rolled him over. She gasped when she saw his face crossed by scratches and deep wounds. She smoothed the blood away with her wet hands, fear making her fingers shake.

"Osborn."

Nothing.

Breena leaned closer, getting her nose almost to his. "Osborn!" she yelled.

His eyelids snapped open. "If that's your idea of healing skills, you've got a lot to learn." He groaned.

Her shoulders sagged in relief, her damp hair falling and shrouding them from the sun.

"Thank you," she said.

"For what?" he asked, his breath fanning her cheek.

"I slowed you down." *And nearly got you killed.*

"I wouldn't have made it, anyway."

A realist. She liked that. Sort of. It would certainly take some getting used to. Breena was used to life in the castle where she rarely saw the struggles of others. Was protected from it. Osborn would never lie to her. *That's* what she needed.

"Those things were too fast." His words were grim. His eyes narrowed and his expression turned stony again. Whatever fog he'd been in since she'd rolled him over was dissipating. Her angry warrior was back.

He pushed himself up.

"You shouldn't be trying to sit yet. I think you need to rest."

He only glared at her, and flexed his arms, then his legs, checking for injuries. He hissed in a breath. He'd obviously found one.

She reached for him. Breena had only meant to pat his shoulder, offering a touch of compassion. But her intended comforting brush of her palm turned into a near caress. She'd never been so close to a man before, especially not one who was naked and so, so fascinating. At least, not while she was awake. She still had the taste of him in her mouth.

Every tendon and sinew of his body was tight and defined. Powerful muscles roped his chest, and bunched at his arms. Scars—some old, some new—ran along his body. And he'd have new ones today. "I'm sorry," she told him again, already leaning forward, her lips just inches away from his skin.

His fingers circled around her hand, drawing her touch away from his warm skin. "What have you done?"

The anger lacing his every word broke her from her daze.

"Done?" Breena began to shake her head. "I haven't done anything."

Yes, her angry warrior was definitely back, this time tinged with a streak of suspicion.

In one quick movement, his hands were at her hips. He rolled her over, her back pressing into the damp sandy bank. He straddled her, blocking any opportunity for her to get away.

"What have you brought here? To my home?" he bellowed at her, his finger digging painfully into her shoulders.

"I don't know."

He leaned in, their noses almost touching. "Those creatures…those *things,* that was magic. Blood magic."

Her heart began to pound, and her throat grew dry. *Blood magic.*

The idea of it repelled her. Every part of her—every emotion, every thought, every memory—rejected it and was sickened by the words.

Blood magic could only work by taking of the blood of the unwilling. Forced. Drained until dead.

"You know of these?" she asked. Dreading his answer, hoping it was something he battled on a regular basis here in Ursa and not something she'd brought down on their heads. But a memory, a flash of recognition of the magic, nagged at her. Then the pain returned.

"In places, but not here. *Never* here."

His confirmation made her shake. She'd brought the magic of death to this peaceful place. For a moment her thoughts lingered on the poor soul whose blood had created such a thing. How they'd experience excruciating pain, and then praying, even begging, for death. A death denied.

"Those things travel in pairs, so one can always lead more here. To my home."

With his weight pinning her to the ground, Osborn moved his hands from her shoulders. She began to shake as his fingers traveled over her naked skin, traced the line of her collarbone until meeting at her neck.

"When I came here I made a vow to kill anything that threatened Ursa ever again. Endangered what was left of my family."

His thumbs caressed the soft skin of her throat. One press, that would be all that it would take, just a little force from his thumbs, and he'd deny her breath. His gaze slammed into hers. "Tell me, Breena. Tell me why I shouldn't kill you."

CHAPTER FIVE

HE'D NEVER KILLED a woman.

It was his rule when he hired out his sword to any-one who had the coin. His only rule. An Ursan warrior never fought until forced and only to protect his family and his homeland. What he'd done to survive, to ensure his brothers' survival, would have brought shame to his people. In those early days after leaving Ursa, he'd sunk to the lowest depths. He lived with other mercenaries, men who'd kill him in his sleep to get his job, or just for the pleasure of watching him bleed.

He'd worked for the grasping, greedy overlords who cared more about securing their own power than tak-ing care of their people. They starved while his people, whose rulers were just and fair, died. But those thoughts always led to madness. Hell, he had been a little crazy after he fled his homeland with his brothers. The harsh, pained sounds of the dying people echoed in his ears. The echoes only silenced when replaced by the cries of his young brothers begging for a mother who wouldn't come to comfort them. Would never come.

Only cheap ale and a few moments' pleasure in a paid woman's bed drowned out the noise. A part of it.

Then he'd broken his own rule. He was paid to kill a young girl, no more than ten. All for the sake of more power. More coin. The girl's only crime was her mar-riage alliance. She was promised to a boy who'd one day be king of his lands. A rival family had a daughter of their own they wanted to see sitting upon the throne.

He located his intended victim sleeping in her bed. Her tiny hand curled around a doll. He'd found his own sister this way many times.

What had he become? The blood of honorable warriors flowed through his veins. He was one with the bear…and he was about to cowardly cut the neck of a small girl. He'd stuck his dagger into the wooden chest next to her bed as a warning to her family, grabbed his brothers and fled into the night.

He prayed to the spirits of the bears that they might let his family enter their sacred grounds, and he vowed to protect those lands with his life, even to kill any trespasser who dared to enter the domain of the bear.

And here she was. The person who dared to defy the warnings staked on the outskirts of this isolated land and intrude where she had no right to be.

Osborn looked down at the woman stretched naked beneath him. Her very presence mocked his vow and his rule—to never kill a woman—and yet he must kill. She brought menace, blood magic, the worst kind, here.

Her breasts rose and fell as she took one ragged breath after another. The tight dusky tips invited his touch and his tongue and he was distracted for a moment. Her hair splayed all around the ground, like it did when he dreamed of her. She wore only an odd timepiece around her neck. Her soft lips were parted and a pulse hammered at the base of her throat.

He was distracted longer than a moment because she slammed her knee into his side. His breath came out in a grunt, but he didn't budge. It would take more than a small woman's shove to overpower him. He gripped her wrists and tugged them high above her head to prove his point.

"Are you daring me to kill you, Breena?"

"Let me go!" She bucked her hips, trying to shake him off, but only managed to shift her legs so that she cradled him. He felt the slick heat of her woman's body, and his cock stiffened. How long had it been since he'd touched a woman? Since bringing his brothers here, he'd driven every emotion, pounded every desire and drove every wish he'd once had for himself into creating something on this land. Raising his brothers, keeping them alive, making sure they had a life so that when he left to seek revenge on those who'd brought down the destruction of his family, his brothers could and would carry on without him.

In an attempt to dislodge him, Breena jerked against his cock, and his breath came out in a hiss. Years. It had been years since he'd sunk himself into a woman's inviting warmth. But the female beneath him wasn't just any female; she was the woman of his dreams.

No. She was the woman who'd invaded his dreams and made him dream of her.

"You cannot best me."

"I can try," she told him, meeting his gaze. Defiance and something like desperation mingled in the green depths.

He knew those sentiments.

Felt them.

Lived them.

She shouldn't have to feel that.

Why he should even care, he couldn't fathom. But for some reason, Osborn cared. It had been a long time since he'd really given a damn about anything.

Her bottom lip trembled for a moment, and he

couldn't look away from the tempting softness of her mouth. Then he felt her spine stiffen. "If you're going to kill me, do it now, otherwise—"

Her *otherwise* was punctuated with the top of her head meeting his chin. His teeth snapped together, and his head reared back, but the shock of her action didn't loosen his grip. Instead, he shifted both her wrists to just one of his hands and gripped her chin to make her meet his eyes. Just to prove that he could.

"A moment ago I was thinking I wouldn't kill you. I'm back to thinking I will."

"I…" But her sentence trailed. Had he expected her to apologize for wanting to live?

Her one word drew his glance back to her lips. The tempting seductress of his dreams, or the sleepy enchantress come to life. Now Breena was a woman. Naked. And under him.

Osborn lowered his head, and took from her what he'd wanted. And she gave it to him. Her lips met his, her mouth opening to welcome in his tongue.

She tasted like promise and better than his dream.

He wanted to taste all of her.

"Please," she said, her voice broken and needy.

Please what? Please don't kill her? Please make her feel something other than fear for a moment? Fear he'd caused?

He slumped against her, burying his face in her drying hair. The drive to explore her body died, and was replaced with something less primal. Guilt? Regret?

He didn't need more of that in his life. He had enough for a dozen lifetimes.

"I won't kill you."

He felt her sag beneath him, the fight draining from her limbs. He released her hands, and balanced above her, Breena's sweet, soft curves still cradling him. "But I need answers." He eyed the sky, noting the position of the sun. "It will be dark soon. You can stay tonight, but you leave tomorrow after I'm satisfied I know all I need to about this threat. And, Breena…"

"Yes?"

"Don't come back."

She nodded, and a smile almost tugged at his lips at the quickness of her agreement. "Don't worry."

With one more hard glare, he gently pushed himself off and away from her.

Don't look.

With a new determination, he began to examine the wounds on his arm. Already a dark bruise had formed, mimicking the shape of the creature's snakelike body. The bleeding had stopped, though. The poison's ache had been reduced to a throb, and the burns would fade. He'd had worse. Osborn heard her rolling to her knees.

Don't look.

He felt the gash on his forehead, and wasn't surprised when he pulled back his hand to find it red with blood. That bang to the head might require his brother to take a needle to it.

Leaves crunched beneath Breena's feet as she raced quickly toward her clothes.

Don't look.

He looked. And groaned. Breena's slight frame was perfection. Made for a man's touch. *His* touch. Her backside was made to cup a man as he entered her from behind. His favorite position. His cock stiffened again.

"One more thing."

She turned, shielding her body from his eyes with

her clothes. But she'd never be able to block the image of her soft curves from his memory.

"Until you go in the morning…don't let yourself be alone with me."

BREENA DRESSED AS QUICKLY as she could with shaking fingers. Shaking everything. Even her knees felt weak. Her nipples ached when she pulled the shirt Osborn's brothers had loaned her over her head. The fabric felt rough and abrasive against her sensitized skin. Sensitized from his hands.

Don't let yourself be alone with me.

She closed her eyes and steeled herself against the hot wave of desire that coursed through her. The pleasure and the thirst for his touch narrowed her focus to only him. Her warrior. Osborn.

She licked her lips, finding them swollen. Breena lifted her fingers to touch where he'd touched. To trace along her bottom lip the spot he'd nipped.

Don't let yourself be alone with me.

A powerful warning. An order. And Breena had been raised to be an obedient girl. She'd never broken a rule or voiced a disagreement. Looking over her shoulder, she stole a glance at that man who'd issued what basically amounted to a threat—to her body. She began to shiver.

Osborn stood watching her. More like stood guard. His arms were crossed against his chest, the muscles coiled and ready for combat. His wide-legged stance instantly instilled caution to any observer.

I'll chase.

Run you down.

Render you defenseless.

He didn't care that he still stood naked. A flutter tick-

led her stomach. She'd never seen what made a man a
man before, and she couldn't help but look. That part
of him stood out and seemed to rise higher and bigger
under her inspection.

Her imagination played with the idea of taking off
at a run. He'd chase. He'd catch her. She'd be helpless
against his strength. And while he'd threatened her with
death a moment ago, she knew that was the last thing
he wanted to do to her. He *did* want to do things to her.
Forbidden deeds. She shivered again. Her skills were
few, but along with hairbrushing there was the reading
of people.

And she could read this man.

Probably the only weapon she had against him.

He was angry. He saw himself as betrayed by her
and by his very dreams when he was at his most vulnerable. To a man like her warrior, such a thing was
probably unforgivable.

She had to make him forgive her. It was the only
way to get his help. Breena desperately needed his help,
but, even more, she wanted him to *choose* to help her
now that she'd kissed him. Been held in his arms. She
craved that almost as much as she needed his skills as
a fighter.

Breena had longed for this man. Ached for him. And
now he stood just feet away from her…despising her.
And wanting her with a heat that made her stomach dip
in excitement.

Osborn's expression grew fiercer. His face was as
hard as the stone that made the walls of her bedchamber at home.

Her fingers stilled. A new image…a memory of her
home. And it came without pain. A rush of images and
feelings nearly overwhelmed her. A peaceful kind of

hope settled in her chest, and she smiled, barely realizing she was still staring at Osborn.

His hands fisted, and the muscles of his legs bunched
as though he was about to stalk over to her and help
her dress. Or remove what she'd already donned. Her
mouth went dry, and she turned away, quickly returning to her task.

The thoughts of her home gave her peace, but menace tinged the calmness and the longing. She tried to
concentrate, grab the memories, which seemed to be
fluttering just out of her reach. This time the pain splin-
tered behind her eyes, and she stopped trying to recall
the elusive thoughts of home. But she'd try again. She'd
managed to survive another day. She'd found her warrior, and soon she'd understand why she was so far away
from her family.

She tugged on the rest of the clothes Bernt and Torben had given her, although *tugged* wasn't really the
right word, since the garments still hung down past
her fingertips, and she had to roll the pant legs up several times. Osborn was dressed in half the time it took
her, and for that she was grateful. How was a girl, long
shielded from males, supposed to react when encoun-
tering a naked man? And one so beautifully made? She
still had to suffer staring at the broadness of his back,
and how the pants clung to his seat. Was a woman supposed to find a man's backside attractive? She'd heard
the maids in the castle gossip about a man's flat stomach, speculate on the largeness of his feet, or discuss
the strength of his arms, but never specifically his—

"Hurry."

Startled, Breena met Osborn's gaze. *Caught.*

"We have a good ten-minute walk back to the cottage, and the sun will be setting soon. I want to be prepared if those things come back."

She nodded, and quickened her pace. Maybe he hadn't noticed her gawking at his body.

"And, Breena…"

"Yes?"

"You can look at that later. All you want."

Why did that sound less like a threat and more like something she'd want to do?

THE BROTHERS STOOD OUTSIDE the cottage examining the waning daylight as they approached. Osborn had led the way, with her following close behind. The boys looked a little shocked to see her beside Osborn. Curiosity radiated from their young faces, and they loped down the stairs to meet them in the clearing.

"Did you see that thing in the sky?"

"It got all dark."

"What happened to your arm?"

Both boys spoke at once, and she smiled. Her brothers when they were younger also charged all over each other's words.

Her breath came out in a gasp, but the three males didn't seem to notice. Another memory without pain. Were her brothers safe? Where were they? Dayn had been outside, and Micah… She tried to picture his sweet face and remember. Something about his nanny. A shaft of pain forced her to stop digging for the memory of that night. It seemed she could recall the events much easier when she wasn't even trying. Perhaps she shouldn't try to force anything. Maybe she could ease into her past like she did her dreamhaze. Relax, picture a door in her mind and, instead of a dream, walk into her past.

"*We* were attacked."

Torben and Bernt didn't miss the emphasis Osborn placed on the word *we*. Subtlety was apparently not one of his skills. The brothers glanced at each other, and suspected they would have rolled their eyes if Osborn hadn't been standing right there.

"We sent them away."

"Just like you said," Bernt defended.

"I found her splashing around in the lake. That's where we were attacked."

"What were those things?" Torben asked.

"Scouts. Created by blood magic. I've seen them before, but only once."

"I've never seen anything by blood magic," Torben said, excitement lacing his voice.

A little too much excitement. Osborn glared down at his younger brother. "Pray that you never do."

"There's rumors you can hear the cries of the souls of whose blood was taken," Bernt added, clearly not wanting to be left out of the conversation.

Osborn's face turned grim. "It's a sound I have no wish to hear again."

"Their shrieks were horrible," Breena added, and she couldn't repress the shudder. She didn't know if the wailing came of the soulless or not, but she recognized misery, unbearable pain. So evil...

"That's because you are a girl," Torben replied. He turned his attention back to Osborn. "I guess they didn't shriek for long after you were done with them."

Breena bit back a smile at the pride the youngest brother felt over Osborn's prowess and fighting skill. Micah had been the same about Dayn and Nicolai.

Another thought of home without pain. Yes, the key was to let it flow naturally, and not work too hard.

Osborn cut a quick glance in her direction, then focused once more on his brothers. "I, uh, didn't have my pack."

"But, Osborn, you're never without your pack," Torben said. The boy sounded incredulous.

"You always keep it within reach."

Did she see a hint of color along Osborn's cheekbones? He cleared his throat and crossed his arms against his chest. What kind of move was that? It was as if he were trying to shield himself. Finally the man didn't have the upper hand.

"Yes, Osborn, why did you have your pack so far away?" she asked sweetly.

His brown gaze narrowed. "Turns out I didn't need it," he said between clenched teeth.

She met his stare. "Oh?"

Osborn shrugged. "Breena killed the beast."

Breena stood a little straighter. Yes. Yes, she had killed the thing. Of course, she had the help of a little magic.

The two boys stared at her for a moment. Then Bernt began to laugh. His younger brother quickly followed. Breena might be wearing borrowed clothes, not have much memory, but she knew one thing...she didn't much care for being laughed at.

The energy she'd felt at the lake began to swirl within her.

"Ouch," Torben said as he backed up a step.

Bernt stopped laughing long enough to look at his brother. "What— Ouch!"

"It's like someone pinched me right on the as—er, backside," Torben said.

Osborn cut a quick glance her way, but he didn't look angry at her use of magical powers.

"What was that?" Bernt asked as he rubbed his rear.

"Looks like you just got a taste of what those blood magic scouts received."

Both boys glanced her way, their faces going from incredulous to betrayed. Then both boys slammed their attention back to their older brother.

"But you said girls were good for one thing. And that wasn't magic or fighting."

Now it was her turn to turn her attention to the big man at her side. "And what one thing is that?" she asked, almost afraid to know.

Osborn's expression turned blank. "Cooking."

"Cleaning," the boys said at the same time.

Osborn shrugged. "I guess there were two things."

She shot him a look full of venom. She'd never even glanced at another person in a cross manner in her life. Half a day in this family's presence and she was shooting energy daggers. At least he didn't suggest to these two boys that girls were only good for what happened once the chamber door was closed. Especially since her body was the only thing Osborn had showed much interest in when it came to her.

"You can't take help from a girl," Bernt said. "A warrior defeats alone."

Osborn dropped the pack at his feet and draped an arm over the shoulders of his brothers. He bent his knees so he'd be on eye level with them.

"There's no shame in a man accepting help from another warrior, even if she's a girl."

All this talk was beginning to fray on her nerves. Her father would be lost without his wife. The queen and her husband always stood side by side. He listened to her counsel, and shared the responsibility of ruling. At least Osborn seemed to have an inkling of how it was supposed to work. Unfortunately, he hadn't shared that with the two boys he was responsible for until apparently this moment. Her magic began swirling again, but she quickly tamped it down.

"Let's get inside. I'm hungry, and Breena has a lot of questions to answer. Bed after supper. I'm taking Breena into the village at first light."

"To the village? Can I go?" Bernt asked.

"It's been so long since you've taken us to a town."

Osborn shook his head. "Not until I know the threat."

The two boys slumped, then lumbered up the stairs. She was hungry again, too. Strange how the body had a timetable all its own. Her family was lost, she'd wandered around in a wilderness, been attacked, and yet, she could eat like it was any normal day.

"Why do your brothers think so little of girls?" she asked when they were alone.

His gaze lowered to her lips. Then fell to her breasts, and her nipples tightened and poked at the material of her shirt. "If you tell yourself a woman is good for only one thing, then you don't miss all the other things you desire from her."

His voice was filled with yearning, and so much loneliness she lifted her hand to cup his cheek.

His fingers grasped hers. His palm was callused, his grip tight, reinforcing her earlier musings that he hadn't spent a lot of time with females.

"Remember what I said? About not being alone with me?" he asked, his expression fierce.

She nodded, unable to take her eyes off his lips.

Osborn lowered his head, his mouth just an inch from her ear. "You're alone with me."

A warning, a threat, a promise... His words were all three. A shiver slid down her back. She squeezed her eyes shut tight as the soft touch of his tongue traced the curve of her neck.

"Breena?"

She nodded, wishing for more of this kind of caress. Wishing he wouldn't send her away in the morning. Wishing for so many things lost.

"Get inside."

Breena slipped out of his unresisting arms, and shut the door firmly behind her. She slumped against the rough wooden door, dragging in air and willing her heartbeat to slow down.

Survive.

Revenge.

She'd do both with Osborne's aid. Her dream magic was not wrong. Now all she had to do was get him to see it, too.

"DID YOU SEE THAT?" Torben whispered. "She touched him, and he didn't even yell. Or push her."

Bernt nodded. "I don't think things are ever going to be the same again."

CHAPTER SIX

DINNER WAS A SIMPLE meal of tough bread, dried meat and berries she suspected were picked near the cabin. It was also completely silent. At Elden, dinner was a grand affair, with numerous courses, entertainment and lots and lots of laughter. Here, the three males regarded their food seriously, heads over their plates, and eyes steady on their meals.

"Does anyone know a funny tale?"

Bernt looked at her as if she'd suddenly begun speaking in another language. Her father always told such funny stories about his travels as a youth. Her mother could charm anyone with her tales of legend and myth. Nicolai told a great joke about a traveling king, a chastity belt and a trusted knight complaining about the wrong key.

Her gaze darted to Osborn and she felt her cheeks heat. She'd always thought that the funny part of that joke was that the king handed over a key that didn't fit. Now she realized it was the knight trying to remove the chastity belt and that the king had purposefully given the wrong key—that was what made the tale funny.

Breena would smack her brother when she saw him. She'd told that joke at least three times. A pang of homesickness chased away her anger. No, if she ever saw Nicolai again, she'd hug him.

"Do *you* know a funny story?" Bernt asked.

She was alive, she was safe for the moment and her belly was finally getting full. One meal. Breena could snatch one meal, and not worry about her brothers, her home or how she was going to survive tomorrow. Pushing the plate aside, she lowered her voice to that same conspiratorial tone her mother's took when she was about to relay something interesting.

"Well, did you hear about the king of Alasia who was most displeased with his fortune-teller?"

Both boys leaned forward. "No."

"He told the king his favorite horse would die. And sure enough, the animal fell dead two days later."

"Fortune-tellers aren't real," Torben said, his voice turning skeptical. She could only imagine where he'd acquired that attitude.

But Breena only gave what she hoped amounted to a mysterious shake of her head. "The king didn't trust him, either. In fact, he suspected the fortune-teller poisoned the horse so that his prediction would come true. That way, people from all over the kingdom would know of his skills, and give him money to relay their fortunes."

"What happened next?" Bernt asked.

"The king confronted the fortune-teller and dared him to reveal the date of his own death."

Bernt was practically squirming in his chair. Had no one told these boys stories? "Why?"

"Because the king was going to kill him," Osborn said.

Breena smiled over at the clever warrior. "Your brother is right. The king would kill the fortune-teller so that any answer he gave would be wrong, and no one would remember him."

Torben was off his chair raising an imaginary sword. "So what did he do? Run or challenge him to battle?"

She bit her bottom lip. No wonder her mother had so much fun telling stories around the table. "He did neither."

"What?" both boys asked.

"He looked the king in the eye, and said, 'I don't know the exact day of my death, but I do know that the king will follow me to the grave just two days later.'"

Osborn began to laugh, the sound of it delightfully rusty. She glanced his way and their gazes met. The desire in his gaze made her smile fade. Oh, she knew he wanted her body, but some other need for her lingered in his brown eyes. Her lips parted, and some elemental part of her wished to give him what he hungered for.

"Time for bed," he told his brothers without breaking his stare.

"What?"

"It's still early."

Osborn sighed heavily. "You'll need your rest if I decide you can go into the village. *If*."

The brothers scrambled to clear the table and head into the room where she'd found the three beds earlier, and in just a few moments, she was alone with him. Again.

"Join me by the fire," he said. It wasn't much of a request, and when he offered her his hand, there was no way it could be disguised as courtly manners. She *was* going to sit next to him by the fire and she *would* be telling him everything he wanted to know.

Every great hall held a large fireplace, and even though the cottage was small, Osborn's hearth seemed to dominate one entire wall. An inviting, fluffy rug lay before the large, flat stones in front of the firebox. She sank down on the throw, seeking its softness. It was thick enough to be a sleeping pallet. Osborn's brothers had added extra blankets. At home, most people slept before the fire, warmed their hands near the flames and danced in front of it during celebrations and heated their ale over it. Osborn seemed to prefer to stare into it. Glare.

"You'll be leaving here at first light."

Was he telling her or himself? He'd already announced he'd be taking her to the village in the morning. It was all decided. Wasn't it?

"Already things are changing, and you've only been here a few hours. My brothers are unused to the gentleness a woman brings into a home. They're wanting things. Things that are impossible." His expression grew grimmer as he continued to peer into the flames. "You have to go."

Yes, yes. He'd already said that.

"No matter how many times you ask to stay."

Breena hadn't asked. Her heartbeat quickened, and she felt a little tingle all the way down to her toes. She was doing a pretty poor job of reading the strong man in front of her. She couldn't fathom his thoughts. No, she'd missed understanding his thoughts again.

Breena left the warmth of the rug and stood beside him. His height dwarfed her. The broadness of his shoulders filled her vision. She placed her hand in the middle of his back, and felt his muscles contract under her fingertips.

"Are you wanting me to ask, Osborn?"

He turned then, catching her off guard and imprisoning her hand between his. "I need to know what dangers you have brought here. Tell me how you got here."

The solid strength of his hand was exactly what she

yearned for after wandering around hungry and tired and full of fear. "I don't really know. It's the truth." Half-truth. Why did she still feel the need to keep all of what she knew to herself? *Survive.* Some instinct told her to tell Osborn only what he needed to know so he'd help her.

"Then tell me what you do know."

"My home was attacked, the details are fuzzy. I woke up in this strange land."

"So you didn't see the markers telling you to keep out?" he asked, his voice filled with hostility and disbelief. His eyes scanned her face, searching for truth.

"I saw the bear skulls, so I figured I was on Ursa land, but they all died out. Years ago. So I assumed I was alone."

"Not all," he said, taking his gaze from her face and returning it to the fire.

Now Osborn's suspicious nature and overprotectiveness of his brothers made sense. They were the last of their kind. The last of the Ursans. Would she be the last of her people? Was she? A tragic trait to have in common.

But at least she had hope. Hope that her brothers and some of the people of Elden had escaped. Osborn had none. "I'm sorry" seemed so insignificant to say about his loss, but she told him, anyway.

His throat tightened. "You're the first person to tell me that."

Sensing that was all the acknowledgment Osborn wanted to give to the tragedy that took his family, she went on with her story. "My people are magical. Not blood magic. Never. But my mother's powers are very strong. I believe she cast me from our kingdom."

"Why here?"

"Maybe something inside me chose the location. We'd been connecting through our dreams...."

His gaze burned for her as hot as the fire warming her cheek. Then his eyes narrowed. "You said you lost your powers, but you defeated the blood magic scout."

"You remembered that." Since he hadn't mentioned it, she thought he'd forgotten she'd told him her magic no longer worked.

"Another one of your lies?"

She shook her head. "When I woke up here, there were just two thoughts in my mind. To survive and to kill. Avenge. My magic was gone and whenever I try to concentrate and really remember what happened in my home...all I get is pain. It's like something is stabbing me behind the eyes, it hurts so bad. Believe me, if I could have used my powers when I was wandering around in that forest with no shoes and nothing to eat, I would have."

The corner of Osborn's lip turned up in a half smile.

"When your home was attacked, did you hear the cries we heard today? Creatures of blood magic?"

Breena closed her eyes, and tried to remember what she could before the pain hit her. All around her had been confused commotion. The sounds of battle and the wails of the wounded and dying. A flash of something sinister. A creature with razors for hands. A thing more skeletal than man. She sagged to the floor, and drew her knees up close to her chest.

"Yes, it was blood magic."

Osborn's breath came out in a heavy growl.

She looked up at him quickly, his face as harsh as it had been at the lake. "I'm so sorry. I never meant to bring danger to you or to your brothers."

He swallowed, closed and opened his fists a few

times, then he nodded. "I know you didn't. Tomorrow I take you to the village. The scouts will be coming after you again. I don't want you leading them here."

"You really won't help me?" she asked, more for her benefit rather than needing confirmation from him. She needed to say the words, so she could know she was truly alone. So her heart could accept the truth, and even the tiniest of hope she still held within her would die.

His silence was her answer.

"I'm sorry I brought all this down over your head. You are not the man I should be dream sharing with. I guess my magic got it wrong," she told him with a shrug. "I really thought you were the one for me."

Osborn pushed himself away from the hearth with a hard shove. She was surprised the cottage wall didn't give way. "I'll find you a pillow," he said, and stalked toward the chest in the corner where they kept the extra winter bedding.

HIS BROTHER WAS ON HIM the moment he entered the room. "She should sleep in here," Bernt told him, his glance roaming to the door. "It doesn't feel right. She's a girl. She shouldn't have to sleep on the cold floor."

Osborn sighed at his brother's misplaced gallantry. "You set out enough blankets to rival a mattress. She'll be comfortable enough in front of the fire. Besides, you willing to give up your bed?"

Bernt squared his shoulder. "Yes."

"*I'm* not."

"I just said I'd sleep out there."

Osborn shook his head. "And her sleep in here with two males? That's even worse." He tossed his shirt at the foot of the bed and made a show of stretching his length along his mattress. "Either the three of us sleep out there or the three of us sleep in the comfort of our own beds. You know what I'll choose."

Bernt's breath came out in a huff. His little brother knew when he'd been beat. And he didn't like it. He slowly peeled his shirt up and over his head and then slid beneath the pelts covering his bed. Osborn blew out the candle, and darkness surrounded them. He felt his brother's uneasiness. It would keep the boy awake all night.

"You worried about her being a girl, think what sleeping in the house with us unchaperoned will do to her. Far worse than sleeping on a pile of blankets in front of a warm fire. The sooner she's out of here the better."

Soon the even breathing of his brother's sleep filled the room, but Osborn couldn't force his muscles to relax. If anything he grew more tense.

I really thought you were the one for me.

Her words were like a deep cut.

When he dreamed with Breena, he was someone else. When she admitted she put herself into his dreams he wrestled with temptation. He wanted to be the man in the dream for her.

But in his dreams, his blood never covered her hands. She'd brought this danger, but he brought much more. His dream girl didn't belong with him. But for the first time, Osborn wished he could mean something to someone.

What he'd told his brothers was the truth. The sooner Breena was gone, the better it would be. For all of them.

BREENA AWOKE IN THE morning in front of the dying fire. Dawn crept over the line of the trees, and she heard a few birds begin their morning song. So normal. So idyllic.

She glanced down at her hands. They looked the same as they always did. Same nails. Still the same little freckle on the back of her hand. Her pinky finger stretched just a tiny bit crooked at the end.

But with her hands she wielded powerful magic. She pointed in the corner. Nothing. With her hands she wielded powerful magic *sometimes*.

Why did her magic power suddenly appear—now? Why not days ago when she could have put the power to use helping her family? What had changed?

Osborn. He was what changed. Did his presence have something to do with their onset? Would they grow stronger the longer she stayed? Or was it all coincidence? Would her powers eventually have appeared?

Breena stretched her arms high above her head. Her neck was stiff, and her back ached, but it felt good to be alive. She glanced around the tiny cottage.

Loud whispers echoed in the bedroom, and she knew the three Ursan men were awake. It had seemed so perfect when she'd stumbled upon them yesterday. She kicked the covers off, and began folding the blanket. Breena didn't want to be accused of dawdling. The door opened, and Osborn stepped out of the bedroom. "You're up."

Turning, she made herself busy straightening the blanket. She wanted to avoid seeing his handsome face. Now that she knew he wasn't her warrior, she didn't want to…

She didn't want to still desire him.

Bernt and Torben pushed themselves past their brother, fully dressed and ready for travel. "I didn't think you were coming with us," she said, thrilled there'd be some kind of buffer between her and Osborn.

"I don't want the boys alone in case any more of those creatures come here."

Cold. Logical. "I'm ready," she told him, unwilling to meet his gaze.

After she used the privacy area, the four of them set out after a simple breakfast. Despite the boys' attempts to cajole her into sharing more stories, the camaraderie of the evening before was definitely over.

"How long does it take before we get to the village?" she asked Bernt after they were well into their walk.

"We can usually arrive by noon," Osborn answered instead.

Some time later she stumbled over a dead tree limb hidden in the brush. Three different male hands offered assistance. She grabbed for Torben's and Bernt's. Osborn's eyes narrowed, and he glared at his brothers.

Around midmorning, they stopped to take a break around an old fire ring obviously used by travelers. The boys ran off for privacy while she plopped herself on a wooden stump as far away from Osborn as she could get.

A large figure blocked the sun. A shadow fell across her lap as she was rubbing her feet. An Osborn-shaped shadow. But she didn't look up. "You've been avoiding me all morning. Why?"

Her shoulders slumped, and instead of feeling lighter that Osborn would soon be out of her life for good, the knowledge weighed on her heavily. She understood his reasons for not helping her, but she wasn't going to make it easy on him.

He wore his longish hair tied back for their trip to town. Black seemed to be his color of choice; he wore it again today. He kept his appearance modest, but there was nothing simple about the huge sword strapped to his side. All together Osborn was devastating to her senses. Never had a man looked so strong, so powerful and so capable to her than the warrior. And right now she needed all of those things. Desperately. How could she not respond to him physically? Emotionally? And now he wanted some kind of explanation about her avoidance of him.

After steeling herself against the pull of his dark brown eyes, she met his gaze. "What do you want from me? I came to you for help. To find my family, to avenge their deaths. You won't give it to me—I can accept that—but I don't plan to sit around and discuss the weather or something with you now."

He glared down at her. "You tried to get your magic to trap me."

"If that's how you want to view it," she told him, her voice tired. If that's how he still thought of her, she'd never convince him otherwise.

"I won't be used. Ever again. By anyone."

"Good for you, Osborn. In fact, go back to your cottage and just seal yourself from the rest of the world. Forget how to live, and die alone because you'll eventually run your brothers off, too. Just point me in the direction of town, and I'll handle the rest."

"I'm taking you," he said between clenched teeth.

She put the uncomfortable shoes back on her feet. "Then let's not waste any more time here. The sooner you discard me at the village, the sooner you can be away from me."

Breena began walking in the direction they were originally headed, and when Osborn's brothers fell along beside her, she let out a small sigh of relief. After her big talk to their brother, she'd hate looking foolish by having to turn around and walk a different direction.

The sun was almost directly overhead when they crested a small hill. Below them a green valley stretched to the horizon, and there, nestled at the bottom, was a village. Having always been kept behind castle walls, the idea of exploring, even for just a few moments, took away the gloom of Osborn leaving her and what she must surely face in the coming days.

"Let's go," she told the boys, and they looped arms and charged down the hill, laughing all the way. Osborn followed behind, his hand never leaving his pack, his gaze constantly scanning around them.

The village was charming; the houses were similar to Osborn's cottage but sanded and painted bright colors. A central road divided the small town, and booths and stalls invited her with enticing smells and beautiful fabrics. She remembered a story her mother once told of a boy made of wood tempted by all he saw in the village. The sights and the smells in town awed the boy, but he was also not careful and lost his money to a crafty fox and cat. The need for caution rang true now more than ever, but so did the lure of all there was to see and explore.

"What do you want to do first?" she asked.

"Eat," both boys replied in unison.

She laughed until Osborn's booming voice interrupted her. "Bernt, Torben, you go along. Breena stays with me."

Torben looked like he might want to argue with his older brother, but the temptation to explore was just too great.

"Back in two hours."

With a quick wave, both boys abandoned her. In a

flash they were out of sight, and she felt the heavy presence of their brother at her side.

"I have a little money. It's not much, but it should keep you from stealing anyone's breakfast," he said, his voice almost kind.

Breena smiled despite not wanting to. Why did he have to be nice? She really wanted to dislike him. It would make his leaving her so much easier.

"Thanks," she managed to mumble. This would be the last time she would see him. She'd never dream of him again. Wouldn't let herself. She began to stare at the booths, hoping he'd just leave.

"Breena—" he said, then stopped.

His voice was so raw, so full of yearning, she couldn't help but meet his gaze.

"Breena, I—"

Raising up on tiptoe, she kissed his cheek. "Me, too," Breena whispered in his ear, then she turned from him, and charged into the crowd.

HE WATCHED HER WALK AWAY. Forced himself to spy the back of her blond head until she was swallowed up by the people of the village bargaining for deals at the various stalls lining the dirt-packed road.

Osborn stood searching the crowd for her, but finally turned his back. Breena was gone.

He might as well enjoy himself while he was here. Eat something neither he nor his brothers cooked. Maybe find a woman to drive his thoughts of Breena out of his mind.

The idea of it made him shudder, and he knew thoughts of her would always be close by. His hands turned to fists. He'd tasted something close to perfect. Held her in his arms, felt her soft body respond to his touch, his kisses. Her nipples hardened in his palms with just the barest caress. And she was walking away from him? The *berserkergang* in him raged, turned protective. Going to find herself another warrior?

Not. Going. To. Happen.

"Breena," he called, but received no response. He was taller than most of the villagers, so it was easy to scan the crowd, but many of the women here sported blond hair. He quickly passed by each stall, bumping shoulders with some, sending others scurrying out of his way. Nothing on the right. He crossed the street and began his search on the left side of the booths. He almost missed the narrow alley between buildings, but something drew his eye.

Maybe it was that his eyes automatically locked on anything blond.

Perhaps it was the glint of the sunlight off a knife blade.

Whatever it was, he turned down the alley to spy Breena, surrounded by three burly-looking men.

"Breena," he called, growing anxious.

That's when he saw the knife at her throat.

A swift chill invaded his arms and legs and his gaze narrowed into a tunnel. Every emotion—all his desire for Breena, the aching need for whatever it was she offered that had lodged in his chest—focused into anger. His *berserkergang* stirred and in less time it took for the man with his blade at Breena's throat to take a breath, Osborn's Bärenhaut lay around his shoulders with the knife removed from his boot and at the man's throat.

He didn't live long enough to take a second breath. The would-be abductor fell at Breena's feet. She screamed, backing away from the body, and the two accomplices rotated to face him. Their eyes rounded in horror, their hands shaking in fear.

Osborn's *berserkergang* always liked the fear. Thrived on it. The walls around them shook with his growl, and he went after the man closest to Breena. "Dare you harm a woman?"

"Just after a bit of fun. We had no money for the paid women. You can have 'er first."

His offer was the last thing he spoke as Osborn snapped his neck with one hand. He rounded on the last, his knife in his hand. But the *berserker* hungered for barehanded combat.

"I wasn't gonna do anything. My brother made me come."

The man's crying words didn't slow Osborn from stalking toward him. His prey dropped to his knees, not much older than his own brothers, and Osborn paused.

"D-don't kill me. Please."

His *berserkergang* forged images of his dead mother and sister. Osborn wrapped his fingers around the young man's throat. "Never touch a woman like that," he ordered, his voice more of a snarl.

The young man shook his head. "No. I won't."

Osborn tightened the grip he held around his neck, watching as his face turned purple and his eyes grew more fearful. "Never harm a woman."

He could only nod in response and Osborn let him go. The alley filled with the man's deep gasps of breath.

Osborn never took his eyes off him. "You live. As a warning. Go."

"Thank you," he said, running as fast as he could down the alley and out of sight.

He turned on Breena, who lay on the dirty cobblestones of the alleyway. Her eyes were filled with confusion, and terror lined her soft features. His *ber-serkergang* bristled and swelled, at first thriving off her fright. Osborn stalked toward her. Breena shrank away, crawling backward, doing what she could to get away from him. To survive.

The *berserkergang* inside him recoiled at the sight of her fleeing. His rage weakened suddenly, a different path from the slow fade his anger usually took. The day before, when he'd found her invading his lake, he wanted her to be afraid of him. Now the idea repulsed him. Made him feel ashamed.

Breena had backed herself into the wall, her eyes darting, searching desperately for a way to escape. He shucked off his pelt, tossed his knife to the side and sunk on his haunches.

"Breena." His voice still shook with traces of his *berserker* rage. He closed his eyes, concentrated and forced the *ber* spirit inside him to settle. He'd never battled against his own *berserkergang*. Had never needed to. He glanced down at Breena. Never wanted to.

He gently touched her arm, the warmth of her skin chasing away the cold his *berserkergang* always left behind. Osborn watched as she took a deep breath, and forced her back to straighten. He hid a smile, because he knew Breena was girding herself to do battle. With him.

After a moment, she finally met his gaze. Accusation laced her green eyes, and any idea he'd had earlier of smiling vanished.

Breena was looking at him like something unworldly. Despised. It was something he was used to. Only he hadn't realized he didn't want *her* looking at him that way.

Few outside of Ursa understood the nature of his

people. One of the reasons they kept to themselves. Most of the inhabitants of the other realms were afraid or relegated them as little more than animals. Things to be feared, yes, but also abhorred.

Osborn's stare never wavered from hers. His expression grew brutal. Distrustful. He wasn't in the practice of guarding his expression, and now was too late to start. But Breena's beautiful green eyes were only filled with curiosity. That full bottom lip of hers curved in wonder.

"What are you?"

CHAPTER SEVEN

SO *THIS* WAS HER WARRIOR.

Breena had never seen anything so savage. Osborn fought with a ferocity unmatched by anything she'd ever witnessed. The knights who'd pledged themselves to her father prided themselves on their skill with a sword, jousted and battled from the lists at tournaments with precision and pride. But Osborn's raw strength and power during the attack was brutal and ruthless.

Almost like an animal.

The perfect challenge to one who wielded blood magic.

A tide of denial and horror swept over her abruptly. Her knees weakened, and she doubled over. Osborn was at her side, his long stride getting him there in two quick steps. His strong fingers tangled in her hair, soothing her, and her stomach calmed.

"They were going to kill me."

The man beside her only nodded. No words were needed.

"Tell me what you are, Osborn," she urged.

He looked into the distance. "I'm a man."

"You're more than a man, you're something else. Tell me."

"I'm *berserker*. I fight with the *ber* spirit."

"But how can that be? No one has spied a *berserker*

for years. They've vanished. I almost believed it to be a legend."

"Gone. Forgotten as if they never lived," he said, his words bitter and biting. "I have vengeance of my own to think about."

She shrank away from him.

His sigh was heavy and he rubbed the back of his neck in obvious frustration. "Are you okay?" he asked after a few moments of taut silence.

The man didn't want to care.

But he did.

As if the sun had shot out bright rays to illuminate the truth, Breena knew she had her weapon against Osborn…if she wanted to wield it. She sucked in a deep breath and squeezed her eyes tight in relief. Breena had the weaponry, but it was his need to protect her that made her heart race.

She swallowed past the lump that had lodged in her throat. "Yes. Thanks to you." She flashed him a grateful smile. He blinked at her, settling on the backs of his heels. Was he surprised? How did he think she'd react? Afraid? He looked over to his side, examining the dead bodies to verify that, yes, they were indeed still dead. He wouldn't meet her gaze. Osborn *was* afraid that she'd reject him or be frightened by him.

She gripped his arm, giving him a squeeze. Her own magic hadn't been wrong to draw her to this man. He *had* to be the one who'd help her reclaim Elden.

But the man maintained a real aversion to the notion that he was being used for his sword. Something had made him hard and suspicious, and she was going to find out. Her mother often complained of men stifling their emotions and that half the time a woman needed to come along and give them a good pop just to release the pressure. Osborn seemed to be holding himself tighter than a sealed drum. Maybe what he needed was for her to give him a good figurative smack.

Maybe he needed her just as much as she needed him.

Now to get him to aid her without him knowing. She searched her mind for ideas, quickly discarding and refining until she hit on a scenario Osborn just might agree to.

She brushed the hilt of his sword. "Teach me."

He glanced down at her fingers wrapped around the handle of his sword, then up at her. "What?"

"Teach me what you do."

Osborn shook his head. "It cannot be taught to a woman. At least, I don't think so. There were never any women with the *berserkergang*."

"Then teach me to fight. I've never seen anything like what you just did. You were strong when you fought the creature in the lake. I doubt any man could walk away from that battle as you did, but in the alley you were invincible." What was it her mother always said? That there was nothing wrong with spreading a little flattery when it came to a man?

At least he seemed less...unrelenting.

"There will be other men bent to attack me now that I'm out on my own. I have to be able to protect myself."

Her fingertips bumped into his, and he jerked. *Good.*

"You won't be my warrior, I can accept that, but at least give me a chance. Surely there are methods I could learn from you—how to use a knife...something. Anything, Osborn. I have to find my people. To avenge." *To survive.*

His shoulders slumped. *Yes, she was wearing him down.*

He stood, towering over her, then extended his hand to help Breena to her feet. "I don't wish to talk in this place of death."

She glanced over at the two dead bodies and then quickly looked away. "What about them? Are we going to leave them here?"

"Vermin like that? Anyone who'd prey on the helpless, especially women and children, deserves nothing less. This is where they belong."

After wiping his blade, he slammed his knife home in his boot scabbard. Reaching for her hand, he guided her toward the entrance. He scanned the scene past the alley, keeping her in place against his back. A protective move, and she allowed herself a small bubble of hope.

Apparently satisfied no one would witness their escape, he pushed them forward, joining the bustling crowd. Osborn routed her in a direction leading away from town, winding through the streets of the village, and avoiding contact with strangers. She tried to reclaim her earlier enthusiasm for this visit before she'd been attacked, wanting, *needing,* something normal. Maybe if she concentrated on the wares at the various stalls and booths. But Osborn led her past each one, refusing to pause even at the ones selling delicious pastries and pies, despite their tantalizing smells.

"Pretty lady, over here."

"A ribbon for her, sir?"

But Osborn ignored them all, and kept them walking. Once out of earshot of the townspeople, she couldn't hold her questions in any longer.

"I've heard the *berserkers* were crazed. Couldn't control themselves when they were..." She didn't know the word. Few did anymore.

"Under the *berserkergang*," he supplied for her. "And if we couldn't control it, that'd make us poor warriors."

"I could sense it, that *berserkergang.* You're the most powerful fighter I've ever seen, but you knew who I was and didn't hurt me."

"No, I wouldn't hurt you," he told her softly.

Did she mistake hearing that near whisper of his? *Not on purpose.* "What happens to you after the rage has passed? I've heard *berserkers* are at their weakest, but you were invincible after the fight."

"Nothing is invincible. The wolves have their silver, the vamps have their sun. I am just a man, but with my Bärenhaut, my pelt, only raw materials of the earth can hurt me. If the battle is long, then yes, I cannot go on without rest."

"And if the battle is short?" she was almost afraid to ask.

"Then I seek the relief only a woman can give." She felt her cheeks warm with embarrassment. As he'd intended her to feel. That was the last question she planned on asking, and she had so many about the man. She suspected most would go unanswered. Was that why she found him so intriguing? That she'd never fully know the story of this *berserker?*

"What other things have you heard of my kind?" he asked.

So he *did* want to have a conversation. "That women aren't—"

She stopped her words in time. Was she about to actually tell him that?

"Breena?" he asked, using a voice she suspected few had dared argue with.

Something flickered in his eyes. Heated.

"That women aren't safe around *berserkers.* That

they take what they want. Who they want. Make a sport of challenging men with daughters."

He halted and gripped her shoulders, forcing her to face him.

"That rumor's true," he told her, his eyes on her soft lips. He grasped her chin between his fingers, rubbed the tender skin with his callused thumb.

"Do you feel safe with me, Breena?"

She chose not to answer. Breena pulled her chin from his clutch, and they continued down the path.

Not too far on the outskirts of town, a peaceful green-grassed clearing stretched near a quiet river, and Osborn finally stopped. The line of the forest stood only a few steps away, and the fresh pine smell scented the air.

"This is beautiful," she told him, remembering the story of the girl who stayed too long in a meadow picking flowers. She'd enjoyed the sun on her face so much that she'd lost her way, finding only a wolf to trust to lead her home.

"It's easily defensible."

"What does that mean?"

"With the river to my back, I only have to defend three sides. The forest can provide coverage for a potential enemy or if I need to regroup."

So many things to know. Where she saw a place to kick off her shoes and run, Osborn saw a good place for battle. "See? I'm already learning."

Her warrior met her gaze, and the smile on her face disappeared. The fierce passion simmering in his eyes made her swallow. "I will teach you, Breena. But what will I get in return?"

"Wh-what do you mean?"

"Everyone must earn what they eat. What can you offer?"

"Well, I can…" She tried to remember all the important duties she maintained in the castle that could translate to Osborn's home. "I can sew a beautiful tapestry for the cottage. Maybe one depicting your greatest victory," she told him, warming up to the idea.

He raised a brow. "What would I do with a tapestry?"

"The fabric holds the drafts at bay. It will keep the cottage warm at night."

The brown in his eyes darkened. "I want other things to keep me warm at night."

Images of them together, skin to skin as they were at the lake, warming each other with only the heat of their—

"I can carve candles that can light the cottage at night," she rushed out in the hopes of chasing the idea of them intertwined out of her mind. "The candles are bright enough to work by."

"My brothers and I work sunup to sundown. We have no need of candles, we're already in bed when the moon is out."

Osborn seemed so much closer than he had just a moment or two ago. The clean, crisp scent of the woods that surrounded the cottage filled her nose, and her arm felt warmed from the nearness of his big frame. Too near.

"Give me your hand," he told her.

With a reluctance she didn't want to show, she offered him want he wanted. His long fingers engulfed her hand, and he turned it over to examine her palm. He gently rubbed his thumb over a scratch at her wrist. The feel of it sent shivers down her arm.

"How'd you get this?" he asked.

"When I was wondering around in the woods, I fell and landed on a stick."

His fingers glided along her palm, and she found it hard to breathe. "How about this abrasion to the heel of your hand. How did you get this?"

"I was trying to climb a tree for some fruit. The bark wasn't very forgiving."

He brought her palm to his lips, and placed a kiss to her injury. Except nothing on her body was in pain anymore. She'd never felt so…well.

"Your hands are soft. When you cup my cheek, it feels like the petals of a flower against my face."

Those shivers he'd started with his thumb, they were now generated by his words alone. An awareness of him, of his strength and scent and beauty as a man, made her tremble. He placed her hand on his neck, and her thumb began to explore him in tiny circles. The way he encouraged her touch in his dream. Their dreams.

"You don't have the hands of a woman who works to earn what she eats. You do not prepare the meals in your home, do you?"

Breena shook her head.

"Nor do you wash the clothes or even sweep the floor."

An edge to his voice took her out of the soft haze his words had seduced her into. Osborn was trying to prove some point here. She just didn't know what it was.

"You can't cook. You don't know how to do laundry or mending or take care of a house. How will you repay me for my training time?"

"You could teach me those things and then I could do them for you."

"That would take more time and I'm not inclined to waste."

"There's got to be something I can do to get you to teach me," she said, hating how her voice sounded so near a plea.

Osborn lifted a brow. "I wonder what that could be." Then his gaze dropped to her breasts.

Her breath hitched. Her nipples tightened, and pushed at the rough material of her loaned shirt. An inner warning told her Osborn's actions were far more calculated than only desire. He was challenging her, trying to intimidate her, and make her wary so that she'd back off and not seek the killers who murdered her family. Breena would not be intimidated. She shrugged her shoulders, not realizing until afterward her movements would make her breasts push even more against her shirt.

His eyes narrowed at the changes of her body. He seemed to grow bigger, more tense, if such a thing were possible, right before her eyes. A ripple of want rushed through her. Breena longed for the feel of him. His touch chased everything from her mind but him, and the way he made her feel. Breena forgot to be afraid, to worry and to mourn what she couldn't fully remember but knew was lost.

He reached out a hand and cupped her breast. Filling his palm, molding her to his liking. She gasped when his thumb slid over her nipple in a gentle caress.

"Why'd you come back for me?" she asked, needing to know the answer almost as much as she needed his hands on her.

"This," he said, and he tugged the large shirt down, exposing her breast. He leaned down and took it into his mouth. Breena clutched his shoulders at the exquisite feel of his lips on her skin, the warmth of his mouth and the gentle graze of his teeth on her nipple. Her knees felt weak again, and she grasped him tighter, losing her fingers in his hair and rolling her head back to allow him more of herself.

"You taste so good," he said against her skin, and he tugged on the other side of her shirt, giving him free rein to her other breast.

"You feel so good," she echoed.

Osborn made a little growly sound, and he circled the tip of her nipple with his tongue. Warmth and wetness pooled between her legs. This was better...

"What's better?" he asked.

Breena hadn't realized she'd spoken her thoughts aloud. "This is better than in our dreams."

He cupped her backside in his hand. "Because it's real."

Yes. Her imagination could never conjure up anything this frantic or exciting. Yet what would it mean for him? She didn't know much in the ways between a man and a woman, but she'd observed enough to see a man pair himself off with a different maid of the castle every night.

"I'm nothing to him," she'd heard one girl sob to another, "just a body."

That's what Breena would be to Osborn. A bartered body. Someone to steal a moment's pleasure with to forget whatever pain made him so hard and mistrusting. Then she'd be forgotten.

She didn't want this man to forget her.

Breena pushed Osborn away, her wayward senses protesting his leaving. After righting her shirt, she smoothed a hand over her hair. His unruly hair was now free of the leather binding, probably her doing.

His stare never left her face.

"Okay, Osborn. I'll do it for your training."

His face drained some in color, confirming her suspicion that he'd started the intimacy between them to shock her into changing her mind about facing battle. Then his eyes lowered once more, her nipples still tight points and clear against her shirt. His nose flared and he reached for her.

She quickly sidestepped his advance, fluffing the shirt away from her chest. "I will do the mending. I did mention that I could sew."

YEARS AGO, ROLFE HAD made a vow to the King of Elden. To protect the king's family with his own life if needed. And he would have faced any battle, raised any sword against any who threatened the Royal House, but this—

This wasn't battle, and he didn't face his demise. It was worse than any death. Any pain. Any suffering.

It was a living death. Unremitting agony. A soulless life. Others had gone mad from the threat of it. Rolfe's own fright had kept him clinging to the shadows of the castle. As a guard he knew the best ways to go unnoticed, slipping around Elden, squirreling away food like a rodent. He'd become someone he didn't recognize. A man who valued going undetected over honor. But what were honor and principles here? That had all died with the king and queen.

Maybe the depraved death the Blood Sorcerer offered would be simpler than this pitiful existence. It was easy enough to be caught. Catching the attention of one of the blood minions, maybe steal something in plain sight. He knew some of what happened to those who refused to give their allegiance to the Blood Sorcerer. Drained of blood, used as target practice and blood sport, or fed upon by something so hideous the screams started before the feeding even began. But the screams eventually ended.

That's what Rolfe wanted. Needed. What came after the silence.

He'd failed. The king and queen were dead. The three princes vanished, even the sweet princess he'd tried to save now all gone. His heart constricted at the pain. His defeat.

What was his life worth now to Elden? Better to face the end now than to go on living with the failure. He heard voices in the hall.

THE BLOOD SORCERER SAT on the King of Elden's throne. The former king. The body had been removed, but the stains from his blood still covered the floor. One of the castle servants tried to clean up the carnage left by her dying ruler's body, but the sorcerer quickly put a stop to that. He thrilled at walking through the spilled blood of Aelfric. The dead king's pain, the anguished cries, energized the great hall. The sorcerer still felt the traces of Aelfric's fear for his children's safety, and his growing need for vengeance, even as his life's blood drained away, seeping onto the cold stone floor for the sorcerer now to plod through.

A wish for vengeance that would be denied. Even now the Blood Sorcerer's minions were verifying the deaths of the heirs of Elden.

Leyek entered the great hall and bowed low to him. The sorcerer demanded the same displays one would give royalty. He *was* royalty. Better than any crowned monarch born of birth. The sorcerer had *earned* his right to walk exalted among the people. Killed until he reigned above all others. Drained the blood of many to sit on this gilt-and-jeweled throne.

"One of the scouts has returned, my lord," Leyek informed him.

He unfurled his long index finger. "Only one?"

His minion nodded. "Yes. Your creature is weak. He must be fed before his questioning."

The Blood Sorcerer stood, anger simmering around him. A visible mist. "Then see it done. There are plenty of Elden's citizenry in the storehouses."

"Already done, my lord."

The mist began to dissipate. Leyek had earned his second in command years ago, and was bloodthirsty enough to not let his position weaken. "Good. Which heir?"

"The scout was too weak, but this pairing was after Dayn. Or the sister, I think."

The Blood Sorcerer began to fondle the dark red rubies embedded in his chair. "Let's hope it's the girl, and that she's still alive. I relish the draining." He closed his eyes and shuddered in anticipated pleasure.

Agonized cries echoed outside. "Good. The feeding has begun. Let me know when he's finished off with his stock. I want to be one with my pet in the questioning."

Leyek nodded. "Very good, my lord."

The Blood Sorcerer gave a disinterested wave of his hand. "Make sure the draining is slow and extreme. My pet deserves a treat."

SOMETHING KINDLED WITHIN Rolfe. Some spark...some return to life. The desire to survive.

One of the heirs still lived.

Lived only to be hunted and slaughtered. But Rolfe

might be able to prevent their capture. A small, sliver of a chance, yet he'd take it. He'd make himself invaluable. Learn all he could of the blood scouts, and steer them away from the heir they hunted.

OSBORN WAS SILENT BESIDE her as they traced their path back into town to buy supplies. Silent but certainly not forgotten. Breena had tried, forcing herself to enjoy the freedoms that awaited her. She'd focus on only the good experiences to be had in town, the booths, the food, the newness of it all. She'd forget about the men who dragged her in the alley. Their deaths. She had to put those thoughts aside, and block every painful experience she'd had since Rolfe shook her awake. It all seemed a different lifetime ago. Happened to a different person. *Good.* It was the only way she could face what was next to save her family and her people.

More villagers filled the streets and small groups clustered in front of the more popular booths. A surge of excitement quickened her steps, and soon she and Osborn were among the crowd. Even without the *berserker* she knew lurked below Osborn's very prickly surface, he was one intimidating man. Tall and broad, there was no hiding the raw strength of him. The shopkeepers, eager for a sale, took a step backward as he approached, and she'd seen several people cross to the other side of the narrow street to avoid accidentally getting in his way. If he were one of her brothers, she'd tell him to remove that ever-present scowl on his face, he was scaring the townspeople. Or maybe it was those dark brown eyes of his that made those around his wary. He was constantly scanning the crowd, assessing the level of threat.

She may have grown up a sheltered princess, but

Breena knew that kind of alert wasn't instinctual. Her brothers were fighters after all. No, a man with that kind of guardedness and suspicion was like that because he'd brought danger down upon himself. His own doing.

The tales she'd read as a child always hinted at the softer side of the beast, but Breena suspected whatever soft side Osborn once had, he'd stomped to the ground and then did a little dance on its remains.

A smile tugged at her mouth, and Breena laughed at the foolish image she'd conjured in her head.

Osborn glanced at her sharply, and she laughed out loud. She'd blame her silly behavior on lack of sleep and the bone-deep weariness of her aching body that made her laugh with such little provocation. But it felt good to laugh. He stopped at a booth and she continued on, knowing his eyes would not stray from her for long.

"Do you need help?" the lady asked her quietly, darting a quick glance in Osborn's direction. His attention was on the rope he was inspecting, but it would only be a distraction for a moment or two. His vigilant gaze would be upon them both soon.

"Help?"

"To get away," she explained, her voice a quiet hiss.

Tears filled her eyes, as Breena realized what the woman before her was asking. The shopkeeper was trying to help her, escape from the terrifying man who always kept her in sight. She quickly blinked the tears back. Crying would only alarm the woman further, and draw Osborn's watchful eye. Breena managed to shake her head, overwhelmed by the kindness of this stranger. She'd faced a warrior and battled a creature of blood magic, but it was this one woman's compassion that nearly reduced her to a shaking mess.

The woman's gaze narrowed. "There are rumors of that one. He's a killer. Ruthless."

That's exactly what Breena was hoping for.

"We've struck a bargain," she told the woman who, despite her obvious fear of the man, would help Breena if she could.

Osborn had finished his transaction, and had turned his attention back to her. That fierce battle face of his firmly settled.

The woman beside her sucked in a fearful breath. "You're sure?"

Her magic led her to this man. Breena was as sure as she could be.

"I'm here every other day. I've helped other women in the past. Just send me word, and I'll do my best to get you free of him."

Breena shook her head again. The rough fabric of the shirt rubbed at her nipples.

"Actually, there are a few things I need."

IF BERNT AND TORBEN THOUGHT it was strange to see Breena at their brother's side at the rendezvous point, they didn't show it. They walked together as a group, silent, as Osborn bought additional supplies from the vendor. No one asked what she carried in her package, and she didn't volunteer the information. These men didn't need to know the intimacies of her underthings.

She caught snippets of agitated chatter from time to time.

"Did you hear? They found Unwin and Dudley dead. In one of the alleyways."

"Thieves, the both of them. Surprised it hasn't happened sooner."

No one seemed to mourn the loss. A few days ago,

the thought of someone dying, seeing someone killed before her eyes, would have been horrifying. Now she viewed the ruthlessness of others in a far different light, and the death of those who would murder without conscience did not bother her.

At another booth the vendors speculated on a suspect. "Who could have done it?"

"With so many strangers pouring into the village on market day, who's to know?"

Both stall keepers quieted their speculation as she approached with Osborn and his brothers. She couldn't help following her nose to the origin of the amazing scent, and the warrior had indulged her. The tradespeople eyed Osborn with wariness, but not suspicion. Relieved, she smiled at the baker who offered her a sample of the bread. "It smells delicious."

Some time later when the sun was lowering in the sky, Osborn announced it was time to return to the cottage. As they walked up the hill, she couldn't help stealing glances back at the village. So many things to see, and taste and smell. A few days ago she would have yearned for this exact experience.

It was almost dark when she spotted the roof of Osborn's home. The boys quickly set to work, preparing the fire while another returned the pillow and blankets for her to use. Last night, she'd made a pallet on the floor, and apparently that was to be the arrangement again tonight. Probably another one of Osborn's attempts to make her change her mind. It didn't matter, the wooden floor of the cabin wasn't soft, but she slept in front of the warmth of a fire, and her stomach was full.

Osborn walked over to her carrying a large woven sack, usually used to carry potatoes. He dumped it in front of her, and out spilled a pile of socks, shirts and pants. The mending.

"All this?" she asked, before she could stop herself.

Osborn raised an eyebrow. "There is a different deal we could make." His gaze lowered to her breasts, and then moved still lower. To between her legs.

Breena's mouth went dry. Never had a man looked at her so carnally. Acknowledged her secret woman's place with such possession. Her hands began to tremble so she sank them into the bag.

"I love to sew. Mending even more. All I need is a needle."

Osborn's lips twisted as if he were attempting to hide a smile. "In the bottom of the sack. Good night."

She rummaged among the cloth until she found a hard wooden case. Breena tugged it out and opened it to find several silver needles and a small pair of sheers. She reached for a woolen sock, sporting a rip in the heel.

"And, Breena?"

"Yes?"

"I'd like to wear those in the morning."

He turned and left, closing the door firmly behind him. The man apparently didn't believe she could sew. She'd show him; her stitches were always tiny and neat. Osborn the warrior may be something amazing when he fought, but he still only had two feet, and he needed only two socks for the morning. Not the dozens stuffed into the sack.

She was also growing tired of his habit of calling her name after the conversation was certainly over—just to give her another order.

Survive. Yes, that's what she was doing.

Breena closed her eyes and breathed in the woodsy scent that hung in cabin. The smoke from the fire. Once again she'd live through another night. And beginning tomorrow she'd start the second command that echoed in her mind. To avenge.

But first…she picked up a sock and threaded her needle.

A HAND TO HER SHOULDER WOKE her up the next morning.

"Wake up."

She squeezed her eyelids tight and rolled away from the voice, sinking deeper into her pillow.

But the voice was insistent. "Time to train."

Breena slowly opened her eyes to see Osborn's familiar strong jaw and firm lips. Kissable. But then her thoughts were always a bit fanciful in that place between sleep and wakefulness. His hair was damp, and his cheek smooth. She reached up to slide a finger across his face.

He jerked back from her touch. Mister Prickly today.

Osborn stood, once again dressed in black, his scabbard slung low on his hip. "There's something for you to eat on the table. I'll be waiting for you outside so you can dress. Bernt and Torben are gathering wood and water. Five minutes."

A hunk of cheese and dried berries waited for her, and she devoured them with pleasure. She'd discovered a smaller pair of drawstring pants in the mending bag last night and, after some trimming with the shears, managed to craft something that didn't drag on the ground. She finger combed her hair, and nearly laughed at the idea of the maids who'd once chosen gowns of silk and fashioned her hair in elaborate styles and adorned her with ribbons and gems.

Who'd recognize her now?

And that was a good thing. She suspected she'd used

up most of her allotted time. The impatient look on his face told her Osborn was just about to charge into the cottage and get her. "This way," he said, and guided her to a clearing not too far from the cabin. Breena hadn't discovered this place when she was wandering around his home on that first day. Targets and woven sacks filled with straw littered the area, and Breena realized this must be where Osborn kept up with his training.

Osborn tossed her a stick.

"I thought you were going to teach me how to use a sword," she said, eyeing the sword at his hip. Her gaze slipped lower until she forced it back where it belonged.

He crossed his arms in front of his chest. "Have you ever held a sword?"

Breena shook her head. As if her mother ever would have allowed it. Her brothers wouldn't have dared to let her carry a weapon. Even the adored sons would have been afraid of the queen's ire over that infraction. "No. Never."

"Then that's why you're using a stick. Now, you've seen swordplay?"

She was quick to nod. "My father loved nothing more than to host a tournament. The knights on horseback brandishing their swords with a flourish were a thing to behold."

"It's the flourishing knights who are the first to die."

Breena bit her lip to keep from smiling. Could that have been jealousy? She stood straight instead. "Okay, definitely nothing fancy."

"Hold your sword like you're about to face me in battle."

She lifted her stick. Osborn moved to stand behind her, his big chest warming her back he was so close.

The chestnut smell of the soap he must use to wash his hair made her want to breathe in deeply.

He lifted his arm, framing her body with his. "Bend your elbows," he told her, "and bring your arms in close to your sides. The weight of your blade will only increase, and you want your sword to do the work, not your arms."

The new stance did feel more comfortable.

Osborn positioned her arms out from her chest. "See how you've left this entire area open?" he asked, trailing his fingers along her collarbone, and down between her breasts.

Breena could only nod. Her skin turned goose bumpy.

"This is your most vulnerable area. You must always protect it."

She was definitely feeling vulnerable. And she was *really* enjoying her lessons. That hand down between her breasts would be worth a pile of sock mending.

Osborn dropped his arms, but not before brushing the sides of her breasts, her waist and her hips. Breena couldn't help but tremble. "Now turn and face me. Always keep in mind that the first blow is the most important."

"*My* first blow?"

"Doesn't matter," he told her with a shrug. "Either you strike and hit or he strikes and misses—*that's what* determines who walks away. If you strike first, make sure you connect. Otherwise, you are off balance and an easy target for his strike. Which *will* kill you."

Breena began to bristle at that assumption.

"You will be smaller than any man you fight. Not as strong. Those are the facts, Breena. I'm not saying you can't defeat your opponent, but you have to be twice as good as they are. Twice as prepared. You have to find their weakness, and use it to your advantage. What do you think my weakness is?"

Breena ran her gaze along Osborn's broad shoulders, powerful arms and muscled thighs. Heat suffused her cheeks as she imagined her hands following the same path as her eyes—over his firm mouth with the full bottom lip. Down the strength of his brawny chest roped with muscle. The flat tautness of his stomach. And below.

"What's my weakness, Breena?" he asked, his voice less instructional but low and husky.

Their gazes clashed.

"I can't see any."

"Then you're wrong. I'm tall, so that leaves my legs exposed. I'm big, so once I'm off balance...that's a disaster. And I'm a man."

Deliciously so.

"And all men are vulnerable in one spot. Do you know what that is?"

She shook her head.

"Between my legs."

She knew what lay between his legs. Couldn't miss the hard male flesh as he stood watching her dress two days ago at the lake. Stood guard, more like. Flashes of what she'd seen stole in her mind at the most inappropriate of times, and refused to be driven out.

"A knee or a good swift kick will bring most men down, and give you a chance to escape. And, Breena?"

"Yes?"

"Trust me, do not wait to see if he falls. Just get out of there."

This mysterious place on a man was growing more and more interesting.

"But most men are protective of that area. You'll really only get just one chance at him, so make it count. Connect."

A twig snapped, and Breena turned her head. Bernt and Torben were crouched behind a bolder, watching them.

"It looks like we have some company," she remarked with a grin.

Osborn rubbed the back of his neck. "Judging by the sun, they've been there for some time."

Breena glanced at him in surprise.

"You must always be aware of your surroundings. What's hiding in the distance. Who's hiding. Where the ground is loose and rocky. Your position to the sun. An opponent with bright sunlight in his face is at a disadvantage. You can lose your footing easily on an uneven field. The time and place of the fight is almost as important as your weapon and skill."

She'd never doubt her magic again. Her powers had provided quite a warrior.

"What about our two spectators?" she asked, angling her head in the boys' direction.

His face turned grim, and his shoulders slumped as if weighted.

"How old were you when, uh, you became responsible for them?" she asked.

"Fifteen, maybe fourteen. It seems like a different life—" his voice was a tired sigh "—the childhood I had was something distant. As if it didn't happen, and was just a story like those stories you enjoy telling."

When her brothers turned fifteen, the king rode with them daily, supervised their study in the classroom and on the mock battlefield. What kind of men would her brothers have turned out to be without the guidance of their parents? Her heart constricted for little Micah. Still so young, and with no one. She swallowed past the lump in her throat.

She had to get to him. Find him soon.

Breena remembered why her magic drew Osborn to her, as well. He definitely needed her, and so did his brothers.

"Maybe you can ask them to join us," she suggested, her voice light as a gentle wind, so her proposal wouldn't seem so monumental.

Osborn stared at her for a few moments, but his thoughts were not on her. With another of those heavy sighs, he whistled. The two boys stood, appearing plenty guilty and a little worried.

"Do you want to learn how to fight?" he asked.

Two heads nodded enthusiastically.

"Grab a stick."

Bernt gave her a tentative smile when he stepped beside her, stick in hand. "Thanks," he whispered.

"He knew it was time. He just needed a push."

"If the courtly manners class is over, we'll go back to sword fighting," Osborn called loudly.

There. That's how she remembered her brothers teasing and talking with each other. It was good to hear, and her heart lightened for the first time.

THAT EVENING, OSBORN LED three exhausted would-be warriors back to the cottage. The night air had turned chilly on their walk, and once inside Breena removed the protective metal screen on the hearth, stirred the embers and added a log. Then she sank onto the rug before the fireplace, closing her eyes as she went.

Even Bernt and Toren stumbled to the bedroom, too tired to eat—an occurrence he'd never seen once since his brothers entered their second decade of life. They were on their own, but Breena...that was a different matter. She was unused to this kind of physical activity, and while he knew he must push her, she didn't have to suffer.

With quiet steps, Osborn crossed to the kitchen and began cutting up an apple. He grabbed a piece of the dark rye bread he'd bought at one of the village booths after Breena had remarked that the wares smelled particularly delightful.

Breena lay in a ball on the rug, a strand of her blond hair across her cheek. Dirt smudged her forehead, and her soft skin was pink from her exertion of the past several hours.

And he'd never seen anything more desirable.

The mystical woman who floated into dreams as he slumbered was ethereal and perfect.

The Breena in real life was far from perfect. Her nails were ragged from her wandering in the wilderness. Her palms growing callused from her work with a stick and finally a sword. And although he knew she was raised to be a gentle lady, he suspected a temper, only needing an excuse to flare, lurked beneath the surface....

Osborn wanted to give her that excuse. To be exactly who she was meant to be. And very definitely have the freedom of *his* body. Explore him until her curiosity ran out and his took over.

He'd spent hours of his daytime thinking on this woman who haunted his nights. Now, after meeting her and touching her supple skin, kissing her inviting lips and holding her welcoming curves against him, he knew she would torment him forever.

She burned to avenge her family. In many ways, she was not unlike him. Only the thought of killing the

butchers of his family kept him sane. That and knowing he must keep his brothers alive.

Was he doing the right thing in training her?

He didn't even have to search for the answer. It was a
quick no. He thought of his mother and his little sister.
If they had been the ones to escape and were alone and
doing whatever it was they could to see another day,
he'd hope someone would help them. Breena needed
his help, and all Osborn knew how to do was fight. So
he had to train her.

He slid down next to Breena on the floor. The rug
was more comfortable than he'd expected and the fire
warmed his cheeks. She stirred beside him, scooting
closer to him in her sleep. Osborn gently shook her on
the shoulder, and her eyelids fluttered open.

"I brought you something to eat."

"Too tired," she said, closing her eyes, and resting
her head on his thigh. The *berserkergang* roused, but
he willed himself not to react.

He smoothed the hair away from her face, not wanting to move, but knowing she had to take care of herself.
"Eat just a few bites. Tomorrow will be even harder,
and you'll need to keep up your strength. Come on, I'll
feed you."

With a groan, Breena pushed herself into a sitting
position. She stretched out beside him touching hip to
hip, shoulder to shoulder and thigh to thigh. He felt his
body harden at her touch. She smelled of warm breezes
and hard work. The scent was heady.

Osborn reached for a bit of apple. "Open."

Breena dutifully opened her mouth. The first time
she didn't argue. Or raise some kind of a counterpoint.
Or make some kind of difficult suggestion.

She doesn't challenge you when she's in your arms.

Oh, yes, she did. It was just a different kind. One he relished.

He managed to get three more bites fed to Breena, then her eyes drooped again, and he knew her body demanded sleep over food. Her head slumped on his shoulder. He shifted his arm to get her into a more comfortable position, and she snuggled close against him.

Why the hell had he done that?

Feeling the softness of breasts pressed against him was agony. His cock hardened, and he made it all the worse by caressing her arm and sinking his fingers into her long hair.

"That's nice," she mumbled into his chest. "Feels good."

He should go.

Right now.

He should stand, settle her against the pillow and never think of doing something so stupid like being this close to her ever again. Breena was too much of a temptation. Especially because she'd made it clear she'd rather stitch up a pile of socks before crawling between the sheets with him. Oh, Breena desired him, but she didn't *want* him. And for some reason, desire wasn't enough.

He should go.

Right now.

Breena wrapped her arm around his waist, seeking his warmth. Seeking him.

Maybe he could just lay here with her for a few minutes more.

CHAPTER EIGHT

BREENA WOKE UP WARM and so, so comfortable. Which was completely ruined by the glowering, accusing brown glare coming from Osborn. With no *berserker* change in sight, the rage tightening his face had to be all him.

"What's wrong?" she asked.

"You invaded my dream last night."

She scrambled away from him, shaking her head. "No, you told me to stay away."

"You were there. Kissing me. Touching me. Feel me, Breena. Feel what your dream did to my body. Give me your hand."

It sounded like an order, but it was still a choice. What had she done to him? Curiosity…it had ruined many a princess. It would probably ruin her, too. She placed her hand into Osborn's outstretched palm.

She met his gaze as he tugged her hand downward. "Feel me. Feel what you do to me."

Do not… Did.

He placed her hand between his legs. "Feel how hard my cock is for you."

The word sounded lustful. Sensual. Lascivious, and she wanted more and more. He wrapped her fingers around the hard ridge of him. Her body got that hollow, achy feeling again. She needed something, and knew Osborn could give it to her.

"Touch me like you did last night," he urged, his voice barely more than an aching groan.

"Show me," she told him, wanting to learn how to give him pleasure. How to keep that aching sound for her in his voice.

"Slide your hand under my pants. Yes, that's it."

Her fingers smoothed over the hard ripples of the muscles lining his stomach, down over the hair at the base of him. With a tiny thrill, she gathered Osborn's cock into her hand. He was long, and very hard, and yet his skin was smooth. His muscles tensed as she explored the length of him.

"That's it. More. Like last night. Up and down."

Breena walked her fingers up and down the length of him.

"You were perfect in my dream. As if you knew exactly how I wanted it before I even told you."

With another groan, Osborn stilled her hand.

"Did I hurt you?" she asked alarmed.

He gave a strangled little laugh. The room was filled with the harshness of his breathing. He opened his eyes. "It really was my own dream. That's why you knew exactly how I wanted your touch."

She nodded, and waved her free hand. "See, I didn't use my powers. There's no trace magic."

"What?" he asked as he slowly removed her hand from his body.

"There'd be some kind of residue, an energy all around us." She felt her face drain of color. "Oh, no. I used my magic at the lake when we fought those blood magic scouts. I have to get there."

Breena shoved her feet into her shoes, and raced for the door, Osborn a step behind her. Once outside he took the lead, running along the path until the lake came into sight. She waved her hands, alarm coursing through her. "It's still here. Not much, but I can still feel it. Those monsters will be able to follow it to us. To the cottage. To the village. That's how they probably found me in the first place."

"Can you disguise it? Make it go away?"

"I never learned how. My powers weren't this strong back at El—er, home. My energy came from fear and anger. We'll have to blanket it with something good. Happiness."

She glanced over at Osborn, his face bleak.

"This is going to be tough." Not much happiness there.

"Come here, Breena."

Why was he always asking her to go to him? She was getting tired of being the one to do the moving. She shook her head. "If you want me, you come to me." Besides, she had to discover a solution to this problem.

Breena realized what a huge mistake she'd made by offering that kind of challenge to her warrior. Osborn's eyes darkened. His lower lip grew more full, and curved into something that might be considered a smile on anyone else, but on him, it could only be considered predatory.

"I will," he told her, his voice filled with determined intent. His steps toward her were driven and steadfast. He never dropped her gaze.

Don't back up. Don't back up.

He only stopped when the softness of her breasts grazed his broad chest.

"Do you know what else you did to me in that dream I had with you last night?"

"It wasn't me doing it."

"It will be." Osborn's thumb traced a path along her

lower lip. An overwhelming urge to lick his skin, taste him, took her over. She felt hollow inside. Achy.

"Your nipples did exactly what they are doing now. Hardening. Begging for my touch. My mouth."

She shook her head. "It wasn't me."

"It will be," he promised again against her lips. His mouth took over, his tongue pushed inside and she met him with her own. Twining and dueling again and again. She couldn't breathe. Her heart raced. Breena grabbed his shoulders, needing the solid strength of him to remain steady.

She'd never felt this way before. Never responded to anything with so much intensity or reacted so strongly, hungrily. Osborn made her feel alive and warm and grasping for something more.

"What are you doing?" she asked.

"You said we needed to change the energy in this place. We are."

She *so* wanted that to make sense. To continue what they were doing.

"Take your shirt off for me, Breena. I hate seeing you in something that ugly."

Osborn was so big and strong. As a *berserker,* he could take anything he wanted. Even her.

That's why he always asked. Asked her to go to him. Her warrior didn't want to take; he wanted what would be freely given.

And right now he wanted her shirt. Off.

No man had ever seen her undressed and exposed in that way. Osborn had plenty of opportunity two days ago in this place while they were both naked and battling a creature of blood.

But this was different.

Freely given. Breena gripped the hem of her shirt

and then paused. What if he didn't like what he saw? If he found her form undesirable? She fiddled with a loose thread on the borrowed tunic. Of what she'd observed in the castle, the knights never complained of a woman's naked body, always clamored to see more. And Osborn hadn't looked away in that secluded clearing outside of the village.

He'd wanted more.

After stealing a deep breath, she grabbed the bottom of the shirt and tugged it over her head. She tossed the garment out of the way of the water, and straightened her back. Almost daring him to dislike what he saw.

His gaze lowered, and his face tightened with longing. "You are so beautiful," he said, his voice filled with a kind of agonized need. He cupped her breasts, molding them to his hands. His thumbs caressed the tips into tight points. With one arm, he gripped her hip and hauled her off her feet, up against his body. The hard ridge of him, heated and full, surged against the bare skin of her stomach. He ducked his head, capturing her breast into his mouth.

She moaned deep in her throat when his teeth gently grazed her nipple.

"More?" he asked against the fullness of her breast.

Breena could only nod.

With obvious reluctance, Osborn let her slide down his frame until her feet touched the ground again. He swept off his cloak, and spread it on the green grass. "In my dream, you shared all of your body with me."

She sucked in her bottom lip, toyed with it with her teeth. "It really wasn't me."

"I want it to be."

She wanted it, too. *Want.*

He leaned close. "Make it be for me."

His warm breath sent a ripple of sensation down her neck. Her fingers shook as she reached for the drawstring keeping the baggy pants in place. It should be awkward to remove her clothes in front of a man who just a while ago she thought would kill her. Now it seemed the most natural thing in the world.

With a jerk, the pants loosened around her waist, and with a shimmy of her hips, the material slid slowly down her thighs.

Osborn's eyes followed their progress.

Breena kicked the pants aside, now fully bared to his eyes. And to his fingers. His lips. His tongue.

He reached for her hand, and drew her down with him to the cloak, its soft material protecting her naked back from the twigs and rocks on the ground. After cupping her breasts one last time, he allowed his hands to explore. His fingers trailed down over the curve of her stomach and along her thighs.

"So soft. Your skin warms to my touch."

Yes, she wanted his hands everywhere on her.

Osborn stretched alongside her, his mouth finding her collarbone, moving along its path until he discovered a place below her ear that when he kissed it, her entire body shivered. He groaned at her response.

"Do you like that?"

So much she wanted to do it back to him. "Yes," she told him, her voice drawn and tight to her own ears.

Osborn added his tongue.

Wetness rushed where her thighs met. Her whole body seemed to be curving toward him, craving more of what he could give her. She lifted her knee, and ran the tips of her toes down his molded calf. She gasped when his fingers sank between her legs, the feeling of his gentle invasion exquisite.

"You're so wet for me." His voice was little more than a growl. With a swipe of his tongue to her earlobe, Osborn began to slide down her frame, stopping to give a gentle nip to her breasts, and he continued lower.

He tasted the skin under her breasts, circled her belly button with his tongue. Went lower still.

"What are you doing?" she asked.

"Changing the energy."

She felt his warm breath on the curls between her thighs, and she began to shake. He nudged her knees farther apart, exposing her woman's body to his gaze.

"So slick for me."

With one tiny kiss, her every muscle locked. His head descended, and he licked. Her moan filled the clearing around the lake, echoing off the trees.

"I love to hear your pleasure." Then he gave her more. He laved every part of her, and plunged his tongue within her. Every muscle, every part of her that could feel, tightened and narrowed, just waiting for more of his touch.

He began to seek inside her with his finger. The tip delving where she ached to have him fill her.

"So tight."

"That feels so good."

"It's about to get a whole lot better." He lowered his head again and began to suck where her sensations seemed to be the most centered. And her world burst.

Breena dug her fingers into Osborn's shoulders as crest after crest of pleasure slammed her senses. Her cry sailed up to the trees and she arched herself toward him until the amazing sensations died away.

With one last kiss, he rolled to his back beside her, and stared up at the sky.

She rolled toward him, draping her arm over his

chest, and cuddled as close as she could. She'd remember this forever.

Osborn tensed when she began to play with the fine hair covering his chest. "You've never done this before, have you?"

Breena shook her head. "That was incredible. You made me... I felt... It's hard to find the words."

She expected Osborn to bask in her praise. Encourage her for more. If anything, his expression grew grimmer than when they'd first returned to the lake.

"Before the invasion of your home, what was your training? What were you meant to be?"

"Be? I don't understand what you mean."

He pushed her hand away from him, and braced himself up on his elbow so he could look down at her, not up. "You're not a servant, or someone who works out in the field. We've already established that. You're something more. You're meant for something. Some-*one*. You're a virgin, aren't you?" His tone sounded accusatory, like he suspected she kicked small animals for fun.

Unease settled just below her heart. She nodded, confirming his question. Breena didn't like the direction this conversation seemed to be taking. She didn't know what she was hoping for after an experience that was so intense and personal for her—maybe a hug, but certainly not an interrogation.

Osborn scrubbed his hand down his face. "Should have known. You had that wholesome look about you."

Wholesome?

Men didn't teach women battle skills they found... wholesome. It was a loathsome word.

"You're meant for another." His words were low, spoken into the ground.

"What?" she asked, not sure she heard him correctly.

He aimed his gaze somewhere in the vicinity of her forehead. "Get dressed. You're meant for another. Not me. Never me."

Breena snapped her legs together. A wave of embarrassment and confusion shuddered through her. "You're not making me leave you?"

His breath came out in a heavy sigh. "No, you'll learn what you need to, and then I'll send you on your way."

Relief chased away the confusion, but the embarrassment still warred inside her. She reached for her discarded pants, and quickly stepped into them.

"And, Breena?"

They were back to that. "Yes?"

"Remember the warning I first gave you?"

Maybe. Which one? There were so many.

She nodded instead. Seemed a safer response now that he was back to being so prickly.

"Don't be alone with me. I don't want my touch to defile you."

Tears filled her eyes, but she quickly blinked them back. "How could what we just shared be defilement?" His caresses had brought something out in her. She felt connected to him. Intimate.

He obviously did not feel the same way.

Osborn finally locked his eyes on her. Her lips. Her breasts. Between her legs. Then his gaze clashed back with hers. Hunger and desire and passion so carnal and raw blazed in the brown depths. "What I want to do with you, yeah, you'd definitely come away defiled."

And she bet she'd have a smile on her face, too. Turning her back to him, she tugged the shirt he hated on her back in place. What did he want her to wear? They were shirts *from* his household.

"And, Breena?"

And again just to make sure she was truly flustered. Now it was her turn to sigh. "Yes?" she replied sweetly.

"Stay out of my dreams."

"I wasn't in your dreams," she told his retreating back.

AFTER THE MORNING CHORES, Bernt and Torben met them on the practice field. Osborn paced across the grass, once more the stern and frightening man she'd woken to days ago.

"Balance is the most important aspect of your fight. Once you lose your balance you lose the opportunity to protect yourself, defend…and lunge, your offense. And then you die."

He pointed to three large round stones, each with a plank of wood beside it. "Place the wood on the stone and step on. Balance until the sun is directly overhead."

Osborn stalked away and both Bernt and Torben shot her accusatory looks. Breena just shrugged. They knew their brother didn't need any actual real provocation to be grumpy.

The three of them did as they were instructed. Balancing didn't seem too hard. She'd seen plenty of dancers at the palace, and one even walked along a rope suspended between two chairs. Fifteen minutes in and she hated those dancers, and knew the rope balancer had to be a fake. She fell off her plank over and over again. At least she was having better luck than the two boys. They spent more time on their backs than they did standing on their plank. By the time Osborn returned, she was hot, sore and really, really anxious to grab her stick so she could whack him with it during their mock swordplay.

He tossed each of them a green apple and a pouch of water. "Water first."

Despite the fact that their backsides must be sporting a permanent imprint of the ground, Bernt and Torben laughed and teased each other while they ate. Osborn wouldn't look at her, and even though she was surrounded by three other people, Breena felt the loneliest of her life.

Their taskmaster couldn't have given them more than ten minutes of rest. The core of her apple had barely shown itself when he had her up and holding a sword. A real one this time, no sticks. Maybe he'd suspected she'd been entertaining dark thoughts with that stick.

"Take it out of the scabbard," he told her.

She slid the blade from its holder, the sun glinting off the silver edge. There was nothing ornate about this weapon. No jewels encrusted on the hilt, no elaborate carvings marring the blade. A simple weapon. So unlike those of her father and brothers.

"It was my first sword," he told her. "Take good care of it."

And even though she looked up to meet his gaze, Osborn never lowered his eyes to meet hers.

"Thank you," she said. The steel in her hands meant something to the man who'd given it to her. She'd always protect it.

He shifted to face all of them. "In a surprise attack, the fatal blow is often struck before the victim's sword is even drawn. The rest of the afternoon, I want you to practice pulling your sword from its scabbard. Quickly. Quietly. Over and over again until it's second nature to you. You should be able to do this in your sleep. One day you may have to."

For hours they honed this particular skill. She stood

still, and pulled the sword from the scabbard; while running, with her scabbard at her side, she pulled the weapon out; when the scabbard was beside her on the ground, she unsheathed the sword. Breena performed the maneuver until it was perfect. Then Osborn instructed her to switch sides and use the hand she didn't favor.

"If you're injured, you may be able to fight off your aggressor."

Every muscle of her body ached by the time Osborn called a halt sometime before the late-afternoon chores. If she thought she was sweaty and dirty after the balance torture Osborn had conceived, she wouldn't be fit to sleep in a stable tonight. She followed him back to the cabin, barely able to hold her sword and scabbard, but not about to ask Osborn for help.

What she would seek his aid in was finding a bar of soap. His lips firmed and that hungry look returned to his eyes when she told him she wanted to take a bath.

"Naked?" he asked.

"That's generally how it's done. How do you wash off?"

She watched as he swallowed slowly. "I usually hop into the lake."

Breena shook her head. "Probably should avoid that place, now that the energy is less...magical. It's too bad you don't use a tub. Sitting in sudsy warm water in front of the fire is one of life's real pleasures."

Osborn looked like he wanted to be anywhere but in this conversation. Too bad. "I'll just grab a basin and wash off in back. Soap?"

"In the cabinet under the window."

"Thank you," she told him with a smile. "No one comes outside," she yelled, so the boys would know to stay inside the cottage. When had she become a yeller? Since meeting up with a family of *berserkers,* the rage must be rubbing off on her.

The water she'd pumped into the basin was cold, but she knew it would feel fantastic against her hot and sticky skin. The soap, however, was another matter. It smelled like Osborn. Warm chestnuts. She breathed it in deep, rubbed the soap between her hands until she built a lather, then began running the smell of him all over her body.

OSBORN SPENT THE REST OF his day wondering about her bath. How she took off her shoes. Her shirt. Her pants. How the fading sun must have glinted off her naked skin. Her hair. He imagined wetting her skin with a sopping cloth, grasping his soap and rolling it along her arms. Over her breasts. Down her stomach. Between her legs.

He envisioned stepping behind her, shedding his clothes and standing before her naked. He *felt* the slick soap and her soft hands along his chest, over his back and gripping his cock. He was in performance mode in record time. She'd slide her hands up and down the shaft of him as she slid her tongue into his mouth. The movements of her hands and mouth mimicking one another. She'd rinse away the soap and sink to her knees. Kiss the head of his cock, tongue the shaft, then slide him all the way into her mouth.

He groaned, nearly coming with the erotic visions. He was going crazy. Osborn had to get her out of his cottage. His life.

But how could he when he wanted her more than almost anything in his life?

He found her later that night, curled on her side in

front of the fire. The blanket lay at her feet and he crouched down low to tug it back over her slim frame. Her hair was still damp, but would soon dry before the fire. She shivered, and he worried that she might be cold. Rolling to his side, he fitted her back against his chest. The way her soft curves formed to his body was sweet, sweet torture. One he'd gladly endure over and over.

Breena smelled fresh and clean, and…a little like him. His soap. Possession arced through him, and he curved an arm around her waist. She snuggled toward him in her sleep as though it was natural. Where she should be.

He buried his nose in her hair, the delicate strands sliding over his cheek. Breena shouldn't smell like a man. And he shouldn't be holding her. Wanting more. Needing more. But he'd steal just a few moments. Then he'd pick himself up and go to his bedroom and shut the door. Firmly.

CHAPTER NINE

BREENA IMAGINED A DOOR in her mind. Two doors. The second door was new. Menacing. While the first stood familiar, opening that door and walking through had been forbidden to her. She went to it, anyway. Leaned against the closed entry. She longed to go inside. Days had passed since she'd last crossed the threshold and found pleasure. And passion.

But she could not go in.

She turned to the second portal. The entrance was ornate while the other gate was plain. Timeworn carvings in the ancient Elden language adorned the mahogany door. Jewels and rubies, sapphires and diamonds, were embedded in the knob. It should be the most desirable doorway in the world. Instead, she looked again at the simple entry, but that was not her path. That way had been barred to her.

Steeling herself, she gazed once more upon the door that should be inviting. A crimson haze seemed to surround it on all sides. The color of blood. Breena didn't want to go inside. Didn't want to know what lay beyond once she turned that bejeweled knob.

Yet this was her destiny.

Her fingers shook as she reached for the handle and turned. A film of oppressive hate dropped over her, smothered her. Her legs buckled, and she wanted to turn back, but knew she couldn't. Steeling herself, Breena stepped inside.

She was in the great hall of her home in Elden. Beautiful tapestries hung on the walls, and fat tapers illuminated the room, just like always. But instead of the friendly chatter of people, the bustle of the servants and the laughter of the king and queen, she heard only agony. The wailing of the wounded. The fearful cries of those left behind and being rounded up by creatures of unimaginable horror. The smell of blood was heavy in the air. It sickened her, but not as much as the sight of her people, dead and dying on the cold stone of the castle floor.

Breena reached to pick up her skirt to rush to their aid, but found she wore pants instead. The outfit of a boy. Strapped to her waist was a sword and scabbard. Her fingers sought the timepiece she wore around her neck. She examined the gift her mother had given her at the age of five. A sword was stamped into the face, such an odd symbol to entrust to a little girl. Breena slid the sword out of its scabbard. It was identical to the image on her timepiece.

She *was* on the path of her destiny.

The queen. She thrust the sword in its scabbard, and raced across the room, avoiding the pools of blood and the dead that she could not help. She ran until she reached the dais upon which her parents always sat during the formal times at Elden. She found them strapped to their thrones, a mockery of their honor. More blood flowed at their feet. Thickening.

They were dead. A slash at both their throats. The pain of it so great she sobbed.

Something warm and soothing patted her shoulder in her dream. On instinct, Breena drew her sword quickly and with intent. But no one stood behind her. She returned her sword and braced herself to look at her parents one more time. One last time. They'd each managed to work a hand free from their bonds. They'd died with their fingers intertwined.

Tears began streaming down her cheeks. So many. Too many to wipe away. But someone gently dabbed the moisture away, and soothed her with a soft whisper. "Sleep, Breena. No more dreaming."

She followed the voice out of her dream. Warmth enveloped her, and she crushed herself toward the soothing strength. And she followed the voice's command and went to sleep without dreaming further.

Breena woke up with her memory restored.

OSBORN WATCHED BREENA sleep until the birds began to sing. Her sob had jerked him awake. She still lay in his arms, but she thrashed about and she began to cry. He'd never seen a woman cry before. He'd never expected it of Breena, who'd proved she could take as much training and work as a young man learning the ways of a warrior.

Her tears did something to him. Made him feel weak. Made him want to fix or kill or change whatever made her cry. Instead, he could only cradle her to his chest, wipe her tears and try to soothe her with his voice. She finally calmed and settled against him. Her breathing eventually turned steady, and he could relax then, but never sleep.

As the sun broke over the horizon, Osborn knew continuing to train her to fight would only prolong her pain. After last night, he couldn't bear to see her hurt any longer. Today was the last market day of the week in the village. Breena couldn't continue to stay with three men. Surely there was some sort of position, something completely safe, that would keep her employed.

The blood scout had not returned. Had not brought reinforcements, and Osborn doubted the creature would be back with the change in energy at the lake. Blood scouts were little more than mindless drones, obeying only limited commands. Osborn's cock grew uncomfortable as he remembered how he and Breena had chased away the trace magic. He shifted his legs to relieve the pressure, and glanced down at the beautiful woman in his arms. She was gently reared. Perhaps she could be a nanny or maybe a companion to an elder in town until he sorted out everything. Found where she belonged.

Why was no one in her family looking for her?

He feared he already knew the answer.

Osborn gently slid his arm from around her waist and, after one last glance, left Breena to her sleep. He quietly walked toward his front door and slipped outside without waking anyone inside. His brothers wouldn't worry; he often left the cottage early to train, or to run or secure and inspect the perimeter of the sacred lands.

Without the three of them, Osborn stood on the border in no time. The village marketers were just opening their booths when he crested the hill. He quickly made his way down the incline. The first stall he sought sold soaps and perfumes and fancy concoctions used to wash hair.

"For you or for your lady?" the saleswoman asked.

"My lady. I mean a lady."

The woman laughed, flashing him a hearty smile. "I reckon if you give her something I've created, she'll be your lady. I make the best soaps in three realms." She popped the lid off a glass container and held it under his nose.

He breathed in soft vanilla with a hint of erotic spice. *This* was what Breena should smell like. Not manly chestnut. "I'll take it. And the shampoo," he told her.

He continued to make his way through the stall, listening to the snippets of conversation, hoping to glean information without having to ask for it. He stopped when he spotted a beautiful green cloak. Breena's eyes turned that exact shade of sage when he kissed her. Osborn suppressed an inward groan. He had to have that, too. He pointed to the cloak of his choice.

"Excellent. My wife just finished this yesterday."

A short woman with a toddler on her hip joined them from behind a privacy curtain. She fingered the material and grinned up at Osborn. "I almost didn't want to give this one up, it's so beautiful. She's a lucky lady. But have you seen the matching gown?"

Osborn shook his head, quickly realizing he was over his head. Sword—yes. Bow and arrow—no problem. Dresses...

"It will leave her arms bare, but with these gold bands, she can cinch the cloak to the dress and pull it around her shoulders if she gets chilled."

And when the woman laid the gown before him, he knew Breena must have it, too. The old pants and shirt didn't do her beauty justice. And although he didn't mind seeing the material stretch across the rounded curves of her ass, this gown suited her far more. In a few moments, the couple had the garments wrapped and Osborn continued on his way.

A gold armband in a stall a few paces down the aisle caught his attention. He didn't know if Breena wore such jewelry in her old life. The odd timepiece around her neck the only adornment that made it with her to safety. But the armband fit what he knew of her now, and he purchased it, too.

Three packages in hand, Osborn had done nothing he'd set out to do. Obtain information. He backtracked to the first stall where he'd bought the scents. "Have you heard any word of battles?" he asked.

Osborn ground his back teeth. He'd meant to ask about positions for a young woman. Not warfare.

The woman's face grew alarmed. "Here?"

Osborn shrugged. "Anywhere in the area."

"You'll want to be hiring out your sword, I reckon, by the looks of you. You're a brawny one," she told him with an inspection up and down.

Osborn shook his head. "No, I'm only checking on…a friend."

"I haven't heard of anything, but go to Hagan, the second to the last booth on the left. He sells spices from all over the realms. If a battle is brewing, he'll know about it."

Armed with a true purpose and destination, Osborn weaved through the growing crowd toward the spice man. After he questioned Hagan, he'd go about securing safe employment for Breena, and this time he would not be distracted.

"How is the basil?" he asked the salesman after his other customer left.

"The most aromatic you will find. Here," he said, opening the spice bag.

"Has the price gone up?" Osborn asked, after taking in the pungent, earthen scent of the herb. "I've heard there's been fighting in that realm and the trade routes are blocked."

The spice man shook his head. "Not with basil.

Where you need to be concerned about rising costs is with the olive oil. Elden is under siege, and the oldest trees can be found only in that area. I'd buy all the olive oil you can at the moment, you may not be able to find it later."

A chill ran through him. His *berserkergang* wakened. "Elden?"

"No one can get in, and what news that's coming out is bad. The queen and king dead. The heirs gone, too."

Something satisfyingly elemental burned in his gut. Elden was finally getting its due. He rued that it wasn't by his hand. He'd always taste the regret of vengeance not fully satisfied.

The *berserker* in him called for his pelt. Maybe he could brandish the fatal blow and send those cold vamps to their deaths.

Osborn felt lighter than he could ever remember. At least since Elden wreaked havoc and took away most of his life. Now to complete his final task.

BREENA ACHED EVERYWHERE. Even her ears seemed to hurt, and she didn't know how that was possible. Her shoulders dragged, and it took her longer than usual to make it to her knees and roll up her pallet and shove it out of the way.

The sun shone brightly through the window. Well past their usual practice time. Osborn must have suspected she wouldn't be much use with a sword today. Especially as he was the one who made her this way.

The bedroom door opened, and Bernt and Torben slunk inside the main room, looking not much better than she felt.

"I don't want to be an Ursan warrior anymore," Torben said.

"Yes, you do," she told him with a smile. "Grab some apples and bread. We can take our breakfast outside. The sunshine will do us some good."

Once outside, Breena raised her face to the sun, allowing its warm rays to heat her cheeks. She stretched, relieving the tightness of her aching muscles. A blue bird flew over their heads, and she smiled.

"You seem different today," Bernt remarked. A small frown formed between his brows. "You're not wanting to leave us, are you?"

It had never really occurred to her that the boys would begin enjoying her in their lives. She'd felt more like an intruder, one who'd broken their furniture and stolen their food. But now she realized they'd miss her when she left, and she'd miss them.

Would their brother?

"I'll have to go sometime. This isn't my home."

"But it could be," Torben told her. "I saw Osborn clearing out some old furniture and crates out of the storeroom. I think he's wanting to make it into a bedroom."

"He doesn't like you sleeping on the floor."

The thought of Osborn caring about her comfort, trying to find someplace better for her to sleep, made her heart leap.

"I do like sleeping in front of the fire," she assured them. "At home, I had a fireplace in my room. And besides, I'm too tired to do anything but just fall down on the floor and go to sleep."

The boys laughed.

"I like it with you here," Bernt informed her.

"Osborn does, too," Torben added. "I can tell."

"He's a lot nicer. He doesn't yell nearly as much."

Really? Because she thought he yelled a lot. All the time.

"And he finally began our training."

"He was already a warrior by the time he was our age, I think." Torben bit his lip. "He doesn't talk much of what happened to our parents and the rest of our people."

She squeezed the boys' shoulders. "I can imagine what he's suffered. Is still suffering. Remember, he wasn't much older than you when he took on the responsibility of two little boys. When you lose those you love, it changes you. But every day seems better than the last."

That was a lie. A comforting adage she so wanted to believe, wanted these boys to believe, but suspected it would never be true. Each day didn't diminish the hurt, only added more time and distance so that it would be easier to forget.

Avenge.

Breena couldn't forget. Something inside wouldn't let her.

The man who was the topic of their conversation entered the clearing. Osborn never failed to make her breath catch. He looked different somehow. Less grim, and with an added resolve. She hoped that didn't mean more balance practice. He'd tied his hair back, and wore the town clothes from just a few days ago. In fact, he carried several large packages in his massive arms.

"Didn't know if you crew would make it this morning," he told them, something similar to a smile curving his lips.

Bernt and Torben quickly scrambled to their feet.

"Ready for more?" he asked, but his eyes were

squared on her. "Get your swords, and head out to the practice field. I need to talk with Breena."

The boys raced to get their scabbards and then flew around the corner of the cottage, leaving her alone with Osborn. He carefully placed his packages on a crate that stood next to the front door, and the dream of last night hit her full force. The pain of it. The anguish. Every vivid detail. But mostly the comfort given as she cried.

Osborn had given her that comfort. Wiped her tears. Breena knew that now. He'd soothed the ache in her heart. If only for a few moments.

Avenge.

Only she could not be truly consoled. Not until the need planted in her consciousness had been relieved.

For the first time, Breena felt uncertain around him. Not sure how to act or where to look. Something in their uneasy relationship had changed in the night while she slept. She twisted her hands, then quickly thrust them behind her back.

"I've been to the village," he told her.

"I can see that," she replied, eyeing the packages.

His eyes narrowed, and his gaze scanned her face, brushed over her every feature. He rubbed his hand along the back of his neck, a gesture she'd seen often enough now to know something heavy weighed upon him.

"I think I found a place where you can go," he finally told her, his gaze dropping.

"Go?"

"There's a woman in the village. She fell last winter and has trouble taking care of her home now. You'd have the entire second floor to yourself, and a little spending money."

"What are you talking about?"

"You can't continue to stay here, Breena," he told her with a shrug. "It's not right. Not a woman with three men."

Breena made a scoffing sound in the back of her throat. "Are you actually going to talk to me about appearances? Propriety?"

He tugged loose the rope that held his hair in place, freeing the strands. There was her Osborn. Wild and untamed. "I'm trying to do what's right for you."

She marched toward him. Breena wasn't about to let him get away with making decisions for her. "By sending me away? We had a deal."

Breena watched him swallow. Then his gaze turned to hers. "You cried last night, Breena. You cried in my arms." His voice sounded raspy and strained.

A lump formed in her throat. The warrior who'd tried not to care about her worried for her. A lot.

"This isn't good for you. You're not meant for this life."

And she was not meant for him, he was saying.

"I don't want to see you grow cynical and so consumed with vengeance nothing will ever be right for you again."

"I'm consumed with vengeance now."

"And it will eat away at you until there's nothing left but hate. I don't want you to end up like…me."

Breena shook her head. "I can't turn it off. My parents are dead. I saw them die. There was so much blood." She covered her face with her hands. "I didn't even get to bury their bodies. Something calls out to me. I can't let it go."

"How do you know this? Your memory—"

"My memory came back," she interrupted.

SHE MET HIS GAZE, AND WHAT he saw in those green depths made him pause. Made his breath hold and his chest constrict.

"Last night I put myself in a dreamhaze. I went back to the night my parents..." She swallowed. "I went back to the night my parents died. I saw the blood. Their blood. The wounds to their bodies."

Her lower lip trembled, and her eyes filled with tears he knew she fought not to shed. "So you see, I do know the pain of losing something. Someone."

He understood that pain. *Lived* it.

"I know that I can't do anything with my life until I somehow fix this. Vindicate the memory of my family. Keep helping me, Osborn. Please," she urged.

Osborn had left the village with plans and so much anticipation. He wanted Breena to follow a different path than the one he'd followed all his life. He was tired. Tired of his own pain and regret and thirst for a revenge he'd had to put off to raise his brothers. The weariness seeped down to his bones, and the little emotion he had left inside ached.

He didn't want Breena to feel this way. To carry the burden of avenging the dead alone. To live what he lived.

He rubbed his hand at the throbbing muscles bunched at the base of his neck. He didn't understand until this moment how much like him she actually was. She'd always burn with her need to make right what had happened to her family, because he always burned. "I'll help you."

Breena squeezed her eyes tight and her shoulders slumped with relief. "Thank you."

He doubted she'd be thanking him for long.

THE REST OF THE AFTERNOON they spent in training, and Breena didn't utter one complaint about pains or aches or stiffening muscles. She had survived. She'd convinced Osborn to continue helping her and she was grateful. Her magic had drawn her to the man who'd teach her how to fight who or what had killed her parents.

She'd have to dream her past again. Her body began to shake at the idea of revisiting that night of death, but it was the only way she could find the truth. Would Osborn hold her again tonight?

That evening the boys showed her how they prepared dinner while Osborn closed himself away in the storeroom off the side of the tiny kitchen.

"I can't believe we're having to show a girl how to make us dinner," Bernt grumbled, but it was all in good-natured fun.

"Yes, I thought you would *want* to cook for us," Torben added, and they all laughed.

"I'll just show you how to dance in exchange."

Two matching horrified expressions crossed their faces.

Osborn opened the door of the storeroom, and stuck his head out. A faint smile crossed his features when he saw her. "Breena, come here."

There it was. An order for her to move toward him. She'd almost begun to miss them. Almost. But she was too curious about what exactly Osborn had been doing in that tiny space. She wiped her hands on a dish towel and moved toward where Osborn waited.

"I, uh…" he began, and stopped.

Was Osborn nervous? Breena hid a smile and angled her head inside the place Osborn had kept himself so busy. The store area was small to be sure; four of these rooms would fit inside her bedchamber at Elden. The walls stretched bare and there was nothing on the floor except a tiny blue rug, the color of the blue flowers that grew around the cottage. Not the kind a man would choose for himself, but exactly what a man would buy for a woman. Now she knew what had been inside one of those mysterious packages.

"Nothing much will fit in here but a mattress, but it will be private and all yours, Breena. If you want it."

Osborn's voice was solemn, and she knew he offered her more than just a tiny space inside his cottage. He was offering a place in his life. She nodded her head. "I do want it."

"I have something else for you." There was that smile again. Who knew her *berserker* warrior was such a gift giver? He came back carrying a small package. She hadn't noticed this one earlier today. She untied the twine and the rough cloth fell away to reveal two glass bottles containing mysterious liquids.

"It's shampoo and soap," he told her.

Breena would have expected cleaning oil for her sword or a new knife, not something so distinctly feminine. She quickly popped off the cork, and inhaled the delicious scent of vanilla and alluring spices.

"Thought you might tire of smelling like a man."

She replaced the cork, and hugged his gifts tight to her chest. "I can't wait to use these. Tonight."

Heat and hunger for her sharpened the features of his face. She lifted up on the tips of her toes, and kissed him on the cheek. "Thank you."

"You're welcome." And there was a promise in his voice that made her stomach quiver.

After dinner, she raced to the small clear spring not too far from the cabin. It wasn't the lake, but it was certainly private. A fact she'd announced to all the *ber-serker* men earlier. The spring was hers.

She grabbed the washbasin and filled it with the clean spring water warmed by the sun and wet her hair. At home, she'd always used the floral soaps and scents her mother preferred, but what Osborn had chosen suited her infinitely better. She popped the lid and breathed in deeply of the scent he'd purchased for her. The soft sweet smell of the vanilla combined with the zest of faraway places. This was what Osborn liked, and she poured a small amount in her hand, and cleaned her hair. Did he view her as sweet with a touch of spice?

She ran the soap over her breasts, and the tips puckered. Her nipples did the same when Osborn kissed and licked her there. Breena ran the soap over her skin the way he caressed her breasts. She slipped a soapy finger between her thighs, touched where Osborn had kissed with his lips. Licked with his tongue. She gasped as she imagined him doing that again. Of her licking and kissing him.

Breena wanted that again. And more. He'd barred her from his dreams. Would he still?

OSBORN HADN'T MEANT to spy on her bath. He'd only needed to grab more firewood, but then he heard Breena's gasp. The *berserker* in him roused, and he raced to ensure her safety. But Breena's cry wasn't that of a woman frightened, but of her deep arousal.

How much agony did one man have to endure? He leaned against the trunk of a tree, forcing his body to relax. Minutes passed, and she rounded the corner, stopping when she spotted him. Her cheeks were flushed, her bottom lip fuller. A fine sheen of water filmed her skin, and she wore only a towel held together loosely over her breasts.

Her face reddened further, and he knew. Knew that when she'd gasped earlier, she'd been caressing herself and thinking of him.

He had an answer to his earlier question. Apparently a man had to endure a lot of agony.

"Osborn, the soap you bought for me was…wonderful."

Her voice was husky, like a woman not yet fulfilled. He imagined her sighing to him in those low tones as he drove into her.

She's not yours.

Breena was loved and protected for another, certainly never a man like him. He was once destined to be something better than he was, an Ursan warrior. With all the honor and distinction that rank held. All he could offer her now was a legacy of shame and a life filled with the need for vengeance

Breena's own steps were aimed squarely at that same path. He'd tried to dissuade her earlier.

Try harder.

But how could he when she was reaching out to him? Lifting her shoulder right under his nose? "It smells different on my skin than it does in the bottle."

The scent of the soaps he'd bought smelled good, but Breena the woman smelled better. He was so close. Too close. He could nip at her shoulder. Run his tongue along that tantalizing curve of her back.

"I have a favor to ask."

Gods, anything…if he could just keep breathing in her scent. Prolong the torture by imaging how he could curve his hand around her hip, drawing her backward to cup his erection.

She took a deep breath. "I have to go back to dream of my past, to the night of the siege."

He shook his head, and she gripped his biceps. Hard.

"There's still more to learn about that night. I couldn't continue after, well, you know how you found me."

Crying in her sleep.

"When I put myself in a dream, I always envision a door and then I walk right through it in my mind. There's only ever been your door in my mind.

A possessive satisfaction settled into his chest.

"But last night there were two doors. My past and, next to it, yours."

Osborn stiffened.

"They have to be side by side for a reason. I think it's because when I go through your door to be with you... nothing frightens me."

"It should. *I* should frighten you." What he wanted to do to her body, what wanted from her, that should all frighten her.

"But it doesn't." She ran her fingers along his jaw. "You would never hurt me. I've known that for a while."

He didn't know it. In fact, she could almost count on him hurting her. It was inevitable. His past. His decisions. *Those* would hurt her. When his brothers were ready, he'd leave this cottage and seek those who killed his family. His plans were not those of a man who would make life easy for a woman. He gripped her fingers to still her touch.

"Remember how we are together in my dreams?" she asked, refusing to let him push her hand away. "How perfect?"

He could make love to her in that fantasy world she created as they slept. His cock hardened at the thought. Yes. He could caress every part of her body. Brand her with his touch. Drive into her as his body demanded. And he could hold her.

Yet no matter how amazing their coupling would be in the dream, Osborn knew he would wonder and crave the real thing until he was mad.

"Those dreams were lies," he told her, his teeth clenched.

"Aren't you even curious?"

Hell, yes, he was curious. Curious if she'd meet his gaze when he joined his body with hers. Ached to learn the feel of her softness as she welcomed him into her. Dying to know—

"Lies," he said again. Just to stay sane.

Her hand dropped and her expression turned sad. "If it makes you feel any better, sometimes those lies I shared with you were the only thing I really looked forward to." Breena turned on her heel and walked away from him

The blood pounded in his head. Those dreams were the only thing that brought anything even approaching happiness into his life. Until he found her sleeping in his bed.

All she wanted was to dream with him. *Be* with him in a dream. How could he refuse?

He reached for her shoulder, his fingers curving into her skin. "I'll do it."

BERNT HAD GIVEN UP HIS bed for Breena. He and Osborn would begin building a new frame for him the next day. It was a tight fit in the storeroom, but after some shifting and one banged-in corner, the bed finally sat in the storeroom for Breena's use.

She kissed both their cheeks. "Thank you so much," she told them, her voice as happy as if Osborn had bestowed on her the rarest of jewels. Somewhere out in one of the realms there was a man who would be giving Breena gifts with gems and gowns and all the things women liked.

But she was his for now.

Breena quickly dressed the bed in warm blankets and pelts. They wouldn't be sleeping before the fire, and she'd need more coverings to keep warm. There also wasn't nearly the kind of room for the two of them on Bernt's old bed. Breena lifted the blankets and crawled to the edge of the bed, which was pushed up against the wall.

"How do you want to do this?" he asked.

Her lips turned up in a grin. "Not a lot of space for you," she said, eyeing the broadness of his shoulders and the length of his legs. When she looked at him like he was the strongest, most powerful man in the world who could best anything, he wanted to be exactly that for her.

"I like it when you stretch against my back," she told him.

And cupped her breast. And fit his cock against her curves. He liked it, too. A lot. And it was starting to show. The bed creaked under his weight as he settled in beside her. Osborn wanted to bury his face in her hair. Lose the nightclothes that separated her skin from his. He settled for draping his arm over the rounded curve of her hip.

He closed his eyes. Forced his muscles to relax. Imagined smelling rotten food to chase away the erotic scent of her. Anything so that he could doze.

"I can't sleep," she whispered to him after a few moments of silence.

"Nor can I."

"Talk to me. Tell me a story."

She wiggled against him, and he quietly groaned. Every one of her soft curves cupped his body. Osborn concentrated on her request, but could come up with nothing. "I don't know the kind of stories you do. No fairies. No wolves hiding in the woods with their eye on a girl in a red cloak."

"Then tell me something real. From when you were a little boy," she suggested.

Osborn tried not to think of those times. Warriors didn't feel sad. They pushed those emotions to the side. Obliterated them. "There's nothing to tell."

"What about a grand party? Tell me about one of those times when you wore fancy clothes and musicians played."

He breathed in the scent of her hair again, and tried to remember. His people preferred a simpler way of life. Little politics, few dignitaries and lords. They were all just Ursan. They prepared for battles, for when their allies called. Few dared to go to war directly with the Ursans. At night they built large fires. Their entire village would talk and sing along with the drums. A smile played about his lips. He'd forgotten about those nights when the elders pointed to the skies and taught how to use the stars for navigation. He'd forgotten about the songs. Osborn should carve a drum and teach his brothers some of the old Ursan songs. Maybe one day his brothers would marry and teach those songs to their daughters and sons, and hope flooded his chest.

For the first time, guilt and pain didn't rush right behind the memories.

"No banquets," he told her, "just families around the campfire."

"Not even marriage feasts? At home we took every

opportunity to host a celebration. My father told us the work in the fields and in the trades could be rough and sometimes bleak. It was our responsibility to provide as much joy and brightness as we could to our people."

"He sounds very wise."

Breena nodded. "He was," she said, her voice quiet and low.

"We didn't celebrate marriages openly," he told her, trying to pull her away from thoughts of her dead father…until she forced herself to dream of him tonight.

"You didn't?" Shock and a trace of scandal laced her voice, and Osborn couldn't help smiling again.

"When a man wished for a woman, he'd ask her to seal her life with his. On a full moon, they'd go, just the two of them, into the woods that surrounded our village. There, with only the stars to see, they'd share the vows they'd written for each other."

"That sounds beautiful. And meaningful."

The yearning in her voice made his gut ache. "That's not the kind of marriage you would have?" he asked, needing to remind himself she was for someone else.

"No," she said on a heavy sigh. "My marriage will be of alliance. It will be an honor to serve my people that way."

"And just how many times have you been told that?"

Breena's muscles relaxed against him. "A lot," she confessed. "In fact, my father was to do the choosing the weekend of the attack."

"Do you think that had something to do with it? An angry suitor?"

"More like a disappointed negotiator. I've never even met any of the potential husbands. Less for them to object to that way."

"And what could they possibly have to complain

about with you?" He was incredulous at the thought. Breena was perfect. Perfect for hi—

She only laughed. "I seem to remember you complaining a lot about me. The danger I brought. The added expense."

"My socks are nice."

Breena laughed again, the sound of it thrilling, like he wanted to make her laugh again and again. Forever.

"Stick to fighting, Ursan. That kind of compliment will never suit you at court."

Another warning. He'd never belong in her world.

After a few minutes, Breena's breathing deepened, and he knew she'd soon be entering her dream. And then his.

CHAPTER TEN

BREENA WAITED BEFORE the two doors.

The plain door stood in front of her, no longer forbidden. It was even slightly ajar. For a moment she was tempted. Only pleasure awaited her on the other side.

Reluctantly she tore her gaze away and over to the ornate frame. With its jewels and promises of wealth, this would be the door most often chosen. But she knew what awaited her once she crossed the threshold. Death and destruction.

She made herself reach for the handle, turn and walk through.

This dream didn't have the usual haze, every deathly image and sound and smell was clear and stark. The zipping wisp of a razor blade caught her attention. Made her shake. She remembered. The hideous spiderlike creature that only blood magic could create. Breena swallowed back the nausea, forced herself to relearn every detail her mind had earlier wanted to reject. She looked to the stairs and saw herself there, as she was, the night of the attack. She was dressed in the beautiful gown she'd woken up wearing in Ursa. It was perfect, no longer ripped and shredded. The Breena on the stairs tried to be brave and show no fear, but each new terror, all the horror she saw before her, left its scar.

Then she saw him. A sight so frightening, so grotesque, she was almost pulled out of her dream. The

Blood Sorcerer. The man responsible for it all. He was speaking to her parents, taunting them. They lay near death, their blood fueling his strength. She saw them touch hands, and she knew before she felt the zap of energy that they'd sent her away. With their combined magic, they'd planted the commands that rang in her mind more like a curse: survive and avenge. The force of her father's will and the power of her mother's magic overcame the Breena on the floor and she disappeared.

And Breena was now in Osborn's dreams.

He was waiting for her, his features no longer obscured by the dreamhaze. His firm lips, long brown hair and dark eyes familiar. She ran to him, and he caught her in his strong arms, spinning her in the air, and then allowing her to slide down the firmness of his body. She had to touch him now. Wanted to chase away the dream from behind the other door in her mind...just for a few moments.

Before, Osborn had been the aggressor. But she wasn't the same Breena that had crept into his dreams in the past. She slid her fingers into the hair at the back of his neck and pulled his lips to hers. Breena parted her lips and sank her tongue into his mouth.

Osborn groaned, holding her tight against him, meeting her forceful kiss with a growing need of his own.

"It's been so long since we've been like this," she said against his mouth.

"Too long," he echoed.

"Your choice."

"I'm an idiot," he said, and lowered his lips to hers once more. The kiss they shared was raw and passionate and filled with everything they'd denied themselves away from this dreamworld.

Breena tugged the shirt from his pants and slid her

hands to his bare flesh. He sucked in a breath when her fingers trailed over his stomach. Her hands grew restless, caressing and seeking every part of him. When her palm cupped his cock, he went completely still.

"Does that feel good?" she asked.

He could only nod.

"I want to make you feel amazing. The way you made me feel by the lake," she told him as she reached for the drawstring of his pants.

Osborn stilled her hands. "No, I want to pleasure you."

"Let me," she urged. "I need this. I need to give right now." His pants loosened and she pushed them down the strength of his legs, the hair of his thighs tickling her palms. His erection sprang forward and she reached for him. He shuddered when she wrapped her fingers around his shaft. She circled the head of him with her thumb.

"Does that feel good?" she asked, loving that she already knew.

"Yes." His voice was a tight groan, and Breena felt the same kind of thrilling power that only a surge of her magic could give her.

"But it will feel better with my mouth."

His eyes flew open. The ache and the yearning for what she could do to his body was stamped on his every feature.

With a gentle push, she sent his back against a tree trunk in their dream clearing, then she sank to her knees in front of him. "Tell me if I'm doing this wrong."

"You won't."

She smiled against the soft skin of his shaft. Kissed the tip. His legs trembled for a moment, and then he locked his knees.

Breena's hand shifted when he moved, and he grew harder between her fingers. She glided her hand up and down his rod, then found a steady rhythm, bringing the tip of him back into her mouth.

She circled him with her tongue the way he'd circled her. His harsh breath told her that no, she wasn't doing this wrong.

Breena had never seen a man so powerful, so strong, as her warrior, but he was like melted wax before her. It was exhilarating. She worked her mouth faster, and Osborn threaded his fingers through her hair, pushing himself deeper past her lips.

"Breena…"

His voice was like a strangled cry, and she quickened her pace. "Breena, you've got to—"

She awoke suddenly in her new bed.

Osborn sat on the edge of the mattress, his feet on the floor. He cradled his head in his hands, his breaths rough and uneven.

She brushed his shoulder. "Osborn?"

He flinched from her touch. Shot up from the bed like she'd zapped him with her anger-charged energy.

"Did I do something wrong?"

He shook his head, but he still wouldn't glance her way. Bracing his hands along the trim wood of the door, Osborn kept his back to her. "We can't do that again." Then he pried open the door and left her alone.

Breena pulled the covers tight under her neck and crawled into a ball. Sleep took a long time to overcome her, but when it did her dreams bordered on nightmare.

LATER THAT MORNING she found Bernt and Osborn building a new bed. "Are we going to practice?" she asked.

"Tomorrow," Osborn grunted at her, not bothering to look up.

Bernt flashed her a look that said something like "Save me" and she nodded. The frame they worked on appeared sturdy and solid. Unlike the chair in the kitchen from…just a few days ago? It felt like a lifetime away.

"You do good work," she told them both.

"After about thirty tries," Bernt mumbled.

"Shut it," Osborn shot at his younger brother.

"I'd rather be practicing, too. We're not meant to be woodworkers."

"You are now."

"If you want to take a break, I wouldn't mind scabbard practice," she suggested, trying to defuse the situation, although she looked forward to scabbard practice just a little above balance work. Which was none at all.

"Breena, go away," Osborn said, his teeth gritted.

He'd never spoken so rudely to her before. Prickly, she could tolerate, but not this.

"Bernt, if you'd please excuse us. I'd like to talk with your brother in private."

Bernt dropped his hammer to the ground as if it were on fire.

"Come back here," Osborn called after his brother, but Bernt pretended not to hear. Good boy.

"One day you're going to push them away for good. Bernt and Torben look up to you. They want your approval. Why they still want that from you, who knows? Especially since you're always such a grouch to them, but they do."

Osborn's mood soured more, and his frown deepened.

"Would it hurt you to give them a smile? To say

something more than just orders?" She rounded on this fuming man of hers. "Why are you so angry?"

Osborn stalked toward her, grabbed her hand and pushed it down between his legs. "This is why. Because all I can think of is shoving my cock into your mouth. Driving it into your body. Me on top. You on top. You on all fours like the beasts in the woods." He dropped her hand. "Don't be alone with me. Again."

The warning had returned.

"Be ready to work after lunch," he tossed at her as his long strides took him into the privacy of the woods.

Breena began to tremble. All those things, every word that she knew Osborn meant to sound as a threat... she desired them, too.

OSBORN HADN'T BEEN exaggerating when he'd told her to be prepared to work. Sweat ran down her temples and covered her back. He sparred with her, parrying and thrusting his sword. Expecting her to block his blade.

"You just died right then," he told her as his stick touched her shoulder. "Again."

She raised her stick, holding it in the position he'd taught her, but he powered through her defenses, his mock blade at her neck. "You're dead."

Breena shoved him away and whacked him across the legs with her stick. Then stopped and held her stick at a point just above his heart. "One plunge and you'd have taken your last breath."

"True, if you'd awoken from the dead. But it was a good surprise attack. You need more."

They bouted again and again with Breena losing every battle. "How do you expect to render justice with skills like this?" His voice was almost a taunt. He was trying to make her give up.

"My opponents won't all be Ursan warriors with a thorn in their side."

"Oh, it's way bigger than a thorn," he told her crudely.

She shoved him away. "Cool off, Osborn. Your temper is your own problem. Stop making this all my fault."

Osborn dropped his stick. "Practice is over."

"Good," she called after him. Wishing she had something more cutting to say at her disposal. Breena wiped a tear from her cheek. Who knew she could cry out of sheer irritation? She marched back to the cabin, grabbed the soap he'd given her, hating the scent as she bathed. Breena quickly dressed, needing to get as far away from the cottage and its inhabitants as fast as she could.

Torben had showed her a path that led to the bushes where they gathered ripe berries. That sounded just as good as any place. Besides the bushes, she discovered several patches of wildflowers, and she reached down to pluck a petal from one, rubbing it between her fingers and releasing the sweet scent.

How long she waited there among the flowers she didn't know, but she stiffened when she heard the footsteps she now recognized as Osborn's. He rounded a tree, his hair still wet. Probably from a soaking in the lake. Her cheeks heated at the memory of what they'd last shared at the lake, and she faced the other way.

He crouched beside her, stretching his legs out in front of him. "I've never been in a situation such as this," he told her after several moments of silence.

She expected this was Osborn's attempt at an apology, and her anger dissipated. Breena had been instructed how to behave on every conceivable social situation. But her mother had definitely missed this one.

Osborn slid something big toward her, and she

glanced his way. It was one of those mysterious packages he'd brought home with him after his trip into the village. "I, uh, got this for you."

She loved gifts, and as surprising and perfect as Osborn's first present to her was, Breena couldn't wait to see what was inside this one. She pulled the end of the twine and smoothed the protective material away to reveal fine green fabric.

"It's a cloak," he told her. "The color reminded me of your eyes."

Her throat tightened. Courtiers had said charming things to her over the years, but Osborn's compliment was the most perfect. Because she knew it originated from his heart. Tears filled her eyes, and she blinked them back. How could one man send her emotions and the reason for her tears careening from one extreme to another? And so quickly?

Breena spread the cloak around her. The fashions she wore at home in Elden were much more elaborate, with tiny embroidered flowers and crystals and other small gems sewn right into the designs. But this was far more beautiful to her than anything she'd ever worn in the past. "I love it," she told him.

"There's a matching gown."

Breena reached for it, her fingers finding something round and hard instead. She plucked it out of the package to see a golden arm cuff in the shape of a snake. What an unusual adornment for jewelry. She'd never seen such a thing. Was this an Ursan custom?

"It reminded me of your first fight. How you defeated those snakelike scouts, and saved my life."

Now it made sense. Breena slid the armband into place above her elbow. "I will never take this off," she vowed to him. Just like her timepiece.

Possession quickly flowed into his brown eyes.

"Thank you," she told him as she stood. Breena clutched the gown to her chest, twirling around with the fabric. "I will wear this gown the day I return home, Osborn. The day our house is restored, and my brother Nicolai is crowned king of Elden. That's how much your gift means to me."

"Elden?" he asked, the color draining from his face. All traces of possession faded from his eyes. His gaze narrowed, and his shoulders tensed. "Did you say Elden?"

Breena nodded slowly. "That's my home. My father is—" she swallowed "—was king."

Osborn sprang to his feet. Away from her. Something icy inched down her back, and she hugged the gown closer to her chest. Needing protection. Osborn no longer gazed upon her with desire and possession in his eyes, as the man she was growing to love. No, now he looked at her with something close to hate in his eyes.

"It all makes sense now," he threw at her. His words biting and hard.

"What does?" she asked, marveling at the newest change.

"I should have known when Hagan told me of Elden's fall so close to your arrival. He'd even mentioned the missing heirs. You. That is why you never told me where you were from. Elden. You knew what your people had done to mine."

"What are you talking about?"

Osborn made a scoffing sound. "Oh, you might have a problem with your memory, Breena, but not me. I remember everything. Your father chose the time of his attack well. I'll give him that. The Bärenjagd, when the warriors journeyed to our sacred bear lands. Our vil-

lage was defenseless. It's a time of truce," he shouted,
his voice anguished.

Breena didn't know what to say, what to do. She
sucked in her bottom lip, hoping he'd continue with his
story. To release all that anger before she responded to
him.

"Elden was our ally. Your father saw to that," he
accused. "We arrived to a massacre. And an ambush.
I killed as many of your people as I could. Enjoyed
watching your dead sizzle in the sunlight when it came.
I taught you to fight. I brought you into my home, I
shared—" He cut off his own words. "All this time
you knew. You encouraged me to share my stories of
the people your family killed." He stalked toward her.
"Your lies won't protect you now."

Breena shook her head, backing away from him.
"That's not it at all. Something inside me said not to
mention Elden, some instinct." The evasion sounded
terrible even to her. "But I swear, Osborn, it's not because of that. My father is an honorable king. He's a
diplomat, not a fighter."

Osborn made a brutal sound. "Tell that to my mother.
To my dead sister. I swore vengeance on you. On all of
Elden. And I kept my hands off of you. Thinking you
were something more than…Elden."

The way he said her homeland packed a punch of bit-
terness and venom. His hands fisted at his sides, and
he lunged at her.

Breena stumbled backward, her feet catching in
the folds of fabric of her gown. She landed against a
tree; the rough bark poked into her shoulder blades.
She could go no farther. The man had taught her many
techniques when in battle with an opponent bigger and
larger than herself. He probably never expected her to

use any of those on him. Breena cupped his cheek. Distracting him. "Osborn…"

He paused. For one crucial moment.

"I'm sorry," she told him at the same instant she kneed him between the legs. *Hard.*

Osborn groaned and doubled over, gripping his stomach. Breena took the opportunity to push him to the ground, grabbing from her boot the knife he'd instructed her to keep hidden. She straddled him, pushing her nose to his. "I could be running away at this moment. Your instructions were to not stick around, remember?"

His eyes blazed with something past hate.

Breena lifted the blade to the beating pulse in his neck. "I could also cut you right now. See? You did manage to teach me quite a bit."

His lips thinned. She felt his skin chill and watched as his pupils began to narrow and focus. She'd triggered his *berserkergang.* But she wasn't scared. Breena had just spent her last moment of fear. She'd die before she felt frightened again.

And that fearsome thing inside him would not hurt her. She *knew* it.

The harshness of their breathing blanketed around them. The sun overhead created gruesome knife-wielding shadows. "My people did not attack yours."

Some of his wrath cooled. "I can see that you believe it."

It was a beginning. "You said the attackers burned in the sun?"

"Those that didn't flee. Cold-skinned cowards."

"Elden's vamps can walk in the sun. My brother Nicolai is as warm-blooded as you and me. My father was arranging an advantageous marriage to secure Elden's future. *That's* how he did things. Not through battle."

Osborn squeezed his eyes tight. She knew he was fighting her, fighting what he'd held to be true.

"They wore Elden's colors."

"It must have been a tactical move in case there were any survivors."

She watched his swallow. Emotion warred in his eyes. "Clever, because I planned my own vengeance against your people."

And with his *berserker* power, he would have taken the lives of a lot of her people. Although it would have been a much more merciful death than that from the Blood Sorcerer.

"I wonder if it's the same enemy. But to wait all these years...it seems unlikely."

She wanted to tell Osborn what she'd discovered in her dream. That the Blood Sorcerer killed her parents. But now this was all about Osborn.

"I'm going to drop this knife. Toss it out of the way."

That was the plan she had, nothing much more than that. Breena rolled off his big frame.

He trapped her hands before she could scramble completely out of his reach. "You know I could have overpowered you at any time."

She'd guessed it. "But you didn't."

He dropped her hands, and leaned against the tree. She watched as he scrubbed his hand along the back of his neck. "No, I didn't."

"Why not?"

His brown eyes met hers. "Because I wanted to believe you. Because I want...I want so many things since I found you in my bed."

Her stomach dipped, and her heart began to race.

Many times she imagined the lover of her future. A man with courtly manners. A man who'd kiss the back of her hand. A man who'd ask for the honor of dancing with her.

Never had she imagined the man she'd want by her side to be conflicted, guilt-ravaged and so, so fallible. And yet perfect.

As a princess, Breena had two jobs, stay a virgin and marry well.

She was about to fail at one of her princessly duties.

CHAPTER ELEVEN

OSBORN FLINCHED WHEN she stroked his arm. His hand instantly grasped hers, stilling her fingers.

She gave him an encouraging smile. "Let me." And his hand fell away. Breena traced the arch of his eyebrow. Ran her fingers down the length of his nose. His lips. The stubble covering his cheek. The muscles bunched below her fingertips. His strong body trembled for the briefest of moments.

"Let me love you," she urged.

The man before her tensed. Every muscle, every force of his body, tightened like her words were a physical blow to him. His eyes closed and his fists clenched at his sides. Who was he fighting now? Her or himself?

Then his lids lifted, and his gaze bore into hers. She saw all the hurt and anger he'd suffered since the attack on his home. He allowed her to see it.

"I want to love you tonight," she whispered against his neck, and she felt him shiver.

But he didn't push her away.

Her heart lifted in relief and she placed tiny little kisses on his neck, the line of his jaw and finally to his lips. Breena tugged his lower lip into her mouth with her teeth. Sucked on it until he moaned.

"Take me to your lake," she invited him. Without waiting for an answer, she tugged his hand to her mouth, kissed his palm, then drew him to his feet. They walked the short distance to the place that would always be so special to her.

After removing her boots, careful to tuck her knife inside them, she turned to him. With the water at her back, she lifted her shirt and raised it above her head, drawing the woolen fabric against her skin in sensual slowness.

"You said you hated me in boy's clothes."

"Glad they're off of you."

Her nipples puckered before his heated gaze. Osborn's brown eyes turned almost black in the dying light.

Breena walked to him slowly, loosening the pants and kicking them out of the way. He was reaching for his own shirt, but she stopped his hands of further movement. "Let me take care of you tonight."

He swallowed. Hard. She lifted his shirt up and over his head. His pants stretched tight against his growing cock.

"These can't be too comfortable," she told him with a click of her tongue.

"Growing more uncomfortable by the moment," he told her.

She smiled at this amazing man before her, feeling happy and desirable and very, very wanted. Hooking her thumbs around the material, she drew his pants down those defined legs of his, finely muscled and strong.

Osborn was magnificent. His body was honed, and crisscrossed by scars, some small, some brutal-looking. She traced a jagged one beneath his collarbone. The one on his face was new, and from the night they'd first met when they battled the creature of blood magic.

Breena ran her fingers along his fine features, his jaw, his eyebrows. He gripped her hands in his, lowering his head. A breath separated their lips, and she raised on tiptoe to kiss him. He clutched her in his arms with a groan. Osborn's kiss was a burning, searing thing, filled with pain, hope and so much passion.

His hands turned bold, palming her breast, caressing her hip, taking a lazy path down the sensitive skin of her spine. Goose bumps formed along her arms and her nipples tightened against the rough-haired strength of his chest. She couldn't get enough of touching him. Just running her hands over the roped muscles of his arms shot little thrills through her body.

"Look at me," he urged, his voice raw with passion.

Her lids drifted open as his questing fingers rounded her hips and cupped her bottom. With a jerk, he brought her flush against his naked skin. The hardness of his erection left no doubt how much he wanted her, and her knees weakened.

Osborn scooped her up into his arms, and stalked to the soft sandy bank of the lake.

"I was supposed to be taking care of you," she told him with a laugh.

"Next time," he promised, his voice rough and filled with need.

"Yes." She nodded. Now and quickly. She looped her arms around his neck and drew his head down to hers once more. His lips parted hers, and his tongue surged inside her mouth. Their kiss was urgent and hurried.

He drew her down with him; the gentle lap of water at their feet was warm and sensual. Osborn stretched alongside her, his mouth and hands seeking her breasts. His lips teased and tormented her nipple until he finally drew her into the warmth of his mouth. Breena arched to meet him, her body aching and slick for the joining of their bodies. She'd been ready for this man a lifetime. Across her dreams to his.

"We have to take this slow, Breena. This will be your first time, and I don't want to hurt you."

"Then touch me." She ached for his hands in her most secret of places.

"Here?" he asked, skimming the skin of her rib cage.

"Lower."

Now his hand smoothed over her belly. "What about here?"

"Lower," she urged.

His fingers slid easily along the wetness between her legs.

"Yes." Her voice was a moan. A wave of sensation flooded her at his caress.

"Touching is good, but I'd rather taste." Osborn hooked one of her legs over his shoulder, then kissed where her very awareness seemed centered.

Osborn circled his tongue, ramping up her pleasure. She felt the gentle probe of his finger. He slid inside her, and her inner muscles clamped.

"This is going to be so good," he told her, then proved it by laving her with his tongue.

A second finger joined the first, and he gave a tiny thrust that left her aching and needing release. Her whole body began to surge and tremble.

"Don't make me wait anymore, Osborn."

A line formed between his brows. "I don't want to hurt you. I'd do anything not to cause you pain."

"I don't care. I need you. Need you inside me. Now."

He moved between her legs, his cock so long and thick she almost rethought her readiness. He positioned himself where his fingers had been.

"Watch," he told her. "See your body welcoming mine."

With gentle pressure, he thrust inside her, found the barrier of her virginity and broke through.

There was pain, but there was so much more. The weight of him on her body. The gentle kiss he placed on her temple. The pleasure shaping his beautiful face. And then the pain was gone. Replaced by a blissful frenzy. The fullness of him. The length of him inside her. Osborn began to move his hips and her tender body grew used to the motion.

"Harder?" he asked.

Breena didn't know if harder was what she wanted but she was willing to give it a try. "Yes," she whispered.

Osborn complied. Yes, harder was definitely what she wanted. He thrust again and again, going faster, the sensations growing more intense. Breena raised her hips to meet his hips. Needing more of him. She'd experienced pleasure with him once before. She craved that now. Her thirst for the thrill building and building.

"Wrap your legs behind my back," he instructed.

The change brought the core of her need hard up against his thrusts. Osborn licked below her ear. Squeezed her breast. He was everywhere. Over her. In her. She breathed him inside her with each breath she took.

"You feel so good, Breena."

The raw pleasure in his words sent her over the edge. She gasped. "Osborn, I'm—"

"Yes, Breena, yes," and he surged within her.

A current of sensation shimmered through her body, and she squeezed the hard length of him. With a groan, his back stiffened and he poured himself into her.

Spent, he slumped against her, balancing the bulk of his weight on his arms. They lay there together, unable to move. Then Osborn rolled to his back, taking her with him, and cradled her head against his chest.

Breena couldn't imagine sharing something so intimate with anyone but Osborn. When Elden was restored, she'd refuse any match Nicolai would make on her behalf. She wanted no one but Osborn. His arms holding her tight. His lips on hers. His body giving her pleasure.

She trailed her fingertip along the warm skin of his chest. "Does your *berserker* ever come out when…you know."

Osborn laughed, and she closed her eyes in pleasure. *She* had done this to him. Made him happy. Lifted him from the agony he'd consigned himself to. Breena had never truly understood or appreciated the gift that was her magic.

"Give me a few minutes and we can try."

All that force and strength and power, it was a little daunting. "How did you become *berserker?*"

Osborn twined his fingers with hers. "Our ancestors tell us man and bear were once one *bermannen*. *Bermannen* and his mate were clever, too clever for the gods' liking. They captured the secrets of lightning and made fire. They stole the key to the clouds and could control the weather. *Bermannen* and his mate even grew wise enough to discover the mysteries of the soil to grow their own food. The two needed nothing from the gods."

Breena propped herself up on her elbow to gaze down at Osborn. "What happened?" She knew many tales, but none that involved the Ursan deities.

"The gods grew jealous, so they separated the two.

All the strength and power went to bear, while wisdom went to man. *Mannen* and *ber* cried to be united. Then grew angry. The *berserker* rage comes from our need to be as one, and it cannot ever fully be. Feeling pity, the gods gave man the gift of his use of fire and knowledge of the land. Bear received strength, and sacred lands where they are free to roam."

"You did know a story."

"*Ber* and *mannen* were broken, but they were still clever and discovered a way to defeat the gods and their interference."

"How?"

"Through death the two spirits merge. Bear and man battle, but only one can win."

"You fought a bear to become *berserker?*"

Osborn pointed to the scar crossing his body. Breena gasped, then traced the path of the scar. Leaned down to kiss it.

"I am one with *ber,* but only through his honorable death. The *berserkergang* is always there, but it's the pelt that merges us, makes me what you saw in the alley, and why I couldn't kill the scout here at the lake."

"You were naked. And that pelt you wear was the bear's. That's so sad."

Osborn raised a brow. "Are you wishing the bear had won? Often they do."

She shook her head quickly.

"Man can merge with bear, or bear can join with man. It is our way." Osborn lifted her hand from his chest. "I love your tender heart."

Her heart slammed into her ribs. Love. He loved her heart. It was a start.

He kissed each one of her fingers. Sucking on the last.

"Yesterday when you were bathing, I heard you gasp. Were you thinking of me, Breena? Were you touching yourself and thinking of me?"

She swallowed the lump that formed in her throat and willed herself not to blush. Breena could only nod.

A slow satisfied smile spread across his face. "I'd like to watch."

His request sounded so outrageous, she sputtered.

"Feel how the idea of it gets me." Osborn took her hand, and placed it on the hard length of his cock.

Moisture gathered between her legs. "You really want to see that?"

"Gods, yes. Here—" he tweaked her nipple "—and here." His fingers delved into her woman's heat. "Sit up."

Breena braced herself off the ground, and Osborn reached for her hips.

"Straddle me."

Me on top. You on top. You on all fours like the beasts in the woods.

Those words of his had hollowed her. Intrigued her. Made her burn.

Breena lifted herself up onto him, and he grew in length.

"Put me inside."

There was that weak feeling again. Breena reached for his cock, smooth and hard. She gripped him gently and he groaned. "I wanted you that day as I was bathing," she told him. "Wanted it to be you touching me."

"Me, too," he told her, his body shaking with the need to plunge.

"Watch," she urged. Now it was her turn to give the orders. Breena positioned the tip of him where their bodies met and sank down his length. Filling her. She shivered with the exquisite perfect sensation of their joined bodies.

Osborn's eyes closed on a deep moan, his hands lifted to cup her breasts.

Her breasts heated at his touch, her nipples tightened. She lifted herself high, until he almost left her body, then she slammed back down again. His hips bucked, and he gripped her waist, trying to take control.

"Touch yourself. Like that day," he told her, his voice raspy and tight. His eyes dark.

Her whole body trembled at his request. Bracing herself on Osborn's broad shoulders, Breena sat back on her heels, her fingers lowering. She circled her nipples, feeling them pucker even more. Slowly, she let her fingers drift down. Osborn's heated gaze followed the slow, sensuous path she took. Down over her rib cage, past her stomach, until she met the curls that hid where they joined.

She gasped at the first light touch between her legs.

"Yes," her lover encouraged, and thrust.

She rubbed herself more forcefully, feeling the crest surge. Her inner muscles clamped down hard on his length. Osborn gripped her hips, keeping her in place as he thrust. Breena's fingers grew more frantic.

Her nipples tightened, every muscle in her body stretched. Reached for him and what he could give her.

"Harder," she demanded.

He gripped her tighter, his every movement bringing him deeper inside her body. With a gasp, he drove her over the edge. Crest after crest of sensation poured through Breena. His name came from her lips in a moan.

She felt Osborn's chest strain and his fingers dig into her skin. In one quick movement, he rolled her onto her back. Hooking her legs behind his back she drew him closer to her still. Reveled in the feel of his weight over her, his strength pinning her to the ground.

"Yes. Like that," she encouraged.

He surged inside her, his thrusts deeper. Harder. Every muscle of his body stiffened as his climax hit, and triggered something deep inside her. Tingles of another peak flared, and she held him to her as hard as she could.

Breena returned to herself slowly. The lapping of the lake, the wind in the trees, the call of a distant bird and the welcome weight of the large, loving man above her. Her heartbeat slowed and she could finally draw in breath without sounding like she'd just sparred with Osborn on the practice field.

Osborn rolled onto his back, taking her with him and tucking her against his side. He kissed the top of her head.

"I love you," she whispered to him. Then fell asleep.

Osborn squeezed his eyes tight. He hadn't known how much he needed those words until she'd uttered them so delightfully in her sleep. He hugged her tight. She deserved a better man than he was. Someone more honorable. Someone who could give her the same words.

She deserved more, but that didn't mean he wouldn't fight or kill to keep her at his side. Osborn wasn't an idiot.

ONE DAY MERGED INTO ANOTHER far too quickly. By day Osborn would continue with Breena's and his brothers' training. Her magic was growing stronger, and she could control small bursts without needing emotion as her medium. The nights were his and Breena's. Most evenings he joined her in the tiny sleeping room. Other

nights they spent near the lake and under the stars…
and he thought about full moons.

Bernt and Torben were growing to be fine, strong
men, despite him. He'd introduced the tradition of ending each evening in front of a large fire, as his people
had when he was a boy. There he told his brothers of the
bermannen and his mate and their angering of the gods.

He shared the traditions of their parents, how they
sealed their life together, and how their father had
trained and prepared Osborn for his Bärenjagd.

The unsettled anger within Bernt lessened each day.

The three of them had lived on the sacred bear land
all these years, with only Osborn's vow to protect this
place. No bear had stalked Bernt to become *bermannen*.
To become *berserker*. And yet Bernt had to be the age
for his Bärenjagd. Well past. And yet he grew powerful.

Had Osborn changed the destinies of both *ber* and
man when he came here to live? Once when sparring,
Osborn thought he'd wounded his younger brother with
his blade, but there wasn't even a scratch. *Berserkers*
couldn't be harmed by steel. Dare he test Bernt with the
only substances that could defeat a *berserker?* Weapons
made of tree and fire. Tree, because it grew from the
ground, and fire, because it was the gift to man by the
gods. Those jealous deities must have found it ironic
that their gifts could also bring about death.

Osborn imagined a life for his brothers with no
Bärenjagd. Strength and honor without the struggle
and blood? But those thoughts would have to wait for
another time…after. But after what, he couldn't say.

LATER THAT EVENING HE followed the sound of his brothers' laughter. He found them around the fire, laughing
with Breena. "What's so funny?" he asked.

"Breena was just about to make good on her threat of teaching Bernt to dance."

"That's not a threat," she told them with mock sternness. "Dancing is an important life skill."

"Mother liked to dance," Osborn said.

Bernt looked up sharply, his expression eager. Right now he was more boy than man, hungry to hear more.

Osborn had cheated them. Took away from them the comfort of their memories and the stories he could tell of them because he was selfish. All because *he* didn't want to remember. *He* didn't want the pain. It wasn't his brothers' guilt. It wasn't their shame. Torben and Bernt should be able to love a mother and father.

"When did she dance?" Torben asked, his voice quiet, as if he were almost afraid he'd anger Osborn and this moment would vanish.

"During the first night of the full moon, we'd gather in the center of our village. The elders would light a large bonfire, and we'd eat, and sing and dance. You liked to chase each other around the fire, which always made mother worry."

A smile spread across Bernt's face. "I remember."

"Did you dance?" Torben asked Osborn.

He shook his head. He would have been dancing. The year after his Bärenjagd. "I never learned."

"Breena should teach you."

"Oh, I doubt your brother would want to learn anything like that," she said, clearly hoping to discourage any further attempts. For his sake? Or hers?

Now he smiled openly. That seemed very much like a challenge, and he never backed away from a dare. He brushed his palms along his thighs and stood, extending his hand toward her.

"It's time I learned."

BREENA FELT THE MUSCLES of her face fall in astonishment. Osborn could have said a lot of things at the moment, but she never would have guessed he'd ask her to dance. Or want a lesson. He'd never stop surprising her.

"Show me how they dance where you come from, Breena."

His voice was pure invitation, and she couldn't resist. She placed her hand in his, and allowed him to direct her to a clearing while his younger brothers poked each other in the ribs. He made to gather her in his arms, which finally snapped her to the task at hand. She'd taken his barking instruction, his incessant demands she work harder and performed the maneuvers again and again. Now it was her turn to issue a few commands of her own.

"A gentleman doesn't just grab a lady and jostle her about."

"There's something obvious I could point out here," he told her.

Was that actually humor lacing his words? She chose to ignore it and flashed him her best imitation of Osborn's I'm-training-you-so-pay-very-close-attention expression.

"You stand beside me, and only our shoulders touch." She'd better amend that to *side*. None of her previous partners had ever towered quite as tall as Osborn. Breena twirled her finger in her hair. "And we face opposite directions."

Osborn dropped his arms from around her shoulders and rotated so that he aligned himself against her side. She was sure this particular dance was designed so that young men and ladies would remain respectable and refined, and Breena had never thought of it as anything untoward. But his hip brushed against hers in a way that was anything but harmless and breathed in his heat and the earthy scent of him.

"Now what?" he prompted.

She glanced up to see his dark gaze boring into hers. "You raise your arm, and I drape my hand over it."

He followed her direction and Breena realized that sometime in the last few minutes she'd lost the upper hand. And she didn't like it. She cleared her throat. "It's important to remember that once on the dance floor, the woman always leads."

The biggest lie she'd ever told, but she doubted Osborn would ever know. Besides, it was fun to tell this warrior what to do. "This particular dance has very precise movements timed to the music. First we circle to my right. Then to my left."

Osborn moved slowly, his gaze never leaving her face.

"Next you drop your hand to my waist, and we circle again."

His hand slid slowly, intimately down her body. She adored dancing. It was her favorite thing to do at Elden.

Not anymore.

"Go to bed, boys," Osborn ordered.

IF THE DAYS PASSED TOO quickly, the nights flew. Each morning he woke up with a sense of foreboding. Something sinister loomed in the distance. He intensified the level of Breena's workout. She'd made herself into an excellent swordswoman, but he feared this strong, brave woman would never have the brute strength to defeat soldier after soldier. They had to focus on her defenses.

Osborn raised his weapon. "Distract me," he ordered.

"Have you ever made love with your pelt on?" she asked.

OSBORN NEARLY DROPPED his sword, and the hilt fumbled in his palm.

Breena couldn't help but smile, and took the opportunity to advance. But he countered her thrust.

"No," he told her, his bottom lip growing more sensual.

"Oh." The idea of it had intrigued her ever since he'd explained it was only in his pelt that he was fully *berserker*. She'd hoped he might know how the *ber* spirit inside him reacted in passion.

He was so strong and powerful and solely focused when enraged. How would it feel to have all that strength and force and attention centered on her?

She knew man nor *berserker* would ever harm her, but would making love add an edge of danger?

Soon she'd have to leave this cottage and face the threat in her realm. Despite Osborn's training and the growing strength of her magical powers, she had to face the reality that she might not live. She might die the last heir of Elden. Breena had a lifetime's worth of experience to cram into only a short time. And making love to her man in full *berserker* frenzy was something she wanted to experience.

"Osborn?" she asked as she parried.

"Yes?"

"Did you notice I'm alone with you?"

He lowered his weapon, and rammed it home in its scabbard. Clearly there'd be no more training this afternoon. "I seem to remember warning you about being alone with me."

"And here I am, disregarding your warnings. Do you remember what you promised? I mean, threatened?"

He shook his head, but his eyes grew narrow and the air around them chilled.

"You on top. Me on top. You taking me on all fours like a beast."

"I remember now." His words turned heavy with desire.

Breena lifted the pack that was never out of reach and tossed it to him. "I'm going to run now."

She dropped her sword to the ground, and took off, hoping the animal spirit in him would not be able to resist a chase. Breena didn't stand in the practice clearing long enough to find out. She raced along the path with a laugh, removing her shirt as she ran. Her pants were a little more difficult to take off, but soon she managed to be running only in her light undergarments.

The air around her chilled, despite the sun's rays over her head. *He was* berserker. Excitement and the thrill of the danger sent her faster down the path. Behind her the leaves of the trees rustled, announcing he wasn't too far away.

"Breena," he called, his voice tight and otherworldly. Not completely human. She'd never heard him speak in full *berserker* rage.

A thick arm curved around her waist and her feet no longer raced along the path. Osborn shoved her against the trunk of a large tree, the bark pressing into her breasts. His hands sought the tiny bows at her hips and ripped. The cloth hiding her woman's places fell to the ground and his fingers slipped between her legs.

He bucked up against her when he felt her wetness, and his cock nestled against her backside. He nipped at her shoulder with his teeth. His love play was rougher and tinged with danger. More wet heat flooded between her legs. He gripped her breasts; they were hard and needed his touch. He pinched at her nipples and she shivered all the way down to her toes.

"Are you mine, Breena?" he asked, his voice was ragged and uneven.

"Yes." *Always.*

"Lift your leg."

She raised her knee, the bark rubbing against her inner thigh. He probed her with the tip of his cock, then sank inside her with a groan. "Mine," he said, squeezing her breast. He thrust and her whole body shook, the length of him so hard and thick with this new angle. His pelt shrouded them both. Osborn rocked inside her, the waves and crests of Breena's desire building and building. Her moans echoed throughout the trees. She was so close....

Osborn pulled out of her heat, his breath harsh behind her.

"On the ground. On your knees," he bit out, the words difficult to get out over his hunger.

She turned and leaned against the bark and stared at her *berserker*. His eyes were nearly black. Strain and tension molded his face. His hands fisted at his sides and his muscles were coiled, ready for battle. Osborn was beautiful in his rage, a fearsome yet awesome sight. His cock stretched straight from his body.

Breena lowered to the ground. Osborn dropped to his knees behind her, smoothed his hand along her back and kissed her shoulder. His fingers found the place where her pleasure centered and he caressed it. Her senses blazed. She needed him inside her.

"Osborn. *Now.*"

With an aching groan he gripped her hips and brought her to his body. She felt the heat of his probing erection, and then he thrust inside. Breena began to shiver and quake at the sensation. Osborn moved inside her, in and out, and once more she was moaning in pleasure.

"More," she urged. She wanted every part of her lover. Needed her warrior.

He pushed his hips more forcefully and finally she slipped over the edge of her desire. Her muscles clamped around his length and she could do nothing but feel. Around her the air swirled, and with a harsh groan, his body was racked by his climax.

Osborn collapsed on the ground, nearly too worn out to tuck her into his side. After a few moments, he kissed the top of her head. "I never lose control like that. I didn't hur—"

Breena lifted up on her arm and placed a finger across his lips. "You didn't lose control. I knew you could never hurt me."

She hugged this man tightly to her chest, her body still fluttering. Osborn had brought so much pleasure into her life. New experiences. She wouldn't be who she was right now if it weren't for him. A part inside her sobered. Was this the woman she was meant to be? If the Blood Sorcerer hadn't attacked, everything would have stayed the same. She would have gone on being Princess Breena.

But the attacks did happen. Her parents were murdered, her realm most likely destroyed, the people who looked to the royal family for protection and continuity dead or enslaved. While she found bliss in the arms of a man.

BREENA WAS QUIET THE rest of the day, and he grew more worried. What if he really had hurt her, and she was trying to hide it? Why had he done it? Worn his pelt and chased after her? It was insanity.

Because she asked you.

And Osborn would do anything Breena requested of him. But not that again, he vowed. Never again. The idea of causing her harm made him hurt.

He watched her, helpless as she suffered through dinner. She had no stories to share at the campfire. By evening he was filled with guilt over his weakness. Osborn had to fix it. He followed her to her room that evening.

"You've been quiet all day," he said as he joined her in the bed. She hadn't told him to go and leave her alone, so he took that as a good sign.

"I was thinking about how happy I am."

A rush of relief almost made him shake. Osborn laced his fingers with hers. "That's a good thing."

Breena shook her head. "No, it's not. I shouldn't be happy. Not when my people are suffering. When my parents are dead."

Cold streaked through him. Not the kind that signaled the return of his *berserkergang,* but from panic. It was happening. He'd feared Breena would become guilt plagued…like him. It would eat at her now that it had taken root. The blame she'd heap on herself would tear at her soul, leaving her anguished and filled with regret.

He wanted to take her into his arms, and assure her that the death of her family was not her fault. Smooth the line forming between her brows, and tell her she had nothing to feel guilty over.

But he didn't, because he knew she wouldn't believe him. Just as he didn't believe those same things about his own life.

They didn't make love that night. Instead, they lay side by side, barely touching.

HE AWOKE THE NEXT MORNING with that same feeling of doom.

Osborn disentangled himself from the bedcoverings, and stared down at Breena's beautiful face. He'd never grow tired of gazing at her. Even if he were privileged enough to grow old with her, see lines fanning from her eyes, and more gray than blond strands in her silky hair. It wasn't her features that made her beautiful to him. It was her spirit. Her capacity to love, both him and his brothers, despite all that had been ripped from her life. Breena hadn't feared the *berserker* in him. That's when it all changed for him. She wasn't afraid of anything.

While he was filled with fear.

He'd lose her. He knew it to be true now. Osborn had probably held on to her a little too long already.

After slipping out of her bed, he quickly dressed. He could no longer put off journeying into the village and seeking news of Elden. That was what loomed in the distance. Breena's revenge and her dreams of seeing her brothers, if they were still alive, restored to the throne. It was time for her to fulfill and silence the commands—no, the curses—her parents instilled in her mind. Survive and avenge…survive *to* avenge.

The village was quiet as he crested the hill, most of its residents still asleep. All but the merchants. Osborn found the spice man unpacking his wares, and arranging the items for optimal display. The man smiled at his approach. "I told you to stock up on olive oil before my supply dried up. Now it's all gone. Elden is a fortress."

"What I need is information."

The merchant only smiled. "The cost is the same. I'm a businessman, after all."

Osborn dug in his pack, and handed over the coin.

"I'm afraid the news is not good, my friend. Can't

get anything in and out of Elden now. There's talk the land is cursed by blood." The merchant shuddered. "I will not go back, not even for the fortune I'd make."

Cursed by blood. The snake scout made by blood magic. It all confirmed Breena's dream memory. The Blood Sorcerer was behind the attacks on Elden. "What of Elden's people?"

The spice man shook his head. "Of them I know even less, although with such little information, I'd suspect they were all dead."

Osborn had suspected as much, too. Breena's beloved brothers…Nicolai, Dayn and little Micah.

"There are rumors of a resistance."

Finally. Some good news.

"What?"

The merchant held up his empty palms. Clever ploy. Dropping his story at its most suspenseful.

Osborn slid more coins the spice man's way. "If I learn your talk was all lies to gain my money, you'll find yourself joining the dead of Elden."

"No, my information is solid. Those loyal to Elden's memory are gathering in an outbuilding along the border. Each day more return to gather arms and plan an attack. A fool's last stand, if you ask me."

And Breena should be there to lead her people.

Osborn had still been foolish enough to hold a small sliver of hope that Breena would stay. Hadn't realized it until that hope just died. He should have known better. In the stories she shared around the firelight at night, the princess never remained in the cottage in the woods.

On his way out of the valley, Osborn secured the provisions they'd need for their travel to Elden. To the place where her people gathered, very likely awaiting a leader. He'd learned the positions of the stars as a child, and could easily lead her home.

The walk through the tree-lined path that would lead him back to Breena did not take long. With a quick knock to her bedroom door, he stepped inside. She smiled up at him, and stretched her morning sleep away.

"I was just wondering where you'd gone." She scooted to the side and flipped back the bedcovering. "Now you can come back to bed."

He did not move.

Her welcoming smile faded. "Osborn, what is it?"

"I have news of your people."

Her beautiful green eyes widened.

"They're forming a resistance. They hope to take back the castle."

Breena squeezed her eyes tight. "Yes." Then she whirled off the bed, quickly retrieving fresh clothes. "We've got to get there as soon as possible."

"I've readied our packs."

"I must gather my things. Do they know that I'm still alive? What a foolish question. Of course not. How would they even know? I wonder who's leading them? And I'm talking so fast you can't catch up."

His lips turned up in a grin despite his souring mood. "You're excited. It's okay."

Breena gripped his elbow. "It *is* going to be okay, isn't it? I can feel it."

"Finish packing what you need. I'm going to give some instructions to my brothers."

Bernt flashed Osborn an accusatory glare when he stepped outside, blinking under the sun.

"I want to keep her," Torben told him, sounding more boy than man.

"She doesn't belong to us," he tried to explain.

Bernt shook his head. "But you could make her stay. Tell her what she wants to hear."

I love you.

Please stay.

I'm dying inside at the thought of you leaving me.

He ground his back teeth. "This is her path. We've always known that."

"What about after? She'd come back if you asked her to."

"I have no right to ask. Besides, she's a princess. Princesses belong in castles."

Bernt turned on his heel and stalked into the wilderness. There'd be no goodbyes from his younger brother.

CHAPTER TWELVE

THEY TRAVELED FOR THREE days. Osborn didn't want to rush their pace, despite Breena's urge to run.

"At the end of this journey there *will* be a battle, Breena. We can't afford to be worn out before the first strike," he warned.

At night they made love where they camped, their couplings sometimes fierce, sometimes savoring, but always tinged with a touch of desperation. Osborn would hold her long after she fell asleep, staring up at the stars.

"What are you doing?" she'd ask sleepily.

"Willing time to slow."

Sometime after their noon meal on the third day, he discovered the whereabouts of the outbuilding. Breena gasped when she spotted tents dotting the area and her people milling about—families, soldiers, workers of the castle.

"My people," she whispered, filled with so much relief and love she could hardly breathe.

"There's Rolfe," she nearly shouted, and Breena rushed toward him before Osborn could stop her.

Breena charged across the field with new energy, the breeze lifting her hair and cooling her face. The people working outside stopped to stare, their jaws dropping open in shock and their eyes filling with tears. Her people crowded her, welcoming her.

"Word of my brothers? Has anyone heard anything of them?" she shouted above the din.

But the Eldens continued to rejoice that one of the heirs had been returned to them.

"Rolfe," she called.

The man turned at the sound of his name. Rolfe had once been an important member of their household, part of the security that guarded her parents. Age had crept over him since she last saw him. He looked drawn and defeated. His eyes grew larger and joy touched the edges of his face when he recognized her. Then his face drained of color.

Guilt. She knew that emotion well.

"It wasn't your fault," she rushed to assure him. "How could a small personal force defeat the Blood Sorcerer?"

"You shouldn't be here," he warned.

How silly for Rolfe to be worried about propriety right now. "Nonsense. These are my people. This is exactly where I belong."

"How'd you get here?" Rolfe's gaze searched the crowd, spotting the other newcomer, Osborn. "You—" he pointed "—get her out of here."

Osborn's hand immediately went to the hilt of his sword.

The door of the outbuilding opened, and out stepped a man, and the crowd hushed. Breena recognized him as a member of the group who'd once protected Elden's perimeters. "What's all this commotion?" he shouted. It was a loud booming voice coming from someone so gaunt.

Instantly the Eldens began to shrink away and cower.

"Why are you yelling when all they are doing is enjoying the day?" she asked, her voice stern.

"Cedric has been, uh, leading the people."

Breena suppressed a shudder. Cedric had always seemed a particularly nasty sort, but then war made strange allies, and she glanced at Osborn. He was scanning the crowd, his hand remaining on his weapon.

"Sometimes a little force is needed to quiet and keep things orderly. You understand, I'm sure."

No, she didn't understand.

"I want no more of it. These people are scared. They've lost loved ones and fear for what's in the future. We need no more strife and anger."

Cedric's lips curled over his teeth in what she supposed was to be a smile. It looked more like a snarl.

"Thank you for all that you've accomplished, Cedric. Your deeds will not go unnoticed," she added. And warned.

Osborn stepped forward. "Tell me your resources."

Cedric stiffened, as if he was about to argue, then his gaze took in the strength and breadth of Osborn's shoulders, and the massive sword at his hip.

"Nicolai is gathering a vast force in the south."

The joy and relief of hearing that news almost made her double over. "My brother is alive?"

Cedric nodded. "Dayn, too. He's leading an army, as well. Word is the Blood Sorcerer's hold on Elden is already weakening. These will be our lands again," he said, loud enough for the entire crowd to hear.

A great cheer sounded, and Breena understood why they followed Cedric. Perhaps her first impression of him was wrong. Times of trouble could often bring out character in a person, and add inner strength. With her, it brought out a fighter.

Cedric's glance fell to Osborn. "Thank you for escorting the princess back to her homeland. You will be greatly rewarded for your troubles. Rolfe, bring me the gold we'd set aside. We feared if you'd been captured, we'd have to pay a ransom."

She glanced at Osborn, whose eyes had narrowed, his stance on alert.

"I'll have you escorted away from here in a few moments. I'm sure you can't wait to be on your way. There's a village half a day's walk to the east. I'm sure you're anxious to spend your coin."

"You're confusing Osborn for a mercenary," she told him. "He didn't bring me here for a reward."

"But you *are* a mercenary, aren't you?"

Osborn nodded slowly.

Rolfe returned with a purse heavy with gold. Cedric grabbed the bag and tossed it at Osborn, who caught it against his chest.

She glanced toward her warrior but he wouldn't meet her gaze. His stare was locked on the man who'd just called him a mercenary.

Cedric grabbed the shoulder of a passing boy. "Fetch Asher and Gavin." Cedric met Osborn's stare. "They're our two best soldiers. They'll escort you off Elden lands immediately."

"What are you talking about?" she asked. "Of course Osborn is staying."

"Are you staying, mercenary? With a princess?" His question was more of a sneer. Cedric was making Osborn sound like an opportunist. One only out for himself.

Her stomach began to tense. "Osborn?"

"She's with her people now. Two great armies are on their way. There's no reason for you to be here."

Tense silence stretched between them. This was so very silly. She opened her mouth to tell—

"No. There's no reason for me to stay."

"What?" she asked, hurt and confused. This had to be a strategy, some kind of ruse Osborn employed to test the security.

"Here come our soldiers now," Cedric announced, his voice betraying his delight.

"I'll have a word in private with my mercenary," she informed them all.

Cedric looked like he wanted to argue, but then bowed his head in acquiescence.

Osborn followed her to a tree away from Cedric and Rolfe. "What's your plan?" she asked.

Her warrior scrubbed his hand down his face. "Walk back home. Train my brothers."

She felt sick. "You really *are* leaving?"

Osborn angled his head around camp. "They seem to have everything in order here. Your brothers are coming."

"And you're just leaving me here?"

His nod was her answer.

"But...but you're my warrior. You belong with me."

He gripped her arms. "You've built me up in your mind, made me something I'm not. You've made me into one of your fairy-tale heroes." His dark eyes burned into hers. "But I'm just a man. A man who wanted you any way he could have you."

"Like a soul mate?"

At least that sounded romantic.

But Osborn the warrior only shook his head. "I don't believe in soul mates. I don't believe in anything but pleasure and passion."

Her body began to tremble. She didn't want to look at him. "I've just been fooling myself that you care, haven't I?"

Osborn swallowed and his gaze clashed with hers. He looked like he wanted to argue with her words. *Please argue. Please tell me I'm wrong.*

"We've enjoyed each other. Now it's over."

Breena would not cry in front of this man. She would not cry over him. Ever. "Go," she told him, turning her back.

He waited a moment, and she almost turned around to grab his hand. But then she heard his boots rustle in the fallen leaves. Osborn was leaving her.

"And, mercenary…"

"Yes?"

"Don't come back."

After gulping in several large breaths, Breena turned toward Cedric and Rolfe.

"Come inside, princess," Cedric invited. "See what's been prepared for your family's return to the castle."

With a nod, she followed him into the outbuilding. Dayn had told her this had been the original keep of Elden, when their realm was new and not so vast. The ceiling only topped to a second floor, so much smaller than the high-beamed castle that was her home. Would be her home again…until she was matched with a suitable marriage prospect. Her heart tightened, knowing that it would not be Osborn at her side. In her bed.

Made of stone and wood, the walls of the outbuilding were stained black from the years of fires in the hearth. A fire now blazed once more for the people who'd sought refuge here. Over the years, this had become a storage house, filled with the casks of wines and oils produced on their lands and sold.

"I've brought you a gift," Cedric told someone in the shadows.

"Is that what all that cheering was about outside?"

Breena shuddered. Goose bumps raised on her arms and along the back of her neck. That voice induced chills. Evil. It was all she could think.

"Leyek, I present Breena, the princess of Elden."

"Alive, how delightful," the voice said, still hidden in the shadows.

Cedric was working for the Blood Sorcerer. His gaunt appearance made sense now. How the Blood Sorcerer's minions were able to break their outer walls—the area Cedric protected. Now she understood Rolfe's words when he first spotted her. *You shouldn't be here.*

The people she thought warming themselves by the fire were tied to hooks in the floor. Men and women and two small girls not much older than four, their faces frightened. Their fate was a blood draining.

"That vast army you spoke of, it's a lie, isn't it?" she asked. But she knew the answer. No one would be coming to save her or her people. The saving was all up to her.

"Your brothers are as dead as your parents," Cedric sneered, and spat on the ground. "I rule here now."

"As a minion. And to the Blood Sorcerer. Both of you."

"Take the princess," Leyek ordered, still not coming out of the shadows. Demonstrating his low opinion of Elden. "Tie her. She'll make a delicious meal for our Blood Lord."

She truly valued Osborn's insistence she practice sliding her sword from her scabbard over and over again. The only time she could make a stand would be now. It would be her one chance.

Her fingers gripped the hilt.

Why the hell was he going?

These were new times. Different and desperate

times. A menace threatened their world—all the realms. It could be years or only days away, but soon they'd all face the reckoning. There may be little left after the battle. What pleasure, what *love,* anyone could grab… *he'd* grab that now with both hands. It didn't matter that she was a princess, and even if it did…he wouldn't care. Osborn would offer anything of himself she'd take. Breena was his pleasure. His love.

Those responsible for the deaths of his mother and sister and father, and the people of his village…he may never know their identity.

Something ripped inside him. A painful acknowledgment that there may never be an opportunity for him to avenge his family. That understanding hurt so fiercely, so brutally, that he almost keened over the loss of what had been his steady companion since returning from his Bärenjagd. Osborn gulped in deep breaths, forcing his heart to slow, his stomach to settle.

But there was still a chance for Breena.

Still a chance for her to free her people. To find her brothers. To do something, *anything,* to shake the ever-present need for revenge.

Why would he leave her now? He would fight alongside her. Fight to bring peace to her land or die, sword in hand at her flank.

But Osborn didn't plan on dying.

Osborn turned on his heel, ready to charge into the outbuilding where he'd left her. Ready to seal his fate to hers.

The steel clang of Breena sliding her sword from its scabbard slowed his step.

He *knew* it was Breena's sword. He'd heard that sound many, many times. Made her practice often enough until her movements were fluid and smooth.

So that she'd draw her sword quickly enough to spring a surprise hit.

Why would she be drawing it now? Among her welcoming people?

Cold began to creep up his legs and spread throughout his body. He dropped everything but his sword and his pelt. His *berserkergang* was alert and anxious for a fight. Osborn slipped into the outbuilding through a side door. He spotted Breena as she stood in battle stance, her sword protecting her body, her eyes alert. She was magnificent.

And she was *his*.

The man who'd welcomed his princess back so heartily a few minutes ago, gave Osborn gold to leave, now raised his weapon to her.

Rage pounded in his chest. Anger flashed white-hot in front of his eyes. With the cry of his *berserker* rage, Osborn raised his sword and charged. In less than a heartbeat, the man's sword clanged to the floor, his body not much farther behind.

Osborn stalked in front of Breena and raised his sword. "Who dies next?" he asked.

A low whistle sounded in the back of the room. Osborn felt Breena stiffen, and knew whoever made that sound was the threat.

"Show yourself," Osborn commanded.

"Or you'll what? Kill these fine Elden citizens? Do it. You'd be saving me the effort. Although…"

The slow scrape of a chair across the floor alerted Osborn he was about to see who'd tried to harm Breena.

"I do like the idea of you getting a good look at my face—as it will be the last thing you see." A tall, thin shell of a man walked out of the shadows.

Osborn's *berserker* stirred again. He'd heard the rumors of what blood sorcery would do to a person. Drain them of what once made them human. First their senses, until they craved hearing only the agonized cries of others and hungered solely for the taste of near death. Then all emotion would flee from their souls—first empathy, then remorse, until finally only hostility and greed remained. Lastly, their bodies would change. The curves and planes and every range of compassionate expressions of the face vanished until finally only a walking, breathing carcass remained.

"Leyek is strong. And brutal," Breena whispered, and Osborn understood. This minion of the Blood Sorcerer might look frail, but that was an illusion. His power was indomitable, tinged with great evil.

Osborn became one with the *ber* spirit.

"Are you what I think you are?" Leyek asked.

Osborn steadied his shoulders.

The Blood Sorcerer's minion let out a delighted laugh. "You are. You're Ursan. A *berserker,* in fact. Thought we'd killed you all."

His fingers locked on the hilt of his sword. "You thought wrong."

Leyek flashed him a smile. "Good. Your women died crying and screaming, by the way. I'll enjoy your death just as much."

His *berserkergang* raged inside him, but Osborn tamped it down. He knew Leyek's words were lies and meant to provoke him.

Leyek made a show of examining the length of his nails. "Surprised you would be helping an Elden princess. Thought disguising our changeling vamps as those of Elden was a particularly clever bit of deception designed by my master. Although I will admit I did think the subtlety of the ploy would be wasted on a beast."

A coldness crept into his body, and invaded his chest. This wasn't the focusing chill of the *berserkergang* overtaking him—this was something different.

Kill.

Avenge.

Hurt.

Breena rested her soft hand on his shoulder. Quieting him.

His woman was right. This creature, this bearer of evil, wanted to anger him. Push him to make a mistake because this thing knew that, despite his command of blood magic, Osborn could still kill him. Would still kill him. With the power of his *berserker* ancestry and Breena's nearness.

Osborn raised his sword, calmly and with perfect balance.

CHAPTER THIRTEEN

EVERY LESSON, EVERY WORD of caution and instruction, Osborn ever gave Breena now ran through her mind. She'd never been so afraid. She'd awoken not so long ago with only two commands echoing in her mind. To survive and to avenge.

Now she added a new one on her own: win this fight with Osborn.

Leyek raised his sword, waving it around in an elaborate dance.

It's the flourishing knights who are the first to die.

The air around her chilled. Osborn's *berserkergang* grew in strength. The Blood Sorcerer's minion charged. The clang of steel on steel rang through the air as Osborn blocked his blow. With an upswing of his sword, her warrior almost sent Leyek reeling to the floor.

She searched the crowd until she met Rolfe's eyes. Signaling toward the door, she mouthed the word, "Go!" With Leyek fully immersed in battle, now would be the time for her people to escape. With a nod, Rolfe silently gathered the Eldens who awaited their deadly fate and ushered them away.

With her people secure, Breena reached for her own sword. Two on one might not be a fair fight, but when did a wielder of blood magic deserve honor and respect?

Osborn charged forward, his sword slicing through his prey's shoulder. Leyek screeched at the pain, the sound horrible to hear; the walls began to shake, and dust rained down on their heads.

"That's the sound your vamps made as I killed them," Osborn shouted at him with a sneer. He thrust again, but Leyek was able to sidestep the blow.

The Blood Sorcerer's minion began to shake and mumble. Words, dark words, reverberated off the beams of the ceiling. A revolting menace permeated through the small hall. Nausea made her stomach roil.

"He's summoning his magic," she called.

Leyek moved in a flash. A slash appeared on the right side of Osborn's pelt. Then the left. With a gleeful cackle, the pelt fell to the floor and caught on fire.

Osborn's connection to the *ber* spirit was severed. Gone.

With a roar of outrage, Osborn rushed toward the minion. But some invisible force repelled him back, and left him bleeding. A nasty gash appeared across his chest, and blood seeped from the wound. Blood magic.

Osborn glanced down at his injury, and wiped across his ribs. His hand came back red with his blood. He stilled at the sight, and the room seemed to warm.

Then her warrior's face changed. The unrelenting rage lining his features softened. Replaced by determination. Osborn thrust, parried and thrust again.

Leyek stumbled backward, blood pouring from a gash across his face, and another wound to his side. Osborn charged once more, burying the blade in the minion's stomach. Leyek fell to the cold stone floor, his blood pooling around him.

"Tell me how they died again," Osborn ordered.

Leyek struggled to breathe. "I'll give you power. Great power. We'll bring the girl in together. My master will reward you greatly."

"Tell me how they died."

The minion's eyes turned the color of decay. He knew there'd be no ally in the Ursan standing over him. "I gave free rein to the vamps. Torture, devastate, torment…they did it all." Leyek's words began to slur, a murky haze surrounded him. The wound on his cheek began to heal. She would not let this thing live another day.

She ran to Osborn's side, and grabbed the steel of his sword. Breena gripped the blade so hard it cut into her flesh. Energy stirred within her, swirled and grew. With a snap it left her fingers, forging itself with the steel.

"My magic with your strength," Breena said. "It's time to finish him."

"It's only right," he answered.

Osborn steered her aside, kicked Leyek's blade toward him, then backed up. Her warrior eyed the Blood Sorcerer's minion. Waved him forward.

Leyek grabbed the hilt of his sword with bloody fingers. He chanted as he stood, but Breena no longer feared his brand of magic. He lunged at Osborn, and with only one strike from her warrior's sword, Leyek fell to the ground dead. Her magic had destroyed him.

Osborn wavered on his feet, and Breena ran toward him, looping his arm over her shoulders and helping him out the door. He needed to be in the fresh air, away from the death and magic of the blood.

"You did it, Osborn. And without your pelt."

"We did it together."

"You belong at my side, Breena," he told her once they'd crossed the threshold, loving the feel of her strength and trying to not let on that he was as hurt as he appeared.

"Don't you mean you belong at *my* side?" she asked, a slow beautiful smile curving her lips.

"Yes." His breath flowed out as a relieved groan.

Her kissable lips turned pouty. "I was doing pretty well in there. You didn't have to turn all *berserker*."

"I am a *berserker*."

"Even without your pelt."

He nodded. The *ber* spirit would always be part of him. He understood that now. A lesson he could one day teach his brothers. "And yes, I did have to turn 'all *berserker*.' For you."

Breena stood on tiptoe and kissed his cheek. "That's why I love you. And him. Mostly you," she teased.

Osborn grabbed her hands. "You know I must go with you to Elden. The Blood Sorcerer killed my family, too."

Breena nodded. "I was hoping this was where you said you loved me, too."

She tried to pull her fingers from his grasp, but he wouldn't let go. He would never let go. "And I'm trying to tell you that I would have followed you to Elden, anyway. Even without knowing he was responsible for what happened to my people. I was returning to convince you, uh, that I belonged at your side when I heard the sound of your blade."

He let her hands drop. Her decision. Her choice.

She reached up and cupped his cheek, her thumb running along his lower lip.

"There will be another full moon tonight. Breena of Elden, will you join me under the stars and seal your life with mine?"

After gripping his hands in her tiny ones, she gave his fingers a squeeze. "I don't know what we will face tomorrow, but tonight will be ours. Yes, Osborn."

"And, Breena?"

She gazed into his eyes. "Yes?"

"I love you."

EPILOGUE

THE NIGHT OF LEYEK'S defeat, Breena insisted they have a feast. She said it was in celebration, but Osborn knew she sensed her people needed festivity. The music, the dancing and the tales around the fire. To feel normal again. United as Eldens. The Blood Sorcerer had nearly broken them as a people. Truthfully many of them would never be the same, but tonight they would eat and laugh and forget.

Tomorrow would be for battle plans. Breena had already questioned every Elden in an attempt to ferret out news, even the most vague of rumors about her brothers. Osborn knew she'd never fully rest until she had her answers, even if they were tragic.

As the sun set, the fire blazed higher. By the hour more Eldens crept from the shadows to join her. Each one was greeted with laughter or tears and sometimes both. Families were reunited while others learned the knowledge of loved ones with stern acceptance. Grief would be for later. After the Blood Sorcerer's death.

As the stars filled the sky, Breena began to tell stories of Osborn's bravery, and the Eldens were thrilled to have a legendary *berserker* join them in the upcoming battle. They laughed as she relayed his skills at dancing and he found himself smiling.

Osborn had hated these people of Elden for most of his life, wanted to annihilate them like his own people had been by the Blood Sorcerer. Now, for the first time in his life, Osborn found he was content. But not so content he didn't wonder how long they would be obligated to sit around the fire. He wanted nothing more than to draw Breena into the darkness of the night. To seal his life to hers as she'd promised. To lay his cloak on the ground and draw her down beside him and make love to her beneath the stars. He wanted nothing more than to hear her cries of pleasure.

Earlier today he'd thought he'd never see her again, or hear her sweet voice again. Feel her touch. Sleep in his arms.

Rolfe moved to stand behind Breena. His steely gaze challenging as he crossed his arms over his chest. The message was clear. There'd be no sneaking away this night, or any night, until they were wed.

He gave the older warrior a nod of understanding, his intentions were honorable—marriage-wise that was. What he wanted to do to Breena's body was wicked.

Even though their most dangerous days lay ahead of them, Osborn looked forward to the future. For the first time since he was a young boy of fifteen. Breena had given that to him.

Thankfully, Breena had moved away from stories of him and on toward tales of her training with the sword. Laughter settled around him, and he saw it took a moment for her people to wrap their minds around the changing image of her from sweet heir of Elden to warrior princess.

Two more men joined the circle around the fire, and he heard Breena gasp. His hand was instantly at his side, his fingers curling around the hilt of his sword.

Bernt and Torben stood there.

He raised to his feet. "How did—?"

Breena rushed to his brothers, kissing each one on the cheek. "Magic. I left clues only they could follow."

Osborn didn't like the idea of them joining the fight, but they were almost men now. It was time he began accepting them that way. The Blood Sorcerer was responsible for taking away their childhood, and they had a right to the fight. His brothers settled around the fire, two more *berserkers* quickly welcomed. The people would entertain themselves long into the night.

"I can do more than just leave clues. I don't know if it's that I'm on Elden land again or that the battle with Leyek released something, but I can feel my power growing. Look."

Breena brought her hands together and he felt the change in her. Something powerful and elusive formed between her hands. Grew. Light pooled between her hands. "I can fully control my magic now. I don't have to rely on intense emotion."

His mind strayed to the intense emotion they'd used to mask the trace magic from the blood scouts at the lake and he nearly groaned.

The ball of light grew and she tossed it up into the air above her head where it separated into three distinct spheres. With a wave of her hand the spheres zipped across the sky, and he surveyed their progress until the light faded into the horizon. "I'm sending that out to my brothers." A smile spread across her face. "I sense they are alive. I know it."

He'd been gifted with this incredible woman. He'd stay by her side until his last breath.

"The moon is full overhead," she whispered.

His heart pounded and his body hardened. In a few moments she'd be his forever. With a laugh, she lifted her skirts and took off at a run. "I'll be yours, but only if you catch me."

Osborn was too quick for her and reached for her hands. "Just try to get away."

LIKE MOST LITTLE GIRLS, Breena had often dreamed of her wedding day. She'd wear a stunning dress, formal and beaded with a long train the colors of Elden. Her husband would, of course, be courtly and handsome, and he'd take her to his palace after the wedding feast and the dancing.

Never once had she expected the man who'd one day be her husband would be more inclined to growl than to dance. And tonight, she wore the sage dress her future husband had bought for her, the golden snake armband securely in place. Better than any imagined wedding finery.

Instead of a great hall filled with a long list of aristocratic and highborn guests to view the royal proceedings, they walked hand in hand, just the two of them, surrounded by the trees and under a canopy of stars. The reality of Osborn was more perfect than anything she'd ever dreamed or imagined.

Osborn, her wild *berserker* of a man, loved her.

Once they'd reached a small clearing, he stopped and turned toward her, twining his fingers with hers.

Glancing up, she gasped when she saw his appearance. "What happened to your hair?" she asked. All of Osborn's long brown locks were gone, his hair cut close to his head.

"Another tradition of my people. On his wedding day, a man cuts his hair. A taming, if you will."

Breena laughed. She doubted there would be much

taming where this man was concerned. His new look would take a little getting used to, but she liked it.

The lines crinkling at the corners of his eyes smoothed, and his expression turned serious. "Breena, my love. I seal my life with yours."

Such simple words. No elaborate vows or flourishes. Just a man taking the woman he wanted out into nature and declaring himself as hers before the stars and under the moon. A swell of love and emotion made her eyes tear. But she would not cry. Her warrior deserved a warrioress.

"Osborn, my love," she told him in a clear, strong voice. She met his brown eyes and smiled. "I seal my life with yours."

Once upon a time there was a beautiful princess who only really lived when she dreamed. Then one day she woke up surrounded by three glowering bears. With patience and love she tamed the fiercest, and with a kiss transformed the beast into a prince.

* * * * *

This book is dedicated to my husband and daughters—I love you all!

Thanks so much to Gena Showalter, Jessica Andersen and Nalini Singh—you were so much fun to work with from beginning to end!

A special thanks goes to Tara Gavin for making it all happen.

A shout out goes to Deirdre Knight, and everyone at TKA, whose support is invaluable.

And a trip down memory lane—thank you to Missi Jay, who first introduced me to berserkers back in school when we played the game on her Atari 2600 instead of studying.

PRIMAL INSTINCTS

As always, thanks go to my husband and family, who are always patient. I love you, Pink!

To Gnomey, may you someday find your way back to me. To Lobby, may the day come soon when I can give your brother to Gena. But never you.

You I'm keeping.

Thanks always goes to Gena Showalter, Sheila Fields, Donnell Epperson, Kassia Krozser, and Betty Sanders. Kassia—I put the serial comma in there just for you.

To Jeff Z, my BFF and all my friends from PCHS—you rock!

CHAPTER ONE

Middle of Nowhere, Oklahoma

WHAT WAS SHE DOING? Or had just done? Miriam Cole sucked in a breath and squeezed her eyes tight. It didn't change a thing. *He* was still there.

Miriam peeked over her shoulder at the man smushed up against her body. His legs were tangled over hers and his hand gently gripped her breast. The angle was awkward, but she could make him out perfectly in the morning light.

She sucked in a breath as she gazed at his sexy, slightly curling dark hair. That full bottom lip that did such dangerous things to her body. That face that looked almost boyish in his sleep.

Boyish, because the man beside her was twenty years old.

Twenty. Twenty? She had to get out of there.

How had this happened? Two days ago, getting a rental and driving from Dallas to see a prospective author in Oklahoma had seemed like such a great idea. A couple of hours in the car with the top down. See a part of the country she'd never seen before. Relax. Take a break.

But the clean air smelled weird, the wildflowers untamed, and after mentally going through her to-do list, she remembered why she hated time alone with herself. She had nothing but work on her mind.

When she returned to the office, she'd fire the person who'd suggested she take a vacation. Even if he was her brother.

The man beside her shifted and snuggled closer into her pillow, burying his face in her hair. She closed her eyes again, loving the feel of his skin against hers. Miriam began to curve her hand along the hardness of his biceps. Nothing felt as good as a man's strong arms. Jeremy's strong arms especially. Maybe a quick—

Her body jerked. *Stop.* If she went down that road again, he'd be awake. What had it been, four? Five times? Besides a little bit of sleep, the man didn't need much else to be up and raring to go. As tempting as round five or six sounded—escape was what she needed.

She slowly tugged her hair out from under him and slid gracelessly to the floor. He shifted, and she made every muscle in her body go still. She held her breath. After counting to ten, she slowly stood. Although way more prudent, she refused to crawl. Some dignity must be maintained. She was a major player in the publishing industry after all.

Oh, her brother, Ian, would laugh his head off if he knew she'd tiptoed naked to the bathroom. Brought down. Brought down by a temperamental sporty little red car and no bars on her cell phone. Stranded. Stranded somewhere in the middle of a place called Arbuckle Wilderness.

Her cell phone beeped and she dashed for it. No way did she want Jeremy waking up. He'd want to do something gallant like fix her breakfast or slay some kind of dragon.

"Hello?" she answered quickly.

That's when she realized that what she held in her hand wasn't her phone. What had seemed so funny the day before, that she and Jeremy had picked out the same built-in ring tone, now was another in an ever-growing list of events that had led her to the colossal mistake of falling into his arms last night.

The long pause on the other line was ended by a strangled throat clearing. "Who is this?" the woman demanded, her tone clearly not expecting any subterfuge.

Rather than answering, Miriam padded across the floor and shook Jeremy's shoulder. "Phone call for you," she told him as he opened his eyes and she met the blueness of his gaze, reminding her just why she'd kissed him that first time.

With a sexy shrug, he sat up in bed, and the sheet slid down his legs. *Don't look.*

"Hello?" His voice sleepy and so appealing to her.

Oh, what did she have left to lose really? Her gaze drifted lower.

And Jeremy sat up straighter. "Oh, hi, Mom."

She shouldn't have looked.

She was going to be sick.

Two Weeks Later

"You look like hell," Miriam said.

Ian Cole slumped into the burgundy leather chair in front of his editor's glass-and-chrome desk, ready for his latest assignment.

"That's a bit harsh," he told his sister.

"It's true. Have you seen yourself in the mirror?"

Maybe she had a point. He certainly felt like hell, and he probably looked it, too. Yeah, well, what else was new? "I've just spent three weeks tracking drug runners. You're lucky I caught a shower before catching the red-eye back to the States."

"Maybe you should try catching a shave and a haircut. And three days worth of sleep."

"The boys gave me a good send-off before I broke for the airport. A little R & R," he said, rubbing his temples, and trying to remember just what they'd done.

Maybe too good a send-off.

Miriam's lips thinned. "I'm not sure the parties those guys cook up could be cataloged as either rest or relaxation. They're certainly not good for you."

"We were all of legal age, and you didn't *have* to bail me out of jail, so I'm calling it good," he said, blinking against the light beaming through her large office window overlooking Manhattan.

Miriam shuddered, as she walked toward the window to close the blinds. "Thanks for the reminder. You should have heard me explaining to our accountant that bail money was a legitimate tax expense."

"You're lucky you got to bail me out. There are quite a few pissed-off officials who'd just as soon kill me as have me share the luxury of their penal system. There'll be no welcome mat for me in Mexico."

"True," his sister said, reaching for the wand on the blinds.

"Come to think of it, there'll be no welcome mat for you, either."

Miriam turned on her heel and glared at him. "You're right, and I have a time-share in Mazatlan I'll never see again. I left my skinny swimsuit there, so screw your hangover. It's your own darn fault you're in this condition, so you can live with the sunlight. I like my view and I like my rays."

Ian looked around the office. "You worked hard enough to get here."

"Damn straight," she said, her angry attitude vanishing. He knew his big sister could never stay mad at him for long.

Kicking off her pointy black power heels, she rounded the corner of her desk. She tossed a manila folder on her brother's lap. "I have a new assignment for you. In fact, I think you'll like it. You've talked in the past about doing more feature writing, less fieldwork. I have a book for you to look over."

It physically hurt to make the face that expressed how he felt inside.

"You're going to tell me you're the only reporter who's never secretly longed to write their own book?" she asked.

"A book is a long way from a feature spread in a magazine."

"Think of it as one hundred features strung together. I need this to work. Cole Publishing has just acquired the rights to an exciting new concept book," she told him as she reached for her ever-present bottle of water.

Ian sat up in his chair. "Ah, the side trip to Oklahoma. I see it went down smoothly."

Miriam coughed on her water.

Expanding into books had been a dream of their father's, which he'd inherited from their grandfather, who'd founded Cole Publishing. They'd spun off a few books from their newsmagazine to other publishers in the past, but the dream of becoming a major player had eluded their father. Since Miriam had taken the reins, his big sister had streamlined production, lowered costs and developed a nice, healthy bottom line.

Looked like Miriam thought the time to revisit the dream was now.

Apparently she planned to drag him along, too.

"And you want me to do the writing? Isn't that backward? Aren't authors supposed to bring the completed manuscript to us?"

His sister straightened in the large executive leather chair. It had been their father's. That and the two leather seats in front of the desk were the only things she'd kept. The rest of the office had her stamp: rounded corners, sunburst motif—art deco all the way. "She's an academic, a doctor of anthropology as a matter of fact. Her writing is somehow, well, awkward."

How like his sister. She was tough as nails, battled reporters, distributors and every yahoo who didn't think she could run a company with the big boys. She was all business. But when it came to talent, she never liked to criticize anyone.

Years ago, Ian had found his sister's weak spot; she feared an utter lack of talent in herself. Artistically speaking. And to be honest, her fears were quite well-founded. She couldn't sing, dance, paint and her writing was terrible. Even her carefully worded memos to staff needed a good editor. So unlike their graceful and talented mother. So unlike him, minus the graceful.

Well, he liked to think he exuded grace in one area. In bed. No complaints there.

His sister called the doc's writing awkward. That must mean it read like an academic snooze fest.

"Why me?" he asked.

Miriam didn't meet his gaze. "Because you're my best reporter and photographer."

Ian dropped his elbows to his knees and leaned forward. "*Reporter* being the operative word there. Why would you want me to help write it?"

"You can work magic with words. And this project definitely needs some sparkle."

"Don't say *sparkle* around any of the guys. So what's the story about?"

"I haven't settled on a title yet, but she's calling it *Recipe for Sex.*" Miriam's brown gaze dropped from his.

Ian snorted. "Just to ensure I'll never be taken seriously in the world of journalism again?"

His sister shook her head, her dark hair not budging from the neat knot on top of her head. "You're a crime and war reporter. You're jaded. It's time to do a little something different."

Yes, and here it came. The big lecture on his lifestyle. He'd walk if she called him a danger junkie. But his sister was a businesswoman, and he knew how to fight dirty. He'd attack her bottom line.

He settled back against the leather chair. "Jaded appears to be selling. Readership's up twenty-five percent."

"And my migraines are up forty-five percent. One hundred percent because of you."

She couldn't be serious about yanking him. Hot stuff was brewing in South America. He itched to cover it. "What is it you're saying?"

"I'm saying you've become a pain in the ass. After your last series of escapades, I need to keep an eye on you."

Ian gritted his teeth. "You may be my big sister, but I'm plenty capable of taking care of myself."

"How about three arrests in two years in countries that change names as quickly as the next coup can be organized? How about the broken ribs you got while fighting some rebel over the film you shot? How about the—"

He cut her off before she really got into this topic. His dangerous lifestyle tended to prove a favorite of hers. "Those are occupational hazards."

Miriam smiled, her eyes taking on a serious gleam. Crap. Now he was in for it. A smile was never good from his sister. He'd seen too many smiles induce too many lawyers, investment bankers and arrogant reporters into a false sense of security. She *would* get what she wanted.

But then, as her beloved brother, he was usually immune.

"This book is important to the company. It's important to me. I want this transition to go smoothly, and I know you can deliver it."

His immunity held firm. "Not gonna happen."

"I promised Mom."

Well, hell. And yes, the smile still worked. He'd been sucker punched, and it was a low blow. Miriam was the only one who kept in semiregular contact with the woman who'd left when Ian had been a toddler.

Theirs was a relationship filled with uncomfortable telephone calls, stilted conversations and now an extra drink at dinner to make it all not seem so bad.

Ian didn't need that lone semester's worth of psychology to realize both of them held some strange, undeniable need to gain the distant, nonmaternal woman's approval. The fact that his mother showed even a bit of concern was infuriating.

And gratifying.

"Think of it as a favor," his sister suggested.

He raised an eyebrow.

"A mandatory favor."

MIRIAM COLE WAS NOT a wimp. Although she certainly saw the advantages of acting like one now. Sending her brother to Oklahoma so she could practice her new-found faith in avoidance was really a new low for her.

Oh, well, it would be good for him.

But still…she'd never evaded anything in her life. And if anyone actually commented that the wadded-up pink While You Were Out slip shoved in the back of her desk drawer was a wee bit out of character for her usual tidy self, she'd add denial to her growing list of bad habits she didn't plan to shed.

She should run that message slip through her shredder. It had already been a week since Rich had placed it on the middle of her desk. Why was she still holding on to it? She had no intention of returning the call of good ol' five-times-in-one-night Jeremy. Or was it six?

She suppressed a shiver and smoothed her hair, even though she'd twisted her dark hair into a tight not-a-chance-of-escaping knot. Anything not to remind her of how Jeremy's fingers had sifted through the strands.

Okay six. It had been six times.

Miriam slumped in her chair and gave herself permission to wallow in her mistake. She was due. Why should her torment only be reserved for nighttime when she was alone in her apartment? Why not let Jeremy and his six times invade the one place she'd always been able to control?

She'd never given much thought to Oklahoma as a state. Nothing much more than football, cows and musicals about dancing cowboys. She hadn't been prepared for Jeremy.

The place had brought her down. One moment she was driving and singing badly with a song on the radio. The next she was on the side of the road kicking her foot in frustration at the red dirt aligning the highway.

She'd have the magazine do an exposé on the hazards of scenic drives. They should be synonymous with stranded and not seeing another person for miles. The unsuspecting public ought to know.

One thing was for certain…she never planned to go there again. She could only hope her brother would fare better.

CHAPTER TWO

Oklahoma City, Oklahoma

"Anyone ever tell you that you have too much sex stuff?" Thad asked.

Ava Simms looked up to see her brother unpack a wooden replica of Monolob, the penis god from an ancient Slavic tribe.

"Careful with that," she told him. "It took me weeks to find someone who could craft that out of the native wood. I'd hate for anything to break off."

"By anything, I'm assuming you mean this ginormous penis."

Thad examined the lean figure with the gigantic proportions. Male proportions. There was only one protruding object that could break off. Disgusted, he set the figure on the shelf, then turned it so the statue's large appendage faced the wall. "It's hard enough to get a date without the womenfolk being exposed and comparing others to this."

Ava paused as she broke down another shipping box. "Since when do you have a problem getting a date? Usually there's a cadre of broken hearts left in your wake."

"I'm doing this for other men. We've got to stick together when battling forces like these." Thad flexed his biceps in a symbol of unity.

Rolling her eyes, Ava tossed the now-flattened box

in the pile of cardboard ready to go to the recycler. "For your information, the men of the tribe carved those as they reached puberty. Some would even string smaller replicas around their necks."

Thad laughed, and looked pointedly at the backside of the figurine. "You'll need to do a bit more research on this one, little sister. I can't imagine *any* man, from any century, parading penises around. Certainly not around his neck."

"Ah, yes, sometimes I forget about the male rules of the early twenty-first century. You know, there's a whole anthropological study there in itself. 'No talking in the bathroom,' 'eyes straight ahead at the urinal,' 'never acknowledge another man's penis.' Honestly, it's like ignoring the elephant in the room. Hey—"

Groaning, her brother raised a hand. "Don't even think about asking me to take you back to the men's room at the airport. It was a mistake. You and your scientific study."

"There might be valuable lessons there. Think about what a trained, yet unbiased eye could glean. Maybe true insight into the differences between the sexes."

"Yes, the differences are very obvious at a urinal. You could call it the Stall Theory. Sorry, Sis, but I doubt any serious academic publication would pick it up."

Ava sighed and returned her attention to the boxes. "Well, that would be no change from what's going on now. No peer-reviewed journals want to publish my research on the lost sexual customs of the world, either."

Thad stooped to pick up another box. "So that's why you decided to write it up as a book."

"That, and the fact my research funding dried up, and it's too late now to find a teaching job. No university would take me on until fall. And now the publisher wants to help me fine-tune it, make it more attuned to today's reader. Whatever that means. As if people won't find the way I've written on sociocultural and kinship patterns attention-grabbing."

"Yeah, I can see how that wouldn't be a problem," he told her drily.

Ava glanced over to see her brother's lips twisting into a smile. "Okay, maybe I could do with a little lightening up."

"Face it, sis, you haven't been living in the real world for…well, at all. Mom and Dad toted you around to every dig since you could carry a shovel. Then you went straight to college and basically never left."

"You had those same experiences," she pointed out.

"Except I chose to have a life between classes." Thad placed his hands on her shoulders and she looked into the green eyes so much like her own. "You know what, I think not finding a job is a good thing for you."

Ava scoffed, her bangs ruffling. "Apart from the tiny problem of paying for food and utilities."

Thad wrapped his arm around her shoulders, drawing her beside his tall frame. Why did he have to inherit all the height genes?

They'd always been close. Sometimes they were the only two children on a dig site, and they'd grown to read each other's moods. "Ava, listen. This is your opportunity to fly. Mom and Dad didn't give you that name for you to sit and mope. Avis, our eagle, now's your time to soar. So you're not teaching anthropology to a bunch of freshmen who probably don't want to sit in your class anyway. That's a good thing."

"I just thought I'd always teach and lecture. Share the love of traditions and learning of other cultures to fresh, new, young minds."

Another huge disappointment in the daughter department. She'd chosen to go for anthropology rather than follow her parent's path and continue their research in mythology and the ancient Greek cultures. They'd have loved nothing better than to always have her by their side at the digs in Greece—the magical place where her parents fell in love.

She had no doubt if she'd pursued archaeology she would have found half a dozen jobs at any major university across the country. Her last name alone would guarantee it.

But she didn't want to rely on that last name even on such short notice.

So she didn't have a job. She didn't have anything published impressive enough to get her a job in her chosen field.

So what? She did have a prospect. In two days, Miriam Cole from Cole Publishing would be here to "help" her explore the concepts best suited for her book. Writing her book with a little bit of help wasn't exactly how she'd planned to earn a paycheck...but she'd adapt. Wasn't that one of the cornerstones of her teaching anyway? How cultures, people, throughout time changed to meet the problems that faced them?

She could be flexible. She'd show Miriam just how interesting ancient dead cultures and their sexual habits could be. Show her that they were relevant to the twenty-first century woman.

"That's it," she said, suddenly ready to clear the moving distraction out of her way. She had a stage to set for the head of Cole Publishing.

"What's it?" Thad asked.

Determination filled her, and Ava squared her shoulders. "I'm going to demonstrate that this book can be exciting. That people will want to read it. I'm going to knock her socks off. When Miriam Cole gets here, I'll greet her in the ceremonial wedding attire of the Way-terian people."

Thad lost his smile. "Isn't that basically just pa—"

Ava smiled. "Exactly."

IAN CIRCLED AROUND THE one-way streets of downtown Oklahoma City for a third time, looking for a place to park. Why couldn't the doc live in a normal place, not some converted old warehouse? Like maybe some place that didn't need to be validated.

For that matter, why'd she have to live in flyover country anyway? At least he'd had no layovers. He estimated he'd lost two years of quality life just sitting in a plane due to a lack of direct flights. The skills paid off this time. With no connections, he had some uninterrupted hours to review the project.

Just as on any assignment, he liked the broad details, but kept away from the finer points so he wouldn't be biased in one direction over another. He'd spent the flight to Oklahoma reviewing the doc's work that she'd turned in to Miriam. The writing style was abysmal. Something between technical anthropological jargon and absolute incoherence.

The sex stuff was the only thing that seemed remotely promising. But discussing it with a grandma-like Margaret Mead stretched before him and seemed as tantalizing as many hours of cuddling and spooning.

Finally, he parked in the redbrick garage he'd found, paid his five bucks and hiked the few blocks to her warehouse loft apartment, lugging his camera, minirecorder and laptop. He looked down at the paper in his hand, confirming her address. Top floor. Of course. She buzzed him in, and he headed for the elevator. He hated elevators. Every family member he had insisted on living on the top floor. He'd rather be chased to the border than be trapped in a metal box suspended by a string.

This kind of elevator was awful, one of those large service lifts. He'd have to pull the top and bottom gate closed. He'd take the stairs. He'd hiked through worse, and with all his equipment strapped to his back.

There was no mistaking which apartment was the doc's. A brown ceramic snake stood beside the front door. A snake with large breasts and fake red flowers coming out of its mouth. Weird.

This photo shoot and discussion was going to be worse than he'd first imagined. His sister owed him something good after this. She'd have to send him someplace dirty. Somewhere he could trudge through swamps and fight off rebels as he followed a band of radicals, a camera in one hand, a knife in the other. Ah, good times.

He knocked on the door. A strange exotic scent lingered in the air, tantalizing his nose. Subtle, yet almost…arousing. He took a few more sniffs of the air, then realized the scent came from underneath the door. At least the doc would smell better than the radicals.

Impatient, Cole knocked again. He already hated the assignment. And the doc. Now she wasn't even here to greet him. He'd make his sister cook for that. She hated cooking. He was about to leave when he heard a noise behind the door. Then some strange, elemental music. Was that drums?

The knob twisted and the door opened.

"Welcome," said the woman in front of him, a smile forming along the red fullness of her lips.

"Pai—" he managed to get out, then stopped.

He'd had a thought. It was there just a second ago.

The woman took a quick step backward, the smile fading from her face. "I thought you were someone else."

"Paint."

His eyes lowered, following the elaborate swirls and colors that adorned her skin. Paint and nothing much else. He tried to swallow. He'd obviously prejudged this assignment too harshly.

Her eyes met his squarely. Not a trace of embarrassment or awkwardness in her body language. "Yes, the Wayterian people would adorn themselves in paints before their wedding, signifying their past. After the ceremony they rinse off in each other's presence, starting clean and fresh together."

Her expression became neutral, and the light he'd spotted in her green eyes as she talked faded.

"But you're probably not interested in that. As I said, I thought you were someone else."

He made out a few words. *Paint. Rinse. Together.* This woman had an amazing husky voice to go along with her amazingly painted body.

She made to close the door.

Whoa. Time to get with the program. He stuck his foot out to block it. "Wait. You've been waiting for me. You're Dr. Simms. Right?"

The door opened a fraction wider, and the doc poked her head out. "Who wants to know?" she asked, her expression growing guarded. Maybe she should have thought about looking through her peephole before opening the door nearly naked. Maybe he should volunteer to give her a few instructions on personal safety.

"I'm Ian Cole. Of Cole Publishing." He held up his tripod. "See? Totally legit."

"I thought Miriam would be coming. Is she with you?" She stood on her tiptoes to see behind him. Lots of luck, she only came to his chin.

"I'm her brother."

The woman in front of him nodded, a hint of recognition now in her green eyes. "Ah, yes. You do the reports from the war zones. Gripping photos. I did some research on Cole Publishing." The smile returned to the doc's face, and she opened the door. "I thought this painting ritual might be something good for the book."

With the door open, the full impact of the doc's body crashed into him once more. Paint and a loincloth. That was basically the composition of the outfit.

Cole wasn't a man who was easily surprised. But Ava Simms stunned the hell out of him.

Vibrant colors of blue, green and black in fancy swirls, circles and lines touched every inch of her body. Her breasts stood bare, although entirely covered in paint.

He'd seen his share of naked breasts in his time. Excellent ones. In all shapes and sizes. Large breasts that spilled out of his hands. Small, high breasts that begged to be kissed. But his favorite had to be the ones before him, covered in paint, fully exposed, yet completely covered. Totally erotic.

She seemed to be waiting for something. With an effort he'd brag about later, he dragged his eyes slowly up her body once more.

"Would you like to join me?" she asked.

Hell, yeah.

And reveal his giant hard-on. No.

The doc turned, and Ian almost groaned. He'd always

thought of himself as an ass man. And the doc's ass confirmed it. Firm, as though she'd performed quite a few of those dances she'd described in her manuscript.

Covered in some white piece of cloth that looked as if it had been ripped and tied around her waist. Paint from her body had smudged the cloth in a few places. He couldn't imagine the men of the Wayt—the Wabr—the Whateverian would stay in a shower, washing off paint, when they could be screwing. Had he ever seen such a beautiful pair of breasts?

Heaving the gear on his shoulders, he followed the doc inside her apartment. He'd send his sister a thank-you card later. Coles were always polite and followed proper etiquette. They learned it from the cradle.

Ava pointed to her coffee table, covered by tubs filled with paint. "I was thinking that in the book we could give demonstrations on how to paint your lover's body. That's not totally in the Wayterian tradition, but we could still include the shower."

He didn't spy any paintbrushes. Images of sliding paint on this woman's body with his fingers, of her running her paint-smeared palms against his skin, then warm water cascading down their naked bodies together left him speechless.

The doc turned and raised an eyebrow. "Do you think men would find the ritual interesting?"

Well, *interesting* was one word for it.

He'd expected boring and painful when he flew to this assignment. Boring was out. He adjusted his pants, but it was going to be painful. Definitely painful.

Dr. Ava Simms was nobody's grandma.

CHAPTER THREE

"So why did your sister send you? I thought she was coming herself."

A look of unease crossed Ian's face. Ava saw his lips move. Did he just mumble? It almost sounded like he muttered something about cowardly sisters.

"Mr. Cole?" she prompted.

"I'll be taking the photos for the book, and revising the manuscript." He hunched down to his equipment bag.

Bringing in a photographer was a given. The rituals she wanted to explore were also very visual. Men were very visual creatures and most cultures had adapted to that. Her book would have to include a lot of pictures to be appealing to her target males. "I thought this meeting with Miriam was to refine and make some fixes to my writing. Surely *revising* is too strong a word," she prodded.

He pulled out what looked to be a light meter. Her father often used the more sophisticated photographic equipment while on a dig site.

"Mr. Cole, are you listening to me?"

"Call me Ian."

She narrowed her gaze. This man was trying *not* to tell her something. Something he didn't want her to know. She'd studied cultures from all over the world, and men from one continent to another flashed the same visual cues when wanting to avoid a direct question. Especially from a woman.

The shifting weight from foot to foot.

The suddenly moving hands.

The rapid eye movement.

Yes, Ian Cole was in full avoidance mode, exhibiting the number-one classic sign—sidestepping the question.

"Ian, when you say revising, what you really mean is—"

His gaze met hers finally. Clear, brown and full of truth. A truth he didn't want to tell her.

"Ghost-writing. Miriam feels the pages you sent in have too much of an academic feel to them," he said, cutting her off with a hint of apology in his voice.

At least he was honest. Disappointed, she slumped against a nearby column. The cool wood cut into the bare skin of her back, and she cringed.

Obviously she'd failed in her quest to find the creative "wow" to impress her new publisher. Maybe her *only* shot at a publisher. This was a disaster. No one wanted her work in the academic field. Now it seemed no one wanted her work outside of it, either.

Ava wanted to kick the wall in frustration. She hadn't realized until just this moment how important doing this book on her own had been to her.

"Have a seat," she told him with a sigh.

Quickly, he shifted his gear. With one direct look into her eyes he sat down. Was that concern she spotted in his gaze?

Now that she knew what she was dealing with, she could move forward. Funny, she'd never acknowledged how correctly her mother had pegged her daughter's personality. Mom had always compared her to a triangle: didn't matter which way she pointed as long as she was moving in some direction.

She'd never had her own apartment before. The closest thing she'd had to a home had been her dorm room. She had no idea if she'd placed the couch or the end tables in the right places, but she liked the final result, and that was all that mattered. She watched Ian look around.

He finished his examination with a slow whistle between his teeth after looking up. "Wow, this is some place. That ceiling is amazing."

"It makes me feel like I'm not so boxed in. I like wide-open spaces."

"Yeah? Me, too." A smile tugged at his top lip, and his gaze narrowed.

For a moment, she met his eyes. Where had her instincts gone? She was supposed to be the expert. *She* should be the one to find common ground. *That* was how alliances were formed. And right now she sensed she needed Ian on her side to get what she wanted—to write this book on her own.

On to step two: Slowly layer in personal experiences so that it's harder for the target to say no. Her gaze slid upward. "When I saw the high ceiling, I knew this had to be my apartment. This used to be an old warehouse." She pointed to the exposed ductwork, painted a warm taupe. "The nearly floor-to-ceiling window allows in great natural light, which just feels more normal to me, even though I'm living six flights up."

"You spend a lot of time outdoors?"

Ava laughed softly. "Since I can remember. Not many hotels in the isolated regions my parents took me to. My father liked to sleep under the stars."

"This your first time living in a city?" he asked.

Questions. Of course, she should have realized. Ian was a reporter. He'd be a man who'd ask a lot of questions. Was she slipping that fast now that she wasn't active in the field?

Hmm. He was making her a subject. He'd apparently acquired his own approach—to remain distant.

Questions were fine. She could handle questions. Her mission was to make sure her answers steered him away from viewing her as a writing project.

"Other than college towns, I don't think I've ever lived someplace with over a thousand people. To go to someplace with more than half a million people was a pretty big leap. I thought about living in the rural area of the state, then I figured, what the hell?"

His brown gaze met hers. Did she see a bit of understanding in the depths of his eyes? Clearly he was a man who understood a what-the-hell? sentiment.

"I have a gorgeous view of Oklahoma City's skyline. The city is literally my backyard. And I have plenty of space to show off the artwork and sculptures I've collected from some of the places I've visited. Before he left, my brother installed shelving on almost every available wall space." She loved the results.

Ian nodded, and ran his finger along the fine woodwork of the nearest bookcase. His hands were work-rough appealing. Obviously he didn't use a phone or computer to do his research, he was in the field. Just like her.

Ava smiled when she realized his attention had settled on a small collection of naked fertility goddesses.

"Ah, you've found my harem. As you can see, most fertility deities are shown with large breasts and protruding bellies."

Ian pointed to Danisis, a voluptuous-looking goddess. "She's different from the others."

"She's my favorite. She's the goddess of war and fertility. Kind of ironic, huh? One destroys life, the other creates it. I love the spear she's carrying, the detail work is amazing. There's a very erotic love-play ritual associated with her."

His hand lowered and he went back to his bags. "Where do you want me to stash my gear? I'll need to plug in my laptop. My battery's shot—I used it on the plane."

"We can just use my computer. My manuscript is already right there."

Ian shook his head. "It would work better to use my laptop. First, if we go from your manuscript, it'll be too tempting to use what's already there. We need to start fresh. A total rewrite."

She took a deep breath, steeling herself for her next question. She *had* to know. "It was that bad, huh?"

The left side of his mouth lifted. Was that almost a smile? "A woman who wants me to tell it like it is."

"Always," she replied. She wasn't one for sugarcoating, she wanted total honesty.

"It sucked. And not in a good way."

Ava gasped. Okay, maybe not that much honesty. "Is there a good way to suck?" she asked.

Ian coughed behind his hand, then looked at her strangely. "If you were going for campy humor, then bad writing can make it more fun. Sometimes. Probably never."

She nodded. A flash of alarm crossed Ian's face. His eyes widened, and for a moment Ava was confused.

"Your concept is excellent," he hastily reassured her. Awkwardly. What did he think she was going to do, cry? That explained the alarm she'd sensed in him a moment ago. Often in patriarchal societies, men backed away from tears. Anything squishy, like emotions, were very much off-limits.

"Thanks," she told him firmly. But he didn't need to worry about her. This was science. There was no emotion in science.

"It's just the writing. The rituals and foods you chose were perfect examples of new and unusual, yet didn't morph into the freak zone."

Her eyes narrowed. That would be a relief for the cultures who'd shared their revered customs and ceremonies with her—that they hadn't moved into Mr. Cole's freak category.

Which then drew the question—what *was* Mr. Cole's freak category?

And would it mesh with her freak categories?

No, she didn't care. This man simply didn't get what she was trying to do here. She didn't want his help, plus he didn't have the sensitivity. Although she hadn't expected to spend any time with the man, his name had come up when she'd looked up Cole Publishing. Her search proved him to be a man more in tune covering the world's hot zones. How would a man like that possibly understand what she was trying to do here? He'd have to go.

"We'll go over each chapter. We can take the pictures as we move along or do them all at once at the end. At night in my hotel room, I'll edit."

"*You'll* edit?" she asked, her tone unbelieving.

Ian ticked off these items as if they were on a to-do list. He'd only reduced her life's work and passion into something resembling an inventory sheet. "You can simply crank these out?" she asked, wanting to make sure.

"I'll have this book whipped into shape in no time."

"*You'll* have it whipped into shape?" Yes, and there was her limit. Ian Cole had just stepped over the line. She squared her shoulders and looked him straight in the eye. Ian's gaze lowered a fraction before returning to hers.

She shook her head. "No. I can't possibly have you do the writing."

"Why?" he asked. His voice held no offense. And yet that one word sounded unbending. As if he fully expected to get his way.

"It's clear you don't appreciate what I'm trying to do with this book. You're thinking to spice up the time in the bedroom, not how the act of lovemaking can be enhanced with a few delicacies and rites from other cultures."

Ian moved toward her, towering above her. Something sparked inside those jaded eyes of his, and the firmness of his lips softened. Grew more sensual. For the first time, she felt crowded in her apartment.

"Oh, really?" he said.

She gulped. "Yes, really."

"This book is supposed to be about passion," he said, his voice soft, like warm honey. "Fire. The words and pictures should put a fire in your blood. Bring a woman and a man closer. Sharing the deep-rooted coming together of men and women from the beginning of time eternal. From all over the world. It should connect. It should be elemental. Raw. Man. Woman. Sex."

Ava swallowed. Her blood felt heated, and yet she shivered.

Okay. So maybe this man got it. Her heartbeat quickened with each word from his mouth. With every firm declaration he stated, a picture formed in her mind. A picture of bringing woman and man closer. Of bringing Ian closer to her. Elemental. Connecting and raw.

She took a deep breath. Bad move. He smelled good. Real good, like the rain forest after a heavy downpour. Earthy and clean.

Pheromones. That's all it was. Ian Cole exuded pheromones she just happened to respond to. It was science. It wasn't emotion. Now was the time for her to think logically. To be fair, he'd conveyed the concept better than she had, and it was her creation.

Now *that* made her mad.

"What you have is more along the lines of 'insert tab A into slot B' with a lot of history thrown in to make sure you'd rather mow the lawn than spend hours making love to a sensual woman," he said. His words were laced with amusement.

Though to her they were like a splash of cold water to her heated skin.

Okay, she was not about to have her project be just another in a long line of screwups because of a little estrogen. Maybe Miriam's idea of bringing in Ian Cole would work. He might have something to add. But there'd have to be some ground rules, and *she'd* have to make the final decisions.

"Maybe we can try this," she hedged. Ava tapped her foot. What she needed was some brainstorming, paradigm shifting. She'd planned on this project being solely her creation, she'd not factored—

"Don't you want to cover yourself up?"

Ava shrugged, and looked down at her body. She'd been so used to walking around nearly naked from one setting to another, she'd almost forgotten she wore little else but paint and a loincloth. Most cultures didn't have a fully-clothed policy the way her homeland did. It wasn't uncommon to go topless.

Was Ian a prude?

His gaze never left her face.

Come to think of it, when she'd opened the door to him earlier, there had been a sudden leap of something in his eyes, something base and hot. His jaded exterior had quickly masked that.

Once or twice it had seemed his gaze drifted downward, but he quickly raised his eyes right back up to meet hers. Or he looked at her high ceiling. Or her statues.

This was something telling. Ian Cole wanted to avoid looking at her body. Now this was good to know.

Maybe he did share that erotic picture his words had conjured up in her mind.

IAN KNEW HE WAS IN TROUBLE the moment her eyes turned assessing. Damn it, he was usually much better at hiding his naked interest in a woman. But then, that was the problem. Ava stood before him basically naked. His body liked it. He liked it.

He watched as Ava glanced at her paint-covered body. Some of it erotically smudged right now. She tilted her head and he made eye contact with the brilliant green of her eyes.

Keep looking up, buddy.

"Why?" she asked, her voice not sounding confused or innocent. Just curious.

Why what? He'd forgotten what they were talking about. And he had a sneaking suspicion he was the one who'd started this particular vein of conversation. "Uh…"

Trying to get her into bed while they worked on the book was a bad idea. If he had to work without sleep to get this book written quickly, that would just have to be the price he paid. Hell, he'd go without food, too.

Had he just decided to sleep with Ava Simms? When had he decided that?

About two seconds after spotting her.

That was a bad idea. Really bad. He'd list the multitude of reasons right now. Except none really came to mind at the moment because a nearly naked, gorgeous woman stood before him. How was a man supposed to work in these conditions?

This woman must be covered as soon as possible. Cover. That was it. That's what he asked about. "Don't you want to put something on?"

She shrugged again. "Not really. And this way I can show you some of the pattern work."

It had been his experience that most women had at least one body part they felt self-conscious about. He wouldn't have complained if his former girlfriends had wanted to parade around in next to nothing. It's just that they hadn't. In fact, he'd seen them go to Herculean efforts to cover their thighs with a sheet, or hips with a towel.

It was all ridiculous. Women were beautiful. The key was to find that one part they hated, and then issue compliments. It never failed.

But this woman seemed to have no problem parading around in barely anything.

She lightly touched a rounded circle of blue on her arm. "You see, the woman begins by painting the color blue on her body. This represents the sky and water. Sky and water play a large role in the lore of many cultures around the world."

He nodded, his gaze shifting from her face to her

arm. *Don't look to the right.* Although he already knew what he'd see. Her beautiful breasts painted yellow.

"Now did that bother you? That insertion of a little history?"

Not a bit. He shook his head as his mouth watered.

"That's the approach I think we should take." Ava trailed her fingers along the green lines crisscrossing on her thighs. "The green represents the earth. New and unknown. Ready to be explored."

He grew harder as she touched and stroked her skin. His fingers ached to do the same. To trace the green lines, to smudge the blue paint on her body.

"Yellow is the past. The Wayterian people don't place value on virginity, so a woman may have had several lovers. Do you?"

"Do I what?" he asked, suddenly feeling as if he'd been jerked out of a sex fantasy.

"Place value on virginity?"

"I'm not one if that's what you're asking."

A smile curved along her lips. "Good. I wouldn't want you cowering in the corner."

She was laughing at him.

Toying with him, in fact. He should be irritated. Instead he found himself turned on more. Well, two could play that game. He deliberately lowered his eyes to her yellow-painted breasts. "That's a very bright color."

"The Wayterian women coat the yellow paint on their breasts. Once the new husband and wife are alone, she takes his hands and places them on her breasts."

Her nipples hardened before his eyes. She might be toying with him to get a reaction, but she wasn't immune to him, either.

"The paint never completely dries, so some of the color gets on him, as well. Together they wash the paint, the past, away. They become one, joined by sky, water and earth."

Ian closed his eyes for a moment, imagining washing the paint off this woman's body. And Ava washing the color from his skin. Erotic and charged. It was perfect for the book.

"I think this ceremony is beautiful." Her voice lost its challenging playfulness of earlier. "I'm always moved by the meaning behind the acts."

And surprisingly, he was, too.

She swallowed, and took a step away from him. "Well, since you're familiar with this particular rite now, I'll just hop into the shower and remove the paint. I won't be long and then we can get started."

Ian raised his hand, not bothering to hide the look of disbelief he was sure was on his face. "Wait a minute. Are you about to go and take a shower leaving a man you've known about ten minutes alone in your apartment?"

For the first time since she'd opened the door, Ava looked unsure. She shifted her balance, and crossed her arms. "I, uh, guess that I was."

"Lady, you've been out in the wild too long. You can't be so trusting."

She shrugged her shoulders. "You're Miriam's brother. It's not like she'd send a serial killer. It will only take me a few minutes."

He couldn't picture sitting calmly on her couch waiting while she showered. Imagining her naked. And wet. He almost groaned.

No. Not going to happen. He had to get out of there. "I'll check in to the hotel while you're getting ready. I'm going to grab a bite to eat. The sandwich on the plane could pass for a hockey puck."

"Oh, I'm getting hungry, too. Why don't we meet at one of the restaurants down on the canal for a late lunch? You up for Mexican?"

He was up for anything about now. "Sounds good." Ava turned on her heel, and once again he got a view of her great ass. "I'll pick you up from here."

She stopped and glanced at him over her shoulder. "Is this about the shower thing? Don't worry, I don't need an escort to keep me safe. Besides, you looked pretty trustworthy to me."

Trustworthy. *Trustworthy?* No one had ever accused him of being trustworthy before. Like a teddy bear. Or a cute puppy. That was almost insulting. Ian straightened his shoulders. He was dangerous. A man of the world. Wanted by the law in three countries. At least. He was *not* a teddy bear.

He'd put an end to that. "Let me know if you need some help with the second part of the ritual," he said.

"The second part?" she asked.

"The washing off."

Her full bottom lip curled upward, and a naughty twinkle appeared in her eyes. "I'll let you know," she told him.

Now why did that come out sounding like a promise?

CHAPTER FOUR

WHILE THE WATER FOR THE shower heated, Ava quickly typed in the website for Cole Publishing. She punched his name in the search fields.

"Bingo." Over thirty results popped up on her screen. She selected the one at the top, and her screen immediately filled with his image. Obviously the picture on his bio page must have been taken a few years ago. In the photo, he had a friendly smile and the look of someone ready to tackle the world.

Much how she'd felt five seconds before she opened the door to him.

Now Ian wore that world-weary air. The stress lines around his mouth were deeper now than the laugh lines around his eyes. She'd seen his type in the airport. They huddled around their gates, ready to hit the next political hot spot.

She headed anyplace but there.

A puff of steam enticed her into the bathroom. Tugging off her loincloth, Ava stepped beneath the spray.

The warm water glided around her body, smearing the paint further. The yellows and blues fused together, turning green and pooling at her feet before sliding down the drain. Long, hot showers. Steam and heat and the scent of honeysuckle. Now this was something she had missed.

Ava reached for the soap and bubbled up a rich lather.

Although the paint was easy to smear, it wasn't the easiest to remove from her skin.

Of course Ian had offered to help. She smiled again, thinking how his brown eyes had turned darker when he'd made the invitation. Ava had seen the desire in his direct gaze. He hadn't tried to mask it. She liked that about him.

A direct man voiced exactly what he wanted. Sought to fulfill his woman's desires. She would have hated to take suggestions on her book from a man who couldn't handle the naturalness of sex. Afraid of his own desires.

And of hers.

There'd been sex in his eyes. Sex on his mind. Despite the warmth of the water, her nipples hardened as she remembered that brown-eyed gaze of his sliding down her body.

When had sex come into play? She wondered as she reached for a bright yellow sponge. When did sex *not* come into play between a man and a woman? Despite Ian's obvious assumption that she was a bit on the naive side, she'd studied gender differences enough to know that one thing shared by both men and women was a charged curiosity whenever they were in each other's presence. A curiosity about nakedness. Would he groan? Would she scream?

It all happened within the first five seconds of meeting someone new, the mind and body put that person into three categories. Yes, no and maybe.

And right now her body was thinking yes. What would sex with Ian be like? Sex had been in Ian's eyes, which placed Ava in his hell-yes category.

If they were going to collaborate, attraction between them probably wasn't the best situation. Far off the mark from professionalism. But then, who was she to shy away from sexual attraction?

Come to think of it, sexual tension and desire between the two of them might be a good thing. Heat might translate onto the pages, into their very writing. Craving the carnal would implicitly lace their words with an intense hunger for sex.

A shiver raced down her spine. Now *this* was something that would sell. She should go for it. Why not suffer for her art?

Anxious to get to work, she sudsed her arms and legs, the water and bubbles turning her already sensitive skin into taut nerves waiting to be touched. Caressed. Her skin tingled.

She reached for the soft washcloth, and twisted out the excess water. Ava stroked the cloth against her breasts, wiping away the more stubborn yellow paint. As she rubbed the cloth against her nipple, the skin along her neck and her breasts turned bumpy and sensitive. Tingles from her nipples shot downward.

She washed her other breast, then slowly trailed the cloth down along her rib cage, around her navel. The material felt rougher now against the heightened sensitivity of her flesh. She imagined Ian's work-roughened hands on her. Imagined him caressing her the same way as the washcloth.

A bit of the cloth tickled the skin of her inner thigh and she sucked in a breath. Steam surrounded her, a light caress against her body. The humid air inside the shower filled her lungs and she leaned against the tile wall for support.

The water ran between her legs, and she followed the trail with the washcloth. She clamped her eyes shut when the cloth grazed her clitoris. Delicious sensations quivered along every nerve. She stroked herself and moaned.

Some ancients believed a couple learned to please their mate only after watching them pleasure themselves. She imagined Ian outside her shower door, watching her touch herself. Becoming aroused.

Then she imagined him joining her in the shower, imagined herself watching him take his cock in his hand. Seeing it grow harder and bigger as he stroked himself, showing her how he liked to be touched. How he wanted her to touch him.

She pressed against her clit, her body growing tense. She gasped and her muscles tightened.

No.

If she brought her own release now, some of the tension and heat that zinged between them wouldn't be as strong. She wanted her pleasure to be on the edge, near the top. Not satiated.

An old woman she'd met in Australia once had told her the greatest aphrodisiac for a man was a woman's arousal. Maybe now she would put that woman's theory to the test. Might make an interesting chapter for the book. Goose bumps rose on her skin as the spray massaged every muscle. She'd definitely suffer for that chapter.

With her body still humming, she quickly finished her shower.

IT DIDN'T TAKE IAN LONG to check in to the Bricktown Hotel; a chain hotel that catered to businesspeople, where the staff was usually friendly and efficient. Since his laptop battery was dead, he plugged the computer in first thing. This hotel promised to be the "most wired hotel in Oklahoma City." Most hotel claims were wrong, but he needed this one to be right.

He was used to traveling light. He'd packed for a week, but figured that would be more than enough time to get this book on track.

If Ava Simms didn't kill him. Some women shouldn't be allowed out of the house. She definitely needed a warning label. Loss of blood to the brain.

Crossing to the sink, he turned on the taps. He splashed water onto his face, washing away the travel grime. Ava would be in the shower now. Naked and wet. No matter how good-looking a woman was, she always looked just a little bit better wet.

He imagined Ava wet and nude under the spray of the shower.

With a groan, he wiped his face with a towel. Glancing at his watch he saw he still had about fifteen minutes to kill. His cell phone rang, and he pulled it from his waist to check at the caller ID. His sister. Good. He was in a mood to harass her over this assignment.

"Did you meet the doc?" she asked.

"Two days. I'm giving this two days, then I'm out of hell."

"I have every faith in you."

OVER THE YEARS, HER brother had been shoved into filthy, rat-infested prisons, slopped around in some of the world's most disease-ridden swamps and suffered weather hardships and clean-water deprivation of the likes she could only imagine. All to get the story.

And yet *this* assignment was the one he compared to hell. She almost laughed.

Miriam fingered the glass paperweight on her desk. She should feel guilty about sending her brother someplace she knew he'd hate. She should, but she was in full self-preservation mode.

Her brother's vehemence had been surprising. She'd dwell on it if another pink message slip hadn't appeared under the paperweight. Miriam wadded the paper up into a tight ball and aimed it toward her trash can. She missed by a good six inches.

Her aim was going the same way as her judgment. She was making a poor business decision and that wasn't like her. Things *would* have been smoother if she'd gone to Oklahoma with Ian. That was her element. What she did. Some people could cook. Some could write. *She* could multitask.

Miriam was a whiz at juggling millions of details, all while keeping overblown egos and hurt feelings to a minimum. Nothing was ever personal and people left her office with a smile even if they came away with less than their asking price.

A few days with the doc and her brother and this book would be complete and ready to go into production and she'd be making more money for the company. So why not?

Jeremy.

If she went back to Oklahoma, she would surely contact him.

On the one hand, that wouldn't be such a bad thing. Who couldn't handle six or seven times a night?

Her nipples hardened and her skin tingled under her clothes. What was she mulling over a moment ago? The book she'd risked her reputation and quite a bit of money on. That book.

This was why six or seven times a night would be bad. She'd get nothing done. Her skin grew hot. She felt uncomfortable. *No.* Not uncomfortable…irritated.

She'd think of it as irritated and chafed. In fact, that's exactly what she should be doing. Word association when thoughts of Jeremy popped into her mind. All of them bad.

Those gorgeous blue eyes of his. Same color as the first car that ever side-swiped her.

Those long showers together. Dry skin.

Seven or eight times a night? Bladder infection.

Miriam slumped in her chair and scanned her office walls. Here was her family history, the legacy she was now in charge of safeguarding. Rows of framed magazine covers lined each wall. Some black and white, others in bold color. Through war, the baby boom, flower power, disco to iPod, Coles had guided the company sensibly and competently.

And not a single Cole had ever blown it over a romance. Although her dad had come close when he'd married her mom. Miriam had always thought herself more like her grandfather. Now it was clear she'd inherited her father's self-destructive romantic habits. Obviously embraced them because she couldn't get that man out of her mind.

Her glance hit upon one of the covers. Woman in a business suit, power bun with the buttons on her silk blouse undone to reveal a sexy red bra.

Is All Work and No Play Making Jane a Dull Girl?

She reread the caption once more. Her shoulders relaxed and a smile slowly started to spread across her lips. It was strange how often something on one of these covers would trigger an emotion or a decision.

Yes. She had become a very dull girl. Miriam had been nothing but work for a very long time. When was the last time she'd gone out? How many times had she turned down her friends' invitations to hit the town?

When was the last time *she'd* been inclined to wear a sexy red bra?

What was wrong with her? She lived in the town that never slept. And she'd been in most nights by nine. She needed to get out. Meet new and interesting men. Laugh, dance. Of course, seven or eight times seemed great when you hadn't gotten any in seven or eight months.

This had nothing to do with Jeremy at all. She picked up her cell phone to call Jenna. That speed-dial setting hadn't been used in ages.

Except Rich buzzed in over the intercom.

"Ms. Cole, there's someone here to see you."

She scanned the schedule Rich placed on her desk every morning. She didn't have any appointments. Rich would know not to announce a drop-in. Something was odd.

"It's a Mr. Kelso."

Miriam could tell by Rich's tone that this name was supposed to mean something to her. It didn't.

"A Mr. *Jeremy* Kelso."

Miriam clicked her phone closed.

CHAPTER FIVE

IAN GRIMACED. HE STUDIED his hotel room. Already he had done all he needed to do. And still he felt restless.

So what else was new? Seems he'd battled restlessness for as long as he remembered. Why stay in the same place when something else beckoned around the corner? Hell on relationships.

But then, he wasn't much of a relationship kind of guy.

So then why did the doc get to him?

She was just another woman. Same as any woman from any other part of the world. Granted her parts were naked and covered with paint…but still.

Ian paced toward his window. He needed outside. He needed the sun on his head and a breeze against his face. Sixth-story windows in hotels did not cut it. He pushed himself away from the glass. He'd walk back to Ava's apartment, and skip all elevators. That should burn off some energy.

Like Ava's place, the hotel faced the winding canal of downtown Oklahoma City, and so the walk to meet her wouldn't take long.

He hiked down the stairs and emerged into the sunlight, giving in to the restlessness. The canal waters rippled bluish-green a few feet away from him. Trees and flowers flanked the stonework path beside the water. He weaved among the mothers pushing strollers who seemed to be the predominant occupants of the walk during the middle of the day.

Old warehouses being turned into stunning homes had renewed many an old downtown area suffering from urban blight. Oklahoma City obviously reaped the same benefits. Restaurants bracketed the walk, so he suspected couples would be replacing the moms and joggers once the dinner hour arrived.

A bright yellow boat floated below him, passengers waving to the pedestrians. They waved back. His lips twisted. Flyover country. People didn't wave to one another in the places he'd been.

He found Ava waiting for him outside the entrance to her building.

A blonde.

Ava was a blonde. He hadn't been able to tell earlier. All the paint was gone, and her hair was still damp from her shower. Natural highlights from the sun streaked her hair. He'd never gone for blondes before, preferring the dark and exotic over the coolness of many fair-haired women. And those green eyes of hers were anything but cool.

He felt anything but cool around Ava. She smiled and came toward him, and his eyes were immediately drawn to her body. His normal life felt a world away from the utter temptation that was this woman. His days and nights were filled with the exciting challenges of chasing down people who did not want to be found, rough terrain and hanging out with guys who smelled like something rotten.

So on the blessed, and lately, more rare occasions when he was with a woman, he wanted soft curves, sweet scents and her dressed in pure glamour. When they weren't naked, that is.

None of that remotely described Ava. Oh, he liked her curves, but there was nothing sweet about this woman. And nothing wrong with the casual jeans and animal-print top she wore.

She hadn't bothered to put on any makeup, and he liked her natural like this. A light layer of freckles dusted her nose and cheeks. Like him, Ava was apparently a woman who'd spent some time in the sun.

She also smelled like cinnamon.

And he loved the smell of cinnamon.

"I found the Mexican place on my way over here. You ready?" he asked her. Ready to get back on the move. Bad things always happened when you stayed in one place.

Ava nodded. "At night they cook their tortilla chips, and I can smell it for hours in my apartment. Sometimes I wake up craving Mexican food, and I didn't even do that when I lived there."

"Then what are we waiting for? Let's go." He adjusted his larger steps to hers. Her head just reached his shoulders. The scent of cinnamon surrounded him once more.

"How'd you wind up in Oklahoma?" he asked, digging up a way to get his mind off the smell of her hair. He was a reporter. He asked questions.

"My grandparents live here. In fact, that was their building. I wouldn't have been able to afford this many square feet. My parents were always moving us from one place to another, but we'd always spend our holidays in Oklahoma. It seemed natural to set up a home base here when I returned from overseas."

"Was that often?" he asked. Talk. Talk was good. It took his mind off wondering what she wore under her shirt. Wondering whether she preferred animal print in all the clothes that touched her skin...

Hell, it'd been a while since he'd been with a woman, but usually he could go longer than ten seconds before imagining her naked.

"From my earliest memories. The longest I can remember staying anywhere was two years. It feels kind of weird to be opening boxes instead of packing them. Some of these things I haven't seen in years."

Her apartment had been filled with statues, masks and pictures. It didn't feel like a home base to him. A home base was more like his apartment, a place to sleep and watch football until the next assignment put you in harm's way. There was nothing permanent about a home base, and Ava's apartment felt very permanent.

"Were your parents anthropologists like you?" He did not need to know this. Knowing her background wasn't important for the writing of this book. He'd only meant to talk, to pass the time, to distract himself. But he found himself curious about her answers. He'd met a lot of different people during his travels. Why did he care?

A smile touched her lips, and she laughed softly. He liked the sound of her laugh. "I'm not laughing at you. It's just that it isn't very often people don't know who my parents are, but then, I'm mainly hanging out with a bunch of academics. My parents, Carol and Alex Simms, uncovered a temple to Isis in ancient Greece and set the archaeology world on its ear."

"Oh, really? And how would one do that exactly?" During his flight to meet Ava, he couldn't have imagined anything more boring than having a conversation about archaeology. Now he was intrigued.

"One would do that by saying that that temple proved

the ancient Greeks patterned their gods and goddesses on those of the Egyptians, in the same way that the Romans took over the Greek gods and goddesses. It's not even too far a stretch to get from Horus to Zeus."

He whistled. "Wow, pretty radical."

"And pretty controversial."

"So why anthropology?" There was the curiosity again. He didn't need to know anything personal about her to make this book work.

"It wasn't too far a stretch. Apparently, wanting to uncover something is in the genes I inherited from them. But on the digs, I was always more interested in the people who'd evolved from the particular culture my parents were studying. How many of the same practices they kept, and which they didn't. That kind of thing."

They rounded another corner and found themselves standing in front of the Mexican restaurant. A hostess quickly took them to a balcony table overlooking the canal water.

Ian cut a glance in her direction as she silently perused her menu. His reporter instincts reappeared. There was something interesting here about the doc. Ava had a degree most people only used for teaching. Also, she wasn't out in the field—another possibility with her degree. And she hadn't followed in the family tradition.

Forget about her. Write the book, then move on.

"What do your parents think of you writing this book?" he found himself asking. *Subtle, you jerk.*

She lifted an eyebrow. "The sex research? Well, as they, too, were researchers, sex was pretty much part of the dinnertime conversation with my parents."

Sex *never* figured into his family's dinnertime conversation.

"Just look around a Roman coliseum or inside a pyramid, and you'll see sex everywhere. Both Mom and Dad were very matter-of-fact about it."

That explained a lot. Ava could talk about sex the way some people talked about their laundry. And yet, her voice took a husky dip when she said the word *sex*. Maybe prancing around nearly naked in front of him had affected her, as well. Now *this* was starting to go somewhere.

"You're not answering the question. Do they like what you're doing?"

Her eyes met his, and she pushed a strand of her drying blond hair behind her ear. "They hate it. They think I'll never be taken seriously in the academic field."

"You're writing a book."

"A pop-fiction book. That's like intellectual prostitution in their opinion. Oh, don't get me wrong, they're not snobs, they're just…"

"Academics?" he suggested.

Ava nodded, and that lock of hair fell forward again from behind her ear. He itched to touch the strands. To let them fall through his fingers. "They don't think anyone will ever take my research seriously after this."

"Will they?" he asked, and wondered why he'd be concerned about that. Cole Publishing was in the business of making money, and although he wasn't sure about it on the plane, he knew they could make a lot with this book…with the proper execution.

"Probably not," she said, her tone rueful. "But then, no one has really taken my work seriously. More like facts to parade out at Valentine's Day. Colleges prefer professors who get published in professional journals, and bring in grant money. Groundbreaking—not titillation."

If they didn't take her seriously before, they certainly

wouldn't now. Maybe he should give her one last warning. He'd hate for her to regret writing the book. The enthusiasm had faded from her voice, and a line formed on her forehead.

Then her face brightened and she stunned him with a beautiful smile. His pulse quickened. "Screw 'em. That's why I'm doing the book."

"Beat them at their own game." He liked that about her. He was beginning to like a lot of things about her.

"So why call the book *Recipe for Sex?* That title is all wrong, by the way. I'll brainstorm a list tonight, and give you a heads-up in the morning."

"Why don't I brainstorm a list and give you the heads-up in the morning?"

His lips twisted for a moment, then he grinned. "Going to be like this, is it? Fight me every step of the way?"

"As the writer, I should make the final decisions."

He raised an eyebrow. "I was brought in to fix some of those decisions."

"And I'll take your suggestions under advisement," she told him.

Ian laughed. "Glad to hear it," he said in the tone of a man confident he'd get his way. "The title still won't work. It sounds like a cookbook."

"Well, originally I thought I'd just include the foods that put couples, and particularly men, in the mood."

"Why men?" he asked.

"It's been my experience, and I can document this with culture after culture, that men don't often use food in their seduction."

Now wait a minute, he made a mean lasagna. He'd be happy to make it for her. And if they managed to get a little messy and needed to clean up together...so be it.

"I can see by your face you don't agree. In cultures where couples routinely push back marriage and family, then yes, the male will cook. In fact, most men have one 'signature' dish they believe is the ultimate key to the hookup."

Ian cleared his throat. Okay, he made other things besides lasagna. "That's ridiculous."

She smiled then nodded. "Research only gives us generalities. Individuals can always surprise you. One thing that is a fact is a man's sense of smell. It's very powerful. A potent scent can stimulate blood flow to the extremities, including the penis, and can evoke all sorts of feelings."

"In the book, we'll use another word other than *feelings* for the male readers."

"You know, straying from gentler emotions isn't universal among men."

"It will be for the men we're trying to sell this book to." And if he had to hear the word *penis* from her lips again, he'd have to resort to phoning this book in.

Change the subject. "Let's get back to this smell thing. Why is it women are always wanting to smell flowers? I could care less."

"Because that's the wrong smell for a man. Believe it or not, the scents more attractive to men are food-related. There's something to be said for that old saying about the way to a man's heart is through his stomach. Pumpkin, for instance, elicits very strong responses from men. And the smell of doughnuts."

"We can keep a running list of places for women to meet men. The pumpkin patch. The doughnut shop."

"I can see you're not taking this seriously. Let me do a demonstration." She signaled the waitress. "Can we have some of those churros, please?"

If the waitress thought it strange Ava was asking for dessert before they'd even been served their entrées, she didn't show it.

Ava returned her attention to him. "Have you eaten one of these? They're delicious. Sugar and cinnamon. Mmm."

The way she said *mmm* with such a level of carnal enjoyment made his stomach clench.

A moment later the waitress dropped off a platter of churros, as well as a basket of chips, salsa and queso.

"Cinnamon is another scent men respond to on a primal level. Plus the food has the added bonus of being somewhat phallic." Her voice had turned husky, as if her very words aroused her.

She cleared her throat, her green eyes never leaving his.

"I think it's most effective when a woman teases her face with the food a bit, running it along her chin. Her lips. Makes men think of a woman running her lips along his—"

Her words didn't drift off. He cut them off in his mind. He knew exactly what seeing a woman with something like a churro, seeing Ava do with that churro, made him think. It made him think of her lips on his erection.

"The key is to keep the man in a steady state of semi-arousal at all times."

Semiarousal? He'd just gone from zero to performance status in about half a second.

She dropped the churro onto the platter. "You see? Food is one very important ingredient for sex. You show me a man whose mind doesn't immediately turn to a blow job at the sight of a woman eating a banana or carrot—I'll show you a man whose balls haven't dropped yet."

Or one who wasn't into women. He turned to face Ava, whose expression was teasing. "Okay, you have a point," he admitted, speaking around the lump in his throat.

She smiled, bit off the tip of the churro with gusto, then tipped it his way. "Bite?"

"No, thank you."

The scent of cinnamon drifted back to him. Was that the food or the woman? And more importantly, was she wearing it on purpose?

"Food-sharing is also very erotic. The significance more than likely dates back to when humans were in survival mode. To share your food literally meant to share your life. Now, eating from your lover's hand reveals an innate trust. All this academic talk, I'm not boring you am I?"

Hell, no. If the classes he'd taken in college had been half this interesting, he might have stayed to finish his degree. He shook his head.

"Good. Do you like churros, Ian?" her voice husky again and full of playful invitation.

He nodded.

Once more, she tipped the food in his direction. "See how sexy, almost carnal it can be to eat from my hand? It's especially effective if you've never kissed your partner."

She used the food to trace his bottom lip. He couldn't breathe. He couldn't do a thing.

"To have your lips touch where just moments ago hers had been. Her tongue, her saliva…it's like sharing a passionate kiss. A prelude of more to come."

He bit down on the food, tasting the sweetness. Tasting her. Satisfaction was light in the greenness of her eyes. And he felt as if he'd just bitten off more than he could chew....

CHAPTER SIX

KELSO. SO JEREMY HAD a last name. The Jeremy who should be in Oklahoma but was now apparently in her outer lobby. Miriam cleared her throat.

"Thanks, Rich. Give me about five minutes then send him in."

Miriam stood and smoothed the wrinkles from her skirt. Ahh, if only smoothing out the wrinkles of her life could be so easy. She was avoiding this person. Had done an admirable job of keeping him from her mind. Mostly. Why'd he have to show up?

The covers on her wall mocked her.

The Mistake You'll Always Regret

Forget Your Forbidden Fruit

Are You Replacing His Mother?

Miriam scowled at that last cover. Okay, she was being ridiculous. None of those headlines even had anything to do with dating younger men. There was no reason to panic. She was a grown woman, had responsibilities and lived up to her commitments.

So she'd had a one-night stand.

So her one-night stand had decided to show up unannounced. She could handle this. Handle it with style and grace and confidently explain to Jeremy that the one-night man did not linger.

Long-distance relationship?

Shoot. Why'd her mind have to wander in that direction?

There were rules about long-distance relationships and she'd made sure of it. She flipped to the review copy of the article she'd recommended for *The Rage*. The sidebar had a few "quick-read" suggestions.

Loving Your Long Distance and Keeping It that Way
1. Don't look for them to last.

Okay, really no problem there.

2. Make frequent-flier miles your best friend.

She had some just itching to be used.

3. Communicate clear expectations.

Obviously she'd already failed in that area, otherwise there wouldn't be a twentysomething man waiting for her in the outer lobby.

4. Be especially creative.

Actually, she and her twentysomething lover already had that down.

5. Remember—the odds are not in your favor.

Yes, but when had they been?
All excellent points of policy.

There was a brief knock on the door, and then Rich efficiently ushered Jeremy into her office, quickly closing the door behind him. And there he was. Jeremy of the now-known last name. Jeremy Kelso, who could rock her world eight times in a night.

Her breath hitched, and her hands grew clammy. She was disgusted with herself. Miriam Cole was about to fall into the worst cliché, and she allowed herself to be mentally sucked back into the past.

Suddenly, she was on that nearly deserted, dusty-red highway in Oklahoma. Hot, tired and stranded. An old, beat-up truck had pulled up beside her.

For a moment she felt only sweet relief. She wouldn't die out in the middle of nowhere. Then every article in her magazine ever written about women alone and out in the middle of nowhere flashed through her mind. A car, let alone a pickup truck, happening upon her was far worse than being out here by herself.

"Need some help?" asked the lone occupant after he slowed to a stop.

Miriam flashed him what she knew worked on the dating scene as the polite brush-off smile. "No, no. I'm fine."

The man leaned across the seat, but his face was still hidden in the shadows. "I could give you a lift into town if you need it."

Get into the car of a complete stranger? What did she look like, an idiot? *This* was exactly how people got abducted. Killed.

"Thanks, but no," she told him firmly as she reached for her phone. Cell phones were excellent man-conversation blockers in the dating world. Surely it would serve the same function now.

"Oh, that won't work here. The mountains stop the signal."

Miriam turned away from the stranger and took a

breath. Her ruse hadn't worked. She wasn't in her element here in the middle of nowhere. In Manhattan she knew how to take care of herself. But here she had no Mace and no cell phone. She felt practically helpless.

"Look, you're clearly in trouble. Hop in and I'll take you into town."

Miriam didn't hop into trucks. She glided elegantly into cars. With sophistication and great shoes. She took another deep breath and faced her would-be rescuer or killer. "How far is it into town?"

"About five miles."

She sighed in relief. She jogged two miles in the park every day. "I can walk. Thanks again," she said, clearly a signal to the driver that his help wasn't needed and he could move on.

"Have a nice day," he offered, moved back in front of the wheel and put the truck in gear. He drove away with a kickup of dust.

Miriam slumped against her car. Okay, so probably he wasn't a serial killer or anything bad, but that didn't mean a woman should be reckless with her safety. So she waited another five minutes then headed down the road, and vowed never to rent a car and trek in unfamiliar territory again.

Fifteen minutes into her journey, she spotted the truck a second time. Coming back toward her. Her stomach clenched and her legs tightened. There could be no reason for him to be back out here.

The driver was on her side and she could clearly see him. He'd pulled right up beside her on the wrong side of the road, and she glanced in his direction. In a bar, in a boardroom, she wouldn't have hesitated to give him her number. Dark hair, beautiful eyes...delicious smile. This was even more dangerous. She quickened her pace.

"I understand you not wanting to get into the car with a stranger, but I don't feel right about you walking into town by yourself. So I'll just follow along behind you."

She stopped and stared at him. "Let me get this straight. You're going to follow me into town…just to make sure I get there safe?"

With a nod, he did a three-point turn in the middle of the road and drove slowly behind her as she indeed walked all the way to town.

Her car had bailed on her. She'd been stranded and left without any way to contact the outside world…and yet Miriam had never felt safer.

And now, here in her office, Jeremy Kelso smiled at her. That same smile that had won her over in the garage as she waited for her rental to be towed into town. That same smile that made her open up and talk with him over dinner. That same smile that made naughty promises that his body kept all through the night.

Suddenly, she didn't feel so safe anymore.

MOST OF IAN'S MEALS were caught on the road or out in the field. He lived on beef jerky and cold cans of lima beans. So, when he had the opportunity to sit down and enjoy a well-prepared meal he enjoyed it to the fullest.

Mendoza's had the kind of casual atmosphere that instantly made him relax. From the brightly colored wooden chairs with straw seats to the scent of freshly made flour tortillas in the air, he suddenly missed his time spent south of the border. He'd loved it all. The bustle of Mexico City. The warm, tropical breezes off the coast.

Ian sat straighter in his chair. Maybe that importance-of-food-to-men stuff Ava was talking about wasn't half-baked, because despite being in a constant state of sexual frustration since she'd stroked that churro around her mouth, he was having a great time.

She sat across from him, animated and energized, discussing all the people she'd met. Her blond hair, now dry, moved around her face as she spoke. The meal was leisurely and he was glad she continued to chat about her experiences once their food arrived.

Like him, Ava had traveled all over the world, but her stories seemed far more interesting than his. His natural reporter's instincts were to keep her talking. And the heat he'd felt since she'd opened that door to him wearing paint and a smile finally simmered down to a low burn.

"I think the scarf dance is one of my favorites. The woman spends hours circling her body with the material."

He'd probably never get this story out of his head. His travels hadn't taken him to places where women adorned themselves only with scarves. But instead of some faceless, nameless woman covered solely in ribbons, he pictured only the woman sitting across from him.

Ava's green eyes darkened. "Then she slowly unwinds each scarf from her body and binds her new husband's body with the material. His arms above his head. His legs together at the ankles, knee and thighs."

The scarf-removal thing he could get into…being tied up by a woman…not so much.

Ava smiled. "I can see you don't think much of the ceremony. But the Urmanian men were fierce warriors, often scarred from battle. A young bride might be frightened of her new husband and afraid of what was to happen between them. Most of these marriages were arranged between families, and the bride probably had never seen her new husband before their wedding ceremony."

"So wouldn't stripping in front of a man you've never met be scary?"

"Well, the girls practice the ceremony for many months, so that takes away any performance nerves. Plus, the whole point of the binding is to make the new bride comfortable. There's something very sensual about a big, strong man, a man who could easily overpower you, and bend you to his will…"

Her words drifted off, and she sucked on her lower lip. Was that a tell? He hadn't spotted one glitch in this woman's "sex is sex" facade. Her full lips were parted, and there was a faraway look in her eyes.

Was the woman who had greeted him half-naked and covered in paint, the woman who could converse about sex, phallic symbols and smells that broke a man's will…did the idea of tying a man up make her pause? His stomach clenched as he waited to hear what she'd say. He might just be willing to consider letting her tie him up if he got to see her in that loincloth and paint again.

"Anyway, it's heady thinking about him allowing you to tie him up. Explore his body. Learn the power your body can have over his," she told him, her voice lower and reminding him of a warm wave washing over his skin.

That simmer he'd been operating under turned to boiling once more. He shifted in his seat, trying to relieve some of the pressure in his jeans.

Did she do it on purpose? Turn him on like that?

The sensual softening of her eyes disappeared and she shrugged, returning her attention to her food.

Ian scrutinized Ava as she spread guacamole onto a flat tortilla. She looked innocent enough, but she had to know. Had to know that her words made him think of her slowly taking off her clothes in front of him. Letting her bind him. Feeling her stroke him.

"The binding is an ancient art that's quite beautiful. I think it would make for some great visuals for the book," she said, her tone all business now. "It's interesting how beliefs manifest themselves. The Urmanian culture did not believe a strong, healthy baby could come from unions where the woman did not enjoy sex. The man wanted his wife to feel only pleasure in the marriage bed."

Hell, what man didn't want to see a woman feel pleasure? There was never a sight as sexy as seeing a woman come.

She pointed her fork at him. "In fact, there is some research that suggests when a woman has an orgasm she conceives more easily."

This had to be, without a doubt, the weirdest conversation he'd ever had. He'd usually bolt at the first hint of the word *conception.*

Ava speared a bite of seared pepper from the fajita skillet onto her fork. "Red and green chilies are great for sex."

Was he going to jerk every time the professor said the word *sex?*

"The chilies get your circulation going. I was thinking we could include recipes that had a lot of aphrodisiacal properties. There are several that don't have long accompanying stories, but would be fun to include."

Yeah, he'd like to hear what this woman's idea of fun was. "Like what?" he asked.

"Celery. Good for all your muscles. Did you know that the ancient Tragrils actually devoted celery to their god of sex and of hell?"

He felt the irony.

"Sex is all around us, has been from the very beginnings of culture." Ava shrugged. "You could probably point at anything in this restaurant and we can relate it somehow to sex."

This he'd like to see. "How about that guacamole you've devoured?" he suggested, indicating the now-empty serving dish.

Ava sat back against her chair as if in thought. "Guacamole is made from avocados. Which is also the Aztec word for a certain part of the male anatomy."

"This restaurant."

"Sometimes in Mexico, a rope is placed around the neck of the bride and groom. Physical binding of a newly married couple is quite common in many cultures."

He was kind of liking this naughtier version of the six-degrees-of-separation game. Ava was right—she didn't have to go too far for her examples. Ian picked up his knife to cut off another bite of enchilada.

"This knife," he suggested.

"Oh, that's easy. In Nordic history, when a father had a marriageable daughter, he'd place an empty knife sheath on her belt or around her waist. Interested suitors would place their knife in the empty case. That evokes all kinds of images, doesn't it?"

It certainly did. Ian leaned forward. "How about you, Dr. Simms?"

A tiny smile tugged at her top lip. "Women with

Ph.D.s are twice as likely to have a one-night stand as those with a B.A."

Which made him wonder about *Doctor* Simms.

That's when it hit him. The humor, the passion, the respect she had for all these people she'd met and cultures she'd studied…none of that was in her book. It was dry and dull.

Which she clearly was not.

Her passion, her personality, Ava…that's what would sell this book. Every word, every image had to evoke the enthusiasm and excitement and utter zest that was Ava.

This wasn't going to be just reviewing her notes and taking a few pictures…he'd need to spend real time with her. Earlier he couldn't wait to get out of this assignment. He'd been restless to set off again, to do his own story, live life on the edge as he wanted.

But now something was different. That edgy impatient restlessness led him to Ava, which led him to wanting to stay. And that was the first thing that had ever scared him.

CHAPTER SEVEN

IAN PAID FOR DINNER. It had been a struggle knowing what to do. He'd run across some women in the past who'd felt it was insulting for a man to pay for their meal. Unlike his mother, who'd raised him to believe men paid for everything. That, in fact, *all* men should pay.

Ava just seemed to be clueless about what to do when the check arrived. Something he found oddly… endearing. She nodded to herself when he placed his credit card on the bill, as if mentally making notes of his actions.

Now they were walking back to her warehouse apartment. The foot traffic along the canal had increased so their pace slowed. He wasn't much for leisurely strolls, but Ava was definitely the kind who stopped and smelled the flowers. And she could probably tell him some new tormenting fact about how women strung them together to frame their nipples, or rubbed the blooms along a man's…

What the hell was happening to him? Sure, he'd been covering some out-of-control stories for a while and it had been a long time since he'd been in the company of the opposite sex, but his physical reaction toward Ava was unlike anything he'd experienced before. It was as if every word from her kissable lips and every stretch of her sensuous body was specifically designed to make him think of nothing but stroking her lips with his. Caressing her skin. Palming her breasts. Making love to her fast. Or slow. Whatever. However. Just as long as the action between the sheets lasted for hours.

That's when it hit him. It *was* all designed. Her every move. Her every supposedly subtle, yet utterly sensual maneuver had been intended to keep his mind on one thing and one thing only. Sex. Not that it was a hard task, but to have his easily led thoughts manipulated in that direction... He stopped walking and just stared at her. He was irritated and impressed all at the same time.

Ava stopped and turned around to look at him. "Everything okay?" she asked, the scent of cinnamon slyly hitting his nose as her hair swirled around her head.

"You're using the book stuff on me."

She crooked an eyebrow. "Is that what I'm doing?" she asked, her voice innocent. Her eyes...nothing close.

He shook his head ruefully. Knowing she'd played him for the past hour didn't detract from how sexy she was. How sexy he found her.

"Was it working?" she asked, her tones now sensual and low. And his body responded once again.

"No," he told her.

Her lips curved into a smile. "Good," she said with a nod. "That was only level-one stuff anyway. I'll just have to ramp it up some."

Hell, he was going to die.

JEREMY LOOKED AROUND her office and whistled. "You didn't tell me you were in charge. Impressive."

Yeah, well, there isn't a lot of talking involved when a man's tongue is in your mouth.

Miriam schooled her features to look cool and professional. "What a surprise to see you here, Jeremy."

He quickly shifted his glance her way, the smile on his face fading. "But not a good surprise, huh?" he asked, his disappointment obvious in his voice.

He caught on fast. Not so surprising since he'd so easily interpreted her every quick intake of breath or delicious sigh in bed and understood exactly what she wanted.

She moved so that she sat behind her desk. She needed that barrier between them. "I wasn't expecting to see you ever again."

Now all traces of that sexy open smile of his vanished. "That was pretty obvious by the way you left the next morning without a trace."

She would ignore the hurt she saw in his eyes. *Get this over quickly. No need to prolong anything.* "Then why are you here?" she asked.

He slowly moved toward her desk, drawing her eyes to his tall lean body. She'd stroked and kissed every part of that provocative body of his. Earlier she'd chalked up her momentary loss of judgment where Jeremy was concerned to the strange situation.

She had been on vacation.

She'd been stranded.

He'd played the role of knight coming to her rescue.

Of course she'd fallen into his arms. She could still feel the heat of him as he'd brought her a drink in the town's garage. He'd made her laugh because he'd placed a straw in one of those fluid-replenishing sports drinks.

"Thought you might be thirsty," he'd said. And she was. Oh, she'd been thirsty for just what Jeremy had to give. He'd sat with her the whole time the mechanics worked on her car.

Listened to her and laughed at her stories over dinner.

He'd offered to walk her to the door of her hotel room. Just to make sure she was safe. She was only going to thank him and wish him good-night. But she'd been hungry to know what his lips tasted like.

In fact, she was still hungry and still thirsty. Her breath shallowed. Her heartbeat quickened.

"Thought by now you might have changed your mind about seeing me again," he said. His voice was a sensual caress against her skin. Just a hint of an accent. His blue eyes willed her to rethink her decision to not see him again.

Of course she'd changed her mind. She'd gone back and forth about ten thousand times.

Look away. But her eyes fell across the magazine covers.

Go For It

Take Charge

Do What You've Been Dying To Do

Miriam stood, her breasts only an inch from Jeremy's chest. He smelled good. Like fresh air, lime and hungry man. Hungry for her. Good to know she'd left an impression on him.

She ran her fingertips up his arm, and his eyes heated. "How about dinner?" she asked.

He lifted an eyebrow. "How about takeout?"

AVA SMILED AT IAN. She should probably feel bad about torturing this man. At least she was hoping it was torture. Strangely enough, all her stealth-seduction practices hadn't been so easy on her. Playing the subtle flirt took a lot of energy. And it was hell on her body. She'd spent that last half hour in first-stage arousal.

She turned and began walking again, knowing he'd be beside her. She liked that he'd caught on so quickly. She liked smart men.

"You don't even feel guilty about trying to drive me nearly insane this whole time?" he asked, as he matched his stride to hers.

"Would kind of miss the mark if I were."

Earlier today, she'd been concerned about this project. Greeting this man nearly naked and covered in paint had clearly been the wrong direction this morning. But she'd managed to work it to her advantage.

"You're taking this book seriously now though."

She saw him smile. "Oh, yeah. Was I that obvious in your apartment?"

"It was very clear you didn't want to be anywhere near this project. Not your style?"

He shook his head, a dimple forming in his cheek. "No. But I warn you, you won't be able to fool me so easily next time."

She smiled. Liking that about him, hoping he'd keep working under that assumption. "Good. I wouldn't want you easy."

They walked together silently, enjoying the stroll around the canal. Although she'd been in her new home for a week, she hadn't taken the time to explore the beautiful Bricktown area. The flowers and trees surrounding the canal were lovely, and quite surprising to find in the middle of a busy downtown area. The sun was setting, and the various businesses had turned on their lights, many reflecting in the water. A family of ducks paddled by, swimming toward two children tossing bits of tortilla into the water.

"It's pretty here," she said.

Ian shrugged. "Sure."

Her instincts about this man were right. He was wound tight. "You know, in ancient England, men would collect flowers and wind them into garlands. They'd spend hours examining the blooms, making sure each petal was perfect. Then with great enthusiasm, the knight would place his unique creation on top of his beloved's head."

Ian made a scoffing noise. "That sounds like something a bunch of women cooked up and *told* men they enjoyed doing."

"You seem awfully cynical about the opposite sex." Now this was interesting. Could this be an actual insight into the man? Good, this could be something to use later. For the book or on the man, she wasn't quite sure which.

He stopped and turned toward her. They were under a bridge, and the lights cast amber shadows around his face. "We're talking about knights, right? Armor, lances, raiding castles. You might want to go back and research the whole flower thing."

"It's well documented."

His lip crooked upward. "Men…spending hours selecting flowers? I don't even give that much thought to my socks. And I'm wearing them. What probably happened was that the knight was on his way back to the armory after a hard day's battle keeping everyone safe. That's when he saw some slacker dumbass knight with a bunch of flowers heading toward his woman. He couldn't let that happen, so found some vendor with a cart selling flowers."

"Oh, really," Ava said, flashing him her best skeptical look, the one she'd seen her college professors use a thousand times. All the while she tried to hide her smile.

"The vendor was probably so bored from trying to

sell flowers to a bunch of dirty knights that he fidgeted those blooms into a string, or 'garland' if you will."

She couldn't stop her laugh. "Did you just use air quotes?"

"Shh. You're messing up my story. And I'm on a roll because here's the best part. He speeds past this other knight, and then *tells* his woman he spent hours selecting the right blooms for this twisted-up mess. He even has her thinking garland is attractive. That women actually want garland. Desire it."

"No, your theory doesn't float because now he sets up a standard that he has to beat and that all his sons and grandsons have to meet. They have to actually collect flowers and make garland."

"Not necessarily, because he passes along the DNA that allows his heirs to make up their own BS stories with enough convincibility that women think they're hot."

"*Convincibility* is not a word."

Ian held up his hands and took a few steps back. That sexy dimple appeared in his cheek again. "Hey, no need to get testy just because I blew your whole men-and-flowers scenario out of the water."

Ava laughed. "Are you going to be this doubtful about all the customs I'm putting forth?"

"I'm just glad I'm here to make sure you don't send the men down the wrong path." Then with a wink, he turned and began walking again.

"Just so long as you know you're wrong," she told him as she joined him. She could spot her apartment now, and despite knowing how wrong he was, she was interested to hear what other theories he was going to try and debunk.

Fifteen minutes later, Ava emerged from her bedroom, barefoot and with a box full of scrapbooks and photo albums. She'd spent time in so many cultures where shoes were not worn, she felt confined in straps of leather, no matter how cute.

She found Ian staring outside her large picture window at the canal below. One of the yellow boats floated along the river. This was her first opportunity to really study him unnoticed. He was a man who observed everything. Probably from his journalistic training. He'd notice her examining him. More than likely he'd use it to his advantage.

Strange. She didn't think they were at war or anything. But there was definitely a tension between them. Both of them were wanting to win. Win at what, she didn't know.

He looked good, relaxed in the khaki pants and polo shirt. Ian was a lot different from the usual men in her circle. Who was she kidding? He was totally different from the academic types. Professors had a reputation for being boring and staid, but really that was an unfair stereotype. Usually they were just so focused on one subject they could talk of little else.

Ian seemed like a man who could focus, too. Only the difference was that he could focus on lots of different things at once. She liked that he cared enough about his sister that he would clearly involve himself in something he thought he'd loathe because she asked him to. She knew her brother would do the same for her.

She also liked how he quickly dropped his bias toward her project and even challenged her to think about this book in ways she hadn't thought of before. A man who challenged her mind was definitely very sexy.

Her body reacted, and she closed her eyes for a moment to enjoy the sensation. She'd be making love to this man. Ava didn't know when, but the fact that it would happen was a certainty and she planned to savor the delicious buildup and tension that existed between a man and a woman before they succumbed to the call of their bodies.

So she'd admire Ian's body. And his mind. For now. As for later…

"It's a great view, isn't it?" she asked.

Ian turned, and his eyes darkened when he saw her. "It certainly is," he said.

She smiled, then turned toward the brown couch in the middle of the large front area of her apartment. She patted the seat beside her, indicating she wanted him to sit down.

He tossed aside a decorative pillow and sat. Once again she took some time to appreciate the moment. His bigness, his strength, the heat emanating from his skin. Nature had made her desire these things in a man. Who was she to deny it?

There was a principle she wanted to impress in her book, and that was showing women and men how to appreciate the strength and power of the feminine. Somewhere along the way, that positive reception seemed to have gotten lost. A whole wealth of pleasure and completion awaited the senses when male and female united.

She opened her photo album. "My photography is pretty crude, but this is an interesting union ceremony. Eligible males and females are lined up. Men on one side. Women on the other." She pointed to the rows of people, their muscles tense with nerves, their expressions anxious.

She turned the page, and pointed to a building made of bamboo and leaves. "The elders emerge from a spirit hut after several days of fasting and prayer. Then they join a couple based on what the spirit tells them."

Ian shuddered. "That's awful. No wonder they look as if they're about to face death. The spirit could give a man some woman who's constantly asking what he's thinking about. Or invites him to a musical."

Not taking the bait, mister. She shrugged instead. "It seems to work. Separation doesn't happen very often, although after a year, the couple can petition the elders to dissolve the union. But they have to wait another two years for another ceremony. They're only performed every three years. And two years is a long time to wait and be alone." She turned the page to show newly formed couples holding hands.

She'd spent two years off and on with this particular tribe, one of the last of its kind. "Look, here are some of their children a year later." She loved looking at the proud daddies holding new infants at the naming ceremony.

"But to spend your entire life with someone you don't even know. To put that kind of faith in someone else to choose for you."

"Almost every culture in the world at one time or another has had arranged marriages. It's as if the older people don't put a lot of faith in the judgment of the young," she said with a laugh.

Then she focused her attention on Ian's brown eyes. "In fact, choosing one's own mate is relatively new."

If Ian didn't pick up the message she was communicating with her eyes, he just wasn't getting it. A woman could do a lot of silent talking with her eyes. Dozens of cultures never allowed women and men to talk until introduced, but women had adapted over time so the men they weren't supposed to talk to knew exactly what they were saying. For some societies, it was the language of the fan. In others it was with the eyes. And Ava had learned from the best.

Oh, a man might think he's the aggressor in approaching a woman, but he'd probably been picking up the subtle cues and hints the woman had been throwing his way all along. Men in any culture didn't like to be turned down.

The stiffening of Ian's shoulders proved he'd caught on to the message she was sending through her gaze. What would he do now? Would he take her up on it?

"Well, it probably beats speed dating," Ian said after a downward glance at her lips before he returned his attention to the photo album. His brown eyes were tinged with desire.

She racked her brain trying to find a reference, and failed. "What's speed dating?"

"You haven't heard of it?" he asked, his voice incredulous.

She shook her head.

"Actually, it's not much different than this tradition here, the men and women are lined up, but then the men move from woman to woman in a row, spending about five minutes with each. Then both the men and women mark on a card whether they want to see a particular person again. If both people mark yes, then the organizers will exchange their information."

"Wow. I can't decide if that's a really great idea or a really bad one. Sexual attraction does happen almost instantaneously."

"Internet dating is even worse."

"Internet dating?"

Ian turned on the couch so that he faced her. "You haven't heard of that, either?"

For some reason, she was feeling almost defensive. "Most of my life has been spent out of the country."

"But you went to college."

"Sure, but my course work took me right back in the field mainly. I only lived one semester in the residence halls, but spent most of that time in the library."

"What about before that?"

"With my mom and dad at sites."

"So, you've never been to a prom, never cruised, never hung out at the food court of the mall?"

She shrugged. "What's the big deal about that?"

His breath came out in a huff, ruffling his hair. "You know so much about cultures all around the world, but you're clueless about your own."

She blinked up at him in surprise. "I'm certainly no shy virgin. I've dated plenty."

"What, other students? That's easy. I'm talking about meeting people. That's hard. You're going to be selling this book to people who *have* hung around the grocery store looking for others buying single-portion meals. I think you need to experience a little of their life to be able to write for them."

This sounded like another session of him debunking her theories. It also sounded very exciting. "Okay, I'm game. When do we start?"

"Right now. Where's your phone book?"

"Under the cabinet by the phone. Why?"

Ian shot off her couch and grabbed her Yellow Pages. He ran his finger along the page as he spoke. "Bricktown is a happening place. Surely there's a— Found it."

"Found what?"

"Club Escape. Ava Simms, you're about to have your first experience in a singles' bar."

CHAPTER EIGHT

MIRIAM USHERED JEREMY out of her office quickly. They'd almost made it to the bank of elevators when her assistant rushed toward her.

"Thank God I caught you. It's...your mother."

Miriam's shoulders sagged. She closed her eyes briefly, dragging in a breath. Jeremy obviously sensed something because he took a step toward her, and placed a comforting hand on her shoulder. The tip-off must have been the alarmed glances between her and Rich. Or more likely, her body's natural bracing stance for the emotional combat sure to come.

Whatever it was, she appreciated the gesture. His hand, warm and solid, actually felt comforting and well, nice.

Rich cut a glance toward Jeremy, then back to her. "I could tell your mom you've already left for the day."

Like the former Mrs. Cole would believe that. When had Miriam ever left work—she looked down at her watch—before seven? She shook her head. "No, she'll just track me down on my cell."

Rich nodded. "I'll tell her you'll be right there. She'll be on line two."

Miriam turned toward Jeremy. "I'm sorry about this, but it's something I can't get out of. You don't have to stay—"

He shook his head and smiled. "No, I'll wait," he said, as if there was never any question that he would.

She raised a brow. "This may take a while. In fact, it probably will. You could go back to your hotel. Leave your number, and I'll call you—"

"Miriam, it's okay," he said, his voice reassuring. His blue eyes supportive.

With a tight smile, she turned and headed back to her office, sighing heavily.

Miriam's mom was what some people would call a gold digger. She was smart, pretty, talented and above all—ruthless. Instead of using all that power to carve a career out for herself, she latched onto rich and successful men.

Miriam and Ian's father had been her first husband, but she'd left him, as well as the rest of her family, to marry a rich rancher in Montana. Today she was married to some obscure painter and living overseas, no doubt funding his work now that she was a very wealthy woman.

About five years ago, Miriam had finally contacted her. They'd been doing an article on what drove women to marry for status and position rather than love, and her mother had offered up several enlightening quotes. Anonymously, of course.

Miriam doubted she'd ever connect with the woman who'd given her life, but she understood some of what drove her. Since that interview her mother called her on a regular basis. Miriam had tried to assign all sorts of reasons for the contact: Janice felt guilty for leaving her children or she wanted to connect with her only blood relations, but she really suspected that Janice liked trying on the mother role every once in a while. Hence her concern about Ian's current occupation.

Miriam returned to her office, and picked up her extension. "Darling, you cannot believe what they've been doing to poor Raoul."

Miriam had never met her mother's latest, and it was hard to work up any sympathy for the man—other than for the fact that he was married to her mother.

"They are canceling his showing. The poor man is having painter's block. He can't help it."

She'd heard of writer's block, but painter's? "Well, Mother, it would be hard to have a showing without any paintings."

"Oh, Miriam, if they weren't hassling him so much about his new vision, he wouldn't be having these problems to begin with. He…"

Miriam opened her top desk drawer and pulled out a doodle pad she reserved solely for phone conversations with her mother. She'd never used a doodle pad before, preferring short conversation that encapsulated in five minutes or less whatever pressing business needed to be dealt with. But Rich had purchased one for her after he'd found her mad scribblings all over her desk calendar. He'd not been pleased.

Twenty minutes later, she found herself walking back to the elevator. Wrung out and fully expecting to see an empty lobby. Then she spotted the man leaning against the wall, an anxious expression in his blue eyes. Her mouth went dry and her heart began to race.

"Are you okay?" he asked, his voice deeper than usual, laced with concern.

She glanced up, meeting his gaze, surprised to hear genuine worry behind his words. The skin around his eyes was tight, and his whole big body seemed tense. The muscles of his arms bunched, as though he was ready to engage in battle.

Battle for her?

The tension in her back eased. "You waited," she said, not realizing until that moment that she'd secretly hoped he would, but hadn't really expected it.

A flash of annoyance shot into his eyes. "Of course I waited."

Something happened to her in that moment. Miriam Cole no longer felt so alone. It felt almost natural to have him at her side. She gave him a tentative smile. "I'm fine. I just want to get out of here."

He punched the down button. "I know about mothers."

"Not like mine," she said.

Jeremy gave her a sympathetic hand squeeze. Among her friends, when the topic of bad parents arose, a competition of sorts began. Whose mother had been the worst? Whose father had the most "other" families? But Jeremy did none of those things. Instead he gave her an easy yet comprehensive form of acknowledgment. And he listened.

She gave him a sideways glance as they waited for the elevator. He'd gotten a haircut since she'd last seen him. Had he done that for her? The thought that he might have warmed her from the inside, even though she kind of liked brushing his dark hair out of his eyes.

He was even better than she'd remembered. And lying in the dark in her big, lonely bed for the past few weeks, she'd recalled him looking pretty damn good.

The downward-facing arrow above the elevator lit up and a bell pinged as the elevator doors whooshed open. She followed him inside and punched the lobby button, and the doors closed.

In a stride and a half, Jeremy was at her side, and tugging her into his arms.

His lips came down on hers. For a moment she was too surprised to respond. Then it all came flooding back. The passion. The heat. The hungry wanting Jeremy evoked in her. She'd missed the fervor, that excitement so much. She'd missed him.

Miriam circled her fingers in the loops of Jeremy's jeans and yanked. Hard. But she didn't care. She wanted to feel the solidness of his chest against her breasts. Feel the hardness of his erection pushing into her gray silk business skirt.

With a groan, Jeremy backed her against the wall and his hands cupped her breasts, touching and stroking her in a way that made her wet and hot.

He'd remembered what she'd liked. Just the way she'd liked it.

The rapid descent of the express elevator slowed. They'd be reaching the lower floors now. With obvious reluctance, Jeremy's mouth left hers. His ragged breathing filled the car, as he rested his forehead against hers.

"I've thought of nothing else but that," he said. And Miriam felt another jolt of tingles at his words. She'd never melted against a guy in her life. But here she was, practically liquefying herself against the man.

Her dry mouth hadn't recovered from the sight of him propped up against the wall waiting for her. And now she had to deal with the lack of his lips.

The elevator door opened, and they stepped out. Calm, cool and with a respectable distance apart of almost two feet. No one passing by would suspect the heat that had fired up the elevator only moments before.

Jeremy drew her toward the glass doors that led outside, his hand warm on her lower back.

They walked together in silence. But for the first time,

she didn't feel the urge to fill it, rack her brain for some tidbit of information that would keep the conversation going. Actually, she kind of liked the calm between them.

The calm before the storm.

Because they both knew the minute they were alone, the passion between then would take off full force. There should be some sort of awkward tension right now. Some sort of preintercourse nerves or reserve. Instead she felt an affinity with the man whose body heat penetrated her blouse directly to her skin, and couldn't they walk through this lobby any faster?

Finally they made it outside and Miriam began to flag down a taxi.

"Do you want to walk?" Jeremy asked, his face turning a little green.

Her arm lowered, and she turned toward him. Miriam tried not to look at him as if he was crazy. She really did. But it was cold. She was in heels. It was—

Then she remembered he'd never been to New York before. She could point out a few sights. He could rub her feet afterward.

"Are you wanting to see a few landmarks?" What happened to the hungry guy from her office? The one who didn't want to wait for a meal in a restaurant to have her?

"You think I drove all this way just to see Manhattan?"

"You drove?"

He nodded.

"All the way from Oklahoma."

He nodded again.

Forget takeout. She'd take him. Then afterward, they'd order in.

And yet he still made no move toward the taxi.

Wait a minute. He looked about as uneasy as she'd felt alone and isolated on that lonely stretch of country highway.

That had been his element.

New York was hers. And she knew what every out-of-towner commented on after a visit. She stared in his direction. "The traffic getting to you?"

He shrugged. "What's with all the honking?"

She reached for his arm, and tugged him toward the cab. "Come on, big guy. This time I'll protect you."

AVA DID AN INTERNET search to find out what to wear to a nightclub and fifteen minutes later emerged from her bedroom hoping she'd fit in with the natives. She was usually a lot more prepared than this, spending hours researching adornment and attire.

By the fire behind Ian's eyes, her choice of black miniskirt, sparkly tank and sheer long-sleeved overshirt hit the mark. Going heavy on the eyeliner and sheer lip gloss felt strange, but she went with the advice in an article she'd found in one of Cole Publishing's own magazines. *Dress To Be Noticed.*

"I won't stand out, will I?" she asked.

Ian nodded. Slowly. "That will do," he said, his voice slow. He crooked his elbow.

Unfamiliar with the gesture, she quickly figured out she was supposed to wind her own arm through his, appreciating the solid strength of his body.

"Technically, you're supposed to want to stand out. You're trying to attract men," he said with little enthusiasm.

Ava tilted her head. "Okay to stand out. Got it."

Like most of the attractions at Bricktown, the nightclub was on the canal, and it took only a few minutes to walk there from her apartment.

She heard the pounding synthesized beat of music long before she turned the corner to the Club Escape. Two large black doors bore the word *Escape* in bold, neon blue. Ian escorted her into a darkened hallway, shrouded in pale blue light. After flashing her ID and paying the cover charge, they followed the music down the hallway.

Lights overhead pulsing in beat with the music illuminated dozens of people dancing on a large floor. She'd participated in many types of ritualistic dancing, but nothing ever this…free-form. She preferred her customs a bit more scripted than this.

Ian indicated a grouping of purple couches and she followed him as he led the way, pushing through the crowd.

A waitress quickly stopped at their table and asked for their drink orders.

Ava leaned over to Ian. "What's the normal drink for a woman to order?"

Rather than reply, he told the waitress, "She'll have an appletini. I'll have a beer. Domestic."

"Draft or bottle?"

"Bottle."

"What's an appletini?" she asked as soon as the waitress left.

Ian shrugged. "Hell if I know. It's what my sister always orders."

She sat in silence beside him just digesting the sights and sounds around her. The smell of various perfumes and colognes scented the air. People grouped and clustered everywhere, trying to make conversation and laughing. There was an interesting anthropological study in this experience she was sure. Too bad she hadn't brought her camera.

DAMN ALL THE LOCKS on her door. It took too long for Miriam to enter her apartment. She could have been using tongs to hold her keys her fingers felt so useless. Her heart raced in anticipation. She couldn't wait to get Jeremy alone and inside her apartment.

Finally. Her door swung open, and then Jeremy took over. Except he was even slower. She wanted hard and fast. And eight times in a night.

Instead he closed the door, locked it and gently pushed her against it. He cupped her face, and she met his blue gaze. He stroked her bottom lip with his thumb.

"I've dreamed about these lips," he told her. His voice gruff and full of desire.

He traced the line of her jaw. Slid his fingers down the line of her neck. A small smile touched his mouth as he found her pulse point. He leaned over and placed a light kiss there. An innocent kiss. One that would look almost chaste until he added the tip of his tongue. Then her pulse really began to hammer.

"Seeing how much you want me makes me hurt not to be inside you," he said with a groan against her skin.

"Then why are you being so slow?" Her breasts ached for his touch.

Jeremy straightened, his expression turning serious. "Because I told myself if I was lucky enough to be with you again, I wouldn't rush things like a horny jerk."

"I liked horny and rushed."

A wicked little grin appeared on his face. "You'll like this more."

Then his hands moved. He slid her jacket from her shoulders, making the simple act a carnal caress. She wanted his mouth on hers, his tongue at the base of her neck as he undressed her. Like before.

But now, his eyes never left hers as he began to un-button her blouse. How intimate it felt to have him slowly undress her in the stark light of her entry.

His expression was a mask of tight concentration. His shoulders strained and tense. Jeremy Kelso was perfect. Beautiful.

Before, in Oklahoma, they'd raced to the bed. Two people in the heady throes of passion who couldn't get their clothes off fast enough.

His deliberate movements now were far more frus-tratingly sexy. He clearly was a man who'd thought of nothing else but undressing her slowly, and he planned on enjoying every moment now that he had the chance. Jeremy's eyes darkened, but never left hers. Although she couldn't hold his gaze as he caressed her nipples poking at her bra.

She moaned when he cupped her breasts, molding them with his hands. "Take off my bra," she said, her voice low and needy.

She hadn't wanted to be naked with a man this much since…since the last time she'd been with Jeremy. How he could make her breasts ache without taking off the material that separated his skin from hers, she'd never know.

He finally removed her lacy blue underwire. "I've waited so long to see you. Wanted you for so long."

The cool air of her apartment did nothing to soothe her need for his touch. And once again he was taking too long. Miriam opened her mouth to demand he touch her. She was done being teased.

She sucked in a breath when she opened her eyes and saw his expression. Jeremy looked at her body with intense appreciation. She watched as his breathing grew more irregular. Spotted his pulse beating wildly at his temple. Witnessing the effect she had on him made her feel strong.

"You're so beautiful," he said.

Miriam reached for his hands and unhurriedly placed them on her breasts. "Then touch me," she urged.

She didn't need to hide her lonely desire for him behind the quick, all-consuming passion. Miriam suddenly wanted to savor this, too.

She'd been imagining, dreaming, thinking of being with him as much as he had dreamed of being with her.

He kissed her then. Carnal and hungry. She opened for his tongue, the taste of him so memorable. So wanted. She twisted her hips until she cradled his erection. Her body demanding more from him. Offering more.

One quick weekend. It should have been nothing more, but she'd missed this. Missed him. The slightly rough texture of his cheek. His familiar masculine scent. The heat of his breath on her skin.

His lips left hers, running down her neck, down the swell of her breasts, stopping to give an erotic kiss to her breasts. Then lower still.

He sank to his knees, his fingers seeking out the waistband of her skirt and finding the zipper. The swish of her zipper being pulled down would be branded on her memory as one of the sexiest sounds she'd ever heard. Her thighs began to tremble.

"You make me feel so good, Jeremy." He pulled her stockings, panties and skirt down her legs all in one move. The man had talent. She stood before him naked. Warmth flooded between her legs. Miriam grew slicker with wanting. Jeremy's fingertips lightly guided up her calves.

"The whole weekend together, and not once did I kiss you here. How could I have missed that?"

The idea of his mouth, his tongue on the most intimate part of her body, made her knees shake in delicious expectation. It was hard for her to swallow. "We were busy doing other things," she reminded him, desperately trying not to sound so...desperate.

She watched as he smiled. "True."

Then he looked at the curls between her thighs. "I'm not missing this time."

He tenderly gripped her thighs, worked his shoulders between her legs. Then she felt the warmth of his mouth. He stroked her with his tongue, gently at first, as though she was fragile. As though he wanted to tease her and make her ache for more.

She shivered as he caressed and explored her with his tongue, seeming to want to learn every curve of her, the taste of her.

Her head fell back, and she moaned at how good he felt. How good he made her feel. Her knees wanted to buckle, but no way would she allow herself to break contact.

He circled her clit with his mouth, getting so close, but never fully finding the source of her most intense pleasure. Then he was there, licking her, sucking her. The thrilling pressure inside her deepened. She wanted... she needed...

Miriam's orgasm rushed her. An amazing release that went on and on and on. Jeremy saw that it did.

Finally, the pounding subsided. Her wobbly legs could hold her no longer, and she began to sink to the tile floor. Jeremy stood, bringing her up with him. Then he did something no man had ever done before. He swooped her up into the strength of his arms.

The sensation of being carried by him should have been corny. But she almost reveled in how cherished he made her feel. No one had ever made her feel so naughty and prized all at the same time. Naughty because all she could think of was that she wanted to give him as good as he was giving her.

"Where's your bedroom?" he asked, his voice gruff and tight with need.

"Down the hall, second door."

Jeremy didn't set her down when he reached her bedroom, he carried her all the way to the bed. Her breathing hitched as he let her body slide down the firmness of his until she sat on the mattress.

"Take my clothes off me," Jeremy told her. Miriam scooted to the head of the bed, and snapped on the bedside light. She wanted to see all of him.

Something in his eyes flickered for just a moment. Something wanting and almost vulnerable flashed there before it vanished. Replaced by desire.

Miriam slipped off the bed and took a leisurely tour around him. If he thought she was simply going to remove his clothes, he was wrong. She planned to enjoy this. Halting at his back, she tugged the T-shirt from his jeans. She ran her hand across his shoulders, loving the play of his muscles under her fingertips.

She went up his back with her breasts, her nipples hardening against the smooth heat of his skin.

"I like the way you take off a man's clothes."

"Just wait," she said. Her voice full of naughty promise. Facing him, her fingers went straight to the button of his jeans. The bulge behind the zipper made it a bit awkward to tug the thing down. This sweet, sexy guy wanted her and the knowledge did strange things to her heartbeat.

Zipper dispensed with, she smoothed her hands down his back, past the waistband of his jeans to cup his perfect muscular butt.

His eyes closed as she squeezed and pulled him in to her. He sucked in a breath. She saw his hands fist at his sides. And she understood. Understood he was doing everything in his power not to yank her up against him, toss her on the bed and sink inside her.

Oh, that didn't sound half-bad.

Miriam shoved those jeans down his thighs, dropping to her knees. She followed the path of his clothes with her mouth. Her tongue.

Her hands touched him everywhere, but not where she knew he desperately needed her contact. He growled as she purposefully missed his cock.

Then, when she sensed he'd suffered beyond what any healthy man could take, she wrapped her fingers around his penis and drew him to her mouth.

A more gentle woman might tease him. Draw her tongue around his base. Stroke to the tip of him. Circle the head of his cock. Instead she drew him fully into her hot, wet mouth.

He groaned, his whole body shaking with the force of his need.

His hand sank into her hair, twining it gently around his fingers. The soft glide of him inside her mouth felt amazing. With an aching sound, he pulled himself from her mouth.

"On the bed," he said, reaching for a condom.

She glanced up, confused. "I wanted to give you pleasure this way."

He stopped what he was doing, his blue eyes almost black. "You will, but on that long drive here, all I could think of was feeling your hard nipples against my chest, the warmth of your breath against my neck, and those sexy little sounds you make as I drive into you."

She swallowed, her whole body shivering at his words. She wanted that, too. With a nod, Miriam stood and crawled up onto the bed. She draped herself across the mattress, parting her legs slightly. "What are you waiting for?"

Miriam watched as he ripped open the condom package with his teeth, then tugged the latex down his shaft. Seeing his hand on his cock, stroking himself, made her breath hitch. That hard piece of equipment would soon be in her, giving her pleasure.

He didn't even realize how sexy he looked preparing himself for her.

Task done, he joined her on the bed. He gripped her hips and rolled onto his back, taking her with him. His fingers splayed at her hips, and she straddled him, her dark hair falling forward like a curtain.

"So this is how it's going to be," she said, breathless.

He nodded. "All I can think of now is you riding me, as I watch your breasts. You have amazing breasts. It's what kept me awake instead of exiting the highway and finding a motel to grab some sleep."

"Let me see if I can reward you." Miriam found the base of him, teased herself with the tip of his cock, then she decided to take pity on the poor man. Take pity on both of them. He'd driven all the way up to New York for her, after all.

She positioned him where he'd give her the most pleasure, then let gravity take over.

Jeremy sounded breathless as he fully seated himself inside her. "Miriam, you're amazing. Amazing."

She bit her lip. No, he was the amazing one. He didn't just do amazing things to her body, he made her feel amazing. As if she was more than a head of a multinational company. More than a reputation or money.

No, Jeremy made her feel like an object of desire. She would have slapped the face of any man who'd suggested she was such a thing, but Jeremy's objectification made her feel powerful. Safe enough to want to let her guard down a bit and be nothing but a sexual being in bed.

She lifted herself, then sank down on him again.

His eyes drifted shut, and she took selfish satisfaction in watching his face as he fought the passion. Then his eyes met hers, and there was that touch of something she'd spotted in him earlier. A vulnerability. "I can't hold out much longer. I've wanted you too long."

"Then don't hold out," she whispered and closed her eyes. She didn't want to see that unmasking of his emotions. She rubbed her breasts against his chest, just like he wanted, ground her body against his hardness.

He groaned again, then grabbed her hips, pushing himself into her over and over, until her muscles tensed around him. Until her climax overtook her, and she moaned with the force of the pleasure. Jeremy's orgasm hit him with force. His whole body tensed and shook. Feeling his reaction to her generated a second wave of pleasure through her body.

Afterward she collapsed against him, her body covering him.

"As good as you remember?" she asked.

He nodded, his eyes still closed. "Better," he said, smiling in satisfaction.

Once she regained her breath, she slipped off him, took care of the condom, then snapped off the lights. She'd tug the covers up later. Right now she was still too hot.

Jeremy drew her close, resting her head against his chest. His steady heartbeat lulling her into sleep. "I'd hoped... I'd wanted to make love to you all night long, but after that drive, I'm sorry. I have to get some sleep."

She settled even more closely against him. "Jeremy, it's okay. Believe me, I got my money's worth. I came twice."

He gave her a tired smile.

"How long did it take you to drive?"

"Over twenty-four hours."

Miriam tried to picture the map in her mind, thinking of a logical place for him to stop. Indiana? Ohio? "Where'd you take your break?"

"I didn't. I drove straight through. Thought I might cash in at Philadelphia, but then...I just kept going."

Then, once he'd arrived, he'd had to check into a hotel. Find where she worked, and then she'd made him wait while she talked to her mother. The man must have been in agony, but he'd never let her know it.

She kissed his cheek. "Rest."

His heavy breathing was her only answer.

Her eyes began to drift shut, too. Might as well get some sleep now, because once Jeremy got his second wind, she suspected there wouldn't be much time for sleep. Nine or ten times.

She'd just about joined him in rest when her body jerked and her mind sent off the warning sequence. In fact, it had probably been sending out the signal and flares all along, only to be drowned out by lust and desire.

Jeremy had driven all the way from Oklahoma just to see her. He'd mentioned he'd thought of nothing else. He'd deprived himself in order to be with her sooner.

Had he read more into their weekend together? Was

Jeremy feeling more for her than just passion? If she weren't careful, she'd shift into full-blown panic. And she hadn't panicked since, well, she couldn't think of a time when it had happened.

Actually, she could think of the last time she'd panicked. In a bed. In Oklahoma. With Jeremy.

CHAPTER NINE

IAN NUDGED HER HAND. "Ready to begin your observations? Check out this guy. He's going to try and approach that girl sitting at the bar."

The bar was more brightly lit than the rest of the club. Blue neon and lots and lots of bottles of alcohol backlit in front of a mirror. Dozens of high-backed chairs surrounded the serving area. Two women sat together talking over their glasses as a man made his way toward the pair.

Twenty-first-century man performing his mating ritual. This was exactly what Ian had wanted her to see. She settled back against the cushion of the couch to better monitor the situation.

Ian leaned closer to whisper into her ear so she could hear him above all the interesting noises in the bar. "She's going to blow him out of the water. He didn't do his legwork beforehand," his tone slightly disbelieving.

Ava narrowed her eyes. Prime research, and she'd worn an outfit with no place to hide a notebook. Thank goodness he'd suggested the purse. "What do you mean?"

"Watch."

The music thumped as she noted the predatory male approach the first woman and say something to her. The second female leaned over and spoke to the hunter. The man glanced down at the first woman he'd marked as his prey. She shook her head, and the man left. His shoulders stooped. His walk slower. Defeated.

"How did you know?" she asked, incredulous. And impressed. *She* was the one who was supposed to be the expert.

"First, look at the way he's dressed. He's a slob. You don't dress like that to meet a woman. Women notice crap like shoes. You dress nice for women. Clean, pressed clothes. Nothing in the grill. Comb your hair. It's a respect thing. This is war. You can't give a woman anything that will make her shoot you down before you open your mouth."

"This is fascinating stuff." *War?*

"Now, look at *their* clothes. They're in work clothes. They're here to unwind from a day at the office. Contrast that against your outfit." His gaze angled downward, stopped at her cleavage for a moment before working its way back toward her eyes. "You're dressed for having fun. *You're* the one men approach. Or at least men paying attention."

"How come you don't go over there and explain to that man why he failed?"

Ian shot her an incredulous look.

"In every culture, it's the responsibility of the more knowledgeable to teach the rest. That way their traditions and mores are passed on to future generations."

"In this culture, men don't inform other men how to score. Why give another man the advantage in battle?"

"Battle? War? Scoring? It's almost as if women are the enemy. There's a study in this. I know it." Ava opened her petite sequined purse and pulled out a small notebook.

"I can't believe you brought that."

"I'm always prepared for research." She squinted at

the blank page. "Never mind. I can barely see." Ava replaced the pad in her purse and scanned the room.

"Not much research here anyway. Just your typical bar scene," he stated matter-of-factly.

She scanned the room. "I almost feel sorry for men. It's so dark in here. How can you even see the subtle cues and hints a woman drops?"

"Men adapt. And that's what the beer is for," he told her, lifting up his bottle as if making a toast. "False courage."

"So how did you learn?"

Ian shrugged. "I'm a reporter. My main job is to study people, look for weaknesses so I can get the information I want."

She'd have to keep that in mind. Was he hunting for her weakness even now? Ava shivered at the thought.

"But the main reason he failed earlier is because he didn't take into account the cockblocker."

Ava nearly choked on her appletini. "The what?"

He grinned at her. "Cockblockers are women whose main job is to block, or prevent, any man from infiltrating the group."

"And women are aware of these roles?"

Ian leaned closer as if he were going to impart a big secret. "Ordinarily women aren't around to hear it. I'm betraying man talk here."

Now *this* sounded very intriguing. "So are all men thwarted by the...cockblocker?"

"No, that's when you bring in your wingman. The wingman approaches the women, paying attention to the cockblocker, buying her a drink, chatting, whatever. Now here is how the scenario is played out. Once the wingman is in place, the other man approaches and acts surprised. 'I didn't know you'd be here.' Then the wingman introduces the two women and invites his friend to join them all." He shifted away from her, his smile very satisfied. "Pure gold I just shared with you."

"And you've tried this?" Ava asked, not bothering to hide the skepticism in her voice.

Ian shrugged. "Me? No, never. I prefer meeting women on my own."

"Care to share how? Because *this* I've got to hear." She leaned closer.

"Women don't go for a man who looks like a loser. He has to look like someone who's worth her time. Like I said, it's a respect thing. A man's got to have a game. A plan. You buy them a drink, never ask. You don't feed them a corny line. You say hello, smile, ask them if they're having a good time. Move on."

"Move on?"

"Women are expecting you to hang around. Show them you're interested then go back to your table. Or play pool. Just something else. It makes the woman curious. Confuses her. It's a mystery thing. All women love a mystery."

Ava couldn't help it. She shook her head. "This is horrible. It's like battle plans, miscues and deliberate confusion. There's nothing sensual about it." She scowled. "Wait a minute. You're just messing with me like you did with the knights and the flower garland. I should have known. This sounds too unbelievable."

"Really? You'll never find out sitting here with me. There's only one way for you to truly understand North American mating customs—you have to experience them. You go up to the bar."

"And do what?"

"Wait."

"For what?"

"To be approached. Run a tab, I'll take care of that later." Then his expression hardened. "Don't worry, if anything weird happens, I'll step in," he assured her, his voice a little gruff.

Was he imagining other men trying to meet her and being jealous? Good.

Ava finished the rest of her drink, anticipation making her feel lighter. She adored participating in ceremonies and rituals from all over the world. That's when she felt in her element. Like now.

"Try to work in some of those subtle seduction techniques from your book."

"Excellent suggestion." She stood, smoothing down her skirt. Ian's gaze followed the movement of her hands down her thighs.

That's right, buddy. That's the sensual game. I'll show you twenty-first-century male responding to the ancient techniques.

"And Ava," he said, his voice taking on that husky tone she was beginning to like so much. A tone that showed how much he liked looking at her body.

"Yes?" she said, flashing him a slow smile. She'd even throw in the head tilt.

"Don't drag out your notebook," he told her with a wink. A man secure in his environment and utterly confident.

Two can play it that way. She rounded her shoulders, her nipples pushing out the material of her blouse. "Don't worry. I'll know what to do."

That brash smile he'd flashed her faded. Besides, she'd forgotten her pen. Ava turned on her new high heels and, striding toward the bar, was careful to pick one of the bar stools that was not occupied on either side. After ordering a white wine, she idly glanced up toward one of the many televisions throughout the club. This one appeared to be playing some type of athletic competition.

"If you like basketball, I can show you one of my trophies," a male voice suddenly said.

IAN WATCHED THE MAN approach Ava. He wasn't surprised. The guy had been checking her out since they'd walked in together.

What *did* surprise him was the twinge of unease he felt at seeing another man advance on her. He observed her sneak a subtle glance down at the man's shoes. Ian smiled. The little professor had obviously paid attention to some of his comments. Maybe he should make a few more about the idiots who'd try to pick her up. A couple stumbled in front of him, obscuring his vision of Ava for a moment. The music blared.

The two talked for a few minutes, actually, the man talked to Ava. Idiot. You didn't talk *at* a woman. You engaged them. Tried to make them laugh.

Ian relaxed. This clown would get nowhere. Then he saw a look of surprise pass across her face. Unpleasant surprise.

That unease he'd felt turned into a clenching of his stomach. What in the hell had the bastard said to her? Ian began to stand.

Then she nodded and they both looked around for... something. Finally, the guy leaned over and talked to the bartender, who then handed him a pen. Ian's breath came out in a disgusted hiss. He saw Ava recite something and the man wrote it down on a napkin.

Idiot. This guy didn't deserve her phone number if he didn't come prepared. And what had he said to her to manage to get her number? Maybe she didn't realize she was supposed to be selective when handing out her digits. Then he watched as the jerk kissed her temple and walked away.

That's right buddy, you just keep on moving. Ava was way out of his league.

The jerk was lucky he'd only kissed her temple.

Ava hopped off the bar stool, then lifted her wineglass and walked toward him. Ian liked the way the woman moved. Her hips rolled with the grace of someone not afraid of her body. She smiled, and his breath caught in his chest.

"I think I did okay," she said, her voice brimming with excitement. "Strange, awkward customs, but I could get the hang of it. What's traditional here? Thumbs-up? High five?"

"Ladies' room visit to scrub off the side of your face," he muttered under his breath.

Her brow furrowed in confusion. "And I see what you mean about corny opening lines."

"What did he say?" Ian asked, resentment making his words rush. If that man had said something crude to Ava he'd go over there right now and show him how a lady should be treated.

"Oh, something about showing me his trophies. It was mixed in with a sports reference so I didn't really understand all of it. But the gist of it was to try and be impressive and hint that all his *trophies* would follow suit."

Ian tasted something bitter in his mouth.

"He asked for my phone number."

"Yeah, I gathered that by all the fumbling around."

Her eyes grew sharper. "Okay, I can tell by your voice you're going to tell me he did something wrong. I checked out his shoes. They looked okay to me."

"He didn't have a pen. It looks unprepared. Incompetent. From the moment a woman notices a man, she's judging him. No woman wants to invest a lot of her time and energy into someone who will turn out to be a dud. You coming without a pen leads to questions like, 'What else will this guy forget?'"

Ava nodded. "Or, how incompetent will he be in bed?"

"Exactly."

She drew a deep breath. "Fine. I think I'm ready to return to the bar."

"What?" He hadn't expected he'd have to step back and watch her be approached by other men again. He opened his mouth to stop her, then—

Why did he care if some slob hit on her?

It wasn't as if he wanted her for himself.

He took a swig of beer, but it no longer tasted good. In fact, it was like lead in his stomach. He'd spent too much time alone and in too many dangerous situations not to trust his instincts and lie to himself now. *Yeah, I do want her for myself.*

Hell.

"Do you not think I should try again?" she asked, her fingers on his back.

Hmm? Oh, yeah. He'd just yelled "what" like a lunatic. Instead he offered another reply. Nodding, he said, "Sure, go back. Try some of those body language seduction techniques you talked about in the book." That should keep her busy. Ava didn't know how to talk to a man in a bar. Sure, he'd grant some of her ideas worked in a small way in a one-on-one situation over dinner, but here? Dim bar? Filled with drunk guys? No way. Subtle was not the answer.

"Universal flirting? Great idea." She finished off

her wine, deposited her glass on the table and headed to the bar. Half a dozen male eyes following her progress. Laughing at him because it appeared he'd struck out.

None of these men knew what she looked like slathered in paint and wearing a loincloth. He did. His gut remembered. It tightened at the image.

That flashy top she wore was no match for that black miniskirt. Skirt or loincloth, he'd never get tired of watching Ava Simms's sweet ass.

Yeah, he was in trouble.

Ava smiled as she made her way back to the bar. He may not know it yet, but Ian didn't like the idea of her talking to other men. He wasn't the only observer of life. She was a trained scientist after all, and she knew when she spotted some pre-mate-guarding conduct.

He'd already pointed out the flaws in a potential rival. Classic male behavior. Anything else? Oh, yes, there was a gleam in his eye when he looked anywhere lower than her collarbone, and his hand gripped the bottle hard when she displayed mate-receptive behaviors. All excellent signs.

At the bar, this time she sat right next to a man sitting alone nursing something on the rocks.

Ava glanced toward Ian and noticed him glaring at the back of the man beside her. *Warning him off.* Another good sign. Her body warmed at Ian's behavior.

His brown-eyed gaze then met hers, and she sucked in her breath. There was heat and fire in that gaze. Something tempting and full of sensual promise. Suddenly she began telling herself maybe they didn't have to stretch the sexual tension between them for the benefit of the book.

Maybe they could enjoy the sexual chemistry. As hot as the sensual energy zipping between them was, it couldn't help but make it onto the pages.

Her shoulders sagged, and she angled her body away from the man nearby. She didn't want to practice her flirting skills on anyone else but Ian. She certainly didn't want to make him jealous by leading on another man.

Ava only wanted Ian.

And to know he wanted her.

He'd teased her about some of the universal flirting techniques she'd postulated. But scientists had been studying them for decades, and she'd show him just how easily they worked. Right now. On him and no other.

After ordering another drink, she rounded her shoulders and positioned herself on the bar stool so her breasts were at their most perky, and her hip-to-waist ratio looked proportional. Subconsciously all men noticed that.

Then she tilted her head to the side, making her hair fall over her cheek. With a flourish, she tucked the strands behind her ear. Then slowly, she raised her eyes toward Ian. She knew he would be looking. She still felt his gaze on her. A sixth sense passed down from one generation to another.

Their gazes met again. The tiniest of smiles played about her lips. Then Ava quickly looked away. She adjusted her hair again. Counted to three. Then glanced his way once more.

He'd been waiting for her. His shoulders tensed. His lips thinned.

Ava held his gaze with her own. Held it. Held it until it became just a tad uncomfortable. Counted to three, then dropped her eyes.

She took a sip of wine from the fresh glass the bartender had placed before her, the coolness of the white liquid not putting a dent in how hot she felt. She was supposed to be demonstrating to Ian the power of flirting. Not succumbing to his dark glances.

Ava crossed her legs and angled her body more in line with his—showing affinity. One more coy glance ought to do it. She lifted her eyes.

Slam.

He was standing, facing her. He'd been sitting the last time she'd looked in his direction.

Every part of this man was focused on her. His body was aligned to hers. His eyes, unwavering, never left her face. Anyone seeing his behavior toward her would see the primitive male claiming what was his.

Ava's nipples tightened. Her skin tingled. With a small nod, he moved toward her. His eyes never left hers as he wove his way between the tables and other patrons of the rapidly filling nightclub. The music pounded around them, the sound reminding her of a tribal drum beating a call. Her response to this man was primal and instinctive.

"Hello," he said as he approached. This man didn't need a corny line.

"Hi," she said, meeting his gaze.

"I'll give you my number, but only if you promise to stop flirting with me," he said, his tone lightening, that dimple in his cheek appearing once more.

CHAPTER TEN

"IS THAT WHAT I WAS DOING? Flirting with you?" she asked, chuckling.

This was fun.

She'd only spent a few semesters of college on campus. The rest of the time was spent on internships or practicums. When she had lived among her fellow college students, she'd been studying so much, she'd never had a chance to go for the club scene.

Ian signaled the bartender for another drink. "You know it is. And you still are."

She giggled then sighed inwardly. The female giggle was a flirting classic; one she particularly thought made her seem utterly vacuous. And here she was doing it. Damn instinct.

But men seemed to like it. Certainly Ian did because he began to finger the stem of her wineglass as he smiled down at her. Palming an object, particularly one that belongs to a love interest, definitely signaled his interest.

And also made her think of him touching her. Made her wonder what his hands would feel like on her body. Would he be gentle and seductive? Or heated and filled with passion?

Might as well go for it. She flashed him another classic—the half smile. "You're right. See, I told you it worked. It got you over here. Now, you're supposed to impress me."

He raised an eyebrow.

"So, was that your best line?"

He shrugged. "Usually works."

Ava bet it did. She couldn't imagine it would be too hard for this man to have any woman he wanted. She planned to make him know *she* was the woman he needed at that moment. But disguised of course. Under the guise of "research."

"Now we're at the preening stage," she told him as the bartender landed a bottle of beer in front of Ian.

"Aren't I supposed to teach you about the local dating customs?"

"I learn best by doing. Why don't I demonstrate this stage, and you tell me if I'm doing anything wrong. I'll do stuff like toss my head, flip my hair, maybe dangle a strand around my finger." Ava demonstrated the moves as she spoke, thrilled that Ian's eyes clocked her every gesture.

Ava watched as he took a swallow of his beer. Who knew watching the way a man's throat moved as he drank was sexy? She'd never read this before. This definitely should be noted. "How'd I do?" she asked, as she reached for her purse. "The hair thing seems to be most effective worldwide."

He made some sort of noncommittal sound. What kind of confirmation, or nonconfirmation, was that? At some point, some less noisy place, she'd have to talk to him about clear, concise communication. It was imperative in research, and sometimes his signals were damned confusing.

"So do you plan to tell me what I'm supposed to do next?" he asked.

Her brow creased, and her voice lowered as if she were about to tell him a secret. "Actually, I think the man's next moves are somewhat tougher. You have to show how big and powerful you are. You'll be a little bit louder than I am. Your motions will be broader, demonstrating the strength of your hands and arms."

Ian shrugged, immediately drawing her attention to the impressiveness of his shoulders. Sturdy. Strong. In more primitive times, those flexing muscles would have proven he could protect their home from any fierce sharp-toothed prey that wanted to get her. In present-day Oklahoma, the demonstration of his brawn proved he could carry the heavy stuff out to her car.

The DJ played a new, louder song and it became more difficult for them to talk and be heard. She leaned toward Ian. "But here's the tricky part for you. Your body is saying to me, 'I'm powerful and tough, but I'd never, ever hurt you.' Strength coupled with tightly wielded gentleness is a heady combination."

He swallowed, his hands lowering to his sides. "You'll always be safe with me. Safe *from* me...now that's another story."

Her breath hitched at the promise she heard in his voice. She didn't need to be drawn into him. She was aiming for the other way around.

"I'll try to entice you further. I'll gaze longer into your eyes. Looking face-to-face with anyone demands a reaction. With a member of the opposite sex you find very attractive, it's exhilarating. Does this approach work here in this situation, too?" She held his gaze, her eyes narrowing slightly, her lips slowly parting.

He shifted, coming in closer to her. Right on cue. He probably hadn't even realized it, but he was testing the boundaries of her personal space. She felt the heat of his body now. Saw the lights from the dance floor reflecting in his eyes.

She twisted on the bar stool, facing him. He followed suit. They'd successfully passed the preening look-at-me stage and were now in full-body synchronization. Her stomach muscles tightened.

Now on to real intimacy. "One thing that's almost universal in flirting is a woman exposing her neck." Ava tilted her head, allowing her hair to slide over her shoulder and down her back. "Early research suggested this was a sign of submission."

His eyes widened.

She gently ran her fingers down her neck, traced the line of her collarbone. Her movements were supposed to draw Ian's thoughts to following that same path. With his fingers. His mouth. But it also got her imagination leaping in that direction.

Ava cleared her throat. "But I don't think it has anything to do with submission. I think it's about invitation. There's something about the gentle lines of a woman's neck that draws a man's eye. It's an erogenous zone. I think presenting my neck says to a man, 'This is a place where you can make me feel good.' It's a challenge." Their gazes clashed once more. "Can you make me feel good, Ian?"

Her question was supposed to tantalize him, but teased her with images of him giving her pleasure. With his mouth. With his hands. However he wanted to make her feel good.

"Yes," he replied. His voice was filled with a charged promise. He leaned even closer.

She felt even more of his heat.

"Now I pull back," she told him as she scooted away from him on her bar stool. Ava turned, positioning her chest toward the bar once more, even though she'd liked exactly where she'd been.

Confusion filled his eyes. "Why?"

Ava shrugged. This was the hardest to explain. Even to herself it felt strange. "Ancient female tests. I call it the Promise Withdrawal Cycle. It's the promise for more intimacy quickly followed by withdrawal."

Ian's body stiffened. "I know exactly what you're talking about. Women do that all the time. Why?"

"It's a time-honed combination of playing hard to get and testing your staying power. To see if you'll stick around. Of course, that was a lot more important when women stayed by the fire in the cave and couldn't go out to hunt the mammoth themselves. A typical man will have two reactions. He's either annoyed, or his interest is piqued even further. As a woman I note your expressions and your body language in less than a second. If you get frustrated, start looking around the room, I know you don't have what it takes."

"But if I lean closer, try harder…" His voice trailed off, but he followed up his words with actions. Ian lowered his head, his lips moved just above her ear. "Say something like, 'Ava, I would never hurt you. I would only ever want to make you feel good.'"

His voice was a sensual caress, his words a sexy reminder of his tempered strength. She felt his breath on her skin. This man got what she was saying. A tiny thrill ran down her back. Her nerve endings reared up and she grew invigoratingly aware of his scent, the expression in his eyes and the subtle movements of his hands.

"I'll invite physical contact. Most people think men are the true aggressors, but it's really women who initiate that first touch. A mature man waits for the invitation, knows how to bide his time for the payoff. I might do something like reach over and pull off an imaginary thread from your shirt."

Ava stretched her arm, her fingers lightly brushing his shoulders. She felt the muscles tense below her fingertips. She was affecting him, and that felt very, very good.

"Now that I have your full attention, I'll take my drink, play with the straw, bring it to my mouth."

His eyes shifted to her lips and he exhaled a breath.

Then back again to her eyes.

His pupils were more dilated.

"I want you to think about my mouth," she explained as she sipped her wine. The waiter had looked at her as if she was crazy when she'd asked for the straw, but she knew what she was doing.

He ran a finger along the collar of his shirt. "I never knew how hot this flirting research could be."

Her gaze was drawn to the skin below his ear. Would he be sensitive there, like her? His mouth thinned, as if he guessed her thoughts. Good. He was becoming more in tune with her. Of course, it wasn't as if she were trying to hide that she was thinking about sex. Sex with him.

"Over time, women developed a set of skills to test men in a very short period of time. It's a back and forth. I make a move, you make a move. It's actually quite sophisticated. If it's working, you'll know we'll be on the same page while in bed."

His gaze heated. "You're making me a believer."

"There's only one other sure way a woman can verify she'll be compatible with a man before sex."

His brows lifted. "I can't wait to hear it."

She eyed the couples out on the dance floor. Some

moving with grace, others encompassing the more sensual movements. "We dance."

"I'll order you another drink." Ian signaled for the bartender.

Ava frowned. "Why?"

"Modern dating tip. Men become better dancers as women drink more."

Ava laughed. Not exactly the response from him that she'd been looking for—she'd been hoping he'd nearly yank her onto the dance floor so he could finally have her in his arms. But funny always worked in a man. "How many more drinks before you're out under those flashing lights with me?"

"Oh, I'd say a lot."

The bartender delivered another one of those green drinks and a shot of something for him. She sipped from her martini glass, loving the tart sweetness of it. Silence. It could be uncomfortable and awkward. But right now, it just stretched the anticipation, the wonder of what would happen next.

The tempo of the music changed, from hard drumbeats to soft, lilting guitar. The lights dimmed, and she imagined gliding around on the dance floor, his strong arms around her.

Something like determination molded his features. He downed his drink in a swallow, met her eyes then offered his hand.

With a half smile, she replaced her martini glass on the bar and stood. She lifted her fingers to his, and his hand engulfed hers in warmth.

He found a secluded spot on the dance floor where the lights were dimmer and drew her into his arms. Close, so she felt the heat of him, couldn't miss the sexy scent of him. But not so close she felt intimidated by his size. Somewhere along the way, Ian Cole had picked up how to treat a woman.

They moved to the music slowly. "You're a good dancer." She looked at him with surprise after his dancing protests from a few moments ago.

Even in the low light, she could see the weird face he'd made at her compliment. "My father made sure my sister and I had dance lessons."

"Actually, that's a good thing. I'll give you a tip. A woman can tell a lot by how a man handles himself while dancing. His confidence. How comfortable he feels with his own body. How he moves."

"And how are my moves?" he asked as his fingers caressed the small of her back.

The man gave her shivers.

"Not bad. But it's more than just your moves a woman is examining. You show me something about yourself as a man by not allowing other dancers to bump into me or take up our dancing space. A woman's mind begins to imagine. Is he adventurous with his—"

"I'll give you a tip." His thumb traced her bottom lip and her words died. In fact, just what had she been going to say?

He drew her closer into the heat of his body. His gaze never left hers.

"Just dance with me," he said. "No more talking about flirting. What we should be doing. I want only this."

Ava closed her eyes when his fingers sank into her hair, the caress against her scalp. He drew her head to his shoulder, the softness of his shirt smooth under her cheek.

He was right. With his strong arms surrounding her, the brush of his thighs against her as they moved, the last thing she wanted to do was discuss the social importance of dancing. She wanted to experience the dance. And that was the first time she'd ever truly wanted to be a participant rather than a cultural observer.

The song ended, the tempo of the music quickened, and Ian led her off the dance floor, their fingers twined together. He wore the confident look of a man who had a woman exactly where he wanted her. Lesson number two for her. She finally understood the battle between the genders she'd observed earlier, and which Ian mentioned. The subtle love play that kept one partner as the lead.

She'd had the lead until the dance. She wanted it back. "Ian, I didn't tell you the surefire way a woman secures a man's attention."

"One more might kill me," he said, that sexy smile showing her he wasn't really worried.

She drew her fingertips down his jaw, and his smile faded. "Make him know you're a bad idea. Men always want what they shouldn't have."

He arched a brow. "Oh, yeah, like how?"

"By telling you the truth." Ava tucked a strand of hair behind her ear, licked her lips and shyly met his gaze. Then she held it, angling her body toward him. All at once the shy seductress and bold temptress. "This isn't a good idea. It might ruin everything. Our work," she said, her voice almost a whisper.

Ian leaned closer. His expression determined to know her meaning. "What might ruin everything?"

"Getting involved. Having sex."

Ian swallowed. She almost felt sorry for him. After all, she'd brought out all the big weapons a woman possessed. She knew how to use them.

Ava wanted to make him burn. She wanted him to want her so badly he thought of nothing else.

She wanted to feel it, too.

He flashed her a sexy, crooked smile. Ahh, men must have that move ingrained in their DNA. Crooked smiles made a woman think mischievous. And mischievous suggested all kinds of naughty and delightful things between the sheets.

"Let's get out of here," he ordered, his voice deep and seductive.

"I still have my drink," she told him, not the least bit thirsty.

His eyes grew alarmed. "Leave it. I'll buy you another. That's a modern dating tip. Never leave your drink unattended then consume more."

"It seems such a waste."

"I'll show you what's going to waste." Ian lowered his head, his lips lightly brushing hers. "Still thirsty?" he asked against her mouth, his breath a warm caress against her cheek.

She shook her head.

"Good." He reached for her hand again, leading her through the couples and weaving between the tables until they were outside.

The cold chill of the winter air nipped at her skin, but she didn't feel a thing. That light teasing kiss Ian had given her had heated her from the inside, and she was ready for more.

The Bricktown sidewalks teemed with activity. The bright streetlights illuminated their path as they made their way amongst the other late-night revelers. The street vendors had gone, replaced by rickshaws. A police officer patrolling on his bicycle rode past as they walked toward her building.

Any other night she'd want to take it slow. Enjoy the ambiance and people watch. But this wasn't any ordinary night. Tonight Ian held her by the hand, and she was ready for him to demonstrate the promises his body had made to her on the dance floor.

Everything about him suggested he'd be an unselfish lover. And could there be anything sexier than a man who cared about his woman's pleasure?

In what felt like way too long a walk, they approached her apartment. In the shadows he pulled her into his arms. Ava stretched, looping her arms around his neck, tangling her fingers in his hair. Their gazes locked briefly in the moonlight.

"You want me to tell you how I kiss a woman, Ava?"

No. She wanted him to show her. Right now.

"I touch her face. Cup her cheek. Then I let my hands slide down her shoulders. Her arms. Just a gentle glide. Make her feel comfortable. Let her know I'd never do anything she doesn't want me to do to her body."

His actions, followed only seconds after his words, was utter seduction, drawing out her anticipation, making her ache to feel what he described.

"I stop at her waist. That safe spot between your hips and your breasts is pure temptation. I can move my hands up or down and be in heaven."

When had he stopped talking in the abstract? Now he was talking only about her. How parts of her were heaven to him. Some of those parts started to get really excited about the prospect.

"What shall it be?" he asked, his gaze lowering to her lips for a moment before returning to her eyes.

He didn't wait for her response. His fingers cupped her hips and he drew her closer. The tips of her breasts brushed his chest, her nipples hardening at the contact.

Her eyes drifted shut for a moment at the exquisiteness of the sensation. As a scientist, she'd studied gender response, researched the origins of customs related to sex and observed the intricate human behaviors that led to it, but experiencing her own response to Ian was intense.

His head descended, but instead of finding her lips, the firm softness of his mouth drifted along her neck. Tingles shot out to everywhere in her body.

"Remember you asked if I were up for the challenge? Could I give you pleasure here?" His breath sent a shiver down her sensitive skin.

His lips slid a slow path down her neck. Across the exposed area of her collarbone. She sucked in a breath when he followed with his tongue.

Yes. Ian Cole was definitely up for the challenge.

His hands caressed her through her shirt, running up and down her back. Shivers of sensation crisscrossed her spine.

"A less patient man might go straight for your mouth. A hard, hungry kiss to show you how hard and hungry I am. But I won't do that."

"You won't?" she asked, unable to mask her disappointment.

"No, a woman like you appreciates a man willing to take risks, not give you what you expect."

Ian kissed both of her closed eyes. The tip of her nose. Each time she sensed his lips getting closer to hers, she raised her mouth, tried to finally feel his lips.

When he began kissing her forehead she'd had enough. Ava opened her eyes to see Ian smiling at her. Gentle, as though he knew he'd been driving her crazy, but his eyes were dark, so she understood he had been waiting, just like her.

"Kiss me, Ian."

"Just waiting for the invitation." He lowered his head and his lips lightly touched hers. Brushed hers for a moment. Then his lips firmed and he kissed her. Passion ignited between them. Burned. Ian kissed her as if he'd rather kiss her than breathe.

Her fingers twined in the hair at his nape. Her heart pounded. The blood rushed in her ears. Ava pressed her body close.

Ian broke off the kiss. The heaviness of their breathing filled the night air. She moaned in disappointment.

"Ava, I haven't shared with you the last tip," he said.

Her lids lifted and she looked into his eyes, clearing away the confusion his kiss caused. "What?"

He dropped his arms. "Always leave them wanting more." He leaned in and kissed her forehead. "Good night," he whispered.

After making sure she entered her building safely, Ian turned swiftly and headed back down the sidewalk in the direction of his hotel.

Her whole body ached with sexual frustration.

Irritation.

Aggravation made her movements jerky as she let herself into her apartment.

Annoyed—yes. Disappointed—for sure. But secretly impressed by his ability to turn the tables on her—yes, she was that, too. "Well played, Mr. Cole. Well played."

CHAPTER ELEVEN

AVA SIMMS WAS ONE HELL of an adrenaline rush. Still, kissing her was not one of Ian's best moves.

Actually, it had been a great move.

But walking away before he suggested something stupid like continuing their research up in her bedroom was his best move of the night.

Ava possessed the kind of lips that invited a man's eyes. A call to investigate. Luckily, that fit right in with his chosen profession of journalist. He could easily spend the next few weeks working on her manuscript all the while exploring the woman. Studying the way her body matched perfectly to his. Or discovering new ways to have her make those sexy little sounds she'd made when their kiss deepened. Her soft moans fired something in his blood.

He could better use his time examining why she made him uneasy. As a reporter, Ian trusted his instincts when they warned him something wasn't exactly as it appeared. And Ava Simms was definitely not the almost-mild-mannered anthropology professor she seemed.

Somehow he knew she'd been expecting him to make a move on her, had been building every moment they had together to that point. It was as if she had something to prove about the validity of her theories and ideas, and he was the guinea pig.

Normally, if a smart, desirable and beautiful woman wanted to test her sexual ideas on his body, who was he to get in the way of science?

But he didn't usually *work* with smart, desirable women. Mostly it was a bunch of smelly angry guys alongside him in the field, if he worked with anyone at all. Quite frankly, he didn't have the skill set for this scenario.

Which was maybe what his sister liked about sending him here to Oklahoma. Miriam, she had a sadistic streak in her where he was concerned. Probably payback for the time he gave all her Barbies buzz cuts before he'd allow them to play with his G.I. Joe. Could be the fact her face was plastered across Do Not Allow into the Country posters in at least one South American country because of him. Or maybe it was for allowing her to do all the heavy lifting as far as their mother was concerned. Probably all three.

His sister wouldn't like the idea of him getting involved with Ava. That, of course, would have been incentive in itself, but he'd long since grown up and quit trying to shock Miriam. She was the only person in this world whom he knew who actually gave a crap about him, and he loved her for it.

Loved her so much that he'd be up at six o'clock in the morning in Oklahoma completing a full edit on a sex book that should be titillating but wasn't. That was until he pictured the author.

Which brought him back full circle to Ava.

Damn. His body reacted just to the thought of her. Knowing she was trying out all her theories and techniques on him didn't prevent them from working on him. Since he'd met her, he'd been surrounded by images of sex. Not to mention the scents that also made

him think only of sex. And now he had to read about it.
And damn if that infuriating aroma of cinnamon didn't
turn him on.

Maybe she did have something with that flower
garland story. He had to admit he'd much rather twist
a bunch of carnations together than tell her just how
much work her *Recipe for Sex* needed. That quick read-
through he'd given it on the plane hadn't revealed all
the problems.

He should probably try to figure out why he didn't
want to hurt her feelings. This was work. It wasn't personal. He'd never been one not to tell it to someone
straight. His career was based on just the facts.

Yeah, he should probably scrutinize those feelings,
but he wouldn't. He preferred to keep his emotions in
the shallow end of the pool. A lesson learned early, and
one that had never failed him.

THREE HUNDRED AND twenty-seven manuscript pages.

Three hundred and twenty-seven manuscript pages
she'd written in a frenzy of anguish and drive. Nineteen-
hour days, restless nights and little food had been Ava's
life until she had finally typed *The End*. She'd poured
her heart, as well as every other body part she possessed, into *Recipe for Sex*.

Three hundred and twenty-seven pages that were
now covered from top to bottom, left to right in red
ink. Some of her writing had apparently been so bad
he'd had to make notations on the back. With drawings.
This didn't include the sticky notes. Or the seven pages
of notes he'd scribbled on a yellow legal pad.

She could almost feel his irritation in the large red
X's that annihilated every paragraph in chapter three.

The force from his pen had left an impression three pages down.

"No, no. That's all wrong," Ian told her for about the billionth time as he turned a page. She'd almost stopped paying attention.

He'd showed up at her apartment this morning with bagels, coffee and a determination to cross out months of her hard work with that lethal red pen of his. He'd looked innocent enough, wearing jeans and an Oklahoma Sooners T-shirt he must have bought since his arrival. Innocent for someone who was about to rip her heart out with his critique. Although *critique* was too nice a word because he'd found nothing positive.

His eyes flared a bit when she opened the door to him wearing the ceremonial dress of the Hidali.

"At least it's more than paint," he mumbled as he slid past her into her apartment. But she couldn't tell if he was happy about that or disappointed.

But her attire wasn't much more than paint as the Hidali hailed from Africa and the clothing took into account the heat, and the beauty of the flora that lent to the dyes. The colorful material was free-flowing and quite sheer.

"There's an elaborate meal that goes with this costume. I thought we could try it at lunchtime. I've already prepared the food. One of the dishes has some real aphrodisiacal properties."

Ian raised his hand. "Please. Let me at least fortify myself with coffee before you start talking about phallic symbols and food that's supposed to make any normal man hard while you're half-naked."

He made decidedly for her kitchen.

There was no mention of the kiss the night before. Not that she'd expected it. Today's agenda was apparently going to be all about work. Evidently, Mr. Cole took to heart that not-mixing-business-with-pleasure axiom, because ten minutes later they were going over the manuscript together page by page. That red pen was finding things it had missed with Ian's first read through.

Ava gasped when he proceeded to X out one of her favorite sections.

"This whole section should go. It's dry and boring."

She shook her head. "It is not. Certainly the Bogani people whose culture you just obliterated from the page didn't think so."

Ian picked up the page. "'In ancient times, as now, in isolated communities in the mountainous region of Bogan, the men eligible to leave their mothers and fathers were gathered together in the village square where everyone dropped their heads and snored because these paragraphs would put anyone to sleep, even a boy about to lose his virginity.'"

She took a deep breath. "Maybe it's a tad uninspired."

He looked up from the page. "Uninspired? Ava, when we're talking about sex, the last thing it should ever be is uninspired."

Ava dropped her gaze. She'd acknowledge that he had a point about her writing, but not that the section needed to go. She'd sat silent for too long, and it was time for Ian to do a little compromising. "Okay, let's rewrite that portion."

Ian raised a brow. "We're not targeting virgins or even near-virgins with this book."

"Come on, Ian. You mean somewhere along the line, you wouldn't have wanted some older, experienced woman to show you the ropes in bed?"

"Well, it's been a long time since I was inexp—"

Ava rolled her eyes. "Oh, spare me that. Even when

you know your way around the bedroom, when you're with a new person there are still nerves involved. Premature ej—"

"Not an issue," he said quickly.

"You mean, you've never had your skyrocket in flight long before hers?"

He swallowed. His skin reddened a bit. "My technique might not have been always airtight when I first started, but now..."

"My point exactly. Readers with a wide range of experiences will be reading this book." She refrained from rolling her eyes again. Male pride on prowess in the bedroom also seemed to be pretty universal. Here it seemed to manifest itself by preferring to fumble around in the dark rather than acknowledge suggestions.

"I know you said the other day that men don't give other men tips to score, but surely a man would take advice from a woman."

Ian crossed his arms across his chest, his expression confident. Overconfident. "Okay, shoot me a pointer."

She was up for the challenge. "Hmm. The first thing a Bogani woman shows the young lover is how to pleasure a woman using only his fingers."

"Of course she does." He made a scoffing sound, but his eyes narrowed in interest.

"A woman can be pretty forgiving of three-pumps-and-he's-done if she's already had at least one orgasm. Something to keep in mind if a man wants to be invited back to the bedroom for a repeat performance."

That overconfident expression he'd worn slipped a little. "Maybe you do have a point about this section."

Oh, yeah, she'd show him. Reaching for her remote, she turned on her stereo and selected music from the Bogani region. Her apartment was soon filled with the sounds of drums. Primal. Like the steady rhythm of a heartbeat.

Then she reached and took that hateful red pen from his fingers and dropped it to the floor. "The Bogani are a close-knit, family-oriented culture."

He mouthed the word *boring.* So she reached for the thick stack of pages comprising her printed manuscript. "Obviously you can improve upon my writing, but you need to actually experience this to truly understand what I'm trying to convey."

He cocked his head. A study in disbelief.

"I wouldn't have understood a singles bar until I experienced it."

Ian let her tug the papers from his hand easily. "I've already crossed this section out."

"I'm putting it right back in. The way the Bogani men learn to pleasure a woman will not only be helpful to less experienced men who might be reading the book, but could also be a fun role play. Dual purpose."

"Role play?" he asked. "Now that's some inspiration." His eyes let her know he was more than curious about her next move.

That next move led to her couch.

"You won't need your laptop, either," she told him as she reached for his hand and drew him away from the kitchen table he'd commandeered for the butchering of her masterpiece.

"The Bogani people frown on couples separating, and believe pleasure in the marriage bed makes for a happy union," Ava told him as she tugged him into her front room.

"Sometimes not even *that* can save a marriage."

Mr. Cynicism was back. Good. She liked demonstrating her techniques to him best. Made it all the sweeter when her point was successfully proven. "True, but it's never a reason for a breakup. That's where the widows come in. Some say they make the bed play work. Plus they're going to save this section from your red pen. And this time, it won't be dull."

"Been giving this some thought?"

"Actually it just came to me. Sit."

Ian made himself comfortable against the cushions of her couch while she kicked off her sandals.

"When a man has proven he can support himself and leave his parents, he's also free to be chosen by one of the widows to show him how to pleasure a woman," she sat beside him on the couch, his jeans-clad thigh brushing along her bare skin.

"She'd have to choose the man she'd tutor carefully, for he'd pay a yearly tribute to her until his death. It's actually a nice little social system. It ensures that women without protectors are provided for, while potentially removing one of the major barriers to marital happiness."

"Are there jealousies?"

Ava shook her head. "No. Once he marries, he and the widow don't see one another again. If the widow has done her job well, the wife has nothing but praise for her. Bogani place high importance on monogamy. Although the widow walks a fine line. She knows she's there as a teacher, and strives to make the process without intimacy."

"How does she do that?" he asked.

"By never making eye contact. By never talking about anything other than how to pleasure his future wife. Every touch, every caress, every new sensation is all encased in the future."

Ava deliberately lowered her gaze. Now she'd show

him how lovers could role-play the Bogani teaching times.

"Boys and girls were usually separated from one another, learning the skills needed to keep their tribe thriving, so when they eventually make it back together, there's a lot of curiosity and shyness. So the first thing the widow teacher would do would be to make him feel comfortable with a woman's body. Receiving her touch and giving his. That first meeting he'd usually only stroke her."

Without looking up, she lifted his hands to the bare skin of her shoulder. He was warm and solid, and even with the barest of touches, not pulling off the inexperienced young man illusion very well.

"She'd instruct him how to run his fingers gently along her exposed skin. Softly caressing all the erogenous zones on a woman. Her neck. Her ears. How to sink his fingers into her hair, stroke her scalp. A lot of this can be missed in today's rushed lovemaking."

Ian followed her instructions perfectly. Deliciously. Her skin grew warm under his fingertips, achy for more of his touch. With shaky knees, Ava stood, still not meeting his eyes.

"Then she'd lead him to the small of her back. With even the lightest pressure there, the muscles loosen and it feels so good."

She sucked in a breath when Ian's fingers eased the tension that had gathered in that spot after seeing her book covered in red.

"The more relaxed a woman is, the easier her blood is flowing through her veins, the quicker it is for her to reach her peak."

"Are you feeling relaxed, Ava?"

Like jelly.

Ava wanted to raise her gaze. To see into his eyes. To gauge his expression, and see if it matched the husky aroused sound of his voice. But she didn't. That's what made this experience so unique, so intense and yet slightly detached. Western cultures placed a lot of emphasis on meeting another's eyes. By not, the whole dynamic between two people completely changes.

Like now.

"He could slide his hands down. The skin behind the knee is very sensitive. Or she may suggest he find her inner elbow with his mouth."

Ian did both. The warmth of his tongue was a purely erotic sensation against her skin. Detached? Who was she kidding? She felt fully engaged.

"When does he kiss her?" he asked, his voice rough and low and sexy as hell. Ian had even added a move of his own, gently blowing against the bare skin of her stomach, the warmth making her tingle.

"He doesn't," she said, her voice sounding close to a moan. He tugged her closer toward him and his tongue began to wind a lazy path along her collarbone and slowly moved to below her ear.

Ava was losing the upper hand. She needed to stay focused. *Fall back on research.*

"You know there are many cultures that never kiss, the Inuit in Alaska being the most well-known. Across the world from the Americas, the Pacific areas and Africa, we find many people that never touched lip to lip. Although researchers documented the kiss first in India, dating it as far back as 1500 BCE."

His hands curved around her hips and drew her still nearer to the heat of his body. She lost her balance and landed in his lap. Startled, she finally met his eyes. Dark brown and full of intense heat and hunger. Intimate.

"Good thing that no-kissing rule doesn't extend to my culture." Then Ian lowered his head, his lips on hers. Heaven. His lips were firm and something elemental exploded inside her.

She wanted more, but Ian broke off the kiss. He smoothed the sweep of her hair over her shoulder and kissed her neck. Licking that place below her ear.

"This is not what we're supposed to be doing here. The Bogani women are always in control and would never allow the man to take over like this."

"Oh, yeah?" He nipped her earlobe. "Tell me what else we're not supposed to be doing."

Her fingers traveled up his to grasp the muscles of his shoulder. Then she sank her fingers into the hair at his neck. She'd loved the feeling of his hand stroking her scalp. Loved hearing his breath quicken when she did the same.

"I shouldn't be on your lap like this." His thighs hardened beneath her.

"Maybe you shouldn't press your breasts against my chest. I'd hate that."

Her nipples drew taut, the sheer fabric not hiding her body's response to his words. Ava flattened herself against him, and he groaned.

"A Bogani widow would spend a whole day teaching a man how to touch a woman's breasts. To caress and stroke and finally lick."

"I don't know if I could last a whole day," he said next to her throat. His hand moved to cup her breast, his thumb finding and circling her nipple.

She cried out at the hot pleasure of his touch. "I have faith in you."

"Glad someone does," he said as his lips claimed hers once more.

This was no playful, teasing kiss. Ian almost growled when she touched her tongue to his. She hadn't expected the near-instant sexual connection she'd have with Ian to be so strong. So primal.

But sometimes that's what you got, and it was a rare, precious thing, so why not go for it? His fingers dipped for the ties holding the Hidali costume in place. "I had about a million reasons in my mind why we shouldn't have sex." His whispered words sent a thrill through her veins.

"Me, too."

His gaze sharpened. "You did? You've been thinking about having sex with me, but discounted it?"

She blinked up at him, missing the heat that was now fading in his eyes. "Sure. I want you. DNA programming. I found you attractive the moment you spoke."

His eyes narrowed. "So, it's just biology? Has nothing to do with me...personally."

"That's right. Sex is a normal, natural part of life. If I've observed anything since I've been back, it's that people seem to make such a big deal about doing the deed," she said with a shrug.

He didn't respond for a moment, as if he were considering her words carefully. "Well, if it's just sex, a totally biological function, then let's do it."

"Do what?"

A dark flame lit in his brown eyes. "Let's have sex. Right here. We don't even have to break out the paints. Just you, me and that rumble-drum music."

She tightened her arms around him. "Sure."

Ian made a strange sound in the back of his throat. "I know you've been away for a while, and so have I for that matter, but usually women aren't so...so..."

"So what?"

"So okay with just being biological."

"What do you mean?"

He gently pushed her out of his lap and stood. "We're missing the game playing, the pretending. Me trying to ramp up the action. You countering with a token denial."

"And that's what you want?"

He began to pace. "No, but it's what I'm used to."

"Ian, look. I don't know what to say. Obviously my experience level with dating normal people isn't very high, but it seems to me most problems between a man and woman could be cleared up with one good sit-down conversation."

He stopped his pacing and faced her. "You're right."

"I don't want to give you a token denial, but the truth of the matter is I didn't really act on my attraction to you because this…this tension between us, this heat, I think it will translate on the page of the book. We could get…biological now. I have these great oils I'd love to try—they're all the way from Bolivia. Or we could work on the book and wait."

Strange how at that precise moment the intensity of the drum music lessoned. Near silence descended upon them as she waited for his decision.

Ian sank against the cushions of her couch. His breath came out in sharp frustrated exhalations. Then his gaze cut to hers.

"You have a natural instinct for picking customs that would be interesting and instructional to today's lovers. But you're terrible at choosing chapter titles and you bog down the flow with too much history."

"I won't be left out of the writing."

"I don't plan to cut you out. Before, when you told me of the Bogani women, that was exciting. That was different, and that's what people would want to read about.

When you tell me about these people, their beliefs, you make them come alive. Seem like living, breathing people that anyone can relate to, can swap lives with, even for just an evening. That's what this book needs."

She glanced down at the manuscript pages covered with his red scribbles. "Obviously I'm not very good at putting my thoughts on paper."

"That's where I come in. I'm going to interview you. Every ceremony, every food, every dance you'll share with me. Together we'll get this book written."

She nodded, liking the idea. "I think that could really work."

Ian stood, reaching for all the papers of her manuscript and stuffing them into the empty space in his laptop bag. "We won't be needing these. We'll start from scratch tomorrow, when we're fresh."

Ava followed him to the door. She leaned against the wall after he left, picking at a bead on her bodice.

Ian had chosen the book over making love to her.

She would ignore that let-down feeling.

CHAPTER TWELVE

AVA GREETED HIM WEARING jeans and a light gray hoodie. She'd pulled her hair back in a ponytail, and Ian realized he liked this casual Ava. Hell, he just liked looking at the woman.

Today they'd be working on the chapter on scents. With that damn cinnamon, Ava had made him a believer that a man did respond on an elemental level. At least in a small way. But he wouldn't be lying if he said he'd been looking forward to this day of writing as a relief from the sexual tension brewing between them. Just how out of his mind would he get from smelling a few vials?

She smiled when she spotted his laptop case. "Don't you think we should experience this together before writing about it?"

"I like to be prepared."

"I'll remember that about you," she said with a wink.

She was doing it again. Turning his innocent comments into something that sounded like a double entendre. As if he was prepared for sex with a condom all at the ready. Or maybe that was in his own mind. She spent most of her life out of the country—did she even know what she seemed to be implying? He was going crazy.

"I've set everything up in the front room."

He'd expected vials and incense and containers of oil. Cotton swabs to capture the scents. What he hadn't prepared for was the scene she'd set up. Ava had been very industrious, pushing back the couches and making a pallet on the floor with colorful blankets, no doubt weaved on the bare thighs of women preparing for sex or some such story designed to push him over the edge.

Two large pillows, presumably where he was supposed to sit, were surrounded by lit candles.

Holy hell.

She reached for his hand. "Take off your shoes and come with me," her voice an invitation to be wicked.

Her soft fingers tightened around his after he'd kicked off his shoes, and she led him to the pillows, reclining on the one facing him.

"These candles are unscented so they won't mask the smells we're trying to explore, but set a nice mood. Rather than just list the fragrances that the opposite sex finds attractive, I thought it would be far more interesting to dab the oils on our bodies."

Of course she'd have that idea. Ava Simms had lots of great ideas on how to torture him sexually.

"Are we talking pheromones?"

She shook her head. "As subconscious sex attractants, nothing can beat them, but it's thought that only eighty percent of humans have the organ to even sense them. Some researchers think even less can detect pheromones due to disuse. Those odds are terrible. Why leave something like that to chance?"

He was beginning to think Ava didn't leave much to chance. Him, he'd take a little mystery.

"So humans found a way to maximize the senses we do have." Ava reached for a lighter and lit a thin stick. "Patchouli awakens sexuality, and comes from the tropical areas in Asia. Incense is the easiest way to find it."

He watched as Ava delicately blew out the flame on

the stick and waved a cloud of smoke around them. Despite his late night, he was now wide-awake.

She'd closed her eyes and took a deep breath. His body hardened as he watched her enjoy the smell surrounding them. This woman took pleasure in so many things.

She opened her eyes and smiled. "It's kind of sweet and earthy," she said as she placed the stick on an ornately carved holder. "Patchouli is thought to alleviate anxiety, so it might be a good scent for first-time lovers."

She kept bringing up the topic of first-time lovers, which always brought the prospect of the two of them being first-time lovers.

Ava reached for a vial beside her. "This is ylang-ylang. That means wilderness, and is used as a true aphrodisiac in the South Pacific." She rubbed a small drop of it on the crease of her elbow.

"Every aroma takes on a whole different personality when on the skin. It mixes with our own natural scents and musks and creates something totally unique." She shifted toward him. "Smell."

He'd kissed this woman. Stroked her skin, cupped her breast, but there was something about lowering his head to breathe in the scent of her that was wholly intimate and erotic.

Ian wasn't up on his scents. He couldn't tell you the difference between jasmine and lavender, but he could say that what Ava rubbed on her skin made him think of nothing but raw lovemaking.

A slow smile curved her full lips. "Powerful, isn't it? Ylang-ylang boosts the attraction between a man and a woman. Enhances energy and open-mindedness."

His imagination sure wasn't having any trouble.

Right now his mind was coming up with all kinds of energetic scenarios from pushing Ava back against that pillow to—

"Vanilla is particularly attractive to women." She reached for a brown bottle. "This is pure vanilla extract that you can find in any grocery store. Not good to taste, but if you were to put some on your neck, I would keep getting closer and closer to you as the evening progressed."

And here he'd been wasting all this money on expensive colognes.

"So do you think this will work for the book?"

All Ian could do was nod.

MIRIAM WATCHED AS JEREMY stretched in her bed, the sheets twisting around his flat stomach. She'd taken the day off. In fact she'd taken two. Unheard of. Now she was lazing around in bed past noon. What was with her?

Jeremy. His kiss. His hands on her body. His mouth on her skin. He was sexy, funny and…

And young.

She'd ask herself what did she think she was doing, but the tenderness of her breasts and the achiness between her thighs was a pretty good reminder.

She'd never been with anyone younger than her. Not even by a month. She didn't need to consult Dr. Freud to know it stemmed from watching her father date women who were less than his age. First five years. Then seven. Finally fifteen.

Damn, was she using Jeremy? Using him to make her feel good about getting older? About gravity? About a lot of things? Was she that far off from her father?

Jeremy rolled over, reaching for her in the dark. Grasping her breast. He smiled in his sleep as her nipple hardened against his palm. That wasn't the only thing hardening.

Even half-awake, he'd explored the terrain of her body with ease. His mouth had sought the sweet spot below her ear where she loved to have him kiss. Lick.

The way he made love to her was beautiful. The way he made her feel, amazing. She didn't want anything ugly between them. Anything that remotely resembled the kind of relationships her father had had with his younger women.

"Jeremy?" she whispered. If he didn't wake up, she could postpone this little conversation until morning.

He lifted his head. He smiled at her sleepily. "Is something wrong?" he asked, automatically reaching to comfort her.

She scooted away from him, as if she didn't quite trust herself to get through this without dropping the whole subject so she could make love with him instead.

Okay, here it goes. "What do you see happening here?"

Jeremy nodded, as if he'd suspected this would occur. The mattress squeaked as he sat up and rubbed his eyes.

"A guy driving halfway across the country doesn't exactly speak one-night stand," she said quickly.

"The way you hightailed it out of my hotel room back home tells me you aren't looking for anything long-term." His tone had changed. Slightly negative.

Why should she be surprised? They'd shared a weekend of no-strings sex. Weren't twentysomething men supposed to be into that? And bonus, she'd left him before there could be any weird, awkward parting moments. There'd been no faux "Let's keep in touch" or uncomfortable hug. Leaving that way had done them both a favor. Right?

"It was best that way," she said quietly, dropping his gaze.

"For you?" But he wouldn't let her block him out. He reached for her hands, his body on edge. "Miriam, I was worried sick. I didn't even know if you'd made it home safely."

Something warm and gooey formed around her heart at his words. Yuck. She was a grown woman. Ran a business. She could take care of herself.

And yet, that yucky gooey feeling wasn't all that bad. It was kind of nice to think someone cared whether or not she was stranded by the side of the road. She couldn't help it. She smiled.

"I never thought you'd worry about me."

Some of the tension he'd carried in his shoulders relaxed. His lips turned up in a smile. "Well, I did." His gaze captured hers for a moment, and he swallowed.

"I haven't been able to stop thinking about you. Wondering what you were doing. When I forgot about the blind date my sister had set up, I knew I had to figure out what was going on between us. I'd never stand up another person. I felt terrible."

Miriam didn't. The idea of him being with another woman made her stomach clench, and she'd never been the jealous type. Not once. She'd read enough articles in her magazine to know jealousy was not a productive emotion. But then she'd never been so attuned to a man's every movement as she had been that weekend. And still was, based on their latest performance between the sheets.

"So, this trip is to get me out of your system?"

"The timing was right to see what we have. I'm between jobs right now."

Yes, of course he was. Dad's women never seemed to keep a job for long.

His hand settled on her thigh, sending shivers along her skin, and the fact that he didn't have a job wasn't such an issue at the moment.

"But given the last two days, it might take a long, long time before I get you out of my system." His hands cupped her hips and he lifted her to straddle him. He was already hard and ready for her, and her nipples tightened in anticipation of his touch. Jeremy was a breast man.

His fingers slid into her hair, and he gently drew her head toward him. "This can be whatever we want it to be," he whispered against her mouth.

TONIGHT IAN WAS TAKING her on a date. With him and nineteen other men. They were going on something called a speed date. Once again she had researched what she should wear, but the predominant answer was "business casual," and that was even more difficult to fathom than going out to a nightclub.

Finally she opted for a black calf-length skirt with a bit of a kick pleat at the bottom. Her top was a salmon-colored scoop-neck blouse with a business jacket in case she got cold.

She did a quick turn for Ian when she met him outside the Bricktown restaurant where the event would be held. "How do I look?"

"My sister would approve."

She lifted an eyebrow. "But you don't."

"Maybe I prefer paint."

Her skin flushed as she remembered the way she'd first presented herself to Ian. He'd liked what he'd seen and she reveled in it now. Suddenly she didn't want to "date" anyone. Even if it were for seven minutes at a time.

Right now she just wanted to get to know Ian better. Away from her book. Away from customs. Just the way normal North American men and women met one another.

Unfortunately, speed dating seemed to be the way they did it. What a strange social rite. "How did this whole system develop?" she asked as he opened the door for her.

"Look at us. We spent a lot of our time in school, then out in the field with our careers. A person wakes up one day and realizes they forgot to date. So here's the most efficient way to meet people who might be about your same age, experience and education, who have the same problem."

Ian led her into a banquet room with a large sign proclaiming Speed Daters Welcome.

"Men on the left, women on the right," came the loud voice of a woman standing on a chair and calling to them from the other side of a bullhorn.

"Have fun," Ian said as he made his way to the left, and she joined a group of women dressed similarly to her. Whew, she hadn't blown that.

"We'll take a few moments to get everyone checked in with their name tags in place. There's wine at the front of the room, may I suggest you partake of it?" said the woman with the bullhorn.

Several of the people laughed and made their way toward the wine table. Five minutes later, she was in her seat, sporting her name tag, as well as the number eighteen, just in case the man couldn't remember her name. She had a score sheet and a pen, and was armed with strict instructions not to write anything down until after she'd been on all the dates.

"When I blow my whistle, the men move to the left. Please do this quickly as we only have the room until nine. Let's begin."

A nice-looking man of about thirty or so sat across from her first. He had a sweet, friendly smile. "Hi, I'm Zach. So, do you want to have children in the future?"

Ava found herself longing for the whistle.

Luckily Ian was her fifth "date." "How is it going?" he asked.

"This feels more like a job interview than dating. I've been asked about my religion, my sexual health and my politics."

"Well, you're interviewing each other for the job of significant other."

"Sounds inspiring."

"Do I detect a note of disdain? From the woman who has no problem with a bunch of men wearing penis carvings around their necks, this, *this* is what you find unusual?"

"It's so clinical."

"Remember what you said about how most problems between a man and a woman could be solved with just a simple conversation? Think about how easy it would be if you had all potential dating land mines already out in the open?"

She hated to admit it, but he did have a point. And using her own words against her. How irritating.

The whistle sounded and Ian stood. He was successful. He was smart and funny, and in his chinos and long-sleeved polo shirt he was amazingly handsome. The epitome of what a twenty-first-century woman should want.

And although she sometimes dabbled in ancient cultures, she was all twenty-first-century woman tonight. She'd much rather spend the next seven minutes and the seven minutes after that talking with Ian. Laughing with Ian. That initial physical attraction she'd felt for him was beginning to deepen. She was beginning to want more.

She suffered through the next few men, all decent guys, but biology did strange things to a person. Not one of them seemed as interesting as Ian. Her body had found her bedmate for the time being. It just took her mind a bit to catch up.

Finally the last whistle sounded and they were free to fill out their cards. She only marked Ian's name and number. They were free to mingle for a few minutes longer while the organizers compared cards and readied contact information. She opted for another glass of wine.

One of the organizers came by and handed them each an envelope. "How'd you do?" he asked.

Her sheet was blank. "Not one request. I must have been putting out the wrong vibes."

He flashed her an incredulous look.

"I didn't even score your number."

"You already have my number."

"How'd you do?"

Ian folded the piece of paper and tucked it into his back pocket. "Doesn't matter."

"Ian."

"Fifteen."

"Fifteen?" she asked loudly, her voice drawing the attention of several of the other daters.

Ian laughed. "Come on, I'll walk you back to your apartment."

"Wait a minute, these were only mutual requests. You would have had to list them as wanting their contact information, as well."

"All in the interest of research. I'm sure you can appreciate that."

"Sounds like a male ego needing a few strokes to me," she grumbled.

"Hey, a man's got to take them when he can. The last woman I kissed blew me off for the sake of a book," he said good-naturedly.

She laughed, and they walked along the canal together, the lights reflecting in the water. This being a weeknight, there wasn't much foot traffic, and the boats that floated along the canal were docked for the night.

"Ian, after this book is over, what do you plan to do?" she asked.

He ran a hand through his hair, and looked away as if he hadn't thought much past the book and it shocked him. "Guess I'll head for whichever hot spot is calling and my sister wants covered."

They walked in silence for a moment, the breeze turning cooler.

"What about you?" he asked, and for the first time she heard hesitancy in his voice.

"Maybe start working on some ideas for a new book. Send out my résumé to a few colleges. But I'd really like to take a few weeks off. Take a vacation and just look around at all of what I've missed."

They rounded the corner to her apartment building. She stood on the first step and turned, staring at him eye to eye.

"Been a while since I took a vacation myself," he said.

Ava's heart quickened its pace. She couldn't prevent

the huge smile on her face. He reached up and cupped her cheek, his thumb stroking her bottom lip.

This was the playacting he'd been talking about earlier. The kind he said he was used to. She should look at him and say, "Ian, after this book is over, I'd like to spend more time with you." But for some reason that scared the crap out of her. It was way scarier than telling a man you wanted him sexually.

Her eyes closed and she leaned into him. Ian met her halfway. His lips were now familiar to her. Wanted. His kiss was quick, firm and filled with promise. Then, with a final caress to her cheek, he took a step away.

"Good night, Ava."

He stayed on her stoop until he saw her key into her apartment building. After making sure the door behind her had closed fully, Ava made her way up the stairs to the top floor slowly. She was really rethinking her decision from earlier not to self-pleasure. Her nipples tightened just from her slipping the jacket she'd worn to the restaurant off her shoulders.

In her bedroom, she let her thumbs stroke down the swell of her breasts, circling around the tips. She sucked in a breath, imagining Ian's hands removing her bra. Ian's fingers teasing her nipples.

But no, she'd made a decision to keep the sexual tension high, and an orgasm now would surely lessen the heat between them.

Instead she tried to focus on all things cold. Feeling a little less heated, she kicked off her shoes, slid out of her skirt and blouse and zipped up one of the ceremonial robes she'd picked up from a Polynesian island late last year.

How long she paced in front of her floor-to-ceiling bookcase in agitation she didn't know. Her shoulders were tense, her brow was furrowed, her stomach was tight...and not in a good way. She should burn some incense. Some nice aromatherapy should really make her relax. But after a quick look through her scents, she realized every one of them was geared toward awakening sexual sensations, not relaxing.

They'd be working on the food section next. Maybe she could start preparing some of the more exotic fare.

With a smile, Ava stopped her pacing. She didn't need to concentrate on not thinking about sex, but instead work on filling her thoughts with something completely different. She ran her fingers along some of her books, but not even those dear friends could take her mind off the heat in her blood. That man was a dangerous kisser.

At least she'd given as good as she'd got. She'd spotted the regretful ardor in his brown eyes before she walked away. She'd felt the hard ridge of his penis against her belly. If they could transfer all that sexual tension and passion onto the pages of her book, it would ignite. It might even make her a bestseller.

Her phone rang, and she jumped. Fewer than five people had her number, and—she glanced at the ornamental clock her brother had given her—and it was almost two in the morning.

"Hello," she said, a little hesitantly.

"I was lying here on my bed in the dark, thinking how stupid I was leaving you after that kiss."

Ava smiled into the phone.

"You there?" Ian asked.

"Well, I'm not going to argue with you."

Ian laughed. "I was thinking that instead of kissing you goodbye, you would have asked me upstairs. Maybe offered me coffee."

"Would I really make it?" she asked.

"No. That was just an excuse to get me to come up to your apartment so we could be together."

"Do we need an *excuse?*"

"Ahh, good question. No, but twenty-first-century couples don't just come out and say, 'Why don't you come upstairs with me so we can neck?' We have to be way more restrained than that. Part of the pretending stuff I was telling you about."

"But why? We're living in one of the most liberated times and places of the ages."

"It's the power thing we talked about. The battle lines. You don't tell a woman you're falling for her. Women play hard to get. Men wait two days before calling a woman once he's got her number."

She swallowed. Was Ian falling for her? Or was he just talking in the abstract? Of course it was in the abstract.

"So where does the coffee thing come in?" she asked.

"Sometimes you want to break the rules."

"So new rules were invented. Another dance, but each knows what the step really means." Now this was making more sense to her.

"Exactly. You pretend you're really going to make us something to drink. I pretend I'm interested in drinking it. Instead you're in my arms."

Ava closed her eyes at the idea of being in Ian's arms again. Of kiss— Of necking with Ian on her couch.

"So we missed that opportunity."

"Maybe that particular opportunity, but there is something else we can do. Tell me what you're wearing."

"What?" That was the last thing she'd expected him to say.

"You tell me what you're wearing. Your voice turns all soft and low, like you're half a second away from moaning. You tell me what you like. Where you want me to touch you. I respond by telling you what I'm doing to your body. This is what we call phone sex."

"You're kidding, right?" She'd studied some unusual ways to avoid approaching a potential suitor from her days as an intern on assignment. Anything from having a brother or uncle ask the groom's intended bride for her hand in marriage on his behalf, or the ghost marriage, where the wedded couple never even met until after some type of sign from long-dead relatives that the union was sound. But sex was always done together and in the actual physical presence and with the other person.

"No, I'm serious. And if you study closely, I'm going to rock your world."

She laughed because this guy knew a word like *study* would really attract her attention. "You just had to put it like that."

"I know your inquisitive mind couldn't stand *not* knowing something that has to do with sexual customs."

Her heartbeat quickened. For the first time she was with a man who truly understood what made her excited and grabbed her attention. "Well, bring it on," she invited.

"Tell me what you're wearing."

CHAPTER THIRTEEN

THIS WAS SUPPOSED to rock her world? Although she doubted anything would come from it, she said, "I went upstairs, and changed into something that originates from Hawaii."

She heard him swallow. "Describe it."

Ava glanced down, a little confused. Ian seemed a little more interested in female clothing than most of her male acquaintances. "Bright pink and white flowers. They're very large, but you can still see the canary color of the background material. The costume hangs straight from my shoulders."

"What the—? Are you telling me you're wearing a mu—"

"A muumuu. It's a traditional gown, which is quite comfortable."

"I know what a muumuu is." Ian cleared his throat. "It's very eye-catching."

"I can imagine that it is," he said drily. "When you mentioned Hawaii, I was imagining a grass skirt and a coconut shell top."

She laughed. "You imagine like a tourist. And although Hawaiian residents prefer more muted colors than what I'm wearing, this is pretty standard. I love the puffy sleeves."

"Keep talking about it. It's turning me the hell on."

"Turning you on?" Was *that* what she was supposed to be doing here when describing her clothes? Her breath came out in a frustrated sigh. She'd totally missed that. And she didn't usually miss that stuff. "Ah. Let me try this again."

Ava grabbed the zipper on her muumuu and tugged, lowering the phone downward as she progressed. "Did you hear that?"

There was another long pause.

"Ian?"

"Yes." His voice sounded like pure agonized strain.

Ava grinned. "Thought I'd lost you there."

"You almost did."

Her smile turned contemplative. She loved his honesty. "From the sound of things a moment ago, you didn't think my dress was all that sexy," Ava said, the teasing tone now gone.

"Since I met this seductive researcher, a lot of things I didn't realize were sexy are pretty damn incredible."

Her heart almost slammed into her ribs. All night they'd been playing games, flirting with each other. The dance, the back and forth of courtship. But now, in the early-morning hours they'd finally arrived at the real truth. He wanted her. She wanted him.

She couldn't explain why, but then she really had no urge to. Who a person desired, what made a woman crave a man's touch, what made a man hunger to wrap a specific woman in his arms rarely made sense on a logical level. She'd been studying it long enough to know that.

Ian made her burn. Made her nipples ache for his touch, her skin yearn for his caresses. And despite him leaving her on the stoop earlier this evening, Ian wanted her. The signs were all there. The way his pulse had beat at his temple. The way his brown eyes slightly dilated when he looked at her.

It didn't make sense to want this man. He wasn't an academic, didn't share her interests and looked at her work with a good dose of skepticism. But pheromones and biology said *take this man. Now.*

She didn't have an urge to make it logical.

Ava simply accepted it.

Now she'd embrace it.

The man had suggested that phone sex was twenty-first-century foreplay. She was a researcher...she should experience it. Okay, not right. She wouldn't use that as an excuse to take part. Justification was a strange thing. Sprang up of its own free will. Ava wouldn't rationalize wanting Ian. She'd just go with it.

"Tell me how we get started," she told him. Her voice husky and filled with invitation.

"Tell me where you are."

"I'm in my living room, looking out the window."

"Are you looking toward my hotel? Were you thinking of me before I called?"

"Well, I was thinking of you, but I had no idea where your hotel is."

"It's west of you."

Ava shook her head as she looked out into the night, not even bothering to guess which way was west. "Still not helping."

"North, south, east, west—all simple concepts. Why is it that women can never seem to 'get' directions?"

"Because we didn't need to. Men have to know stuff like herds move north in the fall. As a woman, I just needed to remember that the edible roots usually grow right next to the bush with the pretty blue flowers. Don't worry, you tell me what your hotel is next to, I'll find you."

"Seems like an imprecise way of traveling around. Although I like the sound of you finding me."

"Don't knock it. Sometimes my roots and nuts will save your meat-hunting backside. Survival is a team effort."

"Ready to win one for the team now?"

Her brows knitted in confusion. "Uh…sure?"

"That's an expression, Ava. Sometimes I forget you weren't raised here."

"So winning one for the team means something like giving us both pleasure?"

"Something like that," he said, his voice turning gruff. "Forget the window stuff, just go to your bedroom."

Ava took the few steps down the hallway and into her bedroom. "I'm here."

"Set the scene. Describe it to me."

She glanced around the room, trying to see it through his eyes. "I've painted it a rich, dark green. It reminds me of some of my favorite places I've studied. I have plants all around, small palms and orchids. Waking up to the sweet smell of flowers is one of life's pleasures, don't you think?"

"One of them," he answered.

"I have a sweep of tulle making a canopy. It just didn't feel right sleeping without netting."

"Your bed, Ava. Tell me about your bed," he said, his voice raspy.

She shivered, anticipating how she'd describe it to him. "It's pure indulgence. After sleeping in sleeping bags and cots, I opted to pamper myself. I splurged on one of those pillowtop mattresses. When I lie down on it, I feel like I'm lying on a soft cloud."

"Lie on it now." His voice was a rough command.

Her footfalls were almost silent as she stepped across the hardwood floor. She stretched out against the silken khaki fabric. The material was cool, but her blood ran hot.

"How does it feel against your skin?" Ian asked.

"Cool and smooth. My comforter is silk, another indulgence, but I couldn't resist."

He chuckled. A sensual sound that seemed to come from deep inside his body. She responded to the earthiness of it, her skin growing flushed.

"I like that about you," he said. "I don't want you to resist a thing. Rub the material against your skin."

Ava lifted a corner of her comforter and ran the silky material along the curve of her neck, and moaned into the phone.

She may have heard him groan. "That's it, Ava. Tell me how it feels as you're doing it. Touch your breasts."

She heard the ache in his voice. The need. Her nipples tightened, and she grew wet.

"The fabric was cool at first as I touched my skin, but my body heat has made it warmer. I'm tracing the outline of my nipple. I'm watching it get hard."

"You don't turn off the lights?" he asked.

"Why would I?"

He chuckled again, but it sounded more like an agonized groan. "Not a reason I can think of. Touch yourself with your hands."

"Where?" she asked, not able to resist a small tease.

"Between your legs, but get there slowly."

Dropping the comforter, Ava cupped her breasts. Tweaked her nipples with her thumbs. "My breasts feel

heavier. Warmer. They ache to be caressed. Kissed."
By him.

This time Ian did groan. "Go lower."

Ava wound a wavy path down her rib cage. Her stomach muscles quivered under her fingertips. She'd gone down this path on her body before. Many times. But the sensations were more taut this time. That much more sweet.

"I've come to my panties." Her fingers were toying with the elastic at her hips.

"What color are they?"

"Red."

"My new favorite color. Touch yourself through them."

"Through them?" Surely he meant *under* them. The rushing of her blood in her ears must be making him hard to hear.

"Yes, through them. That's how I'd start. I'd stroke you over those sexy red panties of yours until…"

Her toes curled into the mattress at his words. She slipped her hand down over her body, down past the elastic of her waistband. Ava's hand went lower until her fingertips rested between her legs.

"I'm there," she said, breathless. Wanting so much more. Waiting for what he'd say next. Wondering what he'd have her do next.

"Run your finger along yourself. Along the folds of your skin. Gently. Get yourself used to my touch."

Ava's eyes squeezed tight. Ian had just made it personal, told her how he'd like to touch her. Her legs began to quiver.

She followed his instruction, skimming her flesh. With a tiny gasp, she arched into her hand.

"How does that feel?" he asked.

"Good. So good." Her breath coming out in little pants.

"I think you can do better than that," he said. "You get to feel. I want to hear."

"It feels amazing, but I want more. I need more."

"That's good." The utter satisfaction she heard in his voice made her smile, despite her blood feeling on fire. "Circle around your clit. Don't touch, just circle."

Ava traced around the small area, her body growing tighter in anticipation. "Is this the way you'd touch me?" It was hard to get the words out, she was so lost in the pleasure.

"Yes," he said, his voice clipped and filled with hunger. "When I know you're ready for more, that's when I slide my hand down inside your panties."

"Do you like that?"

"Nothing compares to following that path down your body. Feeling the heat of you against my hand. The wetness that tells me how much you want me. Slip a finger inside, Ava."

She felt the warmth, the wetness. Her hips rose to meet her finger.

"Are you imagining it's me?" he asked.

"Yes," she hissed. The word long and drawn out. She was close, so close to coming.

"Imagine me taking off your panties."

"How?" she asked. But whatever way it was, she only knew she'd want it to be fast.

"Maybe with my hands. Maybe with my teeth."

She sucked in a breath, the image of his dark head down between her legs drawing her closer and closer to orgasm.

If Ian had simply told her what phone sex was in a casual conversation, she would never have guessed a man and a woman could get such pleasure out of the act. There seemed to be a lack of connection and visual stimulation.

But experiencing it was something completely different. Hearing Ian's voice across the line, hearing how her words and actions affected him, it was very, very sexy.

Ava pulled her hands from her body and wiggled out of her panties. She tossed them to the side and snuggled under the comforter.

"Are your panties off?" he asked, his voice desperate, as though he needed to know. Had to know.

"Yes."

"Now I touch your clit. How would you want it, Ava? With my finger or with my tongue?"

"Both," she said. Her voice nothing but a moan.

"Greedy." He gave her that sexy chuckle. "I'll remember that. I appreciate a woman who enjoys oral, who's not afraid to talk about it."

He'd found the right woman.

"Touch your clit."

Ava circled around it for a moment, then found the exact right spot. She gasped.

"It feels good, doesn't it, Ava?"

She nodded, so close. So very close to exploding right there with just his rich, sexy voice to urge her on.

"Imagine me touching you. Gripping you by the hips and sliding inside you."

"Oh, yes." Her muscles flexed. Her body strained.

"In and out I'd stroke. I'm caressing your breasts, licking the side of your neck."

Her motions on her body became quicker, her fingers more urgent.

"And right when you're about to come, I'd kiss you.

I want to feel your gasp of pleasure with my lips. Come for me now, Ava. Come now."

She gave in to his words. Her senses exploded. Her pleasure arriving in wave after wave of tingles, shivers and tremors. "Ian," she moaned.

"That's it, Ava. I love hearing you say my name like that as you hit. Don't hold back. I want to hear every sound you make."

The intensity of her orgasm and his words were overwhelming. Her voice loud. Her body tense and tight. Finally, finally the sensations ebbed. Her hair clung to her face, the sheets tangled about her feet as she'd thrashed on the bed.

"Did you enjoy that, Ava?"

"Yes," she told him, her voice still weak.

"I'll see you in the morning. Good night," he said softly. His voice was like another caress against her overheated and sensitive skin.

"But you didn't get—" But the hum of the dial tone told her he'd already hung up.

Confusion assailed her. Reaching below her feet, Ava tugged the sheets around her body. Her skin still so sensitive to the touch.

She curled into a tight ball.

In protection?

She wouldn't doubt it. She needed something like that right now. Because there was something else biology gave a woman. The knowledge of when to guard herself from certain heartbreak.

And in spite of the pleasure Ian's sexy voice promised, the heartbreak was there, as well.

CHAPTER FOURTEEN

AVA PREPARED THE SCENE carefully. Today was the first ritual she'd be working on with Ian on a one-on-one basis. She hadn't expected to use this one today, but after the night she'd spent with Ian, the unselfish pleasure he'd given her last night, this ceremony seemed perfect.

Although she'd still take heed of the warning signals her body had sent off last night.

The oils and foods had been easy enough. The fresh flowers had been a bit hard to secure on such short notice in the wintertime, but she liked the effect of the deep purple carnations. With the help of a ladder, she'd managed to drape fabric over the windows and across the ceiling, using the ductwork.

Her front room had the very secluded, enclosed intimacy of a hut.

She'd forgone the fire for obvious reasons, but the couples using her book could easily recreate the Dravonian Sending-Off Ceremony environment with various candles, the way she'd done.

After she sliced open several black trash bags, her setting was complete.

"What's with all the plastic on the floor?" Ian asked as he finished setting up his camera.

The man had been all business since arriving at her apartment this morning. Not a word about what had happened late last night. His attitude put her mind at ease that they could remain professional and still be sensual together.

"Oh, it's to protect the hardwood from all the oil."

His hand slipped on the tripod. "Oil?" he asked.

She touched the bag with her bare, red-tipped toe, and eyed him seductively. "A trash bag isn't the most sensual or arousing prop I could have used, but it's easily accessible for most women."

"Did you say oil?"

Ava nodded. "Yes, for the massage. This is the Hero Send-Off. You may remember from my first draft that all the ceremonies in the book are for couples, so they can achieve the ultimate pleasure for both parties."

She made a show of fluffing up the flowers, trying to hide her attempt at gauging Ian's reaction. Although she'd appreciated his professional behavior, it kind of irked her on some level. "You remember, pleasure for both, right?" Her voice lower now.

Ian nodded, then returned his attention to his light gauge or whatever he was fiddling with. His movements were choppy, his motions clipped.

That was more like it.

"But this is the Hero Send-Off. The Dravonian culture has died off now, but we know a lot of their traditions by their extensive cave drawings discovered in eastern Europe." She found herself fingering the props as she watched him finish with his equipment.

"We suspect that the Send-Off developed during times of war, when clashing tribes fought over territory. But with the domestication of some plants, the tribes began to merge, and the women's traditions for sending off their men moved to right before the last prewinter hunt." Ian completed his tasks, and walked toward her. Reluctantly, almost as if he didn't want to get near her.

She'd take that as a good sign. "Of course, the hunt was not as dangerous as going off to fight, but who could blame the men for not wanting to lose out on that particular practice?"

Ian shook his head, his brown eyes scanning the scene she'd set. "No, I can't see any man wanting to give all this up." Then his gaze returned to hers. Heated and curious—her favorite combination.

She had his attention now. Ian was clearly intrigued about what kind of send-off the women would give their men. "Can you take pictures in the hut I made? I think any shots in there would be more effective in explaining the atmosphere to readers."

"Shouldn't be a problem."

"Good. Though I don't want it to seem like I'm discounting the dangers of the last hunt. It was far more dangerous than others. The men would be competing for game with other predators, and the meat would be so important to sustain the tribe through the winter."

A smile tugged at Ian's lips and her heart did a tiny flip-flop. "Told you something more was needed than just fruits and nuts," he teased.

"Yes, the men's contribution was very important. Step inside the hut, and I'll show you how the women prepared their men."

The laughter left Ian's eyes. *Yeah, that will show you to try and tease me.*

With a shrug, the robe Ava had been wearing slipped off her shoulders. The air was cool against her nearly naked skin. "The idea was to surround the man with his favorites. His woman would greet him in what she knew he liked to see her in. I didn't know for sure what you preferred, but you seemed to enjoy my loincloth."

Ian's breath came out in a hiss as the robe fell to the floor. She adjusted the straps at her hips. She'd paired it with a matching beaded top, replacing the paint from a week ago. "If you were facing danger tomorrow, maybe even death, is this what you'd like to see me in the night before?"

Ian nodded, not able to take his eyes off her body.

Satisfied with his reaction, Ava sank to her knees and crawled into the hut she'd made. Ian followed, keeping his distance. A pretty impressive move when her makeshift hut was less than four feet wide.

Her voice dipped low. "The whole point was to make him feel important. Loved and yet invincible. As if he could face and conquer anything come the next sunrise. The woman would take away all his worry, to give him the opportunity to relax, not to think. Whatever her man most desires before he heads off to the hunt."

"You know, if you want, I could go get us some steaks."

Ava laughed low in her throat. She saw the naked desire on Ian's face now. She met his eyes. "Although it seems only beneficial to the man, the woman enjoys it, too. This might be her last night with the one she loves. How better than to spend it in only…pleasure?"

"None better."

"Let's start with the oil." She uncapped the bottle, and poured a generous amount in her hand, warming it between her fingers.

Ian's eyes followed her every movement, and he licked his lips.

"Aren't you going to join me?"

His gaze met hers. "What?"

"I think these pictures would be more effective if they show me demonstrating on a man's body."

"I have to take the pictures."

"Isn't there some sort of autosnap? Come here. How are you supposed to write it without experiencing it yourself? When you think you have a good shot, set it up, then come back."

He paused for a moment, then he nodded. "That might work." He turned his gaze to hers, and she almost gasped at the look of anguished desire displayed in those brown depths.

Ian had the distinct look of a man who didn't want her to touch him. She could only guess he was a man used to being in charge. Too bad. Last night he'd driven her to distraction. That's what she wanted to give him this morning.

His arms slumped to his sides and he crawled toward her.

"You'll need to take off your shirt."

"Why?"

Yeah, that was her question. Why all the reluctance? "Is there a way I could give you a massage with your shirt on?"

With a shrug, Ian lifted his shirt over his head, and tossed it out the opening of her tent.

It was her turn to be reluctant. Ian had the kind of body that drove women to create ceremonies like the Send-Off. He was a man who lived in the field, worked hard with his body, and it showed. He didn't have the bulk of someone who worked for those muscles in a gym. No, his body was lean strength, tight stomach and hardened pecs. A light smattering of hair led temptingly lower.

Her fingers itched to touch his skin. Caress his muscles. She swallowed over the hard lump in her throat. She knew her body must be flashing all the signals of an aroused woman. She felt the blush above her breasts. Knew her nipples were poking at the material of her top.

His gaze turned heated, and she saw his hands fist and flex at his side.

"It's okay, Ian. I'll make sure you enjoy this."

"That's what I'm afraid of," he stated. This was no soft utterance or muttering under his breath. It was that amazing honesty from yesterday. His words made her burn.

Ian was done hiding his desire and also obviously through with masking his reluctance, too. Could his hesitation be rooted in the same reasons as her own proactive gestures of last night?

They wanted each other, but were both clearly cautious. She'd never shied away from anything, and she doubted the alpha loner in front of her had, either. Why now?

As a researcher, she'd love to ponder and contemplate the reasons until she came up with a reasonable answer. As a woman, she just wanted her hands on his body.

"Your pants, too."

He raised an eyebrow.

"It's going to get really oily in here, do you want that on your khakis?"

Ian's fingers moved to the button, and unhooked it. Then he found the zipper, his eyes never leaving her face. But she was too curious, so her gaze slid downward. She sucked in a breath as she realized something about Ian. He didn't like to wear underwear.

The pants slid down his legs, revealing a deep tan with none of the telltale marks of a man who wore trunks when he swam. Already semierect, he was impressive to behold.

She recognized her age-old womanly response. Her lips parted. Her breasts felt heavy.

His pants soon joined his shirt outside the material walls. Ian turned, presenting her his back. Smooth and tanned and muscled, it matched the rest of his body.

The skin of his shoulders quivered as she placed her oil-ready hands on him. His hot flesh felt right beneath her fingertips. "You seem tense," she said.

"Getting tenser by the moment."

She smiled, her skin becoming more sensitive as she grew aroused. Ava began to rub and knead his flesh. "There's no record that the Dravonian women had any special techniques. I think they just did whatever made the man feel good. Does this make you feel good, Ian?"

"Yes." His voice was low and huskier than before.

Done with his shoulders, she poured more oil into her hand. She slid her hands down his spine, watching him flex and move under her ministrations.

She cupped the firmness of his backside. He had the perfect butt, and his muscles grew more taut as she worked him.

"This doesn't seem to be doing the trick of relaxing you. Maybe this will help."

Ava reached behind her and tugged the bow at her neck holding the halter top in place. The bow between her shoulder blades was more tricky with her fingers so slippery, but she managed to get it undone, too.

Her top fell to the protected floor with a whoosh. Ian shifted around to see what had fallen. His eyes widened at the sight of her nearly naked body.

Ava's nipples hardened further under his gaze. She poured more oil into her hands and rubbed it all over her breasts, loving the slick feeling against her sensitive flesh.

"I suspect that after a while the woman did something like this." Ava cupped her body to Ian's back, rubbing her oil-glazed body against his skin. The sensation was amazing. Unlike any she'd felt before.

She began to run her fingers up and down the sides of his body. His thighs. His ribs. With each stroke downward, his frame jerked as she found her fingers closer and closer to his penis.

She would have loved to have done this last night. Touched him for real, instead of in her imagination.

The oil was working its magic. His skin glistened in the candlelight. Finally the slickness became too much and he fell, his arms barely bracing both of them.

"Roll onto your back. I think it's time to massage your front," she urged.

Ian circled to his back, bringing her along with him. "Never understood the appeal of oil-wrestling until now," he said.

"What?"

Ian shook his head. "I'll explain it later. I like what you're doing now."

She smiled, and poured more oil into her hands, rubbing to heat up the liquid. Then she smoothed it onto his chest, running her fingers along his collarbone, his nipples and the muscled lines of his stomach.

When she settled on his hips, his cock jutted forward. Her gaze lowered. His hard length was ready for anything she wanted to give him.

Ava suddenly held a new appreciation for the control Dravonian women must have had. Her skin screamed for his touch. His caresses. His mouth on her body.

She could only imagine how intense the experience

would be for a woman who was loved by the man beside her, and her fearing for his safety. Everything, every touch, every taste, every sense would be heightened.

She needed to take a breather, to get her riotous body more in check. "I have some sliced meats and some traditional bite-size boiled potatoes. Usually the woman feeds her man."

"Nice to know meat-and-potato men always existed."

"What?"

Ian groaned deep in his throat. "No, ignore me. I don't want you to feed me. In fact, I don't want you to stop what you're doing at all. And in case that's not clear enough, I want your sexy little hands back on my body. Touching me. Stroking me."

Her hand reached for the base of his cock. "Like this?" she asked.

He shivered below her, his face a beautiful picture of male concentration.

"Yes," he answered, his voice barely above a whisper.

Ava wrapped her fingers around his shaft, then slowly raised her hand to the tip, the oil making the movement easy and smooth.

His hips lifted, and she caressed the tip of him with her thumb. Then she lowered her hand down his shaft.

His eyes flew open. "Ava, that feels so good."

She lowered her lips to give him a quick kiss. "Enjoy it," she said against his mouth. "I am."

Ava began to move up and down his cock, gradually increasing her speed. The muscles of his stomach flexed and his thighs shook. His hands came up to grip her. To stop her. "Ava."

She shook her head. "No, let me do this. You gave to me last night. Let me give to you now."

The hands that had come up to stop her movements embraced her. Helped her find the rhythm he liked best. She watched his face, fascinated by the tightness of his jaw. The candlelight exposing the strength of his reaction to her touch.

He grew harder in her hand.

Her heart beat faster in eagerness. She knew his orgasm was near, and she couldn't wait to watch him. The core of her ached to have him feel her, but she resisted the urge to rub her clit against his hair-roughened but oil-slick thigh. That would be strictly against the rules of the ceremony.

Instead, she put even more effort into her ministrations to Ian's body. She rode her hand up and down his shaft, using her thumb to tease the head of him.

With a groan that tore from somewhere deep inside him, Ian came.

She couldn't wait to make him do it again.

CHAPTER FIFTEEN

THE LIGHT ABOVE THE BREAKFAST bar in Miriam's apartment flashed off and on. "Oh, I can't believe it. I've called that in. The super told me he'd fixed it."

Jeremy looked above his head. "It's probably just a loose connection. I'll take a look at it after breakfast."

She flashed him a skeptical look. "Don't worry about it. I hire someone to take care of things like that."

He glanced upward again. "Really, I could check that in a minute."

"There you go again, trying to save me. Honestly, the last thing I want you doing is wasting your time here with me fixing stuff."

His neck reddened. How she loved that about him. It was as if he was slightly embarrassed by their reaction to one another.

"When you put it like that…" Jeremy finished off the omelet Miriam had made him, and set the plate aside. "This was great. Thanks."

Miriam smiled, pleased she'd satisfied one of his hungers. "Glad you enjoyed them. Scrambling eggs is about the only domestic thing I do."

He stood, lifting his plate off the counter. "In that case, I wash and dry. You can sit down."

Wash and dry? By hand? What kind of person did he think she was? Miriam waved his comment away. "Just stack it in the sink. I have someone that comes in every morning to tidy up and prepare a meal for dinner. Takeout gets old."

"You're missing out on one of life's greatest times between two people." His blue eyes grew darker. "Outside of bed."

"Takeout?"

Jeremy shook his head. "Dishwashing. My dad insists it's the key to a happy marriage."

Another knock against the institution. Besides, Miriam couldn't fathom for a moment how dishwashing could be in any way joyful. Housework equaled drudgery in her mind.

"I can see from your face you're skeptical. Every night after dinner, my dad would wash and my mom would dry. They'd talk about their day, the meal, whatever. I could usually hear laughter coming from the kitchen."

Miriam squirmed in her chair, uncomfortable with where this conversation was leading. The illusion of martial bliss. "Couldn't they do other things together?"

"I don't think it's the same. Last year, I bought them a dishwasher for their anniversary. I think mom uses it during the day or on holidays, but for the most part, it's them together at night."

Her eyes widened. What was wrong with these people? "I still don't get it."

"I didn't, either. My father told me it's one of those tasks that your body can do on autopilot. So you talk. You're close, and you stand side by side. The way a relationship should be."

This kind of reminded her of the doc's writing that Ian had been sending to her via email. About how generations of men and women spent time together quietly, doing little more than just being together. How going through life's journey seemed somehow easier when completed with someone you love.

Miriam smiled at him, but for some reason felt melancholy. Wow, happy parents in a happy marriage. Who knew they still existed? Certainly none of her friends came from any intact home life.

She was struck, and not for the first time, by how different she and Jeremy really were from each other. Oh, they connected in bed on a level that was beyond believing, but out of bed?

They were so very different, and not only the age thing. She'd graduated from Wharton, ran a company. Jeremy didn't even have a job, and didn't show much of an inclination to search for one, either.

He believed in domestic bliss.

Her business published articles on flings and long-distance relationships.

He—

The telephone interrupted her thoughts. Jeremy handed her the portable phone, his fingers caressing her hand. She decided right there and then she'd get rid of whoever was on the other end of the line. Fast. "Hello."

"So, tell me immediately why you are still not at work." It was Jenna, Miriam's best friend. Best friend and she still hadn't told her about Jeremy. Not about the weekend in Oklahoma, and not about now, either.

"I was due a break." And Jeremy was the long, tall vacation she'd needed. She watched him as he straightened up in the kitchen, running a damp paper towel over the counters she'd left covered in crumbs.

She could watch him unobserved. Jeremy looked fantastic this morning, shirtless and with his dark hair mussed. A flutter of desire began to unwind inside her. Not a bad way to start her morning.

"I'm coming over there."

Miriam whirled away from the sight of Jeremy in her kitchen, trying not to panic. "No, you can't. I mean—"

"Miriam Cole, what is going on over there? Are you sick? Running away from the law? Have a naked man tucked away folding your towels?"

Miriam gasped. Close. Almost naked and cleaning her kitchen.

"You naughty girl, you have someone there right now."

"No," she insisted. In full panic mode.

Jenna snorted. "Okay, however you want to play it. I expect all the juicy details later. Hey, bring him along tonight."

Oh, damn. This was the night of her monthly book club meeting. It was *Pride and Prejudice,* and at her suggestion. She could talk about that book for hours. And despite that it provided not one, but two romantic endings, sometimes she yearned for a time in her life when she believed in love.

Yes, she could talk about that book for hours, but she'd rather be with Jeremy. And it didn't matter what they were doing, in bed, out of bed, he beat out Jane Austen.

Her heart raced. She was getting in deeper than she'd thought. *Remember the article.* The odds of a long-distance relationship working weren't high. That's when she realized she'd secretly been hoping…what? That they could have something that lasted? The idea didn't make sense.

"I'm going to have to cancel out on you tonight," Miriam said slowly, not happy with the way her heart was turning against her logic.

Jenna made a sound. "I understand. Jane Austen not his scene? Bring him around later. I'm making fondue."

"I'll let you know."

"Wow. That means no, and that you're having great sex. Well, at least one of us is. Enjoy it, Mir."

Miriam replaced the receiver in the charger and took a deep breath. What was she doing? Why was she breaking long-standing commitments for a short-term love affair?

For just one second, she'd almost taken Jenna up on her offer to bring Jeremy over. And then it hit her…how could she take Jeremy? He had little enough in common with her, let alone her friends. He was more than fifteen years younger than any of them.

Which raised the question again, just what was she doing? They'd avoided any real discussion of where their relationship was going. Correction, she'd sidestepped Jeremy's every attempt to bring it up.

He'd said earlier he was game for wherever she saw it headed, and she was holding him to that. But the nagging fact remained, there was some real intimacy here between them, and she didn't want to examine their relationship too deeply.

She dropped her head into her palms.

Strong hands gently rested on her shoulders. "Everything okay?" Jeremy asked.

She nodded, not turning around. "Sure." *I'm just starting to act really irrationally around you. Because of you.*

He tenderly spun her to face him. "I couldn't help overhearing. You know, you don't have to change your routine just because I'm here. I know you have a life. I can head back to my hotel, and—"

Her lips stopped his words. It took him a moment

to respond, her actions probably shocked him. Then he hauled her up tight against his chest and deepened the kiss with his tongue.

She pulled back to suck in a breath. "Make love to me, Jeremy."

IAN RINSED OFF ALL the oil from his body in Ava's shower. He'd invited her in, but she'd shaken her head and given him a wink. That wink told him all he needed to know. Later. They'd be together later. Why did she want to wait?

He knew it'd be sensational. And that loincloth would play a large role in it. After last night's episode on the phone, he'd tried to approach the work-time hours with at least some amount of detachment.

Ava had blown that intention right out of the water.

Hell, he even grew hard thinking about sex with Ava, and he'd only just come by her hand. She had something with that sending-off stuff. Right now, he could battle anything. Conquer anything. Maybe even write that book.

If rolling around in the oil with Ava wasn't inspirational, he didn't know what was.

He found her snuffing out the candles, the smoke rising above her head. She hadn't yet realized he'd returned, so he stepped back and did what any good reporter did.

He observed.

Her skin still glistened with the oil. He almost hated the idea of Ava stepping below the spray of the water and rinsing all of that away. She'd put her beaded top back on, and was now stuffing the used bags into the trash can. She was grace and beauty, and any man of any era would want her for his own.

Except him.

Yeah, keep telling yourself that, buddy. You don't want her for your own.

Ava looked up and smiled, surprised to see him.

"Shower's free," he said.

As Ian waited for her, he brainstormed a few possible titles, but gladly put away his pad and pen when he heard her return. He searched her freshly scrubbed face with his gaze. Ava was uncomplicated. Beautiful. No hang-ups.

Who didn't have hang-ups?

"What kind of childhood did you have?" he asked.

"I'll show you." She pivoted on her bare feet and ambled to one of several large bookcases. Her hips rolling slightly as she walked.

He crossed the room to join her at the bookcase. She pulled a photo album from the shelf and flipped through pages until she found a picture of two children with a man and woman in pith hats carrying picks.

"Those are my parents."

"The famous archaeologists."

"The very ones."

"I'm guessing the little blonde in pigtails is you."

She nodded. "And that's my little brother, Thad."

He raised an eyebrow. "Thad?"

"Short for Thaddeus. It means praise, and believe me, he's never let us forget it. Our parents named us from the ancient Greek lands where they concentrated their studies."

"And Ava?"

"Like a bird."

His eyes narrowed, as if he were examining her more closely. "I don't think I see that."

She laughed. "It's more in the vein of soaring to greatness."

He smiled. "Ah, I see. How old were you in this picture?"

"Six. That's a site right outside of Athens. Up until I was seven, I didn't know anyplace else but an archaeological dig. The summer I turned twelve, I came here, to Oklahoma, to visit my grandma."

"She teach you how to knit? That kind of thing?"

Ava made a snorting sound. "Hardly. Grandma was an actress. In fact, I think an old lover must have left her this place. No, we'd have long drawn-out tea parties, dress up in feather boas and put on elaborate shows."

Ian laughed, imagining the girl she'd been. Then the idea of the woman she was now, prancing in front of him wearing nothing but a boa, chased away everything else.

If it were in the name of research, she'd do it. "Ever think you're still doing pretty much the same thing?"

Now it was Ava's turn to laugh. "You're right. Performing all these rituals is a lot like acting. She must have passed down those interests along with her DNA."

"So, you mentioned a lover."

"Just one of many. She was married four times."

Ian jerked. The lady had his mother beat out by one. But give Janice Cole time.

"Quite scandalous in the 1950s I assure you. Actually, what were my parents thinking? She was no kind of a role model for marital bliss."

Silence stretched between them.

"I was just kidding. She was a great role model. Every one of the men in her life left with a smile."

"I can imagine," Ian said, mentally shrugging off the gloomy thoughts his mother always provoked. "And yet your parents managed to make everything work out long-term."

"Yes, they did. And they were determined to make life a family affair. Despite their obvious displeasure with my chosen career, my parents are wonderful, supportive, but sometimes I wonder, especially after spending so much time with you…"

"Wonder about what?" He'd be happy to indulge her no matter what she had questions about.

She casually lifted a shoulder, but he wasn't fooled. Whatever she planned to reveal was important to her. "On what I may have missed. I want this book to speak to the women of today, but if I'm missing some of those universal experiences, how can we relate? My twenty-first-century dating skills are pretty much worthless. I didn't even know what phone sex was. And sometimes I don't understand the slang you use. We're contemporaries. We're supposed to connect."

"I'd say we connect."

Ava gave him a small shove. "Ian."

"And, it's true, you're far from normal."

She stood to her full height of five foot two. "Now wait a minute, I have done a normal thing or two—"

But Ian gave her a quizzical look. "Never went to a prom. Never cruised. Never hung out at the food court."

"Well—"

"How about a football game? Cheered your team in the rain even though they were losing, because your friends were out there getting their asses handed to them?"

Ava shook her head, closing the picture album and returning it to the bookcase.

"Stayed up past your curfew and gotten grounded?"

Ava folded her arms in front of her chest.

Ian made a tsking sound, his fingers stroking her cheek. "Like I said, you've missed so much." He met her gaze, then snapped his fingers. "Let's make a deal. By day we work on the book, by night, I'll work on expanding your education."

"Didn't we do that at Club Escape?"

"We're going back to the beginning. First-date kind of stuff. Ava, I'm taking you to high school. Hang on."

In three long strides, Ian was at his laptop and punching something into a search engine.

Then he turned and smiled at her, a smile filled with the kind of excitement that made her yearn to be part of whatever he suggested. She almost gasped. Like he was about to steal her away on an adventure she couldn't wait to take.

"You're in luck. The Pirates are playing their arch rivals the Panthers on the court tonight. And you're going as my date."

She pretended to consider his offer, though she could hardly keep from dancing. "So, is that how boys usually ask for a girl's time?"

Ian winked. "No. I have a lot more finesse now. Be ready in an hour."

THE ROARING NOISE GRABBED her attention first. From the moment Ian held open the glass door leading into the gymnasium, sounds of every kind assailed Ava.

The pounding rhythm from the drums echoed her footsteps, the beat only tempered by the tinny blast of the horns from the high-school band clad in orange T-shirts and jeans. Teenage girls lined the court wielding large ornamental balls of fluff. The bleachers were filled with cheering crowds clad in orange and black on one side, and patrons sporting the colors of mustard and ketchup on the other. The battle lines were drawn. Tension permeated the scene.

Some version of this scenario played out in cultures around the world and across time. Turf wars or bragging rights, it was all the same. And she couldn't be more excited to be there.

With a whistle and the sound of a buzzer, tall, lanky boys streamed onto the hardwood floor, their rubber athletic shoes squeaking.

"Here we go," hollered Ian. He escorted her to an empty spot among those proudly wearing the orange and black. "Have you ever seen basketball?"

Ava nodded. "Running up and down. Ball in the net."

Ian's eyes narrowed, but his lips twisted. "Basketball is way more than just running up and down the court. It's the teamwork of passing, the grace of running while dribbling. The excitement of the slam dunk. The refinement of shooting at half court."

She shook her head as if she understood. She pointed to the stands, drawing his attention away from her. "Yeah, the boys with the word *pirate* spelled out on their bare chests in black-and-orange paint especially demonstrate the grace and refinement of the sport."

Ian shot her a glance, his eyes crinkling at the corners. "Now you've got it."

Ian was back to flirting with her again. Her blood seemed to heat and thin all at the same time as it rushed through her body.

The buzzer sounded and the players circled their coach while the fluff-brandishing girls took to the court. Loud dance music, similar to what had been playing at Club Escape, blasted over the sound system, and the girls began to move in a coordinated tribal-like dance.

"What is that?" she asked as she pointed.

"Oh, that's the pom squad, and those girls over by the corner are the cheerleaders. They motivate the crowd."

Ava scanned the faces in the bleachers. Every boy had his gaze trained on the dancers now in the middle of the court. "I can see that."

"The pom girls and cheerleaders inspire many fantasies for the adolescent boys. But then in high school, the soccer girls, the tennis girls, the ones who liked drama or sang in choir, they've all starred in one fantasy or another."

"Yours?"

Ian shook his head. "Me? No. I always liked the smart girls with their nose in a book."

Like she'd been. Yeah, now she knew he was flirting. Her pulse picked up its rhythm.

"However, if you did want to wear one of those short pleated shirts, pull your hair into a ponytail and take up some pom-poms, I wouldn't be…turned off."

She laughed, and quelled the urge to remind him that role-playing and dress up was quite popular in romantic love play in long-term pair bonds. No, she just laughed and had a good time in Ian's funny teasing presence. She liked this side of him, got the feeling he didn't share it with a lot of people. She was warmed by the thought.

"So, we're at the game. We're having fun. What's next for the typical high-school kids out on a date?" she asked.

A mischievous glint touched his brown eyes. "Let me show you one of my best moves."

Ian stretched, lifted his arms, then casually draped one arm around her shoulder. "Did you catch that?" he asked.

"That fake maneuver to touch me? Yes, I caught that." *Was warmed by it, also.*

"Glad to know I've still got it."

He had something all right.

"Now, as a high-school girl, to show you like me, you—"

"I think I can handle that without instruction. I probably scoot up against you." She slid along the smooth wood of the bleacher seat until their thighs touched. Her skin began to tingle. "Like this."

"Exactly like that."

Okay, this wasn't so different from the things she'd demonstrated at the club. They had pure body alignment. Did he remember what she'd said about body positioning? How it would mirror a man and woman's attunement in bed?

The warmth of his body heated her side. The scent of him filled her nose.

"What do you think?" he asked, his arm drawing her closer to him. Her head resting against his chest. This was a different kind of seduction. Slower. Less combative. She liked it more. That easing into another person.

"The rituals of high school are not so different from other courtship ones. The sponsored gatherings where grown-ups can keep a watchful eye. The couples who try to be close to each other."

"Maybe there is something to that instinct stuff."

She rolled her eyes. "Now what?"

"Well, throughout the evening I see just how low my hand can slip. That's called copping a feel."

Ava turned her head to see his fingers just at the swell of her breast. Her stomach knotted, probably how it would have if they were actually seventeen, in high school, and here in the gym together on a date rather than filling in a gap in her education. "Seeing no luck in any downward direction, what then?"

He sighed heavily, turning his attention back to the action on the court. "I try to actually concentrate on something other than you."

Her whole body warmed at his words. Then her lips twisted in a secret smile. Her instincts were telling her she should make his goal to concentrate on something other than her very, very difficult.

CHAPTER SIXTEEN

AFTER THE PIRATES SOLIDLY trounced their rivals, Ian took her on a quick cruise down the famous 39th Street. They stopped at a drive-in for an order of Tater Tots and cherry Cokes.

Ava had been on dates before. An awkward coffee date between classes her freshman year in college. Enthusiastic, yet utterly impersonal dates with story-swapping colleagues. Blind dates set up by her parents with archaeologists on dig sites. None of those had felt right. She'd never felt the ease of simply being herself as she did with Ian.

As Ian drove back to Ava's building, they'd talked and laughed and not a single word was about the book. The Bricktown crowd was light that evening, and they didn't have to wait while pedestrians crossed in front of her garage.

Ian pushed the button for the gate to open, then drove the car inside the loading area redesigned to act as a garage. They were acting as if they were a real couple. She liked being with him like this.

Ava reached for her door handle, sad their evening was coming to an end. Not if she could help it.

"Don't go yet," he said, his hand on her shoulder.

He'd turned the car off, but left the music from the radio on. The lights from the dashboard glowed, but didn't fully illuminate his face. She couldn't tell what he was thinking right now.

His fingers curved around her shoulder. "Come closer," he urged, his voice low and seductive. He pulled her as close to his body as the bucket seat would allow.

A small shiver rippled down her back and settled at the base of her spine. "This is called parking, and if I'm lucky, you'll let me get to first base."

"What's first base?"

"It's a baseball term."

She smiled into the night. "Sports. Of course."

"But on a woman, it's this."

Ava's eyes drifted shut as Ian leaned forward. His lips gently brushed hers again. This kiss was different from anything they'd shared before. Slower and yet tentative and less controlled, as if they really were school kids and this was their first kiss.

Then the real Ian, the mature man of the world took over. His mouth teased and tantalized her lips. She sucked in her breath and held it as his mouth opened over hers.

She wound her arms around his neck and curled her fingers into the dark locks behind his ears. The blood zipped through her veins and she released her breath in a sigh.

Ian eased the pressure of his mouth and began to explore the seam of her lips with his tongue. Her breathing came quick and heavy. She opened her lips to him. He groaned and pulled her tighter.

It could have been hours or maybe only a few minutes, but Ian released her, resting his chin on her forehead. His breathing was hard and labored, matching hers.

"So, if that's first base, I take it there is a second?"

"Yes," he told her, his voice strained.

"You up to showing it to me?" she asked, her body on fire with need.

"Believe me when I say I'm up." He swooped in, and gave her another kiss, then his hands slid to her breasts. "That's another move to distract you," he told her. He never dropped his hands.

Her nipples hardened, growing more sensitive against the lace of her bra. "Although I was never your traditional high schooler, I believe I can safely say that the girl wasn't really fooled by your maneuvers."

"And here I was working under this grand illusion all this time." His lips touched hers again, his tongue doing delightful things to her mouth. "My favorite move at the time was the thumb circle."

He circled her breast with his thumb, his rotations getting tighter and tighter until he reached the tip. "If I were feeling bold, I'd move to below her shirt."

Her stomach quivered when she felt his fingertips caress her bare skin.

"I like your bold moves."

"Then check this out," he said. He leaned over and gently sucked her earlobe into his mouth. She felt his hands on her back, then the looseness of her bra.

She moaned as he fully cupped her breasts. "That was some move," she told him.

He chuckled. "Ready for third?"

"There's another base?" she asked, her body beginning to tremble in excitement.

"Oh, yeah."

She almost whimpered as his hands left her breasts. Then she realized their destination. She slid her legs apart as his hands skimmed down her waist, over her hips and to the place between her thighs. She cursed her tight pants for being in the way.

"What I wouldn't have given to touch a girl like you here at seventeen."

"Think of something," she teased.

"I don't know, but I'm feeling the exact same kind of desperation."

She laughed, loved knowing she made him desperate. He rubbed her though her jeans, and suddenly *she* was desperate. His hand created a delicious friction, and she grew warm and wet and ready to take him inside her body.

His lips found hers again, and he kissed her with a hard, passion-filled caress. At the same time, his hand plunged into her jeans under her panties, his fingers discovering her clit.

She pulled her mouth away, moaning. "Ian."

"More? Relax. I want to touch you all over."

"What's the goal of baseball?"

"To hit a home run," he said, his lips lowering to her collarbone.

"What does it mean with a girl. With me?"

He stopped. Glanced at her. "To make love to you."

Her body trembled. She was ready for a home run. "Ian, would you like to come up for some coffee?"

"I can't tell you how much I'd love a cup of coffee."

IT WAS THE QUICKEST he'd ever exited a car. Ian followed her upstairs and into her apartment, nothing and no one around them. They were the only two people in the world. The large front room was still scented by a subtle hint of oil.

Ian locked the door behind them, and trailed her into

the kitchen. "Should I actually pretend to make it?" she asked.

A smile briefly touched his lips as he practically stalked toward her. Ava sucked in a breath. The lessons had stopped. Now they were just man and woman. And primal instinct.

He grasped her head, then brought her mouth to his lips. This kiss was neither controlled nor deliberate, but hungry and ready for her.

This was no slow seduction. Only need and passion.

"You on top," she said.

He almost growled. Ian bent, reaching under her knees and hauling her against his body. He marched into her bedroom, and carefully set her on the mattress. He moved to follow her, but she held out her hand.

"Wait," she ordered. "Watch."

She tugged her shirt up and over her head. She'd never bothered to rebutton her jeans after his ministrations in the car, so with a quick flick of her wrist, the zipper was down and her pants off.

She lay against her pillows wearing nothing but a sexy bra and panties. They matched. Black with little pink bows. His new favorite color.

She also hadn't bothered to snap her bra into place after he showed her his moves in conjunction with second base, so the material slipped easily off her body.

She sat before him in only those skimpy little panties. He'd felt what secrets were hidden behind that tiny swatch of lace. She'd described imagining his fingers there, his cock learning those secrets of hers when he'd taught her about phone sex.

What he hadn't done was see her. Her fingers hooked around the edge of her panties, and she slowly wiggled them down her thighs. She kicked them away, and lay before him naked. Availing herself desirably, his arousal grew.

"Ava, here's another conversation you probably need to learn. The condom discussion. Do I need to get them? I have some in my camera bag. But I want you to know that I always play it safe, and I get tested all the time because of my trips overseas. I'm clean."

"Me, too."

He swallowed. "What about pregnancy? You protected there?"

"You don't want to use a condom, do you?"

"I can think of nothing else but the erotic feel of your skin against mine."

"I'm protected there, as well. Don't worry, I won't get pregnant."

He moved toward her, and she put her hand out again. "Wait. Not yet."

He groaned in frustration, but then his eyes widened as she ran her hands down her body to caress her breasts, circle her navel, stroke her clit. His breathing turned shallow and his heart almost went through his ribs at the site of her fingers touching, drawing pleasure, from the very place he wanted to be.

"You like watching me touch myself, don't you, Ian?"

He nodded. "Most men love to see a woman take pleasure in her body. It turns them on, makes them harder."

His cock swelled against his jeans. Quickly he stripped, and her eyes cut his erection a glance. A feminine smile lifted her mouth.

"You see, for men, finding orgasm comes easily. Not so much for women. It takes a little time. Then women discovered the secret, their true power. It's in their pleasure. A man's pleasure, your pleasure is actually heightened by mine."

He nodded, his eyes never leaving the vision of her fingers caressing between her legs.

"That's nature's way of making sure man took care of woman. And if a woman finds a man who's all into taking that time, she knows she has a winner. Nice how it works that way. Look at me, Ian."

His eyes traveled slowly up her body until he met her gaze.

"You're going to make me feel good, aren't you?" she asked, half question, half demand.

"Yes. So good."

She smiled, rested against the pillows and spread her legs for him.

He took himself in hand, moved toward her and found where she'd opened to him. She moaned at the intimate thrust of his flesh sliding into hers.

She locked her legs behind his waist, her body a perfect fit for him. He began to thrust more deeply inside her. Ava started to move with him, against him. Her face tightened. Her muscles gripped him. He ground his hips against hers, finding her clit. That sent her over the edge.

She screamed, her climax hit hard. Her moans, her grip of his penis, it was all too much. He went right over the edge with her.

Soon their breathing returned to normal. The only other sound was the blowers from the heating unit keeping them warm. She lay in his arms, stroking his skin. Utterly content.

Her fingers found the knot of flesh below his right shoulder blade. The scar.

"I was shot."

Ava gasped, her brows knitting together in concern. "Why?"

He shrugged. "Some people don't like reporters."

"So they shot you?"

There were worse things than being shot at, he'd seen plenty of it. Normally, he wouldn't have a problem talking about it. But Ava, as he was quickly realizing, had spent an idealized youth jetting from one remote archaeological dig to another, then from the protected walls of university to on-the-job research among cultures that were actually getting along. Not his area of expertise.

Deep down—hell, not so deep down—Ava was an optimist. She easily found the good in anything. Five minutes of hearing his war stories could wipe that brightness of spirit right out.

He sat up, reaching for his shirt.

"Where are you going?"

"Back to the hotel. It's late, I thought you might want your privacy." Plus she hadn't invited him to stay.

"Here's a story you might find interesting. The early American Puritans thought one way to gauge if a couple would be happy together was partly based on whether or not they slept together well."

"Sleep together or actually sleep together?"

She paused for a moment. "Oh, I get it. *Sleep together* is a euphemism for sex. No, in this case, sleeping together actually meant sleeping together. Of course, this was a culture where innocence was valued for both men and women, so a board was placed in the bed between the young man and woman. If they slept well next to each other, it was seen as a good sign."

Ian scrubbed a hand down his face. "Ava, I'm too worn out to work on the book right now."

She shook her head. "What I'm trying to say, and obviously not very well, is that you can stay the night here with me, and I promise—no board."

NATURALLY, HE WOKE WITH her breast in his hand. Was there a better way to sleep? Her soft backside pressed into the heaviness of his erection.

He wound a lazy path with his fingers along her skin, inviting her to wake up. He smoothed the hair back from her neck, watching the blond locks fan out against her pillow. He loved her hair. Loved seeing its softness spread out on the sheets, in his hand, across his body.

With her neck exposed, he ran his tongue along its slope, already knowing that particular spot was one of her favorites.

"Mmm," she moaned and tilted her hips, pushing her soft rear against his hardened cock. She stilled. "Oh."

"Yes, oh."

He lowered his hand until he found her breast again. "I love your breasts. How they respond to me. How you taste."

But as tempting as her breasts may be, he wanted the slick feel of her against his fingers. Ian lowered his hand, stopping as he felt the soft curls between her thighs.

Her hips jerked, forcing her harder against his penis. He fought the urge to sink into her. No, he wanted to touch her, savor her.

He found her clit, damp and so responsive to his touch. She gasped with just his slightest graze. His fingers lowered, and he smiled at what he found. "So warm, so wet. Are you ready for me, Ava?"

She nodded. "Yes."

Ava made a small protesting noise when he moved

his hand away. His fingertips skimmed down her thigh and stopped just above her knee. He pulled her leg over his, getting her into position. His penis found her wet opening, and he slid home. Slowly. They both groaned at the wonderful sensation of her body enveloping his.

His entry complete, his hand sought her clit once more. He stroked her and her every muscle tensed. He thrust and fingered her, every part of his body working together to bring them both pleasure.

Her inner muscles began to quiver around him. He knew she was close. "I want to hear you," he said.

Nothing, not one thing was as erotic as hearing Ava find her release. Her body tensed, then with a burst she clamped down, making him moan.

He doubted he could last much longer. Then he felt her, heard her come. She cried out his name, and he changed his mind. Hearing his name on her lips as she reached her orgasm, now *that* was the most erotic thing he'd ever heard.

"We never really set up any ground rules for what we're doing," she said a few moments later as he was about to drift off to sleep.

"We never really set up any ground rules on who was the decision maker over the book, either, and that's going just fine," he countered.

"A technicality."

Ian rolled onto his back and tucked her head against his chest. "You're going to make me talk, aren't you?"

"You know what I always say—"

"Yes, I know. Most problems between a man and woman can be cleared up with one good sit-down conversation."

She lifted her head and smiled down at him. "Most conflicts can be avoided that way, too."

He chuckled tiredly. "Doing this after sex is a sneaky blow."

"One practiced by generation after generation of women."

"My job is too complicated for any type of relationship."

"I figured so, like mine. All the traveling. But I like what we have right now."

His heartbeat quickened. "Me, too."

Her eyes narrowed. "And I don't think we need to worry that us making love will ruin the sexual tension of the book. Not anymore."

"So, as long as we're working on the book together…"

He gently pushed her head back down to his chest, her hair fanning across his skin. "Then we're together." He liked the sound of that.

"Why did you become a reporter, Ian?"

Was he off the hook now? No more discussion talk? And why did he feel…let down that she didn't want more of a relationship from him? He sighed heavily. "I've always been curious, always wanted to know what's around the next corner. That first time I was running across the desert with my camera, being chased, that's when I knew who I was. I felt the most alive."

Except right now. Dog-tired, sated and with Ava lying across his chest, he felt very much alive. They'd said the book, but there was also that vacation. Plus revisions, captions for the photos, suggestions from the copy editor, final proofs…

CHAPTER SEVENTEEN

THEIR LAST WEEK HAD TAKEN on a nice routine of working on the book together in the morning, sending the manuscript pages to his sister in the afternoon and taking pictures at night. They'd made tremendous progress despite being delightfully interrupted to make love and to argue as to who exactly was making the final decisions.

Ian and Ava sat cross-legged on the floor in front of her fireplace as they debated about an ancient warrior class. "I'm telling you it's true."

Ian gave her a skeptical look. "So you're telling me that once they stole the woman and he had her in his possession, it was suddenly okay with her father that she was gone? Her family is hell-bent on protecting her, then all of a sudden all these alpha males just throw up their hands, and say, 'Oh, well, you won.'"

Ava made a face. "Well, when you put it like that it does sound far-fetched."

"I think some of your theories need a male's point of view from time to time."

She glanced up sharply. She was about to ask Ian if he planned to volunteer for the job. As a joke. Then she saw the look on his face. The man was clearly horrified by what had just come out of his mouth.

She searched for something to fill the gulf that suddenly arose between them.

"What I find so interesting," she began, "is that after

they've stolen the woman, they then try to woo her. I mean, she's there…he's got her. But he works very hard to win her love."

Ian cleared his throat. "Makes some sense to me. It's not just about sex. He's taken that woman to be his wife. His companion. It's about loneliness, and the need to spend your time with someone who doesn't want to run away or toss a knife in your back."

Silence stretched between them once more. Since they'd become lovers, nothing even close to resembling an awkward moment had passed between them. Now there had been two.

Maybe she should try to tempt him with the paints. Although the idea was to paint yourself and wash your partner, they'd improvised, taking on both roles. She'd try something else. "Maybe he just needed a friend."

"He'd have been insulted if she'd offered. A woman should never tell a man she just wants to be his friend."

"Don't men want friends?"

"Not the women ones," he said drily.

She laughed, and reached for a newspaper clipping. "Hey, I think I found the perfect thing for more of my twenty-first-century dating indoctrination. It's called a cuddle party."

Ian's eyes widened in alarm. "Have you ever been to one? It's supposed to be great. Hugging and touching. Perfect to shake off any intimacy issues."

"I'm fine with my intimacy issues just the way they are."

"You're in a strange mood today."

His eyes narrowed as he looked at her. An odd smile passed across his lips. "You're right." He stood and stretched his legs. "I'm sorry. Miriam emailed me and asked for a rush on the last chapter. I stayed up late to finish the manuscript."

"I can't wait to see it, and give you my final decision," she said with a smile. But Ian didn't return her grin at the mention of their inside joke.

"I'll go back to the hotel and print it off."

She glanced down at the case he used to carry his laptop. "Why not print it off here? You can use mine."

Ian shook his head. "I need to call my sister, too."

She rolled to her feet. "In that case, I'll walk you to the door."

He turned toward her, his expression suddenly intense. "Let me take you out to celebrate. Champagne, the works."

"That would be nice."

He kissed her cheek, and shut the door behind him.

Something was wrong, and she had a good idea what it was. The book was complete. A dozen questions swirled around them. The one foremost in her mind…what happened next?

THE PHONE RANG JUST as Jeremy had scooped Miriam against his side. He loved holding her that way. With a reluctant kiss, she slipped out of bed.

She'd been receiving a lot of calls lately, mostly from work. She'd gone in this morning, but had taken the rest of the afternoon off, although a lot of calls were still being diverted her way.

"Hey, Ian."

Jeremy recognized the name. Ian was her brother. The only family she spoke of. He watched as she tucked the phone between her head and shoulder and tugged on a robe. Her long, dark hair looked mussed, and curled down her back. All he could think about was the feel of her hair on his skin.

The soft arousing tickle as it trailed down his stomach as her mouth moved closer to his penis.

He hated that she'd stayed cooped up in her apartment for so long because of him. Miriam was a popular woman. He'd gathered that by the number of phone calls, and the lack of any real substantive food in her kitchen.

"No, I'm not doing anything at all." Her voice carried into the bedroom. Well, they *had* just finished.

He watched as Miriam rolled her head from side to side. "Just a boring weekend at home alone."

Just a boring weekend?

Alone?

His mouth went dry. Something dark and bitter broke free in him. No, when had he become so paranoid? So Miriam wasn't ready to share the news about them with her friends and family. No problem. This was all new to him, too. Except he wanted to shout from the rooftops that Miriam chose to be by his side.

Jeremy thrust the sheets away from his body and swung his legs to the floor. He pulled on his jeans and grabbed his T-shirt. Hating what he was thinking of Miriam.

She said goodbye to her brother and returned to him. "Good news, my brother and the doc finished the book, and if that last chapter is as good as what I've already read, it's going to be great."

He knew how much of her company's resources she'd put behind that book, and its success meant a lot to her both professionally and personally. "Let's go out, Miriam, go to a restaurant and cut loose. Maybe we could invite your friends."

She dropped her hand so fast from around his waist, she almost left skid marks on his back. "No, Jeremy. We can't."

"Can't? What do you mean can't?"

"Going out to a restaurant would be too much like a date. I can't have a relationship with you. Date you. You probably think dating is going to the Taco Barn with change you found between the cushions of your couch. Or on the floorboard of your car."

Jeremy made a face. "That would mean I'd actually have to clean. You're serious? You really don't want to go out? Get to know each other's friends?"

She nodded, her face looking tortured. "Don't you see? I'm over fifteen years older than you, Jeremy. Believe me when I say I can't pass for twenty. Hell, sometimes I can't pass for thirty."

"No one's asking you to pass for anything."

"Do you realize what people will say? They'll take one look at us together and make assumptions. They'll call you my boy toy. I'd look pathetic."

"That's easily fixed. You just stare down anyone who's stupid enough to tell you that and say, 'Screw you.'"

She stalked into the dining room and huffed, "Oh, that's really mature."

"Then that fits, because apparently I'm low in adult behavior skills."

Miriam twisted her hands together. "Would you stop acting like that?"

He turned a surprised gaze to her. "Like what?"

"Like you're all broken up about this."

The silence between them stretched taut.

She reached for his hand, caught his fingers between hers. "Jeremy, I never meant to hurt you. I didn't ask you to come here. You did that all on your own. I never even returned your phone calls."

His hands dropped to his sides, and he took a step back. He could accept a woman not interested in him. He was a guy who could bow out gracefully. But with Miriam, he'd planned to at least put up a fight. A fight she apparently didn't want him to make.

"If you'd turned me down right from the beginning, offered to play hostess to me being tourist, instead of us winding up in bed—I would have walked on. That would have been the end of it."

Her brown eyes didn't soften.

"But the minute you fell into my arms, the second your lips touched mine, I knew what that kick in the stomach was all about. What I'd been missing since you left Oklahoma."

Miriam refused to meet his eyes.

"A fire burns between us." He grabbed her shoulders. "If this were no more than a second one-night stand, it would have been through by the weekend. You wouldn't have extended it into this week. It's hotter than it was before."

"Think of this as just getting lucky. You're twenty. You should be into easy lays."

He shook his head. "Don't make this into that…"

"I did. Our time—"

"Our time was all about you and me. It's been there all along. And for the record, I could afford to take you someplace other than Taco Barn. I have a good job back home."

Her eyes narrowed, finally meeting his gaze. "One that allows you to take off and leave for weeks at a time?" she asked. Her voice skeptical.

"As a matter of fact, yes. I own my own business.

I flip houses. I buy them cheap, fix them up and sell them at a nice profit. The housing market is usually slower in February. That's when I normally book my vacation. And don't worry, even if I should lose a job, I can always find another. People are always looking for someone who can fix things. I can go anywhere I want. Men who can work with their hands, cabinetry, plumbing, we're a dying breed."

"OH," MIRIAM SAID, suddenly feeling deflated. She'd insulted Jeremy. "I'm sor…"

Her words trailed off as he brushed a stray lock of hair from her face and tucked it behind her ear. "Don't be too hard on yourself, though. You spent this time with me because you love me."

She jerked away. "Jeremy, don't make this into something it's not. I know you expect to have what your parents had. To fall instantly in love and live happily forever. But they were lucky. It doesn't work like that for everyone. For most people."

"My parents listened to their hearts. And it wasn't just luck. They worked at their marriage. They *made* it work. They became the person the other one could count on. I want you to count on me. I want to be the man who left the world a little better than the way I found it by fixing things with my hands. I want to be the guy who took his kids out for doughnuts on a Saturday morning so Mommy could sleep in. But one thing I don't want to be—the man whose woman was too embarrassed to introduce him to her friends."

She stood away from him. "You don't love me, and I certainly don't love you," she told him.

"Prove it," he challenged.

You went to bed with me because you love me, she answered, but didn't say the words out loud.

Jeremy stepped toward her. "Tell me how you feel about me. Tell me you don't love me."

"I don't love you," she told him quickly. Firmly.

She saw that flicker of hurt touch his eyes. She knew better than this. At least she should have. She was older and supposedly wiser. Miriam had spotted the vulnerability in him. She should have known it would come to this, and avoided it. The responsibility of hurting him cut deeply, she was sick and angry with herself.

"That sounded really convincing."

"The truth usually is."

"Prove it's the truth."

She tilted her head toward him. "How?"

He held out his arms. "Come over here and kiss me."

Sexier words had never been spoken. Desire pounded her body. "I'm not going to kiss you." But her words lacked any defiant conviction.

"Well, how do I know that's how you really feel?"

"I just told you how I really feel."

She couldn't take much more of this. She'd kiss him, prove him wrong, send him back to Oklahoma. And she'd make a vow. Never, ever get involved with someone under thirty. Forty.

"No sly stuff."

"You assuming you're going to lose?"

"No, I'm assuming that you're tricky."

"Tricky? I'm hurt you'd say that. I've always been straightforward with you. I want you. I want to spend more time with you, and get to know you even better. It's you who hasn't been honest. With yourself."

"Oh, come over here, kiss me and get it over with."

"Now darlin', I can say I've had better offers than that."

"Fine." Anything to get this point proven and the whole thing over with.

She walked with slow, deliberate steps toward him. He took a seat at her dining-room table.

So her younger lover wasn't going to make this any easier for her. She had no desire to hurt him. She wouldn't try to lay on him a kiss that would send Jeremy reeling. She'd simply give him his kiss, all the while remaining detached.

After Oklahoma, he'd haunted her nights, but now that was over. She just had to make him believe it. And herself. She'd focus on something completely mundane, *not* on the sexy ruggedness of his voice.

She lowered her head, and her hair fell forward, shrouding them. At the first touch, his lips remained firm. And closed. Miriam pulled away slightly and darted her tongue along the seam of his lips, then traced the outer edges with the tip of her tongue.

Still nothing from him.

The blood pounded in her ears, her mouth grew desperate for the taste of him.

"What are you trying to do here? Why aren't you kissing me back?"

"Maybe if you put some feeling into it. If you trusted yourself to," his voice taunted.

"Maybe it's because there are no feelings involved."

"Then prove it, and kiss me like you mean it."

Miriam braced her arms on the armrests of her very expensive mahogany dining-room chair. She felt like rolling up her sleeves and getting to work on this guy. She trailed small kisses to his ear then licked the sensitive skin below.

He sucked in a breath.

Good. She traced the edge of his ear with her tongue. Jeremy moved his hands to her head and tugged her face to his. He met her lips with his mouth open. Fire shot through her body, tightening her nipples and sending a rush of feeling downward, fueling her desire.

Jeremy jerked her closer, his kiss deepening.

Off balance, she fell onto his lap, straddling his legs. The hard ridge of his cock sent another wave of warmth through her. She pushed herself closer, touching him through their scant clothes. She began to move up and down, mimicking the moves she'd make on the mattress.

Jeremy placed his hands on either side of her face and gently thrust her away. She balanced her forehead on his. Their heavy breathing filled the room. Jarringly, she sat up and shoved the hair from her face. She couldn't pretend that was nothing—her nipples still throbbed.

Okay, it was sex. Just sex. But nothing else.

Through a sensual haze, their gazes locked. His eyes blazed like sunlit sapphires.

"You're right," he said, his tone flat. His expression blank. "You don't love me."

He'd called her bluff.

And then Jeremy Kelso pushed himself up from the chair, collected his things and walked out her door and out of her life.

That's when she noticed the light in her kitchen was working.

CHAPTER EIGHTEEN

IAN LOOKED AT HIS WATCH for the third time. A feeling completely foreign and strange came over him. He wasn't exactly sure what it was until he looked at his watch yet again in the span of less than thirty seconds. That's when the feeling wagged its smug little finger at him.

He was nervous.

Why was he nervous? He wasn't a nervous kind of guy. People shot at him, and he didn't blink at that.

But he knew the reason. He was edgy because his time with Ava was over. He'd typed the last word of the book last night. This morning he'd scanned the last picture and emailed everything to his sister. He expected to hear from her at any moment. But he wasn't worried about her thoughts on the book. He knew that *Sex by the Book*—the new title—was stunning. Ava had created something amazing. But...

He'd faced guns, angry officers of the law and death, but none of that compared with facing Ava when she arrived. He'd said goodbye to a few women in his day, but they'd all been like him, looking for some contemporary company.

And he'd never been in love with any of them.

In fact, falling in love had never entered his mind. *What the hell?*

Had the word *love* just charged into his head? Twice? If it had, he planned to make it exit. Love, if he even believed it existed, didn't mix with anyone with the last name Cole.

But then he thought of the beautiful woman on her way to him. Damn. He'd done it. Or she'd done it. Whoever it was, he'd fallen in love with Ava Simms.

He'd been an idiot not to see it coming. How could he not spend all that time with someone as witty, smart and sexy as Ava and not fall in love with her?

Yes, it was definitely time to go.

Then he saw her walk through the door of the elegant restaurant where he'd booked a table for them to celebrate the completion of the book. Huge chandeliers hung from the ceiling, and the most expensive china and silverware graced the table.

The perfect setting for a breakup.

She smiled at the hostess in greeting. He'd miss that smile aimed in his direction, Ava's blond hair flowing freely around her face the way he liked. Damn, she was so beautiful. And challenging. She made him wish for things. Things he could never have.

It was right to end it now.

Ava removed her sunglasses and he watched as her beautiful green eyes scanned the area. Their gazes met. Held.

Those emerald eyes of hers communicated a wealth of feeling. Each intriguing. But the emotion that called to him, drew him in, was the promise he saw lingering in their lush depths. A promise he couldn't take her up on.

She smiled at him now, and he almost changed his mind. Almost. He didn't return her smile.

Ava slid into the plush seat across from him, her eyes searching his. She seemed to find what she was looking for because she dropped her gaze and sighed. "You're leaving, aren't you?"

He nodded.

"What about taking a vacation?"

"You know that wasn't really real. We just told ourselves that. My flight leaves tonight."

A line formed between her eyebrows. "So soon? Don't I get any say in this?"

He shrugged, knowing he was hurting her. "Why would you?" he asked, angry at himself for being deliberately cruel.

He sighed and looked around the restaurant, avoiding looking at her. Having this last meal with her had been a mistake. Soon she'd have him rethinking his decision to leave. To follow his chosen career path. Like after the sending-off ceremony, when he thought he could do anything.

She lifted her shoulders in a slight shrug. "Yeah, why would I?"

A waiter approached their table. Oblivious to the tension between them, he asked merrily, "What can I get you folks to drink?"

Her green eyes examined Ian once more, then she looked up toward their waiter and offered him a tight smile. "Nothing for me, thanks. I've decided I'm not hungry."

She stood, and Ian stood along with her. "Ava, let's—"

"No, Ian, it's okay. Stay, or go. It doesn't matter. I'll take a walk around the canal. Plan what I'm going to do next. Maybe sort out that vacation."

He flinched. The idea of her vacationing, having a life without him, made him ache.

"In fact, I missed a call from your sister." Ava balanced on her tiptoe and kissed his cheek. "Take care," she whispered below his ear.

This wasn't right. She shouldn't be leaving him. He shouldn't be letting her go. Letting her go? Hell, he'd pushed her away.

They should be celebrating over wine and candles

and all that romantic stuff he knew would make her happy. They should be swapping memories of the last few days of the writing process. Laughing over times they'd argued, because it was done now and the finished product really worked.

Afterward, he would take her into his arms. Lead her onto the dance floor, then later hold her in his arms while they made love. Any normal boyfriend should be thrilled things were beginning to work out for her career.

But he wasn't boyfriend material. His sister called him an adrenaline junkie. A risk taker. And there was Ava, a gentle researcher. An academic. How would their lives ever meet?

Ending this—it was the right thing to do. He knew it. But knowing that didn't make it stop hurting like hell.

MIRIAM SAT FOR A MOMENT and watched the blinking cursor on her laptop screen. It felt good to be back in the swing of things. She knew catching up on work at home would make her return that much smoother.

Work. The one thing that was always there for you. Never left your side.

She'd learned on her father's knee that reaching the top level of a chosen career was the epitome of success. Things like family and kids never really factored in. Certainly hadn't played a key role with her dad, anyway.

Words like *kids,* and *mommy* and *doughnut* seemed to roll off Jeremy's tongue without him even choking. Weird.

Miriam rubbed her temples. She couldn't remember the last time she let someone else handle the particulars. Jeremy had wanted to handle the particulars. He'd been interested in her business. Keeping their home clean. Feeding her. Fixing the things that were broken in her life.

But she'd realized a long time ago, there was no fixing some things that were broken. Especially when the breaks and tears had happened so long ago. She'd been cynical about love, about men, about relationships by the time she was thirteen. A few delightful days spent with Jeremy were never going to fix that.

Yet...she'd wanted them to.

A knock sounded at her door and she jumped, knowing it was him. It had been two long days since Jeremy had left her apartment. Left her.

But she'd recognized his knock. A funny thing to be familiar with, but there it was. She could distinguish his knock as surely as she could make out his scent or the build of his body.

She raced for the door, swinging it open. Jeremy stood there, looking sad and oh, so good on her eyes. "I'm leaving tonight. Thought I'd say goodbye."

She nodded, not really trusting herself to speak.

He rubbed the callused pad of his thumb against the swollen softness of her lips. She darted out a tongue and tasted his skin, unable to stop herself. With a groan, his lips found hers with an urgency that made her heart skip and her toes curl.

She buried her fingers in Jeremy's hair, pulling him closer as she opened her mouth for him.

Thrills shot through her as his tongue entered her mouth and filled her with heat. Jeremy's hands moved from her waist to cup her breasts, and she moaned deep in her throat.

MIRIAM SMOOTHED HER HAIR from her forehead and molded herself to Jeremy, not ready to let go of him yet. She placed a kiss in that sensitive place between his neck and shoulder. "I'm glad you came back."

Jeremy lifted from her, his expression...not one that was typical of Jeremy. "Yeah, me, too," he said as he rolled off her.

Miriam scooted up against the headboard, watching as he reached for his jeans and stepped into them. He'd just tugged his shirt over his head when she finally clued in to the fact that he was actually getting dressed. Dressed to leave her.

"Are you going?" she asked. Surprised.

He gave her a tight nod. "It's time."

She yanked the sheet up and around her body. "Oh, well, you can..." Her words trailed off. What was she about to offer? That he could stay with her? Until when, morning? She recalled supervising the article on women broadcasting mixed signals.

What kind of mixed signals was she disseminating to Jeremy?

That she wanted him?

That she only wanted him for sex?

That she'd only use him for sex because she was afraid of what others would say and think?

When had she become so shallow? When had she become so much like her mother?

Her eyes prickled, and the back of her throat tightened. What a cold bitch she was.

"You came back tonight to show me how I made you feel. To show me what it feels like to only be used for sex."

His sad blue eyes met hers, and he shrugged. "I started out that way, but I could never use you for sex, Miriam. I care for you too much."

Was she so shallow she was about to lose the best thing in her life?

No.

She didn't deserve him.

He tugged on a boot. She didn't deserve him, but she wasn't so stupid she was going to let him walk out of her life so easily. Things seemed so clear now. Sure, the cynical side of herself would say she was trying to pound square pegs into round holes because she wanted Jeremy.

And so what if she were? Wasn't he, wasn't the thing between them, worth fighting for?

"Jeremy, wait."

He turned slowly, reluctantly.

Her stomach clenched. She'd never seen that look on his face. Dejected. Tired. Resolved. "There are a million reasons why this shouldn't work between us."

"You've told me already."

"But I haven't told you why it can."

The next words would be hard to get out. She hadn't said them to another person since she was seven.

"I love you. You were right. I don't know how it happened, maybe that scientist author who's working with my brother is right, and something in you triggered something in me."

She wrapped her fingers around his hand. "I know you'd never hurt me. You'll try to rescue me and take care of me, and I'll just say 'screw it' to anyone who says something about our age difference."

Miriam saw his body tense. Then relax. In relief she realized she was winning him.

His expression lightened. "That's my Miriam."

She reached for him, drew him to her. "That's who I'll be. Your Miriam."

He lowered his head and kissed her gently on the lips.

"I have tickets to the ballet tomorrow. I can't wait to introduce you to my friends," she said.

"Ballet? How about a baseball game? Maybe even tennis? I'll even throw in dinner."

She let out a laugh, and his grin turned into a full smile.

"Tough," she said and touched the tip of her tongue to the seam of his lips.

"Miriam, when you do things like that to me, I can't go slow."

She ran her tongue up the side of his neck until she found his ear, tugging his lobe gently with her teeth.

Jeremy scooped her up in his arms. "I'll wait for slow next time. I want you now."

Miriam liked the sound of that.

AVA STOOD IN THE OPEN doorway of her apartment, only to find Ian leaving a stack of papers she assumed was the last chapter of the manuscript. He dropped the spare key she'd given him on top. She was startled, but not entirely surprised to see him still there. Something between them felt...unfinished. At least in her mind. Perhaps he felt it, too.

He stood slowly and faced her. "Miriam approved the book, it's going into production."

She forced a smile, feeling next to nothing. "That's great."

"You should be getting the rest of your advance now. That should seed you for your next project or your vacation."

"Actually, I pitched another idea to Miriam. It came to me on my walk."

He stuffed one hand into the back pocket of his jeans. "Really? I thought you might try to find work teaching."

"I thought I would, too. But now I find I'm missing doing the actual field research. I think I'd much rather be out discovering new things than writing about them. It was a large part of my life, and I want to get back to it. Like you and being a reporter."

He nodded slowly. "Just like me."

"In fact, something you said gave me the idea. Remember how you said I knew all these ancient customs, but nothing of my own? Well, that's what I plan to work on, the more unusual marriage and courtship customs found in modern times."

"Where do you plan to go first?"

"Miriam and I agreed on Sweden. I want to explore the rituals from colder climates. See how they're different. How they're the same. There's something kind of sexy about spending months indoors under the covers with your love." Her voice trembled. She'd tried to make it detached, but all she could imagine was snuggling under the covers with Ian.

"Maybe when you're done with the research on that we could…" His words trailed.

Her throat began to ache. He was going to say work on the book together. "Yeah. Maybe. I'd like that." She paused. Somehow this conversation felt like that coffee role-play. She'd offer him coffee. He'd accept knowing she was inviting him in for something other than a hot beverage.

Except this time it was about something a lot more close to her than coffee. This was the role-play about not seeing each other again, while pretending they would. This role-play only made her sad.

"Where are you headed?" she asked.

"The jungles of South America. Some interesting stuff brewing down there."

She suppressed a shudder at the thought of Ian in the line of fire. "I'm sure you'll enjoy the pace."

A long awkward silence followed. She should be used to those by now, but she wasn't. Ava folded her arms across her chest. He lifted the strap of his laptop case over his shoulder.

"You know, there's one thing you never talked to me about twenty-first-century dating."

"What's that?"

"How to act when it ends."

Something dark and fierce blazed in Ian's brown

eyes, then faded. His fingers lifted, almost as if he were going to reach for her. But he didn't.

"It ends as friends."

Her heart ached. She didn't want friendship. She wanted more. "I thought you told me men never wanted friendship from a woman."

Ian shrugged, and dropped his gaze. "Sometimes when that's all you can have, that's what you take."

Her throat tightened. "Ian, I wanted to thank you for everything. If you hadn't—"

He shook his head, and his eyes met hers once more. "No need to thank me. It was all you. I just helped you... bring it out."

Ian smiled then, the first genuine smile he'd given her since the end of the book. "Goodbye, Ava."

Two Weeks Later

"PEOPLE AS HAPPY AS you are shouldn't be allowed in public," Ian said, as he cradled his head in his hands.

Miriam patted him on the shoulder. "And someone as miserable as you are should be shot and put out of their misery. What is wrong with you? I thought you'd be happy covering those peace talks. They're not very peaceful, are they? That's right up your alley."

"I was. Am."

"Come on, baby brother. Tell me what it is."

"Drifting from one place to another isn't exciting anymore. I don't get the rush. That jolt of excitement. Chasing danger just feels...silly." Because nothing could ever be as thrilling and challenging as Ava.

"What is it you've been chasing all this time, Ian?"

He lifted his shoulders. "I don't know. I don't know if I ever did know."

"Now you seem more like you're running."

And how. But what was he running from? From Ava?

From his feelings? What if he did find her again? Try for something resembling a normal relationship? Things would eventually fall apart around him. They always did. And then he'd hurt like hell.

He was hurting right now.

At least if he found her again, he'd get to spend the good times with her while it lasted, right?

"Sis, we're in the media biz. Love and happiness, it's all an illusion. Our job is to market happiness, but promote it in such a way that people always want more. We sell a fantasy. How do you know if you're really in love?"

Miriam rolled her eyes. "You know what not being in love feels like, right? Do you feel like that?"

"No." He didn't have the strength to deny it any longer. It was time to face facts. Weeks had passed, and whatever trick passion played on his heart had not faded. Usually he forgot the woman as soon as they'd both said goodbye.

He *was* in love with Ava.

A slight smile tugged at his lip. "What's even more bizarre, I was actually happy with Ava." He knew some people who, when they found their latest "love of their life," became miserable and made everyone around them unhappy, too.

"What's more, you're not happy now without her," Miriam pointed out.

He scrubbed a hand down his face. "You're right, but you know how things are. How could I subject her to me? She's really bett—"

"If you actually say something stupid like 'she's better off without me' and you're backing away to be good to her, I'm really going to scream."

"Look at Mom, Dad. They probably passed along some personality trait that actually makes the person I love better off not being around me. They were bad enough as single entities, but combined together in my DNA..."

"The love-destruction gene? I don't think so." Miriam's lips firmed. "I almost pushed away the best thing that's ever come into my life because I was afraid I was too much like Dad, enjoying a trophy boy toy. You're worried you're like Mom. Are you using Ava to your own selfish advantage? Only being with her because of what she can give you before you move on?"

He shook his head. "No."

"Then what's the problem? The fact that you're willing to push her away, wrong though it is, proves you're looking out for her best interest, and not being a jerk. And screw Mom and Dad as examples. If anything, I think we're better candidates for marriage because we've witnessed firsthand all the things you can do wrong to ruin a relationship."

The tension he'd been carrying in his shoulders, and the ache twisting his gut relaxed. "Right. Who we should be feeling sorry for are all those people who grew up in normal, functional homes and think love is easy."

Brown eyes met brown eyes and they both laughed.

"I do love Ava, and you know, when I was with her I never felt that urge to keep looking over the next hill to see if there was something more exciting."

"Isn't there someone else you should be saying all this to?"

Ian looked up and met his sister's serious gaze.

"You're happy? You really are?"

Miriam nodded.

"I'm out of here."

Miriam reached over and buzzed Rich through the intercom. "Book Ian on a flight to Sweden."

AVA PULLED ON ANOTHER pair of thermal underwear before sitting cross-legged on her bed. Who knew sleeping on a bed made of snow and ice would actually be comfortable? But it was. Everything about the ice hotel was amazing.

She'd lived all over the world, seen a lot of hotels, motels and patches of dirt on the ground, but she'd never slept in a place like this. A hotel in the village of Jukkasjärvi made entirely from the frozen water of the nearby Torne River. She'd loved this amazing structure the moment she'd stepped out of the cold into the warmer reservation area of the hotel. Warmer, but not warm. She appreciated the snow coat, hat and mittens provided by the hotel, and was glad she'd packed so much thermal underwear.

This clothing was certainly different from the attire worn by the cultures she usually researched. The coat might not show a woman's form to its best advantage, but the women of the Artic region still kept their beds warmed at night with the presence of a man when desired. She was looking forward to learning the flirting techniques these women utilized while freezing their backsides off and in the bulkiest clothing ever created.

Maybe it had something to do with the saunas. The Swedes took steam to a whole new level, and she never realized how much she'd enjoy the ice sauna in the hotel. Relaxing in the outdoor hot tub while staring up at the designs the Northern Lights created in the night sky was a nice backdrop for a romantic interlude.

She snapped a few pictures of the interior of her room, the large blocks of ice carved in a gothic style. Each room of the hotel was a work of art, the architecture unique, and she'd stayed in four different quarters so far. The clearness of the ice cast a beautiful light blue hue, and the beauty of the ice sculptures made her forget the cold.

Made her forget almost everything but Ian.

Ava pulled the blanket from the bed and wrapped it

around her shoulders. The window beckoned her, as it did whenever she was alone in here. She faced to the left. That was the right direction for South America, right?

She sighed heavily. Maybe she'd messed up there that last day with Ian. Maybe she shouldn't have taken his word for it, as friends. Maybe she should have fought for what she knew he felt for her. He had felt something, she knew it.

Or maybe it was this beautiful, magical place making her get all fanciful about Ian. This hotel that made her feel as if she was living the life of a fairy-tale ice princess waiting for her misguided prince to wise up.

The hotel would be gone soon. Already she heard the faint drip of the melting ice. Spring would come and begin to claim her room, by summer it would all be gone. Only to be reborn in the fall. A new hotel would be carved from the ice. A new vision.

Ava knew there was probably a metaphor about her relationship there. She'd explore it right now but she had a wedding to take part in. No longer was she just an observer: Ava Simms was living life now. She tossed off the blanket and headed for the door.

She found the excited bride, Penny, waiting for her, already dressed in a medieval gown of lace, her hair tied with garland.

"I can't wait until your book comes out. Can you see what's in my hair? Gavin liked the story you told last night so much, he tied it himself. The flowers were going to be for my bouquet, but who cares? What's a few less blooms?"

Take that, Ian Cole. "You look lovely, and I have something for your bouquet." Ava opened a small plastic bag, and pulled out some greenery.

The bride caught the strong aroma. "That smells."

"I know, and for good reason. The ancients of this

land believed small trolls and evil gnomes would plague young couples. But there was a remedy."

Penny made a face. "I'm guessing that the remedy is what smells."

"You guessed right. The bride and her attendants are to carry herbs and stinking weeds, but I think the gnomes and trolls can be successfully chased away with just a bit tucked into your bouquet."

After a quick hug, they both made their way to the ice church. Ava took a seat and noted the beautifully designed space with arches and an ice altar carved with intricate designs.

The ceremony was beautiful, and it wasn't the first time she wondered about what Ian's reactions would be to all she'd found here. What would he think of the ceremony? Which customs would he want to recreate with her?

About every fifteen seconds she thought of something she wanted to tell him. Whenever she spotted something new, she immediately thought of sharing it with him. When had she ever wanted to share her work with anyone before?

Only with Ian.

Now, for the first time she understood her parents' need to work together.

The happy couple was headed for the ice bar for a celebratory drink, and she was invited. Although the heavy coats were still needed, the large room was a favorite place for all the hotel guests to mingle. The blue lights of the bar reminded Ava of her first experience of a club scene with Ian, although the elegance of the large bar crafted entirely from ice and the drinks served from ice glasses was about as far removed from the experience as Oklahoma was from Sweden.

Which was why she was so surprised to see someone else completely out of place.

"Ian?" she called, unable to hide her shock, her heart pounding from the surprise of seeing him.

She watched him tense as he looked her way. That familiar tight ache she felt in her throat whenever she thought of him slammed into her with a vengeance. A million questions appeared and evaporated in her mind.

He was at her side in five long strides. "What are you doing here?" she asked. "Is there something wrong with the book?"

Ian shook his head. "I came for you."

She blinked. "But what about those things you said? You're the risk taker. How you live to be in the danger zone, and there's no place for—"

He grasped her hands. Were his hands actually shaking? "I don't need that rush anymore. I've discovered a way to feel alive without risking my neck."

She forced herself to be still. Stay calm. Don't give in to the hope. "What's that?"

"Being with you. I love you, Ava."

She closed her eyes tightly as he spoke, savoring his words.

"I've been miserable without you."

His fingers curled around her chin and her lids opened. His smile wasn't as bright. His eyes no longer so hopeful. "Do you need help with how a twenty-first-century woman responds to a man who tells her he loves her?"

She shook her head. "No, I think I have that covered. I love you, too."

He hauled her to his chest, his strong arms surrounding her. Making her feel loved. She glanced up at him. "But where will you work? What will you do?"

"Don't worry about it. In fact, I think I found the perfect setting for my next assignment."

"Where?"

"Anywhere you are, if that works for you. This cold, beautiful place is the perfect setting for a project I had in mind. I've come to really enjoy exploring cultures and documenting courtship rituals. Together. If you want me."

"Well, I don't know about that," she said, her voice taking on a teasing quality. "I think we're going to have to discuss this decision-making process. Set down some ground rules. You know what ground rules are?"

His lips twisted. "I'm familiar with the concept."

"In fact, we can settle this the old-fashioned way. The Swedes have a very interesting custom. Instead of the father giving his daughter away, the bride and groom arrive at the church together. Whoever enters first, that's the person who'll be the decision maker."

"The chapel down that hallway?" he asked.

"Yes."

"Hey," she called, when all she could see was Ian's retreating back. He was trying to get a head start. The cheater.

"You know it won't count because we haven't filled out any of the paperwork," she said when she caught up to him at the entrance of the ice chapel.

Ian looked at Ava and smiled. "Always trying to catch me on a technicality…and I wouldn't have it any other way."

Then he reached for her and brought her into his arms and they crossed the threshold into the church together.

* * * * *

nocturne™

COMING NEXT MONTH

Available OCTOBER 25, 2011

#123 LORD OF THE WOLFYN
Royal House of Shadows
Jessica Andersen

#124 DARK SINS AND DESERT SANDS
Mythica
Stephanie Draven

You can find more information on upcoming
Harlequin® titles, free excerpts and more at
www.HarlequinInsideRomance.com.

HNCNM1011

REQUEST YOUR FREE BOOKS!

2 FREE NOVELS FROM THE PARANORMAL ROMANCE COLLECTION PLUS 2 FREE GIFTS!

YES! Please send me 2 FREE novels from the Paranormal Romance Collection and my 2 FREE gifts (gifts are worth about $10). After receiving them, if I don't wish to receive any more books, I can return the shipping statement marked "cancel." If I don't cancel, I will receive 4 brand-new novels every month and be billed just $21.42 in the U.S. or $23.46 in Canada. That's a saving of at least 21% off the cover price of all 4 books. It's quite a bargain! Shipping and handling is just 50¢ per book in the U.S. and 75¢ per book in Canada.* I understand that accepting the 2 free books and gifts places me under no obligation to buy anything. I can always return a shipment and cancel at any time. Even if I never buy another book, the two free books and gifts are mine to keep forever.

237/337 HDN FEL2

Name		
	(PLEASE PRINT)	

Address		Apt. #

City	State/Prov.	Zip/Postal Code

Signature (if under 18, a parent or guardian must sign)

Mail to the **Reader Service:**
IN U.S.A.: P.O. Box 1867, Buffalo, NY 14240-1867
IN CANADA: P.O. Box 609, Fort Erie, Ontario L2A 5X3

Not valid for current subscribers to the Paranormal Romance Collection or Harlequin® Nocturne™ books.

Want to try two free books from another line?
Call 1-800-873-8635 or visit www.ReaderService.com.

* Terms and prices subject to change without notice. Prices do not include applicable taxes. Sales tax applicable in N.Y. Canadian residents will be charged applicable taxes. Offer not valid in Quebec. This offer is limited to one order per household. All orders subject to credit approval. Credit or debit balances in a customer's account(s) may be offset by any other outstanding balance owed by or to the customer. Please allow 4 to 6 weeks for delivery. Offer available while quantities last.

Your Privacy—The Reader Service is committed to protecting your privacy. Our Privacy Policy is available online at www.ReaderService.com or upon request from the Reader Service.

We make a portion of our mailing list available to reputable third parties that offer products we believe may interest you. If you prefer that we not exchange your name with third parties, or if you wish to clarify or modify your communication preferences, please visit us at www.ReaderService.com/consumerschoice or write to us at Reader Service Preference Service, P.O. Box 9062, Buffalo, NY 14269. Include your complete name and address.

*Harlequin® Special Edition® is thrilled to present a new
installment in* USA TODAY *bestselling author
RaeAnne Thayne's reader-favorite miniseries,*
THE COWBOYS OF COLD CREEK.

*Join the excitement as we meet the Bowmans—four
siblings who lost their parents but keep family ties alive
in Pine Gulch. First up is Trace. Only two things get under
this rugged lawman's skin: beautiful women and secrets.
And in Rebecca Parsons, he finds both!*

Read on for a sneak peek of
CHRISTMAS IN COLD CREEK.
Available November 2011 from Harlequin® Special Edition®.

On impulse, he unfolded himself from the bar stool. "Need
a hand?"

"Thank you! I…" She lifted her gaze from the floor to
his jeans and then raised her eyes. When she identified him
her hazel eyes turned from grateful to unfriendly and cold,
as if he'd somehow thrown the broken glasses at her head.

He also thought he saw a glimmer of panic in those
interesting depths, which instantly stirred his curiosity like
cream swirling through coffee.

"I've got it, Officer. Thank you." Her voice was several
degrees colder than the whirl of sleet outside the windows.

Despite her protests, he knelt down beside her and began
to pick up shards of broken glass. "No problem. Those trays
can be slippery."

This close, he picked up the scent of her, something fresh
and flowery that made him think of a mountain meadow on
a July afternoon. She had a soft, lush mouth and for one
brief, insane moment, he wanted to push aside that stray lock

of hair slipping from her ponytail and taste her. Apparently he needed to spend a lot less time working and a great deal *more* time recreating with the opposite sex if he could have sudden random fantasies about a woman he wasn't even inclined to like, pretty or not.

"I'm Trace Bowman. You must be new in town."

She didn't answer immediately and he could almost see the wheels turning in her head. Why the hesitancy? And why that little hint of unease he could see clouding the edge of her gaze? His presence was obviously making her uncomfortable and Trace couldn't help wondering why.

"Yes. We've been here a few weeks."

"Well, I'm just up the road about four lots, in the white house with the cedar shake roof, if you or your daughter need anything." He smiled at her as he picked up the last shard of glass and set it on her tray.

Definitely a story there, he thought as she hurried away. He just might need to dig a little into her background to find out why someone with fine clothes and nice jewelry, and who so obviously didn't have experience as a waitress, would be here slinging hash at The Gulch. Was she running away from someone? A bad marriage?

So...Rebecca Parsons. Not Becky. An intriguing woman. It had been a long time since one of those had crossed his path here in Pine Gulch.

Trace won't rest until he finds out Rebecca's secret, but will he still have that same attraction to her once he does? Find out in CHRISTMAS IN COLD CREEK. Available November 2011 from Harlequin® Special Edition®.

HSEEXP1111

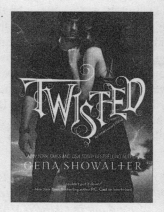